DUPLICITY

IT'S NOT **CORRUPTION**
IT'S JUST THE WAY THINGS ARE DONE

RICHARD EVANS

852 PRESS

852

PRESS

First published in 2018 by Impact Press, an imprint of Ventura Press
PO Box 780, Edgecliff NSW 2027 Australia www.impactpress.com.au

Third Edition published in 2023 by 852 Press,
Suite 12, 12 Eshelby Drive, Airlie Beach Queensland 4802 Australia
www.852Press.com.au

10 9 8 7 6 5 4 3

This book is a work of fiction. The characters and incidents are the products of the
writer's imagination and are not to be construed as real.

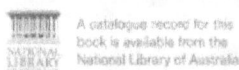 A catalogue record for this
book is available from the
National Library of Australia

National Library of Australia Cataloguing-in-Publication entry:

Author: Evans, Richard
Title: Duplicity / by Richard Evans
ISBN: 978-0-6452823-4-4 (paperback)
ISBN: 978-0-6452823-5-1 (ebook)
ISBN: 978-0-6452823-6-8 (hardcover)

Australian fiction.
Cover Design: 852 Press

Richard Evans' first book, Deceit, is a five-star thriller that brings the Australian political process to life. – *GOODREADS*

Just finished reading *Deceit* and it was gripping; I could not put it down. It was brilliant. I just loved the book and can't wait to read *Duplicity*.' — *FORMER CLERK OF VICTORIAN LEGISLATIVE COUNCIL*

I absolutely loved it, couldn't put it down. I would love to see your book become a movie. – *IAN S., MELBOURNE*

Rich in ideas and provokes much thought about our parliamentary process, abuses of power, corruption, and the need, at times, for ordinary people to step up and take a stand in the name of honour and professional integrity. – *NADINE D., EDITOR*

'The Kill Bill has such a fascinating concept at its heart and you brought the characters to life brilliantly.' – *C.dB, EDITOR*

This is an outstanding debut from Evans, and this terrific read comes highly recommended.' – *GOODREADS*

From former Federal MP Richard Evans comes this exceptional political thriller debut, which serves as the first part of his Democracy trilogy.' *CANBERRA WEEKLY*

I adored Gordon O'Brien. Straight as an arrow amongst those who are only in things for themselves, I couldn't help but cheer him on as he was like a dog with a bone, searching out the truth' *BJ'S BOOK BLOG*

I thoroughly enjoyed the book and did not want to put the book down, but neither did I want the story to end! Congratulations! – *TRINITY MARKETING*

ALSO BY RICHARD EVANS

Democracy Trilogy
Deceit
Duplicity
Doomed

Referendum Series
Forgotten People
The Kill Bill
The Mallee

Stand Alone Books
Out of my Hands
Selfish Ambitions

Non-Fiction
The Australian Franchising Handbook

For Jan

Your love and care for Rena was appreciated and will never be forgotten.

The Major Players

GOVERNMENT:

Andrew Gerrard	Prime Minister
Meredith Bruce	Manager of Government Business

OPPOSITION

Peter Stanley	Opposition Leader
Barton Messenger	Deputy Opposition Leader
James Harper	Member for Moncrieff, former leader
Christopher Hughes	Member for Warringah
Jaya Rukhmani	Candidate for Melbourne

MERCANTILES

Tony Hancock	Hancock Media
Kerry Jameson	Casinos
Felicity Osman	Finance
Frank Lowsonne	Property
Allan Connell	Mining
Sally Verhoeven	IT
Adam Lowry	Retail
Jim Buckley	Cattle
Jonathan Wolff	Covert Campaign Operative
Jack Sinclair-Browne	Wolff alias

MEDIA

Anita Devlin	Hancock investigative journalist, Canberra
Peter Cleaver	Hancock Chief of Canberra Bureau
Cassandra Rogers	Hancock Television

THE STORY SO FAR

Prime Minister Andrew Gerrard had it all. He was at the top of his political game, leading the parliament and the nation with his charismatic style for twenty years. The only thing he didn't have was enough money.

Six months ago, after a boozy dinner with his friend, the president of Indonesia, Gerrard agreed to a funding deal for offshore immigration detention centres. Gerrard would take a clip of the money on the way through. Retirement sorted.

Until two weeks ago, when tragedy enveloped the parliament prior to the crucial vote to approve the first tranche of the funding for the immigration centres. A plane crash killed all politicians on board, and consequently Gerrard did not have the numbers to get his funding legislation through the House of Representatives as the opposition had the majority.

Using his devious influence on the Speaker, Gerrard demanded the entire legislation for the full amount of funding be rushed through the parliament, and thus ensured a plan to provide him $40 million secret commission in the process.

The clerk of the parliament became aware of the manipulation of the parliament and ultimately forced the Speaker to resign over her indiscretions with the prime minister. During the procedural confusion in the chamber, it was determined that the parliament has lost confidence in the government, a very serious action that causes the nation to be sent to an immediate federal election.

CHAPTER
1

DAY ONE – THURSDAY

Robert Wong knocked respectfully on his professor's wood-panelled office door. Finding it slightly ajar, he peered into the gloom and saw her concentrating on student papers. 'Professor Rukhmani? Have you got a few moments?'

The professor looked up and smiled as she recognised the student, pushing her marking pen into her tied-back hair. 'Sure Robert, come in. I've been meaning to contact you about your last paper.'

Wong tentatively ventured into the overstuffed office, wondering where he could sit.

'Grab a seat. Here, pass me that pile of papers.'

He removed the large stack of student work from the chair and the professor slapped them onto another pile behind her. There seemed no order to the paper chaos surrounding the walls of the office, even the floor seemed to overflow with it.

'You seem really busy, sorry to interrupt.'

'No, not at all. I welcome the break. Don't worry about the mess—' The professor laughed, a little embarrassed by the state of her office. 'It's always like this. I seem to know where everything is though,' she said dreamily, perhaps thinking she should be more organised.

Wong sat on the edge of the chair, a little nervous about talking to his politics professor about his grand idea. Leaning slightly right so as to see around a high stack of papers on her desk, he asked apprehensively, 'What did you want to discuss with me about my paper?'

'This interesting idea you have about the legacy of Obama being a reason the Republicans eventually lost Congress and the presidency.' The professor reached up behind her toward another stack of papers, flicked up two assignments and with a quick flourish, withdrew Wong's paper with her attached notes. 'We haven't studied Saul Alinsky and his doctrine for community organising, so I wanted to ask why you referred to him so much in your paper. In particular, his nineteen-seventies ideas of collective community action to achieve political outcomes. Don't you think these ideas might be a little dated?'

'Just like everyone else in the United States, President Obama never accepted the legitimacy of Donald Trump as president, becoming, I think, very protective of his own legacy. It seems to me he encouraged his supporters to resist Trump by strategically initiating a targeted campaign against the president during the first term. It is highly unusual for a retiring president to remain politically active – even more so during the next election campaign. Bush, for instance, never campaigned against Obama.'

Wong opened his canvas satchel and fleshed around, pulling out a tattered book. 'I found Alinsky's handbook in a second-hand bookstore a few weeks back. The campaign methods correlate with how Obama ran his entire administration for eight years – and his community activism after he left office.'

The professor took the dog-eared book and carefully flicked through it. 'Alinsky was considered radical—' The professor paused as she flicked the pages. Without looking at her student she asked, 'Do you think Obama was a radical socialist?'

'Not really. Actually, I don't really know. Probably not, not strictly, but there is strong evidence that Obama was subtly using Alinsky's suggestions to incite division in the community.'

The professor smiled as she leaned back in her chair. 'That's a big claim. Can you cite any examples?'

'Well, in my view, there are plenty.' Wong sat forward, shifting the stack of papers aside to lean on the desk. 'During his time as president, Obama was consistent in blaming wealthy Americans for the social problems that beset the United States, especially after the financial crisis. He often suggested low-income earners were the victims of the greed of the wealthy and was always quick to support accusations of racism against police when black or brown Americans were involved – even when there was little evidence of actual racism.

In other words, he rubbed raw the resentment toward the police and the political system with his rhetoric – which mostly focused on the black community – and agitated almost to the point of inciting conflict. This could be interpreted as classic Alinsky teachings. His rules for radicals basically says: look for ways to increase insecurity, anxiety, and uncertainty in the community. No-one could deny the increased community demonstrations after Trump won.'

'Oh sure, who could forget. Everyone came out to demonstrate and many didn't even know why. They were angry with the result of the election and hate was stoked – it didn't help that Trump was an obnoxious dud either.'

'In my view, a lot of that disorder was driven by one of Obama's supporter groups, Organizing for America,' suggested Wong, pushing his glasses back up his nose.

'What makes you think Obama was instrumental in Trump's ultimate defeat?'

'The OFA started campaigning immediately after Trump won office. Every time Obama spoke, he incited community action to reclaim America. Remember he was out in the hustings on a regular basis asking citizens to resist and reclaim? And he hardly ever mentioned Trump by name; he just referred to the many challenges and lies from the administration.

'Like everyone else, he didn't think Trump was worthy of high office, framing him as an enemy of American values. Everyone spoke against the president, community action groups mobilised, and it virtually became a community revolution, which is classic Alinsky.

'In 2018 there were many congresswomen and men elected for the Democrats who came from a community movement. I found out the OFA recruited over fifty thousand community organisers to be disruptive against the administration by organising anti-Trump events.' Wong paused for a moment. 'They then drove the mail ballot vote and got out and secured those ballots for Biden in 2020.'

Wong reached back for his book, admiringly flicking through the pages before putting it back into his satchel. 'When you think about it, Obama was a little more politically covert than historians give him credit for. In my view, he was very manipulative and massaged his image extremely well. Obama is still loved the world over in lots of ways, but the truth is, he didn't achieve much as president – yet history has been very kind toward him, recording him as one of the best.'

'Interesting. I hadn't thought to link any influence of Alinsky on Obama. I probably wouldn't share your view – there are a lot of differing thoughts when it comes to politics – but you have made a good case for it in your paper, so well done.'

'Don't get me wrong. Sometimes these organised community tactics get things done – it is used a lot more by the major parties in a lot of western democratic countries at the moment.'

'Create division in the community and force the government to provide a solution.'

'Exactly.' Wong leaned back into his chair with a big smile, enjoying the moment with his favourite professor. 'The Democrats in the States, especially in places like Chicago, have been influenced by this kind of community organisation strategy for years – we now see it in action at most elections.

'This is the new power, I imagine. Community groups are getting organised and campaigning on single issues impacting elections. They are usually well organised too, just like these so-called progressive parties emerging in Australia. And it's the reason, I think, Andrew Gerrard has been prime minister for so long.'

'Not because of his policies?'

'I think he's a populist prime minister who speaks directly to the have-nots in the community in order to maintain his power. He wedges policy all the time, but I finally sense a mood for change.'

'You think the electorate is in the mood to change the government?'

'Gerrard has made some really provocative procedural reforms to the parliament over recent years yet remains popular because he subtly drives community division on other policy. He is silent on his parliamentary reforms, which suggests to the electorate there's nothing to see. His party is better organised, using a whole raft of causes to get people out supporting him. Gerrard does exactly what Alinsky suggests – he picks a target, frames it to his advantage then personalises it, polarising the community to get active.'

Professor Rukhmani squeezed a slight admiring smile as she listened to her A-grade student.

'Get discontented voters who believe society is fundamentally unjust to take their lead from community organisers speaking about unfairness and suddenly you have a revolution.'

'One Nation and the other conservative groups?' she asked.

'Exactly. They're growing because the conservatives are not strategically geared to organise the community. They seem too pompous to do anything other than act ethically, which is probably why they have remained in opposition for nearly twenty years. They don't want anything to do with the socially and economically handicapped, which leaves a gap in their policy for One Nation and others to fill.'

Rukhmani's chair squeaked as she leaned back. 'Are you going to use your study to advance a political career?'

Wong chortled a little, then said, 'That's exactly what I want to talk to you about.' The student leaned forward again with a broad, excited smile. 'Why don't you seek preselection for the federal election? I could be your campaign manager.'

The professor raised her eyebrows, flinging her arms out as if on a cross and looking to the ceiling in mock shock.

'You're kidding me, right?' the professor scoffed as she

straightened to address Wong. 'And anyway, the election is too far into the future to even contemplate such a preposterous idea.'

'Haven't you been listening to the news?' Wong said, tossing his hands into the air in bogus exasperation as he sat back.

'If I could find my radio within this mess—' the professor looked glumly about her office. 'I'd be listening to music.'

'Haven't you heard about using technology, Professor?' The student sassed her. 'The government has been sacked by the governor-general.'

'What?' Rukhmani bolted upright in her chair. 'When?'

'About an hour ago. Apparently, the speaker resigned, and the clerk prorogued the parliament, or something like that.'

'You're kidding me?' Rukhmani fell back into her chair. Bewildered by the news, she ran her fingers absent-mindedly through her tied thick hair.

'There's a federal election called for the ninth of December, and it's anyone's guess what will happen. I hope Gerrard loses.'

'They say a week is a long time in politics, and this week has been awful.' The professor slowly shook her head before slapping her hands to her thighs. 'This is unbelievable. First, we lose politicians in a tragic plane crash, and now this – unbelievable.'

'But with every misfortune comes opportunity,' Wong smiled, nodding excitedly with eyes wide. 'So, are you going to run in the election?'

'Me? No! Why?'

'You teach this stuff. Why not get real-life experience from an election campaign?' Wong was almost bouncing in the chair, his tongue squeezed between his teeth. 'We could treat it as a case study and film it for further academic analysis and research. We can have a website with our own social-media feed, and you could publish a daily diary linking back to theory.'

'Hmm, I'm not so sure it's a good idea,' said Rukhmani, screwing up her face as she considered the idea. 'For starters, the university would never allow it ethically and secondly, which party would I even stand for?'

'Does it matter? We could only do this in a seat where you couldn't win.'

'The conservatives would never endorse me, and the socialists challenge me with their extreme liberalism. The Greens, well? Yeah, nah. Not a good idea.'

'Either major party could select you in a seat that no-one cares about – and they think they will lose.'

'Such as?'

Wong laughed like a young child wanting to blurt out a secret. 'Why not run against Gerrard in Melbourne,' he announced triumphantly. 'It would be a fantastic story for the media, and we could have some really great fun.' He was speaking staccato-like, his tone rising and quickening.

'You'll get preselected easily if you make an application, I'm positive. But we'll need to move today. I'll run your campaign for you, and you'll get an applied political experience from the campaigning. This has got to be a great case study for you. We run the daily diary online and as I say link it to political theory. Plenty of your students would be willing to help. We may even get a documentary out of it.'

'What about constitutional issues?'

Wong's eyebrows raised, 'Which ones?'

'Citizenship, and perhaps office of profit.'

Wong considered the question for a moment, pinching his chin between his forefinger and thumb. 'We renounce any citizenship duality immediately just to make sure, and you apply for extended leave from the university, just for a month, before you submit your application.'

'That's a ridiculous idea,' said Rukhmani, punching a pointed finger at Wong. 'Anyway, the conservatives would never select anyone like me to run against Gerrard.' The professor placed her elbow on the desk clutter, tapping her fingers to her mouth and reflecting on the idea. 'It took them years and years to have Italians and Greeks elected who weren't born in Australia – they would never preselect an Indian woman federally.'

'You wouldn't be expected to win Melbourne against Gerrard. And there's always a first time for selecting an Indian woman. Think of the media you would generate.'

'I'm the wrong skin colour for Australians.'

'We've had plenty of people with colour elected. Remember the Kenyan senator from South Australia? There's still a Koori man in the Senate, and Speaker Bagshaw is Indigenous.'

'Yes, but they're not as black as me.'

'It's over.' Prime Minister Gerrard sat at his parliamentary office desk, pinching the bridge of his nose as he gave the news to his friend the president of Indonesia. 'The earliest we can get the money to you will be February.'

'That is not good for me.'

'There is nothing I can do about it now. I'm officially not prime minister for now.'

'That is a sad news, my friend. I will now have to withdraw the order for clemency on your citizens.'

'Amir, come on. You can't execute them now just because you won't get your money until next year. It's only a few months, for fuck's sake.'

'There is no guarantee that the money will be transferred next year. You may not win the election.'

'I will win the fucking election and I'll get you your money!' Gerrard barked into the phone.

'Andrew, I cannot be sure, so I will stop all site works for the immigration detention centre on Ambon, withhold the clemency order on your drug-trafficking citizens, and recall my ambassador. You can forget any deal we may have had.'

'What! Why?'

'My country cannot trust you to maintain your word. If you want to regain our confidence, I suggest you win the election.'

'I blame you actually,' Anita Devlin said as she sipped sparkling wine from a plastic disposable cup.

'For what, exactly?' Barton Messenger had brought a bottle to the second-floor newsroom in the Federal Parliamentary Press Gallery to celebrate the events of the day. An allegedly corrupt prime minister being sacked was definitely something to celebrate.

'I had the chance to get a front-page byline in the national newspaper and now your mob will be plastered all over the first eight pages.'

'You can still run with your story.'

'It's only wild speculation now that Gerrard's funding legislation wasn't passed. The story about him ripping off the government is literally in the bin.' Anita proffered her flimsy cup for more. Messenger obliged with a splash that sent a foam rinse over her hand. She quickly swapped hands, flicking her wet hand dry. 'What happens now?'

'We go to a general election, and hopefully we come back as the elected government.'

'Would you still fund Gerrard's detention centres in Indonesia?'

'Probably, since ironically it remains part of our policy.' Messenger pushed back on the legs of his chair, putting a foot on Anita's desk. 'We'll guarantee to pay the stimulus package to the electorate before Christmas to nullify it as an election issue for the punters, and when we come back to the parliament, we'll scrutinise the Indonesian funding going offshore a little more rigorously than we did this week.'

Anita took a sip and contemplated Barton, a curious smile lingering as she watched him. 'So, you could be deputy prime minister in a month?'

'Seems I could be, yes. Would that create a problem for you?'

'Not at all.' Anita smiled as she gulped down her cup and proffered it for more celebratory bubbles. 'The question is, will I be a problem for you?'

'You already are,' Messenger joked.

'So, no exclusives from you then?' Anita teased.

'I can absolutely guarantee you to be exclusive,' Messenger laughed, as he looked at her. 'If you're interested.'

Anita also laughed, comfortable with the thought of having Barton Messenger in her life. 'Can I get an invitation to Yarralumla sometime?'

'Would you like to live there?' Messenger slyly smiled.

She suddenly sat upright, almost out of her chair. Anita chortled, 'Did you just propose?'

'No.' Barton responded gruffly. 'I'm only teasing. We're yet to even have that first dinner date you promised me.'

'What are you doing tonight?'

'I have a very early flight tomorrow for an emergency campaign meeting in Melbourne, so if it's not a late one, let's go Chinese.'

'Good idea. Let me pack up and have a chat to Cleave. I

can either meet you downstairs at the Reps entrance or at the restaurant, you choose.'

'I'll see you downstairs. In about thirty minutes?'

'Sure, sounds great.'

Messenger crushed his cup and flicked it into the bin. He kicked himself out of the chair, saying goodbye as he left Anita.

She began by tidying her desk, filing scraps of paper into her various resource boxes and trays. Anita assumed she would be assigned to cover major policy announcements during the election campaign and provide political profiles of the leaders for the weekend editions. This would mean criss-crossing the country, living out of a suitcase for over a month, probably from the coming weekend, with little time for a social life. She mused her dinner with Barton might be the last opportunity to enjoy herself before Christmas.

Peter Cleaver was sitting at his desk when she knocked and entered. He looked up and motioned for her to sit as he finished reading what seemed to be an article ready for publication. The experienced political editor supported Anita in her recent pursuit of the prime minister, but parliamentary events overtook the potential exclusive. He pulled out a bent cigarette from a soft pack and lit it, sucking hard and breathing deeply – and ignoring the convention of a no-smoking workplace – before billowing smoke above her head.

'Your story raises an interesting connection between Gerrard and Indonesia and is very good. I can't run it now given today's events, but I think we should file it to use if Gerrard wins the election.'

'There's not much point now. The scrutiny of the legislation will be much better when it goes before parliament again. This alleged secret commission we identified will either be taken out or much better explained by the government.'

Cleaver pulled off his glasses and rubbed his face, cigarette dangling from his lips. 'Even so, I think we might be able to use it, so I sent it off to the boss.'

'Who? Your boss?'

'No, Hancock. I was pretty sure he would be interested, given he's a mate of Gerrard's.'

'Was he?'

'He liked it and asked if you would write more like it for the campaign.'

'Like what?' Anita waved an uncomfortable hand in front of her face to clear the smoke. 'Does he think a conspiracy lies behind every campaign sign?'

'No. What he wants you to do is write special interest stories during the campaign, sketches of the remarkable political things that happen every day. Providing a sort of human element to the lying morons if that is possible.'

'You're kidding me. I'm not a social diarist, we have those in Sydney.'

'Hancock has requested you to do it.' Cleaver replaced his glasses and drew heavily on his cigarette, provoking a rasping cough. He roughly stubbed it out in an over-full saucer. 'Fairly insistent, actually.'

'I'm an investigative journalist, Cleave. I don't write crap, you know that.'

'We're not asking you to write crap, Anita. We want the hard stories from the campaign.'

'You don't want policy analysis?'

'Nope, I've assigned two others to do that.'

'Hard news?' Anita said, sarcastically. 'You want me to write hard news?'

'Yes.'

'Where the hell do you think these stories lie if I don't analyse policy?'

Cleaver leaned back with his hands behind his head and a broad smile. 'That's for you to find out. You're the investigative journalist, are you not?'

'Don't patronise me.' Anita stood. 'I won't accept crap like that.' She stared at Cleaver, angrily gnawing her upper lip. 'Where do you want me to go?'

'Start with the opposition, work your contacts,' Cleaver smirked. 'How is Messenger?'

'Don't shit me, Cleave,' snapped Anita, shaking her head. She looked to the ceiling. 'How many words do you expect?'

'I want something every day. Your pieces can range from a gossip tidbit to a substantial feature – that's up to you.'

'You're serious, aren't you?' Anita began prowling slowly in front of her editor's desk. 'You have no idea how this will work out. It's just a damn demotion. Why?' she whined loudly. 'You know the work I put into the last election. I even got a Walkley for it. This is crap.'

'As I said, Anita, this has come from Hancock himself, so I suggest you get focused on the campaign.'

'Hard news?' Anita chided, a little sceptical. 'You just want puff pieces, that's what they'll turn out to be.'

'That'll be your call.'

'I'm so sick to death of this business and the dark art of mate's politics. This misogynistic crap lies everywhere and nowhere more so than in this fucking office.'

'How do you mean?'

'You've shafted me, just like Gerrard was shafted today, and you have no answer as to why.' Anita stopped pacing and stood before Cleaver with both hands on her hips. 'Gerrard was about to commit a fraud and I broke the story,' she thumbed her chest. 'Now I've been relegated to the back-bench as election campaign social commentator because he's a mate of Hancock's.'

'That's not the case.'

'Then explain why this is happening to me if it's not mates looking after mates.'

'We want a different tone and perspective from the campaign, rather than having to compete with social media. We want you to write stories with a bit of grunt.'

'So, no social crap?' Anita aggressively stood before him, now with both hands clenched on her hips.

'Not as far as I'm concerned,' Cleaver nonchalantly replied, pulling another bent cigarette from his pack.

'Will I be free to travel to either campaign?'

'Yes, but can you concentrate on Stanley's first, before

looking at Gerrard.'

'I can't believe this.' Anita looked to the ceiling, tapping her right foot slightly. 'How do you want me to handle the sacking of the government?'

'Not actually a sacking, was it?'

She sighed heavily and asked, 'What would you call it, a resignation?'

'Politics is only ever about power, Anita. You either have it or you don't.'

'So obviously, as a woman, I don't have any power in this fucking men's cave. Journalistic ethics have little to do with it either.'

'Just do as we ask, please, Anita.' Cleaver implored her, torching his cigarette with a flame, and drawing in the smoke deeply. He managed to get out, 'Then everyone'll be happy,' before rasping a cough.

'Except for me,' said Anita. She turned on her heel and stomped from the office. 'Those things will kill you, by the way.' She slammed the glass door, rattling the entire office partitioning, kicked a nearby bin creating a storm of papers, grabbed her bag and left knowing she would eventually calm down.

'Fucking men shit me!' she barked as she marched toward the stairwell.

CHAPTER
2

DAY TWO – FRIDAY

The opposition leadership group agreed to convene urgently to discuss strategy for the unanticipated federal election at its party headquarters in Melbourne. Delays with Barton Messenger's early commuter flight from Canberra persuaded him to go straight to the meeting, rather than change and refresh at home in Williamstown, a coastal community twenty minutes by train from the CBD.

It was an opportunity for a latte at his favourite city cafe in Bourke Street, just around the corner from the Exhibition Street headquarters. A longtime coffee snob, Barton was looking forward to resuming his love of good coffee missing in most other cities, even more so in Parliament House in Canberra.

Settling at a footpath table, reviewing the lead stories of the national newspaper about the chaos and crisis in Canberra, a latte arrived, and the warming sun began to filter through the trees. It was his favourite time of day to enjoy a good coffee. As he took his first sip, Messenger's phone pinged a message.

> Thanks for last night, it was great spending time with u. Let's do more of it once the campaign is over

Messenger grinned and quickly tapped a response on the screen.

> Looking forward to seeing more of you hopefully before Xmas.

> If you need to know anything about the campaign be sure NOT to call me.

Messenger smiled as he dropped his phone back into his jacket. He trusted his attempt at humour was a subtle reminder to Anita about the restrictions his role as deputy leader might bring during the campaign. Anita had agreed over dinner that communication between them should be scant, and if they had time for a social catch- up, they both agreed not to talk politics. Barton welcomed Anita's ethics and didn't want to compromise their budding friendship by denying her the opportunity of doing her job. It could also very well mean negative press for him.

Messenger settled back into his newspaper, flicking it open, then reading the coverage of the prorogued parliament. He tried to steer clear of articles about himself but couldn't help reading the editorial that supported his promotion to deputy leader, encouraging the party to further promote younger MPs and clear out the stodgy frontbench. Its coverage of the parliamentary crisis was extensive, highlighting the resignation of the speaker that led the parliament to abruptly prorogue and force the nation to an unexpected federal election.

Prime Minister Gerrard was plastered across the front page with menacing headlines that promised political retribution to those who caused the crisis. His fierce look, snapped by a parliamentary photographer as he brushed past the media, would drive fear into anyone with him and his statement made a veiled threat to the governor-general. He claimed she failed to act on his advice, which constitutionally she was required to do.

Gerrard didn't hold back his vitriol, vilifying parliamentary officers, including the Chief Justice, promising there would be changes when he was re-elected. A small assortment of brave commentators implied this crisis may be the end of the Gerrard era, suggesting it was time for the electorate to make a change to the leadership of the country.

Messenger's favourite section of the paper was always the cartoon, which today had Gerrard lounging like an opulent Greek senator from long ago asking, 'What is democracy? Freedom to elect your own dictator.' This brought him a small chuckle. As he sipped his coffee, his phone rang displaying a number he didn't recognise.

'Hello, Barton Messenger.'

'Barton, it's Jaya Rukhmani.'

Barton crushed his newspaper and sat straighter. 'Hello Professor, how are you?'

'I'm terrific. Very enthusiastic about the events in Canberra yesterday. You must be very proud of your election as deputy leader?'

'It's an honour, and to tell you the truth, totally unexpected. I didn't go to Canberra this week thinking I would be voted as deputy opposition leader, that's for sure. But I'll take it.' Messenger scoffed as a tram trundled loudly past and he placed a finger in his other ear.

'Who would have thought a scholar of mine could possibly be prime minister?'

'Not there yet, Professor, and I doubt I'll get the nod for the top job any time soon.'

'Oh Bart, you've always shown potential, and you have the ability, it's just a matter of time now.' The professor sounded authentic with her praise. 'Perhaps you should think about getting married, we like our prime ministers tall and good looking – and married.'

'I probably would be elected prime minister before ever getting married. At this time in my life, at least.'

'What's wrong with you? You're handsome and young, there should be girls falling all over you. I'd even put my hand up for that enjoyable task,' Rukhmani joked.

'Hmm, well the idea of marital bliss is not on my radar at the moment.' Barton was beginning to feel a little uncomfortable with the conversation. 'What can I put the pleasure of this call down to, would you like me to speak at the university again?'

'Hey, that would be great if you could, especially if you win government.' Messenger immediately regretted making the quip, remembering the last time he visited the campus was fraught with student dissidence during his speech. 'Actually, I wanted your advice – and perhaps a little help.'

'Happy to, what are you seeking?'

'I want to run at the federal election.' Messenger didn't respond, screwed his face, and gazed at his paper. 'Are you there?'

'Yes, I'm still here,' Messenger dithered a little. 'Can I ask which party?'

'Yours, of course,' Rukhmani clarified, a little irritated with her former student's indifferent response. 'My colleagues think it would be a terrific case study about the many challenges running an election campaign. It could possibly allow us to develop a teaching unit in the politics program on applied campaign techniques, which we would hope to offer from second semester next year.'

'Sounds interesting,' Messenger replied cagily, engaging the benign political speak he, like most politicians, was skilled at. 'Do you know which seat you might stand for?'

'We want to challenge Gerrard.'

Messenger pursed his lips and breathed out slowly,

thinking through the information. It might be a proposition worthy of further discussion. 'He normally stands without many candidates running against him. I think his primary vote is something ridiculous like seventy-two per cent. We have a hell of a time trying to convince anyone to stand against him, and more often than not, we don't spend any money on campaign materials. We haven't stood a candidate for the last two elections. Why Melbourne?'

'A number of reasons. We think it would be a great experience because of the small number of independents. Plus, we think national exposure might create interest for our project, and we could get media footage to use in the unit. Of course, the university is in the electorate too.'

'Who is we?'

'A number of post-grad students and a couple of tutors from the university.'

'Are you serious about this?' Barton looked about him. 'I mean, it would require an enormous effort. You'll need plenty of people – and money.'

'People won't be a problem. We'll call upon our alumni students and their networks. The money could be problematic, but we're thinking of using crowdfunding websites.'

'Will they let you do that?'

'Not sure, but if we can and we do it well, it may resolve this ongoing issue about fraudulent campaign donors. In any event, it will allow us to include possible funding alternatives in the unit we are hoping to design. We really need to start addressing the many allegations of political favours being given for campaign donations that so many politicians are accused of. You haven't been accused, have you?'

'I had some trouble when I first started out with a property developer wanting to donate to my campaign, but we sent his money back. He then unscrupulously got it to us via another company, which our accounting missed. Caused a bit of pain for me that did.'

'What happened?'

'I was forced to provide an explanation to the federal police. Nothing came of it, but the media hounded me for months and they still raise it occasionally.'

'What happened to the money?'

'I donated all of it to charity under the moron's name.'

'I suppose what we can learn from your experience is that we need to be careful to weed out those who may want to manipulate us.'

'Exactly, and if you do, you will be a rare political candidate,' said Messenger as he lifted his coffee, pausing before sipping. 'Tell me, why do you want to run against Gerrard?'

'I suppose if I genuinely think about it and consider the true reasons, then I would have to concede it's about profile. Gerrard will bring us profile, and with that we will generate more media material to use. If we impact Gerrard's margin in some small way, that would be a huge plus for the development of the unit.'

'So why not run as an independent?'

'We want to include the preselection process in the study and the campaign structures of a major party. We think there are some valid ethical and moral constructs about the distribution of power within politics, especially the major parties, and we want to take a look at it.'

'I'm not sure how the party will react to your application.'

'Am I not qualified? I have been a citizen for almost twenty years now.'

'No, it's not that,' Messenger hesitated, gnawing at his bottom lip.

'Please tell me it's not because I'm a woman?'

'You know our party prefers to promote good women, and you are definitely one of them.'

'And yet you have none in your leadership team?'

Messenger squirmed a little at the retort. 'Not for lack of trying, I can tell you.'

'Yes, I know your position, Bart, so why are you hesitant?'

'We've never preselected an Indian migrant for a federal seat before.'

'Your party has had plenty of mixed Asian diaspora elected to various parliaments and you've had candidates with Indian backgrounds in state elections.' Rukhmani lowered her tone, 'What aren't you telling me?'

Messenger hesitated a little. 'Frankly, I'm concerned about the media and how they will treat you, and how the electorate will respond ...'

'To a woman of colour?'

'No,' Messenger protested. 'That's not it. I mean to a woman with your background. Please don't misunderstand me, I'm only thinking about the consequences should there be a red-neck campaign against you. You must know Twitter haters will go crazy.'

'That is precisely one of the reasons why we want to stand for this election. We want to expose any unethical bullying we may encounter and show how social messages can be misused and manipulated, for example by trolls on Twitter.' Rukhmani was suddenly upbeat. 'This is what I actually love about politics. Democracy is hard work, and we must fight to keep it. And we have to fight for ethical and moral equality.'

'I have to say, you're a brave woman, Jaya.'

'Rubbish, Barton, this isn't about me. It's about our political system and how the community must actively stop post-truth theory overrunning us. We need to constrain the power of propaganda from populist leaders like Gerrard.'

'I can't promise anything but let me talk to a few contacts and I'll get back to you.'

'Today?'

'I'm scheduled for a campaign strategy meeting shortly,' Messenger checked his watch. 'It should take a few hours, but maybe I can get back to you before the end of the day?'

'This is why you will be a great prime minister, Barton.'

'Why?'

'You're unafraid to make a promise, which I'm confident you will no doubt keep.'

'I had a good teacher, Professor. Talk to you later. This is good news, very exciting.'

'Thanks, Bart, chat soon.'

Messenger was somewhat taken aback by the call and

slowly placed his phone on the table, thinking how best to manage the request. The professor would be a terrific candidate for the party, and frankly would be well suited to a safe seat, but to throw her to the political wolves against Gerrard could be a challenge for his party, and indeed, the electorate of Melbourne.

He wondered why he remained overly concerned about a potential backlash against her. Was it a fear for her safety, as he had suggested, or did he harbour a subtle bias against her? The thought troubled him. And if it transpired there was no backlash against her, what did that say about his relationship with multiculturalism? If he earnestly believed in equality of diversity, why was he hesitant to endorse her candidacy? Perhaps he wasn't a strong believer in cultural tolerance after all.

Messenger folded his paper, collected his leather satchel, paid the bill, and walked quickly to Exhibition Street, the centre of state government offices. He waited for the green walk sign before crossing Bourke Street toward the location of the federal opposition's Victorian headquarters, now likely to be the base for the national campaign.

The meeting rooms were on the fifth floor. He swiped his security pass to gain access to the boardroom, dimly lit like a military bunker complete with projector, whiteboard, and flip charts at the ready to flesh out campaign strategy. A solitary colleague waited in the gloom, working his smartphone.

'Hi Jim, when did you get in?' Messenger was surprised to see him.

'Morning Bart,' Harper slipped his phone into his jacket. 'I came down last night for a meeting and thought I would stay.'

'Did the leader ask you to come along?'

James Harper didn't seem too pleased with the challenge. 'You might recall I was the leader just two days ago.'

Messenger sat opposite and considered his colleague. 'I'm not sure the leadership team would appreciate you being here today – the optics wouldn't be good.'

'Like the optics when I was dumped on Wednesday night, you mean?'

Messenger grimaced. 'Jim, that was an unfortunate political decision made by you to move to a vote. You were warned not to do it; you can't blame anyone else for what happened.'

'You certainly didn't help with your shenanigans during question time,' jibed Harper.

'We needed to chase down Gerrard and defer the funding for the immigration centre. You were blocking us.'

'Bart, I was set up by Gerrard to comply in the parliament, you know that.' Harper said it matter-of-factly, confidently leaning back in his chair. 'What happened in the party room subsequently shouldn't disqualify me from strategically assisting in the campaign. I was leader for eight years, for heaven's sake.'

'It's an opportunity for change.'

'What's going to change? My policies? My work in getting us into a winning position? None of that will change. Do I get to keep any of my legacy?'

'Jim, it's not about shunning you, it's the optics of having the former leader driving party strategy. In other words, are the punters voting for Stanley, or Harper?'

'Stop with the fucking optics, will you please,' Harper barked, sitting forward.

'We have promised you a ministry if we win.'

'So, what?'

'We just need clear air around the new leadership group so we can provide a positive message. You must know that?'

'I've had enough of this babble.' Harper abruptly jumped up and moved to the door. 'I'll have a chat to Peter and see what he has to say.'

'Jim, it's for the best. You'll see.' Messenger attempted to placate Harper as he left the room, but he was already gone.

At that moment, Christopher Hughes strolled through another door. Messenger repositioned himself to where Harper had been sitting, by the leader's assigned chair.

'That was truly bizarre.'

'What was?' asked Hughes as he pulled a chair from the table opposite.

'Jim was just here expecting to be on the campaign strategy team, suggesting that as former leader he should be.'

'What did you tell him?'

'I told him to expect a ministry if we win, but to leave the campaign to the current leadership group.'

'Good lad,' said Hughes, the shadow minister for Industry and Member for Warringah in Sydney. 'Strategically it's for the best, and he can play a low profile in his electorate. We don't want Gerrard playing the leadership instability card during the campaign.'

Messenger smiled and cited a previous campaign slogan: 'If you can't run your party, how do you expect to run the country?'

'Exactly. The perfect cliché – I knew you would have one.' Hughes moved to the sideboard to pour a coffee. 'Would you like a cup?'

'No thanks, I don't drink that muck.'

'Coffee snobs you folk in Melbourne, aren't you?'

'Well, when you have the best baristas in the most livable city in the world then you tend to steer clear of the instant and percolated muck.'

'Who else is coming this morning, do you know?'

'Harry is down from the Federal Secretariat. The polling guru, Andres, will no doubt be coming.' Messenger laughed at the thought. 'I've asked Julia Laretsky from the women's division and sequestered Sussan Neilson from Pete's office to handle comms.'

'So just six of us?'

'Seven if you count the leader.' Messenger waved an acknowledgement as Laretsky entered the room. 'I don't see any need to have it any bigger, unless you think we should have a representative from each state. If we did want a national structure then there would be no reason not to have Jim on the team, given he is our best man in Queensland.'

'What, you don't think Tilley is capable?'

'Of course, he is – at a rodeo,' laughed Messenger. 'Hello Julia, thanks for coming.'

'Hi Bart, Chris. Nice day for it.' Laretsky pulled files from her oversized soft leather rose-pink bag and took a place at the table. 'You guys must have had some fun over the last few days.'

'Not much fun dumping a leader, I'm afraid, Jules, but enormous gratification having Gerrard sacked by the parliament and seeing his reaction. We just have to win now,' replied Messenger.

'This is our best opportunity for snatching power from Gerrard, and those unfortunate deaths last week makes it game on as far as I'm concerned,' Laretsky said as she flicked through her paperwork.

'Yes indeed, truly unfortunate for the families and a great tragedy for the parliament. I suppose Andres will apprise us if we benefit from it.'

'Andres can tell you what?' The pollster had just walked into the room, dumped his computer and thick folders at the end of the table and walked to the coffee station.

'We were just talking about the death of our colleagues in the plane crash,' Hughes said as he checked his phone.

'I'll wait until we get into the meeting, but I can tell you there is good news. Is there anything to eat other than these crappy biscuits?'

'Good news about people dying?' Messenger queried, looking askew at Hughes.

'The king is dead, long live the king,' Hughes glumly offered in response.

'And so, the political caravan moves on,' Messenger cynically added.

'Right let's get on with it.' The charismatic voice of Peter Stanley silenced everyone as he strode in with Harry Lester and Sussan Neilson trailing behind. 'We have an election to win.'

CHAPTER
3

DAY FOUR – SUNDAY

'Remind me why we're here, again?'

'You know why,' sighed Miles Fisher, the prime minister's steadfast adviser, a little frustrated with the impatient pacing of his boss.

'Do we really need them?' Gerrard walked to the other end of the overstated corporate lobby, with sweeping views over Sydney harbour, the enormous sails from the racing yachts cutting through the breeze. 'Is that a Whiteley, do you reckon?' Gerrard was now distracted by a painting by the floor to ceiling window.

'It's called Balcony 2 and I believe he did it around 1975.'

'It's crap,' Gerrard turned away. 'He's so overrated.'

An elegant woman entered through a large silent door

and sat at an open desk with only a telephone on the glass top. 'They won't be long, Prime Minister.'

'What's the hold up, luv? I was advised this was supposed to be a 10 am meeting and now it's ten past. I have things to do.'

The woman smiled, 'They won't be long. Would you like a drink? There is water in the boardroom, a tea perhaps?'

'If they aren't ready for me by ten fifteen, we are out of here.'

The woman gave a calm toothy smile in response, saying nothing and referring to a few pieces of paper in front of her.

'Boss, they won't be long, this is important, so let's just stay calm,' placated Miles.

'I am calm. I just don't like these people. Who the hell do these morons think they are?'

'They run Australia, that's who they are.'

'I run Australia you dickhead, not some pampered, precious, privileged group of business owners,' Gerrard spat the words.

'Stay calm boss and choke them with cream.'

'I am calm, Miles, for chrissakes,' Gerrard quietly snarled.

The telephone softly hummed, and the woman immediately answered, softly responding before replacing the handpiece. She then stood and walked to Gerrard. 'The board will see you now, Prime Minister.' She turned to lead him through the access to the boardroom.

'More like a cabal than a board,' sneered Gerrard to Fisher. 'I'll see you soon, young man.'

'Cream, boss, choke them with cream.'

Gerrard tailed the woman as she opened another nearby door and announced him to the room. No-one stood to greet him as Gerrard waited by the door surveying what was before him. Twelve chairs were occupied with a solitary one left empty and alone on one side of the enormous heavy timber table. Gerrard scoffed silently to himself as he took the seat, leaned back confidently in his chair, and waited for someone to speak. He perused those opposite and the image of a bottle of cream came to mind as he smiled.

'Prime Minister, thank you for coming to see us,' Kerry Jameson softly said.

'Pardon?' Gerrard decided he should take control before shoving handfuls of cream down resisting throats. 'Sorry, I didn't hear you.' Gerrard cupped his ear.

The frail owner of five casinos cleared his throat with a phlegmy cough and projected, 'Prime Minister, thank you for coming to see us.'

'No problem, how can I help?'

'You know our group and our interests, so we don't need your help, rather, we would like to help you get re-elected.'

'That's very kind of you, I appreciate it.' Gerrard smiled like a toothy used car salesman welcoming a new client onto the lot.

Tony Hancock, a friend, and confidante of the prime minister chipped in. 'Andrew, we just want to get confirmation directly from you today that a number of our issues will be handled by your government during the next term of parliament.'

'Oh, hello Tony,' Gerrard squinted through an overstated grimace. 'I didn't see you there squirrelled away in the dark, it's a long way down to the end and my eyes aren't as good as they used to be.' Gerrard smiled and then turned away. 'I must say, I'm not very happy with the editorials your mob have been running since Friday. I hope they're not your words.'

Hancock sat back in his chair preferring not to engage his friend.

'Prime Minister, we are concerned about a number of policies you have been promoting in the media over the last few years and we would like reassurances.' Felicity Osman, the respected finance sector executive joined the conversation.

Gerrard begrudgingly turned to look at Osman, pursed his lips as if sucking on a lemon and ran his tongue over his front teeth. 'What policies might they be?'

'Well for one, the refusal of your government to recognise coal seam gas exploration as a legitimate resource investment.'

'Fracking?' Gerrard sat forward leaning on his elbows on the table. 'You want a change in the government's resources policy to allow fracking in Australia?'

'Yes.'

'Breaching every promise and policy we have developed over the years to reduce atmospheric carbon. Ignoring all our international obligations.'

'Yes,' repeated Osman, sternly.

'Like a good fracking, do you?' Gerrard stared at Osman, paused for a moment, fighting the need to add another comment, slightly nodding his head. 'What else?'

'We want you to loosen access to international workers.' The familiar voice of property guru Frank Lowsonne brought a smile to Gerrard's face.

'Good morning, Frank,' Gerrard nodded. 'Expensive penalty rates worrying you, are they?'

'It's not me, Prime Minister, the labour market needs competition.'

'Nothing to do with hospitality workers or casinos then?' Gerrard sassed them, seeming to have misplaced his cream bottle. 'Anything else?'

'We want a repeal of the Native Title Act,' Allan Connell, the mining magnate offered. 'It's too costly as it currently stands, and we have already paid way too much for rights to dig. The compliance requirements and the need to employ Aboriginals are extreme. This new Act is killing us interna-tionally.'

'So, you think it's fair to rip off our Indigenous brothers and sisters?'

'You suddenly get a heart, Andrew?' snapped Connell.

Gerrard looked down the table with scorn. 'Is that it?' There was silence. 'So, if I agree to do what you have asked then you will support the government?'

'Pretty much,' Osman responded.

'What's in it for me?'

'What?' Jameson asked, cupping his ear. 'What did you say?'

'I said … what's in it for me?' Gerrard barked turning to Jameson, then added quietly. 'You deaf bastard.'

'Good media, campaign funds, plus we can provide you people on the ground, and any additional resources you may need,' Hancock smiled as he listed off the benefits.

'I didn't say what's in it for us, Tony boy, that goes without saying. I said, what's in it for me?' Gerrard glanced at Jameson, the leader of the group. 'I want to know what you are prepared to do for me if I do what you want?'

'What do you need?' Jameson hoarsely whispered, his voice beginning to strain.

'No, that's not what I asked.' Gerrard had no cream left. 'I want to know what you will do for me?' Their silence was instructive to Gerrard. The collective tension from the wealthiest, most influential, independent business owners in the nation was palpable as some sat quietly while others fidgeted avoiding engagement.

Gerrard let his request linger for a moment then repeated his demand a little louder. 'What's in it for me, my friends?' Each owner remained silent, preferring not to move nor respond to each other, apparently knowing Jameson would speak on their behalf.

Jameson coughed a wheeze like a smoker before saying, 'We will consider your request and let you know later today.'

Gerrard said nothing as he gawked at the old man, a slight smirk moving his lips. Finally, he said, 'You think I'm going to let a bunch of overstated nobodies who have abused their privileged position in Australia to grow obnoxious wealth, tell me, your prime minister for over seventeen years, what he can and can't do?' The leader stood and politely pushed his chair back into the table and leaned forward, resting his forearms on the high back. 'You folks are crazy brave to think you can seduce me to your will like that. You want action on your policies? Well then, you'll just have to do what everyone else in this country does, and that's grovel at my office – not my house in Canberra anymore, but my office across the bridge. You can stick your sad little offer up your collective arse and get behind my re-election campaign if you know what's good for you.' Gerrard began to walk to the door. 'Hancock knows how things work with me, so I'd suggest you listen to him. And I can tell you this ...' he stopped and turned, pointing back at the group. 'Things don't work with me when I have to wait ten fucking minutes for an audience with you pompous pricks.' He walked through the double door and slammed it as hard as he could, rattling its partner.

'So that went well?' suggested Miles, smiling as he jumped up to meet the striding Gerrard.

'The dairy is fucking closed today.'

'Whenever self-interest is running in a political race, always back it, because you know it's trying its hardest,' Tony Hancock finally said to the quiet group after the door stopped rattling.

'What's his self-interest?' Felicity Osman asked.

'Winning another term, then retiring to Paris.'

'So, if we get him elected and buy him an apartment in Paris, he will do what we want?' Lowsonne asked.

'No,' Hancock sceptically replied. 'We just offended him, and he has no reason to do us any favours. Quite the opposite, I'd reckon.'

'So maybe we should back the other side. Surely, they will finally run a strong campaign,' suggested Kerry Jameson, as he struggled to stand. 'Let's get rid of the prick once and for all and go to work on Stanley. It's time for his mob to be back in government anyway.'

'Agreed,' said Lowsonne.

'What's the first step?' Osman asked.

'I'll initiate media support and perhaps Kerry can contact Wolff?' Hancock asked.

'Sounds like a plan, let's hook up in a few days after the Cup on Tuesday, I'll be in Melbourne trying to win a few dollars.' Jameson began shuffling off to his office. 'Have a great day everyone, sorry it didn't turn out as we expected – and speaking of the races, put some money on the English stayer, Gorgeous Girl, she'll win by a length.'

Felicity Osman hung back to talk with Hancock as the others began strolling out chatting among themselves about tips and plans for their Melbourne Cup holiday.

'I'm not sure that went very well at all. Gerrard seems to be way too cocky for my liking,' Osman suggested. 'I'd have thought he'd have been dead keen to listen to our policy plans.'

Hancock smiled and rubbed a hand against his face, 'Welcome to the world of Andrew Gerrard, prime minister extraordinaire.'

'Will he win?'

'He should, but I don't think he'll stay for the entire term. He is sixty-seven and I reckon he'll pull the pin early, so it may not matter who actually wins, we get what we want no matter the result.'

'It's way better for us to back the winner, I would have thought,' Osman said as she slowly made her way from the room.

'One of my journalists discovered his wife left for Switzerland the other day and is not due back until the new year.' Hancock slowly walked out with her. 'It may mean nothing, but knowing those two, as I do very well, then something is going down. So, if we back Stanley and he loses then it may not make any difference if Gerrard retires soon after the election.'

'I didn't realise politics was this hard.'

'Trust me, Felicity, politics is easy. It's only ever about numbers and simple arithmetic.' Hancock stepped back and let Osman walk through the door. 'Whoever has the numbers has the power. We just strip Gerrard's numbers off him and we get what we want?'

Anita was at her desk in Canberra filing her first campaign story when her phone buzzed. 'Hello, this is Anita.'

'Anita, this is Tony Hancock, have I caught you at a bad time?'

'Mr Hancock, hi. Sorry—' Anita startled, dropped her phone as she sat upright and quickly picked it up again. 'It's fine, I was just filing a story.'

'You work way too hard,' Hancock said politely. 'Say listen, I just wanted to say how much I thought your Gerrard piece the other day developed into a tremendous conspiracy. I must say though, I remain a little sceptical about the notion a prime minister was about to rip off the government with some secret deal with the president of Indonesia, but I liked it.

'Are you ever going to run it?'

'Nope. But this leads me to why I called. I had a chat to Pete Cleaver just a few minutes ago, and he told me you are a little annoyed by the campaign role I want you to do.'

'Mr Hancock, I'll do whatever I'm asked to do – I just thought it was a waste of resources.'

'Maybe you're right,' Hancock waited for just a moment. 'Look, the media group are going to support Stanley. We're going to give him the full five-star treatment and promote him to win government. So, this becomes a vital strategy of the group for you to lead. I want you to begin running the editorial on his campaign.'

Anita couldn't speak.

'I want you flying with him and staying at his hotel, so I've arranged that with his team. They will bill me directly. Just make sure you also get good background and profile pieces from the campaign. He's only been opposition leader for a few days and Australians are never going to elect a stranger. So, make sure you bring him into the homes of voters for me. Can you do that for me?'

'I don't know what to say.'

'You'll be okay, Anita; just do the job I want you to do. Write strong editorials and get the human-interest pieces that will sell Stanley's team. If he wins, we can then talk about you moving up from the Canberra bureau to Sydney, and maybe into television.'

Anita's hand was shaking as she cupped her mouth. She was a little startled, mixed with the enthusiasm of the responsibility she was being handed. 'Thank you, Mr Hancock.'

'Don't underestimate how much value you provide us, Anita, just do this job well for me, please. Will you do that?'

'I'll do my best, sir.'

'I want more than your best, young lady. Call me directly if you need anything.'

Hancock clicked off and Anita dropped her phone on her desk, then knowing she was alone jumped up excitedly screaming as loud as she could. Her first instinct was to call Cleave, but she had someone more important to speak to.

'Hi Barton, guess what?' Anita could not control her excitement.

'What gorgeous?'

'I'm travelling with Stanley, and no doubt you, for the

campaign. I've been assigned to promote the hell out of your lot and get you elected.'

'I'd heard on the grapevine Hancock was going to support us,' chortled Messenger. 'That's great, we can see more of each other.'

'This is the start of something big, Barton Messenger, for you, and for me. This is crazy.'

'I always thought you would be recognised for your hard work. I suppose we can catch up when I link up with the leader.'

'Hancock told me if I get you elected then I could get promoted to television.'

'Fantastic.'

'You don't sound terribly convincing.'

'Melbourne or Sydney?' asked Messenger, a little nervous about what such a promotion might mean.

'Way too early to say. Hey, don't worry, we'll work our way through it. You'll be a heartbeat away from being prime minister by the time I make the move.'

'I had better be on my best behaviour then.'

Anita smiled as she curled a strand of hair. 'It's never personal the things I write about you, Bart, you know that don't you? It's just politics.'

CHAPTER
4

DAY SIX – CUP DAY (TUESDAY)

The sun quickly broke the ocean horizon, filling the bedroom with light. The increasing warmth aroused Jonathan Wolff from his slumber.

A sharp ache in his head attracted his fingers and he gently rubbed the scar of an old wound to relieve his discomfort. Opening his eyes to gaze into the mirror above the bed, he realised his friend from last night was still with him. He slid from the bed without disturbing her to prepare his usual breakfast and plan his day.

Wolff's Gold Coast apartment was only ever used by him as a holiday residence when he wasn't overseeing an election or a political campaign somewhere in the world. The demand for his special services was high and kept him from his favourite place for too long. Covert campaign strategy and assistance was the specialty he offered generous benefactors wanting to win an election or influence government policy, but he never took money from politicians, considering it a conflict of interest.

He padded naked across the marble tiles of the open concept living room to a modern galley-style kitchen and began to prepare a pot of French Earl Grey tea and a bowl of strawberries, toasted oats, and vanilla yogurt. He enjoyed living on the coast, and especially his sub-penthouse that provided commanding views along the famous beaches.

The apartment was full of glass. Bright, airy, and secure, the perfect place for his much-needed breaks from the demands of dealing with people. Gnashing on his oats, he thought about hitting the waves. As he watched keen surfers in the early morning swell, he realised he would first have to rid himself of last night's guest.

Turning his mind to his phone, he found it in his strewn leather jacket and checked his messages. Sitting on a high wooden stool at his marble kitchen island, he scrolled through various messages, spotting notifications from six missed calls. He recognised the number and pushed the redial button, waiting for Kerry Jameson to answer.

'Wolff!'

'Mr Jameson, how are you? How can I help?'

'Always straight to the point, never any chit-chat.'

'Nothing to talk about, Mr Jameson.'

'Can you get to Melbourne today? Where are you?'

'I arrived back from Zimbabwe on Saturday. I was expecting your call sometime this week.'

'Zimbabwe? Did our boys win?'

'Yes, the opposition leader is – shall we say – no longer relevant.'

'Don't tell me anymore. I would prefer not to know,' Jameson said quickly. 'Are you able to get a flight?'

'I'll check, but it should be okay. Who are you backing?'

'Self-interest.'

Wolff chuckled. 'No, not in the cup, I meant in the election.' He walked to the boiling kettle and poured steaming water into his white teapot. 'Are we supporting Gerrard again?'

'No. As I said, self-interest.'

'No surprise. I think he's overrated now. Perhaps it's time for someone new.'

'Someone from his party – or would you recommend the opposition? What are your thoughts on Stanley?'

'Doesn't really matter. In a lot of ways, both parties are mirror images. We don't have the robust politics they do in Africa.'

'We're supporting Stanley, although we retain reservations.'

'Which are?'

'Well, he was only elected leader last week, for one thing.'

'That could be problematic in getting his message out. Most folks in the electorate wouldn't know who he is from a bar of soap.'

'That is why we need you to manage the campaign.'

'I'll do my best. What service do you need?'

'Strategy, and probably recruiting boots on the ground. We're sending funds to them.'

'Any other services?'

'Like what?'

'Like the ones I supplied to your friends in Zimbabwe?'

'Different country, different politics, needing different outcomes.'

'I still have your credit card from the recent job in Taiwan, shall I use that?'

'That should be okay. Have your rates changed?'

'I have a bonus on positive election outcomes now, but we can talk about that when I see you later today.'

'That'll be fine, I'll get a ten per cent, $200 000 advance to you tomorrow.'

'I'll get down to Melbourne this afternoon, depending on flights, and we can go through it. Is Hancock active?'

'He and Gerrard are mates, but he supports us getting rid of the government.'

'Other than the obvious issues, why do you want to get rid of him?' Wolff jumped as he suddenly felt a hand slip around his waist, caressing his naked stomach before moving lower while another clasped his chest, then warm lips on his back. 'Mr Jameson, I have to go. I'll be in touch later today.'

'Righto.'

Wolff turned and the nude girl warmly kissed him. 'Good

morning. How did you sleep?' he finally asked, stepping back. 'Would you like tea?'

'That would be nice,' she said dreamily, straddling a stool. 'You look sharp this morning, no headache?'

'I don't drink. How's your head?'

'The champagne you opened was sensational. Was it local?'

'No, French. Would you like milk?'

'No thanks.' A freshly poured mug of tea was passed to her. 'You must work out a lot, you look in good shape for an old bloke.'

'Couple of times a week.' Wolff climbed on the stool next to her. 'You live nearby?'

'I live in Sydney. I'm up here for a conference. Do you know where my bag is?'

'To be honest, I don't even remember your name.'

'Well, Mr Wolff. Does that mean I didn't leave an impression?' she said demurely from behind his shoulder, eyes smiling.

'Nice one.' Wolff smiled. 'Can I drop you somewhere this morning?'

'That would be great. I'm staying at the Hilton.'

'I'll have to leave in around an hour, so if you want a shower or something, I have plenty of towels and girly things in the bathroom.'

'Well, I do want something. Shall we do it here?' She tapped the marble bench then ran her hand between Wolff's thighs, lingering.

Wolff knew the decision he was about to make might cost him valuable time, but he took her hand and led her to the bedroom.

———

'Barton? It's Jaya. Please tell me, what's going on?'

Messenger was enjoying a coffee after lunch at a cafe around the corner from campaign headquarters. He walked off from the table to take the call.

'Hi Professor, what do you mean?'

'You said you would get back to me, and you haven't.' Messenger scrunched his face, remembering she was right. 'You promised me, in fact.'

'I'm deeply sorry, Professor, but I've been a little distracted with the leadership group.'

'Can I seek endorsement? What do I have to do?'

'Yes, is the short answer. The nominations close tomorrow and preselection for all vacant seats is Saturday.'

'Tomorrow?' yelled Rukhmani. 'Today is a public holiday and you expect me to have this done by tomorrow?'

'I'm sorry, Professor, I can't explain it, I just forgot to get back to you.'

'No other reason?'

'No,' Messenger paused for a moment. 'Like what?'

'Racism is revealed in many subtle forms, Barton, and God knows I've experienced a lot of it throughout my life.'

'I forgot, I'm sorry,' Messenger was a little befuddled. 'That doesn't mean I'm a racist.'

'Barton, you come from a position of privilege, and you wouldn't know racism if it bit you. It's always subtle – the person never thinks they're racist, but deep down in their heart, they are.' The professor paused, Messenger waited, not wanting to respond. 'I'm surprised by your behaviour, but I won't have it influence my judgement. Can I use you as a reference?'

'Of course, you can, and I'll speak to our president about your endorsement and the project you're planning.'

'Is that another one of your promises, or just political spin?'

Messenger squirmed a little. 'I'm truly sorry for letting you down, I didn't mean it.' He rubbed the back of his head. 'I'll talk to the president immediately. If you have issues getting your application in by the deadline, let me know as early as possible.'

'I'll do my hardest to get it in; one of my students will help me. Thank you for your enthusiasm.'

'Professor, I'm deeply embarrassed not keeping my promise, please forgive me.'

'No issue, Bart, as I said, when it comes to these sorts of selection processes, I'm used to the covert nature of bias against me. I get it at the university all the time. Bye for now.'

The phone went dead. Messenger tried to dismiss the points made to him, but the lingering thought of unconscious bias and his commitment to equality was challenged by her. Did he believe the professor – was he really a racist?

'Bad news?' asked Sussan Neilson as Messenger returned to the table a little absent-mindedly to finish his coffee.

'No, I failed to do something for a colleague, and she accused me of being racist.'

'That's a little harsh. Anything I should be concerned about?'

'My politics professor at university wants to run against Gerrard as our candidate. She is planning to use it as an academic case study so she can design a teaching unit on applied campaigning. They want to blog it and film it. Should be fun.'

'What's the problem?

'She isn't preselected yet, which is scheduled for Saturday.'

'Is she suitable?'

'She has a PhD in politics, she's an immigrant, a child bride from an arranged marriage, a single mother, although I think her adult son lived with his father when he was younger, not sure about that. She's a long-term Australian citizen and she is the perfect candidate.'

'What's the problem?'

'She is Siddi.'

'Where is that, I've never heard of it.'

'It's the cultural group in India that originated from Africa.'

'So?'

'They're very dark skinned.'

'Oh.'

'That's what I thought.' Messenger raised his eyebrows and shook his head slightly. 'It seems that even thinking that thought means I might be racist. I'm also worried the party might not accept her, and if that happens, perhaps we are indeed sending xenophobic messages out into the community.'

'Leave it to me. If you think she'll be a good candidate, and if we put her up against Gerrard, and she's doing it as a university case study, it's a win-win for everyone.'

'That's a bit cynical, isn't it?' Messenger gnawed his bottom lip.

'To use your oft clichéd phrase – it's the optics. We'll be seen as inclusive and close Gerrard down from hitting us with immigration as an election issue. Pretty hard to argue politically that we have a discriminatory policy when we are inclusive with our candidates, wouldn't you think?'

'So, we use her for publicity as much as she uses us?'

'Yes, of course. It's politics, Bart. You know that,' said Nelson as she finished her coffee. 'I'll pull in a few favours and get the media ready, just make sure she gets her application in.'

'You travel light.' Wolff dropped his leather backpack on a chair and sunk into a soft leather couch at Jameson's swanky Melbourne office high above the casino.

'When I'm working, I like to move fast, so if it doesn't fit in the bag it doesn't come,' Wolff smiled. 'Did you pick a winner today?'

'I never bet; I just collect.'

'Nice philosophy.'

'It pays the bills.' Jameson presented Wolff with soda water and took his whiskey to collapse in the lounge chair. 'Thanks for coming down, we are keen to make this change of government happen and you're just the guy to do it for us.'

'Always willing to support you, Mr Jameson.'

'And you did a great job for us in Queensland.'

'Beautiful one day, perfect the next.'

'Especially with a change of government,' Jameson smiled broadly. 'What do you know about Stanley and his mob?'

'Not much. I would have thought James Harper had the best chance of winning an election, but this Stanley bloke and his new leadership cronies are hard to get an angle on at the moment. I suspect there isn't much government experience in their team?'

'You're right about that. They have a major headline speech on domestic violence tomorrow at a sporting club out at Mulgrave, here in Melbourne, so let's hope they get traction. Hancock is already primed to promote them,' Jameson said softly. Coughing a little, he took a swig of his whiskey.

'I'll observe their strategy over the next few days and give you a report on what we'll need. I've already spoken to several community contacts to begin to get feet on the street. So, we'll be ready to go probably Monday if you give us the green light.'

'How will that look?'

'We'll begin with community rallies – town hall–type meetings, in the most winnable electorates. Each with the same message, saying the same things every day in every electorate.'

'Every day, that'll be tough.'

'This election against a headline act like Gerrard can only be won at the grassroots. Using Twitter and other social channels will help generate momentum, but it's talking to the masses in the suburbs that will change votes. Our people will be in the audience at meetings, providing vocal support and encouragement to give the perception of a growing community movement. Social media coverage of the rallies will rapidly create a political movement, potentially influencing voting patterns across Australia. But it needs community organisers, and we will need at least one hundred and fifty-five, one for every seat.'

'Do you have those sorts of resources?'

'I can recruit both agitators and organisers, who are easy to mobilise, especially if there's money involved. It'll be up to them to get their own volunteers. By election day we should have a reasonable movement at the voting booths, which will influence voters as they arrive.'

'How much will this cost us?'

'Plenty, but it's not the money, it's the positive outcome we want. We all want good government, don't we?' Wolff smiled.

Jameson took another swig of whiskey, declining an immediate response.

'Do we need any muscle?'

'I wouldn't have thought so, but it's a little too early to say. Let me assess the campaign before I give you an answer. Just make sure Stanley's mob keep any stuff-ups out of the media. I can only do so much – if they're useless campaigners, I can't do anything to help them.'

'We want Gerrard gone – do what you have to do.'

'I haven't let you down yet – or for that matter your international colleagues – have I?'

Jameson smiled and slightly shook his head.

'Trust me, Mr Jameson,' Wolff leaned forward and engaged Jameson deeply in the eyes. 'I'll ensure Gerrard won't be prime minister of this country after the election,' said Wolff menacingly.

CHAPTER
5

DAY EIGHT – THURSDAY

S o Wolff wouldn't be exposed by a curious media tracking him to other campaigns he had managed, he always introduced himself to the strategy team by a pseudonym. This time he decided to add a touch of conservative sophistication and used the nom-de-plume Jack Sinclair-Browne. A hyphenated name would suit the class warriors of the party leadership group, no doubt.

He sat at the end of the table and poured himself a glass of water from the nearby pitcher, opened his well-worn leather folder, preparing a wad of papers. Stanley had been counselled by the party president that a campaign strategy expert would be assigned to the team and nodded his acknowledgement to Wolff when he entered the room. The expert position was donated by an obscure printing company in Sydney's west, and no-one asked any difficult questions. Something for nothing was always welcome in politics, no questions asked.

Stanley started the meeting. 'Right, welcome everyone, especially our new colleague, Jack,' Stanley nodded and smiled toward the end of the table, but Wolff didn't bother looking up. 'We are keen to receive good campaign advice from someone with your excellent campaigning skills and experience.'

When he didn't get a response, Stanley moved on. 'Christopher is an apology. He has urgent business in his electorate, apparently.' Stanley looked to his list, suggesting he was disappointed with Hughes. 'Sussan, can you give a media briefing, please.'

'The Hancock media are doing a great job for us with their lead political journalist, Anita Devlin, so far publishing two profile pieces, yesterday and today, highlighting the policy experience within the ministerial team. I want her to do a piece on Barton, but there has been some resistance.'

'Why?' Wolff asked quietly.

'Perceived conflict of interest with the journalist, but they will get another writer to do it.'

Messenger smiled, slightly embarrassed by the revelation as Neilson continued.

'The domestic violence policy launch yesterday went well and we made evening news broadcasts. Well done, everybody.'

Andres Jorges cleared his throat and said, 'Approval ratings for the party went up overnight based on our announcement of increased funding for agencies directly supporting victims and their families. It was a good strategy to get it into the electorate early. We achieved a significant rise in positive female response, and in eighteen to twenty- fives, we also recorded a strong positive response.'

Wolff jotted a note.

'That's a terrific outcome. It was a great event,' Stanley beamed.

'Leader,' Neilson hesitated. 'I'm taking calls about a remark you may have made last night.'

'Oh, yes? What am I supposed to have said?'

'Did you have a few drinks after a business dinner last night?'

'Yes, I had a brandy with two donors at the Athenaeum Club. I'm staying there.'

'Did you say the domestic violence package was labelled in certain circles as home maintenance?'

'Say what?' gasped Messenger, turning and staring at Stanley.

'Well, you have to take these things in context,' protested Stanley, embarrassed by the disclosure. 'We were having a laugh about what to call various policies and I volunteered the joke,' Stanley laughed nervously. 'Hilarious.'

Tightening his jaw, Wolff shook his head slightly then gazed at Stanley who responded by shifting uncomfortably.

'Okay, it may have been an unfortunate comment by me,

but it was said within a private group of three, so I'm not sure why the media would be contacting you.'

'It hasn't hit the media yet. These were not media calls,' Neilson offered.

'Loose lips sink ships,' Messenger remarked.

'Stop with your fucking clichés will you,' Stanley brusquely snapped. 'Suzie, what do we have to do to stop it getting a head of steam?'

Messenger smiled smugly at the leader's response.

The irony of his own clichéd comment was not lost on Wolff, and he sneered. 'I would suggest you say nothing. If approached for comment, you deny it. Who were the two businesspeople you spoke to? Let me have their details and I shall speak to them personally about maintaining confidentiality and establish if a recording exists. If there is, I shall get it.'

Wolff confidently pushed his way further into the discussion and stared directly at Stanley. 'No matter the circumstance, no matter the location, always consider you are being watched and recorded. This was a dumb thing for you to say no matter the so-called context, as you call it. Don't do it again.' The words were delivered with such confidence and intimidating force that others said nothing.

Stanley dropped his head for a few moments, collecting himself before finally responding, 'I apologise for my mistake, it won't happen again.'

'It better not, or I shall withdraw from the campaign.'

Wolff stared at Stanley, who again shifted nervously. 'Can I ask a few questions?'

Messenger responded, 'Sure, why not?'

'Do each of your local campaigns have a thirty-day plan that can be implemented from tomorrow?'

'Not sure. Is it important?' Stanley replied, looking to Messenger who shrugged his shoulders in response.

Wolff jotted a note. 'Do you have a policy and media plan?'

'I have key dates for media releases and press conferences,' Neilson offered.

'Are you planning a systematic policy launch over the campaign?'

Jorges sat forward to the table. 'We will link policies to the polling, and if we drop our numbers, our plan is to release a popular policy announcement to get the figures back in our favour.'

Stanley nodded, knowing the campaign plan was in keeping with what they had done in the past.

'Who is running your community support programs?'

'We don't have one. We leave that to individual members seeking re-election using their own networks. The new candidates in the other seats have to develop their own,' Messenger said.

'Do you have a centralised information distribution and volunteer recruitment program?'

'We haven't done any of that sort of thing in the past,'

Harry Lester offered. 'We leave that for the candidates to organise.'

Wolff dropped his pen on his pad and rocked back in the chair. 'So, what you are telling me about your campaign plan is that you are planning to lose.' Wolff was blunt. The tension increased around the table. 'You will not get elected if you don't address these issues very quickly, and I mean today.'

No-one spoke.

Lester eventually began justifying their strategy. 'We don't have the resources to do those things, so our strategy is to concentrate on broadcasting messages and maintaining attack pieces against the government.'

'And you have a moron as your leader who stuffs the first policy announcement by cracking a joke about it. Some strategy.'

'Hey, ease up, Jack,' Stanley defended himself.

'This is a clusterfuck.' Wolff was not finished. 'You are a national brand hoping to be handed the keys to the government bank accounts and you think a negative broadcast campaign will get you elected. You have got to be kidding me.'

Lester turned to speak but was cut off by Wolff with the flick of a raised finger. 'Look, think of yourself as a franchise with one hundred and fifty-five site locations. Would you let your franchisees do whatever they wanted in the market?'

No-one responded.

Wolff continued his lecture. 'This election campaign is the same operational model as a franchise. It's not overly hard to implement, and if you do it correctly, you'll be elected. Run a coordinated local campaign in every seat where everyone in Australia has the same message delivered to them every day in their community. No matter where voters go, they see your message. Go to Richmond, see a message, which is the same in Manly, or Cairns, or Perth – the same message no matter where you are, just like a franchised brand.'

'How do we do that?' Stanley asked.

'By ensuring every candidate, and that means no exceptions, uses your campaign operations manual, daily speaking notes, press releases, suggested diary activities and a community meeting program.'

'Why do safe seat members have to do this?' Lester innocently queried. 'We already have the vote in these electorates.'

'As I said, clusterfuck thinking.' Wolff slapped the table, startling the others. 'Do you seriously think these voters who already vote for you in safe seats are not your advocates and have an important role to play in the campaign? Don't they have friends they talk to who live in other seats? Do they not have children and grandchildren who live in marginal seats? You folks are fifty years behind in campaign strategy and the use of community organisers. No wonder this country is struggling to become competitive internationally.'

'We are?' Messenger said.

'Don't kid yourself, economic indicators and trends don't support your view. If we don't get a change of government right now and step away from the oligarchy we have in this country, which your poor election campaigns have created over the years, we will struggle as a nation for another fifty years.'

'What's that got to do with us?' Stanley asked as he jotted a few notes.

Wolff scornfully dropped his head, shook it slightly and gently rubbed his fingers into the scar on his scalp, relieving its tension. He looked up at Stanley with a slight wry smile. 'It is your failed election campaigns over the years that has allowed Gerrard to be in office for so long,' he softly said. 'It is your failed campaigns over the last twenty years, not your policies, that have allowed Gerrard to change the parliament, ignore the constitution, and do whatever he damn well pleases.' Wolff tightened his jaw again and stared darkly at Stanley. 'It has everything to do with you.'

There was no response as they avoided each other's gazes. Jorges bowed his head, scribbling notes.

'Look…' Wolff tried another tact. 'McDonald's has over thirty-five thousand stores in their global network. No matter the country, they provide customers with the same food standard, the same cleanliness, and the same message. You know what you are going to get every time you take the kids for a burger and fries.'

Wolff waited for a moment. 'Their burgers taste the same no matter where you are. But what would happen to their brand if their franchisees didn't all share the same standards?' Wolff looked about the table not expecting an answer.

'They would go bust. It's the same with you folks. You must insist every candidate uses the same message and they do everything in their local campaign in the same way. If we are to create a national community movement for a change of government then we must do the same activities every day in every local campaign.'

'What do you suggest we do?' Lester asked.

Wolff pulled a single typed sheet from his folder and slid it across to Lester. 'This is a schedule of activities I would like to happen over the next five days.' He then pulled out a thicker wad of papers from his folder and slid them across. 'This is a standard thirty-day action plan for each of your candidates with daily activities and campaign standards for them to follow. Send each of the candidates a copy. I have it on a USB for you, although I would strongly recommend you don't send a soft copy. Instead, send it in a campaign folder so they can read it without having to use a computer.

'You will note on the first page that every candidate has to agree to do what the campaign manual advises them to do. If they don't endorse the program, then you'll need to change the candidate before nominations close on the twentieth. No exceptions, whether they are sitting members or not.'

'We can't ask sitting members to sign something they don't agree with,' said Lester, snatching up the papers and flicking through them.

'Yes, you can,' said Wolff, announcing each word slowly and deliberately. 'And you will. If you don't, I can promise you, you will not win government.'

'I can immediately think of five current members of parliament who won't sign. What then?' Messenger asked.

'Disendorse them.' Wolff stared straight at the leader. Stanley almost choked, wildly looking for support from the others as Lester guffawed. 'Gentlemen, if you want to win government then take control of your party.'

'You can't be serious?' said Stanley, uncomfortably lifting himself with his hands firmly gripping the arms of his chair and then lowering himself.

'I am deadly serious,' insisted Wolff. 'To win government you need to win seats. Your new candidates will do as they are told. Why would these candidates be required to follow a campaign when sitting members do not? If these dills don't want to toe the party line during an election campaign to win government, why are you holding on to them?'

Stanley looked at Messenger with a crazed look of despair. 'What do you think, Bart?'

'I think we should at least get them on to this campaign program, and if they resist, then worry about what to do.'

'I suggest you get a local printer to produce a manual for every electorate as quickly as possible, today if you can. In the meantime, I will begin mobilising community organisers in each electorate. Once we have each candidate sign off on the operations manual, I will contract the organisers into the local campaigns to manage the candidate.'

'How much is this going to cost?' Lester asked.

'These things are being paid by my employer as a donation to help you win government.'

'Who are you, again?' Neilson asked.

'I'm the specialist in winning election campaigns, which

seems to be the missing link here,' Wolff retorted, shooting a fierce look at Neilson who squirmed slightly in her seat, avoiding his gaze. 'I have probably worked on more than one hundred campaigns over the last twenty years, so I know what works and what doesn't. I know, for instance, that releasing policy when the polls weaken will go nowhere,' provoked Wolff, looking at Jorges.

'I also know that unless we own the news cycle, we do not get any traction in the polls.' Wolff got up, snapping his folder shut. 'Folks, we have much to do and not a lot of time. Let's meet again in Sydney on Sunday. I expect you to complete the first eight points on my list. If you don't, frankly, it's over.'

'Why Sydney?' Lester asked.

'You have more winnable seats in New South Wales. I would have thought it was obvious that working at the campaign coalface is important.' Wolff didn't close the door as he left the room.

The room instantly became less hostile and relaxed. Julia Laretsky, who had been smart enough not to say anything during the discussion, moved to the coffee station to calm herself. Wolff had shaken her with his forceful language.

'Wow, that was exciting,' Stanley eventually said. 'I heard he was good.'

'Do we really want to be subjected to this type of bullying for the next thirty or so days?' Laretsky moaned. 'I'm very nervous about this type of operative working for the party.'

'As far as I am concerned, we need him,' Messenger responded. 'He's given us the campaign blueprint. All we have to do now is build it, then follow it.'

'You can't help yourself, can you?' Stanley laughed. 'The cliché kid is at it again. If you ever get the top job, you will be pilloried for it.'

James Harper was a despondent man. He hadn't ventured out of his waterside home since he returned from Melbourne. His daily heavy drinking was worrying his wife who encouraged him to freshen up, have a shave, change out of the exercise clothes he had been lounging around in for days and get out into the electorate. 'I can't face anyone at the moment, Shirl. I'm still a little raw about it all.'

Just a week ago, he was the leader of the opposition. Now he was relegated to campaigning in his electorate of McPherson on the Gold Coast, apparently for the greater good of the party. Once a parliamentary rooster, now just a political feather duster, it hurt.

He had been brutally discarded as leader the previous week. His colleagues didn't support him when he needed them most, and now Peter Stanley would decide his career fate if they won government. Ironically, he was considering a lesser ministerial role for Stanley in any future government he was destined to lead. Stanley and Messenger – both now leaders of the party – were great friends, but like Shakespeare's Brutus, they were assassins who came for him with a knife to the back.

He retained many friends in the party, a few close supporters, and co-conspirators within the shadow ministry and most of his former staff were still employed by Stanley, although the number of telephone calls and texted messages from them were fading. So, almost every day, he did what every savvy politician does and continued to strategically gossip with his network, trying to keep informed about the campaign and the machinations of national politics.

The shrill of his phone disturbed his afternoon snooze on the back patio. He knocked over his empty wine glass as he snatched the phone to quieten it. 'Hello? I wasn't expecting to hear from you – ever again. What can I do for you?'

'Just a few delicious tidbits of information for you to do with whatever you wish.'

'Oh yes. More fake news, no doubt.'

'The leader cracked a joke last night with two businessmen.' The informer laughed a little ironically. 'The moron called his domestic violence policy home maintenance.'

'You're kidding me,' Harper laughed.

'No, I'm not,' the caller chuckled. 'Plus, get this – he plans to have every candidate and sitting member sign a campaign agreement insisting they do as the party directs them during the election campaign. No exceptions, including you.'

'He can't do that. Whose idea was that?'

'A supposed campaign guru who has been appointed,

named Sinclair-Browne. He has been engaged to manage the national campaign. Just thought you'd like to know.'

'Can I quote you?'

'Not likely.' The caller clicked off.

Harper was baffled by the call. Thankful for the information, he was confused as to why the caller was giving it to him. Such a Machiavellian thing to do. Leadership ambition still coursed through Harper, and while others were sympathetic toward him, he toyed with the idea that it was a call from a friend who wanted his return to the leadership. After twenty-five years, the dark art of politics never ceased to amaze him.

Contemplating what to do with the information, he stepped back into the house and padded to the kitchen for a cooling glass of water. He pondered his media contacts as he scrolled the list. Who would love to receive this type of information? Who would do the most reputational damage to Stanley with this exclusive? Who would give him a little payback with this information leaked to them?

He looked at his list and zeroed in on two journalists who could do the job for him without having the information come back to bite him politically. One was a political lightweight, yet paradoxically an award-winning gossip columnist, the other an investigative journalist.

He called Mila Dempster first, a whippet-smart celebrity journalist who had grown to become a celebrity in her own right. She had a reputation for trashy stories and revelations penned for various publications. Now employed at the national broadsheet, she won a Walkley award for a story that no-one could ever fathom how she discovered it.

Legend has it she was given a strategic gossip piece on a celebrity who had fallen on hard times and was assigned to search for a scandal. What Mila uncovered was the plight of young male refugees in western Brisbane who had fallen foul of overenthusiastic celebrities organising drug- and alcohol-fueled sex romps. The exposé led to arrests and further police inquiries into a predatory network of highly respected men involved in drugs, pornography, and the procuring of children for salacious activities. She went looking for gossip and came out an award winner.

'Hello James, darling. So sorry to hear the terrible news about your leadership last week.' Mila always spoke with a high-toned aristocratic English accent, which was rather eccentric as she had not yet travelled to England. 'It must be terribly distressing for you and your family, darling. I feel so sorry for you. Is there anything I can do?'

'Can I give you information totally off the record that should only be considered background?' Harper always insisted on the secrecy code when speaking to journalists.

'Of course, darling, total anonymity, as always.'

'Stanley released his domestic violence policy yesterday.'

'Yes, I saw that darling. I expect to see more AVOs from my celebrity sisters in the future, and a good thing too.'

Harper ignored her commentary and got to his point. 'Within hours he was making jokes about it.'

'How can you make a joke about domestic violence?'

'You can't unless you call it – *home maintenance.*' Harper smiled as the words came out.

'He said that?'

'Within hours of the announcement. He was with two businessmen. Not sure where exactly, but it was in Melbourne.'

'Are you sure, darling? It doesn't sound like Peter?'

'Let's put it this way – if I'm wrong, you can expose me as your source.'

'Courageous thing to say, darling. But because you do say it, I tend to believe you.'

'I shall leave it with you then.'

'Thank you, darling. Let's catch up for drinkies when you're next in town. Now, promise me you will?'

'After the election, I promise. Good luck, Mila, bye.' Harper ended the call.

One more call then his work would be done for the day. Harper scrolled through his contacts until he found Anita Devlin.

'Hello Anita, Jim Harper here.'

'Hi Jim, this is a nice surprise.' Like any political journalist, Devlin enjoyed being kept in the loop, especially when politicians rang with news they thought she could use. Anita was challenged by the ethics of it all but understood that sourcing information from senior politicians was an essential part of the exotic daily dance of politics, especially when they want to undermine colleagues and weaken their party's policy. 'I must say, I'm sorry with what happened last week. I know no-one was expecting it, you did such a great job as leader.'

'Your boyfriend wasn't expecting it?' joked Harper.

'Well,' she was quick to respond. 'On the record, he isn't my boyfriend, but off the record, I'm working on it.' Anita smiled then disarmingly added, 'You were never available, Jim,' laughed Devlin.

Harper appreciated her humorous retort and chuckled. 'Am I able to give you some information as background. Can I be confident it doesn't get back to Messenger?'

'You can always be assured I protect my sources.'

'No pillow talk?'

'We've only shared a Chinese dinner and pillows are yet to be seen, so no, Jim, your confidentiality will be protected.'

'What I'm about to tell you may intrigue you, but you can't share it as it could reveal my source. You could dig further and perhaps confirm the information yourself if you know what I mean?'

'I would never compromise Bart like that Jim; you must know that. If I need information, I'll go find it elsewhere.'

'That's what I like about you, Anita, an ethical journalist with the desire to dig and investigate.'

'Thank you. Now what have you got for me?'

'What would you say if the opposition leadership team were about to embark on a new campaign strategy by managing all one hundred and fifty-five seats from head office?'

'I would say politicians do not like to be corralled by

anyone.' Anita quickly began to take notes after stretching for her notepad.

'I have it on very good authority that the party have appointed a campaign expert, and this is his first direction. He has insisted on them doing it, no exceptions.'

'How good is your source?'

'From the inner sanctum.'

'What are they planning to do?' Anita wrote quickly as she framed a storyline.

'They're planning on insisting all candidates and sitting members sign off on a strategic performance management agreement for their local campaign. This will require each of them to execute exactly the same strategy in every electorate, every day. As I said, no exceptions.'

'Sounds a little bizarre, but on quick reflection, it probably is a good idea to get everyone on the same page. But even so, it is a little heavy-handed, don't you think?' Anita paused for a moment, waiting for a response. 'When will this initiative be announced?'

'I know no further detail other than a name of this appointed expert. I must say I know a few good ones about the place, but I've never heard of him.'

'What's his name then, I'll do some checking.'

'It's a hyphen, do you have a pen?'

'Yep, fire away.'

'Sinclair-Browne. I suspect a hyphen name like that would be rather posh and it'll be Brown with an e.'

'Sounds English. You have nothing else on him?'

'No, that's all I have for you.'

'Why are you doing this, Jim? This disclosure may not be good for your campaign.'

'Let's call it karma, Anita. See you.'

Harper tossed his phone aside, pleased with his work, and returned to the kitchen for a drink, a little stronger this time. Devlin was right, it may hurt his party, but it may just help rekindle his leadership chances.

CHAPTER
6

DAY TEN – SATURDAY (REMEMBRANCE DAY)

Anita liked to continue her daily exercise regime when travelling. She always tossed her favourite sneakers, yoga pants and a neon top in her bag, and this morning appreciated the streetscape and sights of the exercise trails around the Williamstown peninsula.

Schwabs Galley Cafe was recommended for a light breakfast by Barton, who was waiting for her at an outside table. As she sat, Anita poured herself a glass of water from the carafe, prompting Barton to fold away his morning papers and hand her a menu.

'Did you walk far?'

'I followed the coastline from the beach, right around the point to the old Timeball Tower, which was fascinating. Then along Nelson Place past the shipyards until here. It was a great walk, plenty of people out with their dogs and the smell of fresh seaweed was great. I just love it here.'

'Where did you stay last night?'

'They have us in the Apartments, just over there.' Anita pointed to the end of Gem Pier on the other side of the park opposite.

'Nice.'

'What do you recommend?' Anita read through the menu.

'Everything's good here, but the frittata is excellent.'

'I'll have that then, and some tea. Do I order inside, or is it table service?'

'They'll come out. Hey, you look great by the way,' smiled Barton. 'Very Sporty Spice.'

'Oh, thank you. What a charmer,' said Anita, squeezing his hand and smiling. 'What's on your schedule today?'

'There's a service at the local cenotaph around the corner at eleven, and then we're off to Sydney. Gerrard is at the Shrine, so we thought we would do a suburban service − the optics will look good on the news. Community service, connecting with the community, all that sort of thing.'

'It seems you're doing a few things differently in the campaign from a few days ago. What's changed?'

'Lester has his act together. He's brought in resources and we're initiating a community campaign aligned with the national strategy.'

'Interesting. That's more diverse than you've done in the

past. What's brought this on?' Anita effortlessly probed, looking over her shoulder for the waiter.

'Lester has been arguing this type of campaign strategy for a few months and he is keen to engage the electorate at a local level, supplementing the national broadcast message.'

'Can I quote you?'

'Yes, please,' urged Messenger. 'We have nothing to hide when it comes to our campaign. The election war will be won in the individual battlefields of each electorate.'

'Nice one, especially on Remembrance Day.' Anita tapped the quote into her smartphone as the Greek cafe waiter took the order from Messenger. When she had finished her note, she asked, 'Have you seen Dempster's column today? Would you like to make a comment?'

'Here we are having a quiet breakfast together, the sun is out, we'll chat and laugh and enjoy ourselves and you ignore all of that lovely ambience just to get quotes from me.' Barton feigned being a little miffed. 'What ego has she smashed today? Celebrity or another socialite.'

'Actually, it's your leader.' Anita studied Barton to gauge a reaction. 'Apparently Peter has been a naughty boy, cracking jokes about your policies.' She only caught a slight flicker at the corner of his mouth, otherwise his face didn't move.

'What's he said?' Barton casually gnawed his bottom lip, superficially having little interest in what she was saying.

'*Home maintenance.*' Anita was impressed with him as she still could not detect any reaction from her breakfast partner. 'You are incredible.'

'Why?' Barton broke into a smile.

'I give you what could be a game-changing revelation about your leader and your face does not move. How do you do that?'

'Why should it be game over? Even if he did say it, and I'm fairly sure he would not have been so stupid, then it is simply a joke, and the political caravan moves on.'

'You don't think calling your domestic violence policy, home maintenance, is a problem?' guffawed Anita. 'You think he can joke about these things and get away with it?'

'It's hypothetical – he never said it.'

'Dempster always has very reliable sources.'

'Take it from me, he never said it,' insisted Messenger.

'You have that political butter wouldn't melt in my mouth look again.'

'Anita, he didn't say it,' Messenger retorted. 'You can quote me.'

'Oh, now you want me to quote you?'

'He never said it.'

'Which probably means he did.' Anita remained a little apprehensive about how this relationship she was keen to explore with Barton was going to work when her prospective boyfriend would always be on the political defensive. 'What else is happening?'

'We finalise all preselections today, which reminds me, have you learned who we plan to run in Melbourne against Gerrard?'

'A pale stale male as you usually do in most seats?'

'Oh yes, very funny. Actually, it's quite the opposite. We have a university professor putting her hand up to run. Of course, she won't win the seat – no-one can win Melbourne while Gerrard remains in the parliament – but she plans to use it as a case study for her political study programs.'

'She teaches politics?'

'She's an immigrant as well, which is just a sensational story.'

'If that is the case, I might be interested in doing a piece on her. What's her name?'

'Professor Jaya Rukhmani. She's based at Melbourne University, and she supervised part of my PhD.'

'Where is she from, sounds like Sri Lanka or Fijian Indian?'

'Actually, she's from India. She came here around thirty years ago to get married, one of those cultural things.' Messenger grimaced. 'Once she had a child, things changed for her, and the marriage didn't last.'

'I'm not surprised, most of those arranged marriages seem to struggle. What is she, around sixty?'

'More like early to mid-forties.'

'Say what? That would mean she was very young when she came here.'

'Her son never lived with her. I think the father obtained custody when he was around two, maybe. Don't quote me. I went to his thirtieth birthday celebrations early this year.'

'I bet she has some interesting stories to tell. How did she end up doing what she's doing?'

'Her husband's family disavowed her. With limited options, she used the welfare system to complete her education, went to university and hasn't left – now she's a professor.'

'Good on her. You're absolutely right, that is a great story. Is she likely to be preselected?'

'We don't normally get candidates wanting to run in Gerrard's seat, but that doesn't mean she's a certainty.'

'No candidates, no certainty – how does that work?'

'She is Siddi, from Karnataka.'

'So what?'

'They are of African descent and her skin colour is much like she might come from the Sudan.' Messenger screwed up his face. 'I'm not so sure the party is ready for that type of cultural diversity.'

'Can I quote you?'

'Hell, no!' chided Barton a little too loudly, nervously checking about him. 'Jaya has already accused me of being insensitive to her, so no, don't quote me.'

'Enough of the colourful language please, Mr Messenger.' The cafe owner arrived by his side with their breakfast. 'We have high standards here.'

'Ah Parthena, thank you.' Barton sat back and removed his newspapers from the table. 'This is my friend Anita, she's from Canberra.'

'Are you a politician as well?'

'No,' Anita laughed. 'I'd rather poke my eyes out with a burnt stick.'

'Ah, just like me. I can't stand them.' Parthena poured

more water for her clients. 'Present company excepted, of course, Mr Messenger.'

'No offence taken,' laughed Messenger. 'Tell me, what are the issues worrying you at the moment.'

'No future for my kids.' The owner offered cracked pepper from the mill she held under her arm; Anita waved no. 'The government lets too many immigrants into the country and they bludge on the system. The government makes it too easy for them and who'll pay the bill? My kids will.'

Barton smiled broadly then sarcastically replied. 'But you're an immigrant.'

'My family came to this country with nothing. We worked hard to establish ourselves. There were no government hand-outs in those days, not like there are now.'

'So, we should just stop letting people in? Is that what you want the government to do?'

'No, of course not. We need immigration to grow, but we don't need to pay money to them so they can sit around all day.'

Barton shrugged his shoulders. 'Oh well, this is the system.'

'Then change the system. You are there, do something. It's not fair for us taxpayers who work hard and see our taxes being wasted.'

Messenger began to feel a little uncomfortable not knowing how to end the conversation, so he said nothing, smiled and nodded his head.

'Enjoy your breakfast, I'll bring your teas out.'

'She's a nice lady, but always has a go at lazy immigrants,' Barton said softly, looking to see if others could hear him.

'Does she have a point?' Anita asked.

'It's the system. No government will clean it up.'

'Is she right when she says politicians are too scared to talk about these things?'

'Talk about immigration policy we're called racists, or some other derogatory phobic word.'

'Maybe you should try and bring the conversation into the public domain and talk about these issues, especially if there are strong views. I suspect the electorate would appreciate it.'

'Yeah maybe,' sighed Barton as he picked up the first section of his toasted club sandwich. 'Have your breakfast.'

Anita looked at him, wanting to change the tone as she unwrapped her cutlery from the paper napkin. 'This Indian candidate is a great story; can you give me her contact details, or should I get them off Lester?'

'Best you go through him but wait until she is confirmed as our candidate.'

The frittata flavour was hitting the spot and Anita squirmed a little in her chair as she always does when her tastebuds are excited by good food. 'This is fantastic, would you like a taste?'

Barton ignored the question but then asked, 'Do you think I'm a racist?'

'What a strange thing to ask.' Anita stopped eating and gazed at him. 'Why would you ask such a thing?'

'Jaya got me thinking about it. She says the privileged white community doesn't grasp the realities of the daily struggle for ethnic minorities and therefore we are inherently racist. Not deliberately, but we just don't see the system as those with colour see it.'

'White privilege assumes race is class based, but I would argue it isn't. There are plenty of white people who don't get access, such as women,' suggested Anita.

'I assume what Jaya means is that because I'm a white male, the system I was born into was a majority construct and therefore I have no idea about the struggles of others, consequently I'm privileged.'

'Well, you're not a bigot, I know that. It's a bit harsh to call you a racist for not having empathy. I don't call you sexist because you have no idea what I want,' smiled Anita.

'I don't know,' worried Barton. 'Maybe she has a point. She certainly has a point within the history of the parliament, it has been mostly a dominate, white-male institution.'

'I'm not sure the dominate culture needs to continually feel guilty about so-called privilege.'

'I'm not sure about that, maybe we do,' said Barton.

'Boy, you really are being philosophical this morning.'

'I just get the feeling there is a gap within the community no-one wants to fill, and we just continue to categorise and create division. It's awful the way we can't discuss issues these days without being called phobic of something or someone.'

Anita decided to change tact a little as she finished her breakfast. 'I feel a little sorry for Stanley.'

Barton sipped his recently arrived tea and looked at her. 'Why would you say that?'

'I think he is going to be a little out of his depth as leader.' Anita closed her knife and fork and sat back in her chair patting her lips with her serviette. 'It's questionable if he ever wanted to lead the party, and only last week he would have been happy for Christopher Hughes to have been elected. I'm not sure he'll be able to handle being prime minister.'

'The party room didn't want Hughes.'

'I'm not sure Stanley has the ticker to face Gerrard.' Anita prodded a little harder. 'This joke thing, true or not, is just an example of the political system getting ahead of him. He's just seems too nice to be a political leader.'

'Maybe you're right, but he's all we have now. I think the election result will be close, and if we win, he'll make a fine prime minister.'

Anita worked a little more to get where she wanted to go. 'The campaign just seems a little out of control. If you are going to Sydney today, why wouldn't you go earlier? Surely there is a cenotaph in a community in Sydney? Why go to one here when you would have had the coverage in Sydney.'

'Lester's following a plan.'

'The Hyphen's?' Anita just tossed it out there.

'Yes.' Barton stopped briefly before quickly recovering. 'And we have other strategic points of view that have been part of the planning process for a number of months.'

She had what she wanted so changed the subject to

Barton's favourite. 'When do you think we can have dinner together?'

'Tomorrow? I know a nice little place in Bondi, we have an afternoon strategy meeting, but dinner would be great.'

'I'll look forward to that but now I have to go. I have an article to write,' Anita said, quickly finishing the last of her tea and bouncing to her feet.

'Have a great day, gorgeous,' said Barton, as Anita leaned in to kiss him on the cheek.

'Thanks for breakfast, I'll buy you dinner, okay?' She knew he would be watching as she walked away; she contemplated doing a few leg stretches in the park for him but reconsidered. Not yet, he wasn't ready. She had more important things to think about than teasing Mr Messenger. She now had a campaign operative confirmed by one of the inner sanctum. She looked over her shoulder to check if he was watching and he waved.

James Harper was no computer graphic expert but considered the result of his work good enough to fool most people, especially political clowns like Peter Stanley. He had worked through his design on Adobe and after printing it a few times to check placement, he reproduced the graphics on quality paper stock and, except for one small yet significant difference (the telephone number had one digit out of order), the prime minister's official letterhead, complete with coat-of-arms, was surprisingly convincing yet an obvious fake.

Harper created the forgery by copying the prime minister's formal letter he had received during the previous week of parliamentary sittings, which validated their arrangements agreeing to no formal votes in the House of Representatives chamber. Legislation for a Christmas bonus for taxpayers was combined with funding for an immigration centre on the Indonesian island of Ambon and agreed to pass the parliament without any opposition obstruction. His agreement with the prime minister had cost him his leadership, and the irony in the plan he was hatching amused him.

The next stage of his scheme was to compose a fraudulent letter addressed from the prime minister to a senior adviser. Harper scribbled notes about various contentious policy issues, briskly crossing out those he considered too unbelievable. He needed something authentic and worthy of the prime minister's attention. Wasting money is always an issue with the electorate and the media jumps at any evidence of unfunded government policy so he centred a dollar sign on a page and whisked lines from it, writing ideas.

Handouts, hospital insurance, capital-gains tax, reduce social welfare, increase education, reduce education, cut defence, increase immigration … the issues kept rolling out for Harper as he wrote them beside a whisked line. The one he kept connecting with was the idea of a tax increase. Harper supposed the idea that the government had a secret plan to increase taxes after the election was credible and provocative enough to gain attention. A secret deal to increase the rate of tax to pay for – he wasn't sure.

Harper drafted his first letter then rewrote it, and then wrote another. He scratched out words and tightened syntax, crafting a message that would deceive those who read it. He wanted the message to sound official with the prime minister's arrogant style, using specific jargon. Once he had completed yet another draft, he thought it was good enough to print on the fake letterhead. He slipped on light white cotton gloves so he would not leave evidence before positioning the paper in the printer and clicking the print button.

To add further credibility to the forgery, Harper scanned a copy of the prime minister's signature from a letter advising of a parliamentary memorial for his colleagues killed in the recent plane crash. The paradox was that the tragic crash had led to the agreement between the leaders to take no formal votes during the last week of parliament.

He smiled as he scanned the signature into his computer software and connected it to his signature printer. The machine, used by many savvy politicians, allowed letters to appear personally signed – thousands of standard letters could be produced quickly. Harper placed his Mont Blanc into the machine, positioned the fake letter and pushed the green button. The letter addressed to the tax commissioner on formal letterhead signed by the prime minister was complete.

Harper then deviously dropped the letter onto the carpet a few times to give it a look of wear, rolled it up then straightened it, and tossed it around his desk until it looked well-handled before carefully inserting it into a benign A4 envelope ready for posting. Keen for the letter to be in Sydney the following day, he couldn't rely on traditional postal services that didn't operate weekends so drove to Brisbane to a Pack and Send freight outlet.

'I would like to send this envelope to Sydney, when can I expect it there?'

'We can get it there tomorrow for you, but there is a weekend premium. Otherwise, it will be Monday.'

'I'm happy to pay the premium. What time, morning or afternoon?'

'Late morning is the best we can do. Could you fill in this docket, setting out the delivery address, and I'll get the process moving.' The clerk began firing up her computer. 'Could I have your name, please?'

Harper hesitated slightly, quickly pondering what to do. 'Keating, Paul Keating.' He smiled at his choice of the former prime minister's name that the clerk didn't recognise. Maybe she was too young. He continued filling out the delivery address form.

'Address?'

Harper hesitated again then made something up before also providing a false telephone number – there was zero evidence to link him in the order trail.

'How do you want to pay for this Mr Keating, card or bank transfer?'

'Do you take cash?'

The clerk paused then looked up. 'You don't have a card?

We normally prefer not to take cash.'

'I only have cash. How much is it?'

'Let me quickly work that out for you.' Fingers flicked across the keys of a calculator. 'That'll be one hundred and twenty-three dollars, which includes GST.'

Harper extracted two fifties, a twenty and a five from his wallet and placed it on the counter. 'Keep the two dollars if you don't have change.'

'We don't and thank you.' The clerk responded and set about adding the completed form to the outside of the envelope. 'Mr Keating, all done. You can follow the delivery status with this code on your receipt, which will advise you when it is delivered. It'll be in Sydney tomorrow.'

'Thank you so much.' Harper left the store satisfied his fraudulent scheme would create a major setback for Stanley, it might even be the pivotal moment of the campaign, potentially destroying his leadership. He wanted his party to win government, but he wanted his leadership position back even more. If not immediately, then in time for the next election.

Harper smiled broadly as he got into his car. 'That should be enough now, James,' he said as he caught himself in the rear-vision mirror. 'I can't do any more. Enough.'

Much later that day, sixty minutes after she filed her column on the conservatives' new-look campaign strategy managed by a mystery hyphenated man, Anita was waiting for a taxi to take her to the airport when her phone shrilled.

'Anita, it's Tony Hancock.'

'Hello, Mr Hancock. How can I help?'

'I've just read your piece for the morning and I'm a little concerned,' Hancock said gruffly, unsettling Anita. 'You say you have reliable sources for this information. Is it your boyfriend?'

'For starters, he isn't my boyfriend, and secondly, no he is not my source,' Anita was a little miffed with the question. 'And thirdly, I wouldn't reveal my sources, anyway.'

'Then where did you get it? I need to know, it's important.'

'All I can say is that I was given the information a few days ago and I needed to confirm more of the details before I submitted.'

'Are you sure the information is correct?'

'Yes.'

'No doubt in your mind?'

'None.'

There was an extended silence and Anita didn't know what to do as she waved to the arriving taxi.

'So, you think there are outside sources at play within the opposition party's strategy and you consider this is a good thing?'

'They need all the help they can get, Mr Hancock. Gerrard is well ahead in the polls and today's story on Stanley will hurt him with the female vote.'

'And this shadowy character you have identified, Sinclair-Browne. Have you met him?'

'No, but I'm going to pay more attention to the campaign logistics personnel over the next few days to see if I can identify him. If I do identify him, I'll try and get a meeting with him.'

'Are you sure about their change of strategy to focus on local community campaigns?'

'Yes.'

'You've cited the Harding campaign in the States as a similar campaign that had a positive outcome.'

'My research on this led me to America. The Republicans had every candidate for a state legislature sign a campaign agreement. I found a copy on the web,' said Anita. 'It just sounds very familiar with what I've been told. I know Lester didn't visit the States during the election campaign – I checked his travel records – so they could have sourced this Hyphen chap from that campaign.'

'And you want to put this out there?'

'You're the owner. You wanted me to write good pieces. I think this is a good piece for the conservatives and indicates Stanley has lifted his game.'

'Let me sit on it for a day, I'll run it Monday or Tuesday. I want to check a few things first.'

'You're the boss.'

'Have you got anything else?'

'The opposition is running an Indian immigrant against Gerrard.'

'And you think this will help them?'

'No, but it positions them as a party of diversity willing to embrace ethnic communities, which is their new campaign theme, apparently.'

'Male or female.'

'Female. She's a former child bride.'

'Geezus Christ, will they never learn?'

'We need diversity, boss, it's good to have role models.'

'Okay, whatever. Anything else?'

'Just one last thing. My private life is a no-go area. I'd appreciate no further discussion on it when we chat.'

'Are you sure you want to talk to me like that?'

Anita hesitated slightly. 'Yes.'

'Fair enough, I won't raise him again. See you.'

Anita needed to sit down, so headed for the back seat of the taxi, letting the driver place her bags in the boot. She knew her boss had to be told to back off on her personal life but worried her tone may affect her chances of promotion to the promised television gig. Hancock had a reputation for burning staff if they didn't meet his high standards, but no-one actually knew what his standards were. It was always a guessing game when dealing with him. Why hadn't Peter Cleaver called her instead?

CHAPTER
7

DAY ELEVEN – SUNDAY

The opposition strategy team assembled as agreed in the Sydney Commonwealth Parliament Offices in Bligh Street, with Christopher Hughes looking forward to meeting the campaign guru he had been told so much about.

Hughes, the rakish Member for Warringah, knew he needed to contribute to the national campaign to be seen as a leader of substance. He was patient, as it was only a matter of time before he would be asked to be leader. If not for the unfortunate quirk of fate of the horrific plane crash killing parliamentary colleagues, his plan to snatch the leadership from James Harper in the new year would have been achieved.

Stanley was the compromise candidate when Harper

tripped up over parliamentary arrangements and unexpect-edly called for a leadership ballot, but he wasn't expected to win the election so his plan to take the leadership early next year was still in play. His time to be leader would come, he just needed to be patient and not be saddled with too much damage from this losing election campaign.

'Okay colleagues, let's start with current polling numbers.' Stanley began the meeting.

'Does it matter?' interrupted Wolff from the far end of the table. 'The only poll that matters is the one on polling day.'

'As leader, I think it might be a good idea to learn where we are after the first week. Does everyone agree?' Everyone else seemed to agree. 'Andres, do you have the overnight results?' Wolff sighed heavily and leaned back in his chair, not happy wasting time.

'Leader, the results are encouraging, but we continue to be weak in an important demographic. The preferred prime minister results are tracking the same. It seems voters want to get rid of Gerrard but results from the focus groups indicate they're yet to know who you are.' Jorges flicked through his results. 'On a two-party preferred basis, we are one point ahead, which if replicated on election day we could just scrape in. We plan to do more marginal seat tracking over the next few days to determine if we are having any traction in those seats.'

'What is our weakening demographic?' Stanley asked, half expecting the answer.

'Women.'

'Which category?' asked Stanley, breathing in heavily through his nose.

'Leader, it's all categories, I'm afraid.'

'So, we've lost women?' asked Hughes, exasperated. 'We have lost women to a misogynist pig?'

'I suppose the domestic violence policy can now be called, home renovation,' jibed Wolff flippantly.

'Sorry, who are you?' Hughes demanded, switching his gaze to the end of the table.

'This is Jack Sinclair-Browne. He is a political campaign consultant generously seconded to us by the Acclaim Group,' Lester said.

'And they are?' Hughes asked, still looking at Wolff but getting no response.

Lester relieved the tension between them. 'They are a major contributor to the party and do most of our printing and posters. Jack joins us from a recent campaign in the States and has had some Australian experience.'

'Had any wins?' Hughes didn't avert his gaze.

'A few,' Wolff replied, his dark eyes now engaged with Hughes. 'Never had a loss as a result of my methods or strategy and I don't intend to have my first with you lot.'

'Well, based on these figures, your first-time loss could be a sure thing,' Messenger interrupted the showdown. 'Let's move on, to try and increase our chances, shall we?'

'We'll get the women back,' Julia Laretsky said. 'The joke getting into the media didn't help, but we'll get them back.'

'Yes, I wonder how that happened?' queried Stanley, then

quickly added. 'After our meeting the other day, Jack distributed a list of activities. Harry, can you give us an update, please?'

'We have distributed the campaign management agreement to all new candidates. They have all agreed to sign and do as we request.' Lester hesitated for a moment. 'The sitting members are another matter. All the backbench agreed, but we are struggling with some in the shadow ministry.'

'When do nominations close?' Wolff asked.

Lester looked to Sussan Neilson, who responded, 'Wednesday, 5 pm.'

'Well, you have twenty-four hours to get their agreement or you disendorse them.'

'That's a little extreme, don't you think?' questioned Hughes, looking to Stanley.

'You weren't at the meeting the other day when we agreed the process,' retorted Wolff.

'To be absolutely accurate, we didn't actually agree to a process of disendorsement,' Messenger offered.

'I'm here to win this election for you,' Wolff said sternly. 'Currently, on those figures, you are well behind…'

'We are one point up,' Jorges interrupted.

Wolff looked fiercely toward Jorges who bowed his head and quickly averted his gaze. 'On those figures you will not win, trust me. You've lost women and they are not likely to come back. They don't know you or what you stand for, so they're not going to vote for Stanley.'

'I can raise those ratings over the next few weeks,' insisted Stanley.

'Your speech in Melbourne the other day was dreadful.'

'It was well received.'

'You talked about GOS, and you said it meant gross overseas spending – it actually means gross operating surplus. You're speaking on policy settings you haven't the foggiest notion of what they mean.' Wolff leaned into the table on his elbows. 'The more you speak, the more voters will know you haven't the character nor the intellectual capacity for the role of prime minister. My expectation is that you will fall further back on the preferred prime minister's rating and won't recover. It will only take one more stuff-up by you over the next few weeks to end the campaign – and if that happens, I'm out of here.'

'So, you think we will lose?' asked Hughes. 'Not much confidence from a guru.' He anxiously chuckled, looking at the others for support.

'I still reckon you can win, but only if you do as I say and disendorse those politicians who do not want to sign a campaign management agreement.'

'What has signing an agreement got to do with campaigning?' Hughes insisted.

'Discipline, and I can tell you this party doesn't have it.' Wolff sneered his response, looking at Hughes with disdain. 'I can assure you the government certainly does.' Wolff looked around the table for a sign of disagreement. 'You will win this election at the grassroots, not at the headline-grabbing national broadcast level where Gerrard prefers to play. You will win by developing a people movement for change in every electorate expedited by community organisers who I have appointed and stand ready to go, but only if every candidate is committed.'

'Have we finalised all the candidate preselections?' Laretsky asked.

'Settled yesterday,' Lester confirmed.

'Did we manage to convince a member of the ominous task of running as a candidate against Gerrard?' asked Hughes.

'We did,' advised Neilson. 'And she's a beauty.'

'That's a rather sexist thing to say, Sussan. I'm surprised by you,' Laretsky said. 'What's her looks got to do with it?' Hughes and Messenger swapped glances, rolling their eyes. Wolff dropped his head, breathed deeply, and exhaled loudly, gently rubbing his scar.

'I meant to say she is a great candidate.' Neilson pulled a profile from among her papers. 'I have no idea what she looks like.'

'Then I am sorry for my remarks.' Laretsky shifted in her seat. 'Please give us an overview.'

'She is a professor of politics at Melbourne University, an immigrant from India, and a single mother.'

'Does she meet constitutional requirements?' Hughes interrupted.

'Yes, we have checked, and she is clear,' Neilson confirmed.

'Then that's a plus – let's move on,' Wolff encouraged.

'A profile like that might be able to raise our vote in Melbourne,' offered Stanley. 'She won't win, of course, but if we keep Gerrard busy on his local campaign it may help the national effort.'

'Being a migrant is a terrific advantage as it will under-mine this idea that we are bigots and racists,' Hughes offered. 'How old is her child?'

'He's thirty. I went to his birthday earlier this year,' Messenger offered.

'An older single mother, then?' queried Hughes. 'Nice one, that ticks a few boxes for us.'

'Well, no, she is actually around forty-three, a child bride, a cultural thing apparently. She was my supervisor for my thesis.'

'People, can we stop with the chitter chat, we have a campaign to win. Let's get to more important news.' Wolff forcefully interrupted, moving the meeting back to the agenda.

Key messages and themes were strategically discussed and developed over the following eight hours. A revised policy release strategy was linked to a workable media plan and the production of local campaign materials agreed. Tasks were allocated with Wolff insisting on deadlines being kept. It was also agreed to disendorse all recalcitrants who refused to sign the campaign agreement. Wolff called an end to the meeting at five by packing up briskly. He left the room knowing he had plenty to do and instructions to give to his community organisers.

As the meeting was breaking, a staff member slipped into the room and passed a plastic file to Stanley with a large red sticker marked confidential. He didn't open it immediately, preferring to say goodbye to his colleagues and confirming the next full meeting in Melbourne on Wednesday.

When the room was quiet, he opened the file and read the letter. Not completely convinced, he read it again, and then yet again before punching Sussan Neilson's number into his phone.

'Sussan, can you call a press conference please, and we should do it within the hour. I want to make sure it gets on the evening news.'

'What's it about boss, shouldn't we stick to Jack's plan.'

'Stuff Jack's plan!' barked Stanley. 'I'm the leader and I've just been leaked news from the government that will guarantee us the election.'

Ferries came and went as Anita Devlin set herself up at an outside table overlooking Circular Quay. Working her smartphone, she made notes, preparing for the following day's editorial column. She was looking forward to her dinner later with Barton, who was supposedly trapped in a strategy meeting in the Bligh Street parliamentary offices. Her phone pinged an email arrival and she opened a message from James Harper.

Harper sought reassurance of total confidence if he were to send her startling evidence of a government conspiracy. Anita thought the request fascinating – it was an odd thing to ask. Confidentiality protocols between politicians and journalists existed to protect everyone who wanted to dance in the cabaret of political secrecy.

She quickly tapped a response, reminding Harper of her ethics and confirming anything he said would never be disclosed. Moments later, she received a blank email from a benign Gmail address with an attachment. She then received a message from Harper confirming he sent it and to open it. When she did, she immediately rang her editor in Canberra.

'Cleave, I've just received information from a senior source who has provided me with a strangely odd letter signed by Gerrard.'

'What does it say?'

'Gerrard is going to increase the GST rate immediately after the election.'

'You're kidding me?' Cleaver exploded. 'This is dynamite!'

'Do you want a copy?'

'Sure, flick it over. I'll have a look at it and ask the legal boys to consider it.' Cleaver was curious. 'What does it actually say?'

Anita quickly swiped the file to a new email and pushed the send button. 'I just sent it to you. It basically says Gerrard is demanding Treasury establish a task force before Christmas to rapidly deal with drawing up legislation to increase the tax rate from ten per cent to fifteen. It's addressed to the tax commissioner and signed by Gerrard, dated six days ago.'

'What's it on?'

'The PM's letterhead.'

'This may change the whole game. I can't see Gerrard surviving this, the punters will go crazy.'

'If it's genuine,' Anita remained sceptical. 'I wonder how my source could have got access to this, and why would he give it to us and not Stanley.'

'Maybe you can ask him.'

'How do you mean?' queried Anita.

'There is notice from the opposition for a five-thirty media conference. Are you near the parliamentary offices?'

'At the Quay. I can make it if I leave now.'

'Ask Stanley about the letter. Ask if he has it, and if he does, he may want to comment. If he doesn't, then disclose you have a copy and ask for a response. Let's get a reaction from them. Get going,' directed Cleaver. 'I'll give Hancock a call.' The phone went dead.

Anita packed up, paid her tab, slung her leather bag over her shoulder and trekked up the hill to the secured government building. As she was making her way, the phone buzzed with a call from Barton Messenger.

'Hello gorgeous, where are you?'

'Stanley has just called a press conference, I'm on my way to Bligh Street.'

'He's done what?'

'Your boss has called a press conference for five-thirty,' Anita was surprised. 'You don't know?'

'No. We just finished our strategy meeting, and I was coming to see you,' Barton was disappointed. 'I'd better go back, see you there.'

'Perhaps we can catch up after the media conference,' Anita pushed her luck. 'Any surprises during your meeting?'

'No, everything was set out and we have a clear media strategy. I must admit, this wasn't part of it.'

Again, this surprised Anita. 'What does he want to talk about, do you think?'

'If I knew I wouldn't be telling you. Bye.'

Anita finished her call and quickly scurried to the building, navigating tourists on the congested footpath. When she finally reached the crowded media conference room there weren't any available chairs, so she positioned herself at the back, keeping clear of cameramen and lighting assistants. Other media people followed her in, squeezing into available spaces along the walls. Messenger walked in, checked the rostrum, then left. Sussan Neilson entered, fiddled with the backdrop, repositioning the five Australian flags draped to add a patriotic tone, then stood to the side. She held a bundle of papers in her arm that seemed like photocopied documents.

Anita scanned the room and wondered who the mysterious gentleman was at the back standing with arms crossed. He wasn't loaded down with pad or bag and was elegantly dressed in black trousers, black shirt, and black jacket. With a tanned complexion, his shaved head revealed what appeared to be a rather vicious scar across his scalp. He didn't seem to fit into the scene, and she hadn't noticed him around the campaign before.

Stanley stalked into the room. Messenger followed, positioning himself behind and to the right of the leader who took his place at the rostrum. Anita thought Barton looked too stern and serious. She tried to attract his eye to give him a relaxing smile, but he seemed focused on being in the moment.

'Ladies and gentlemen, thank you for coming on such short notice,' Stanley began talking to the assembled media pack. 'Everything set? Okay?' Last minute recorders were placed among the tagged microphones at the top of the rostrum. Stanley took a calming breath and then looked straight to the cameras at the back of the room. 'I recently received startling evidence proving Prime Minster Gerrard—' Stanley waved a sheet of paper like a flag. '—has a secret plan to significantly increase the rate of the goods and services tax upon re-election, effective immediately after the new year. The evidence delivered to me less than an hour ago confirms the Gerrard government, if re-elected, will bypass legislation and the parliament and increase the GST tax rate by regulation, ignoring the legislated requirements of seeking approval from all state and territory governments for any amendments to the tax.'

Anita now knew she had a copy of the letter Stanley was quoting and pondered why Harper had given it to her. How did he get it?

'Government is of the people, for the people, and my party is committed to restoring trust into our political system, so long treated with disdain by the prime minister. The information I have confirms Andrew Gerrard does not agree to proper government process, ministerial standards, nor safeguarding legislative direction as he plans to increase the GST from ten per cent to a staggering rate of fifteen per cent. That is a staggering fifty per cent increase of tax on everything Australians buy. If re-elected, the prime minister secretly plans to raise taxes on every purchase, be they consumer or business, all done without the approval of the Australian people.'

Stanley waved his hand and nodded to prompt Sussan to act. 'My adviser is now distributing a copy of the letter on Gerrard's own personal letterhead confirming the plan and counselling the tax commissioner that under no circumstances can they afford to make the plan public during the election campaign. The letter is signed by Andrew Gerrard and dated just six days ago.' Neilson quickly handed copies out from her armful of papers.

'I call upon Andrew Gerrard to explain himself. I call upon the prime minister to explain to the Australian people why he continues to treat them with disdain and why his secret tax plan is so needed by his government. This plan will obviously hurt the most vulnerable in the community, those Australians who cannot help themselves and who struggle to make ends meet. Gerrard must be held to account to explain his secret tax plan, his deception, and his betrayal of all of us.

If Prime Minister Gerrard fails to immediately disclose this monstrous secret tax plan and tell us why he thinks it necessary to increase the burden of tax upon all of us, then he should resign.

'If Prime Minister Gerrard can't explain why he continues to treat the community with contempt, he should resign now and allow this election to be a competition between the ethics and standards of transparent government − not the lust for authoritarian power as this outrageous letter confirms.' Stanley waved the letter high above his head this time.

'It's time for a change in how we are governed in Australia. It's time for the people to take back their parliament. If Andrew Gerrard refuses to provide answers, then he must go.'

The journalists raised their voices to a cacophony to be heard and be the first picked for a question. Wolff took a copy of the letter and left the room, distracted by the shouting. Anita watched him go, wondering if he were the Hyphen she had heard about.

The media conference continued for the next ten minutes with journalists wanting to be heard and Stanley trying valiantly to give them the answers they wanted. Most were sceptical of the letter and demanded the source of the leak for which Stanley stumbled through with hesitant answers trying not to fan the wrong political fire. Abruptly, Messenger stepped forward and tapped him on the elbow, so he swiftly ended the media conference leaving the room as journalists continued bellowing questions.

Anita tried to attract Barton's eye, but his grim, steely look didn't move as he ushered Stanley from the room to the safety of secure offices. She now had more questions than answers about the disclosure and still wondered how Harper had a copy. She had a story to write but didn't know which angle to take, so when she settled by a window in a nearby cosy cafe, she called Cleaver.

'It's a political bombshell – the atom bomb of announcements. That's the only way I can describe it,' Cleaver said after their pleasantries.

'I'm sure you'll write the news, but I'm a little concerned about the opinion piece and need your editorial direction.'

'What's troubling you?' Cleaver asked.

'The campaign operative was at the media conference, at least I think it was him.' Anita had guessed correctly. 'Anyway, if he was there and is such a guru, why would he not have told Stanley to wait to confirm the letter?'

'It's way too explosive to wait and they needed to get it on the national television news tonight.'

'I have it on good authority there was no discussion about it prior to Stanley making the announcement, which may mean the guru was not involved and didn't endorse the media conference.'

'I suppose Stanley was making a leadership decision.'

'But if it is a fake, Stanley is toast,' Anita said.

'Why would you consider the letter a fake? It looks real to me,' Cleaver forcefully said. 'Gerrard is just as likely to agree to a tax hike as try to hide it before the election. He's done that sought of thing in the past.'

'It's all a little too convenient for me and now I wonder how my source got hold of it.'

'You know what to do,' Cleaver demanded. 'We support Stanley, so write a piece that supports his call for Gerrard's head.'

'This could be very wrong, Cleave. I just feel something is missing,' Anita ran her fingers through her hair, scratching the peak of her forehead, her face twisted. 'I just don't think the expert would have approved this announcement, which could mean there may be a political disagreement within the campaign team – that's the angle I want to write about.'

'I respect your intuition, but not this time. Write the piece focused on Gerrard's duplicity and I'll publish it. Anything else, I can promise you, won't get printed.'

After her goodbyes, Anita ended the call and began tapping her keyboard. She wanted to run the conspiracy angle but conceded it would never get past Cleaver, or Hancock for that matter. She wanted Stanley to succeed because it would help Barton's career, but she was confused as to why Stanley puff pieces were relevant when her investigative work was continually rejected.

Messenger never returned her call or responded to her messages.

CHAPTER

8

DAY TWELVE – MONDAY

The front door of the Melbourne Federal Parliamentary Offices in Treasury Place, behind the Old Treasury Building had been roped off to provide enough room for a prime ministerial lectern with an Australian flag on each side of the entrance. Journalists had gathered beyond the rope since being advised a media conference with the prime minister was due, rare in previous election campaigns. They wanted answers to Stanley's accusations and the PM was going to either resign or initiate a withering attack.

Attack the prime minster did from the moment he reached the lectern, ripping into everyone who dared question his integrity. He accused television news departments of bias and demanded why they never sought confirmation from his office before running the spurious allegations against him. Gerrard had been ranting for five minutes – denying the accusation of complicity in developing a secret tax policy and accusing instead the opposition leader of forging the document printed in all newspapers and lambasting the journalists for not doing their work in exposing the fraud.

'Prime Minister, how can we be so sure the letter is a forgery?'

'Mr Weideman, you have been in the Canberra Press Gallery now for more than twenty years, and during that time have you ever seen such tosh written on any letterhead associated with any of my ministers?' Gerrard rhetorically asked. 'I think not. Those journalists accusing me of this fake news are nothing more than desperate corporate news flakes and should not be anywhere near the serious national media. This rubbish, written by Hancock media today denouncing me and calling for my resignation, is nothing more than fake news and these conspiracy merchants should never be allowed to be treated with esteem by the public ever again. The rubbish written be Anita Devlin was reckless and she should be condemned for damaging the reputation of the tax commissioner, and indeed, me.

'I demand a front-page apology. I also demand an apology from the opposition leader Mr Stanley on today's national news broadcasts. I think the people of Australia will now see the opposition for what they truly are – fraudsters and con artists, saying anything and doing whatever it takes to squirm their way into government.'

'Prime Minister, other than your denial, do you have any other proof this letter is a fraud?' queried a journalist.

'Well, yes I do.' Gerrard pulled a smartphone from his jacket and held it aloft like a trophy. 'Let me use this simple device to show you what the media should have done when they first received a copy of this obvious forgery yesterday.' Gerrard then checked the letter and prodded in the numbers, touched it to speakerphone, and placed it as close as possible to the microphones.

'The number you have called is not connected, please try again.'

'That is the message you receive when you ring the number on this Stanley forgery.' Gerrard declared triumphantly with a broad smile; his chest pushed out like a peacock. 'That same response would have happened to any journalist who bothered to do their job and check the letter's bona fides. While it is true the numbers are the same as my office, they are in the wrong order, which obviously means this is not my letterhead and the letter is a blatant forgery.

'Everyone,' Gerrard then pointed at the journalists. 'And that means all of you, including every news organisation in Australia that is associated with this corrupt treachery, should be ashamed of yourselves. The people of Australia deserve better from the alternate government than this fraudulent rubbish and their lies.' Gerrard then looked straight down the barrel of the camera lens directly in front of him. 'And electors know I would never lie to them.'

Several journalists spoke at once. Gerrard ignored them,

not changing his piercing stare into the camera. 'I would never do to the Australian people what the leader of the opposition has just done, and I expect a public apology. Today.'

The journalists fell silent, stunned by the revelation and Gerrard's declaration.

'Do a better job next time and stop believing fake news,' barked Gerrard, storming off, returning to his office.

Wolff was admiring the Whiteley, wondering how much it would be worth now if it were on the market. He enjoyed Whiteley's work and considered him underrated in the labyrinth of modern artists, especially in Australia. More than just a coke head, he thought as he studied the strokes more closely.

'Mr Wolff?'

Wolff turned to see a tall, elegant woman beckoning him. 'Yes, ma'am?'

'They will see you now.'

Wolff moved toward her and, before she moved off, engaged her. 'I was just wondering?' She stopped and looked at him. 'How does one get on your dating roster?'

The woman smiled slyly and said, 'Wait to be asked would be my recommendation. Please follow me.'

Wolff smirked as he followed her. You never know unless you ask was an early mentor's advice and he always followed that rule. He had more spectacular crashes than wins in his tango of flirtation with women, but he always enjoyed the banter his assertiveness brought to the communication.

He stepped into the room to be welcomed by Jameson and eleven colleagues. He had visited the group in their boardroom many times in the past to discuss services and projects and was never intimidated by the crusty atmosphere of the room with its subdued lighting and dull resonance. He sat and smiled as he looked about familiar faces.

'We are a little concerned about the prime minister's media conference and wonder what you might have to say about it, Mr Wolff,' Jameson whispered forcefully.

Wolff 's smiling optimism quickly disappeared. 'Sir, it is my opinion Gerrard will not be beaten by Stanley,' Wolff gravely responded. 'When I first attended their so-called campaign strategy meeting, I was surprised how little organisation they had within their initial plans. It is hard to describe their lack of preparation and to be fair, they were not expecting the election announcement, but seriously, they are grossly inept. This would normally not be a problem as I can work to fix most things, but Stanley is not prime minister material. He is deadset hopeless.'

'You can't win?' Connell, the mining magnate, asked.

'We can win,' asserted Wolff, remaining confident. 'But I'm not sure you will want Stanley as prime minister. I'm fairly confident history will record him as the worst if he were to win.'

'Even worse than McMahon?'

'Worse. Frankly, if he does become prime minister, I would recommend you quickly take action to remove him and change to another who is more competent, as you've done in the past.'

There was no response from the directors. Jameson stared at Wolff, his jaw moving as if rolling dentures about his mouth. Wolff knew to remain quiet when investment news was not as good as expected and options considered.

Finally, Felicity Osman enquired, 'Just run us through what you've done so far.'

'Well, as I said, they had very little organisation plans in place. They were not focused on the battles in each of the electorates and they were luxuriating in the positive media they had been receiving. If Stanley is to win, we must change votes in the suburbs of every electorate. It's a fight we need to do virtually door to door. I've established community action groups that partner with the local candidate. In marginal seats we will ramp up this support with more resources, including getting more people active on the hustings.'

'Who are these people?' Osman asked.

'We recruit community coordinators who then pay agitators to engage with various community groups, who in turn promote disquiet within their own groups. The plan is to build resentment against the government, blaming it for everyone's troubles. They've had it good for too long under Gerrard, but now I sense a willingness for change.'

'What do you need to make this happen?' Osman began taking notes in her folder, others sat listening quietly.

'These community agitators will need money, lots of money. The campaign headquarters will need more people, especially talented social media campaigners. We need to bombard social news feeds with information that will influence young voters. Harry Lester has abilities, but he would be a number three in any leadership team I'd run, capable but devoid of any strategic foresight.' A couple of directors cleared throats as they shifted in their seats, while others shrunk further into their chairs, concerned by the report.

'I have to say working with this mob is challenging, but it is not impossible to quickly turn them around and get them operating as a cohesive unit. I've set up campaign procedures I want done and insisted all candidates and sitting members sign up to it.'

'Take us through your plan,' Tony Hancock quizzed.

'I'm not sure the detail is relevant for this table,' Wolff said confidently. 'But to give you a heads up, it might surprise you to learn I'm Marxist by nature. Not in philosophical terms because the system he espoused proved to be a failure, but more in practical application terms. For instance, I understand his teachings as they are applied to community revolution. Marx said if you want outcomes, people must make the move otherwise they resist poor leadership, and you achieve no result. Marx was really the first to identify the potential people power.'

'I'm not sure speaking about Marx excites this group that much, unless it's Groucho.' Frank Lowsonne interrupted. 'We're very proud capitalists here. We reject socialism outright and Marx is a socialist demagogue as far as I'm concerned. We reject his teachings completely.'

'With the greatest respect, Marx did not teach socialism, he taught community control. He wanted the people to take control not the capitalists, which paradoxically is the basis of modern western democracy,' Wolff said, delivering it with confidence. 'It's not his socialism offshoots I'm talking about, it's getting organised at the grassroots, developing a people movement wanting change and voting for what they want. That's what Marx taught his students to do – to get active in any organisation, including democracies. Lenin and Stalin misunderstood Marx and just did it for their own interests, just like capitalists I suppose,' Wolff smirked at Lowsonne.

'Self-interest wins again,' Lowsonne retorted with a sneer.

Wolff ignored the comment. 'So, to win this federal election campaign we need a community movement wanting change and that means a strong community campaign in every seat. We should learn from David Cameron, President Clinton, and possibly Turnbull in an Australian context from all those years ago. These so-called charismatic politicians concentrated only on their voting base and didn't worry about mobilising the broader community. They eventually lost support because they didn't listen to the people. On the other hand, Obama organised communities to respond to his messages and convinced them to come out and vote. That's what Marx recommended – rally the people on an idea for the future. It didn't matter if Obama didn't achieve much, the people loved him, still do.

'In election campaigns I work with, we mobilise community groups to speak on behalf of the people, and the politicians are there to represent the voice of the people – not their own.'

'Did you work on the recent Harding campaign?' Hancock asked.

'Yes, I did. Why?'

'One of my journalists recently likened it to the Stanley campaign plan.'

'Interesting, what's his name?'

'It's a she, her name is Anita Devlin.'

Wolff took a small notepad from his leather jacket, flicked it open and wrote her name as he continued. 'I believe for every action there is an outcome, either good or bad. Nothing happens without an action, and that is the message I'm getting back about Stanley, he is not a man of action.'

'So, what is the state of the current campaign?' asked an anxious Jameson.

'I have engaged one hundred and fifty-five seasoned community organisers who are briefed and ready to go once I have your agreement. I've refined the opposition's campaign and given them a four-week daily action list leading up to, and beyond, election day. We are ready to go. I just need your approval.'

'Why do we need to wait?' Osman asked. 'Surely we're running out of time.'

'I suppose Wolff is waiting for us to make up our mind

once and for all if we are committed to Stanley and give Gerrard away,' responded Jameson.

'Your call, Mr Jameson. I'm here to serve you.'

'What do you make of this alleged forgery?' Lowsonne asked.

'It's a forgery. I knew the number was wrong yesterday when I first saw it.' Wolff responded. 'We're in trouble because Stanley didn't refer it to the strategy group or me, although I've advised them, I'm always available. He acted against agreed media strategy, independently and frankly irresponsibly, which probably gives you a clear indication how he'll be as prime minister. Gerrard is right when he says it's a stitch-up, although I'm not sure if the original is from him or someone on our side.'

'Will Stanley last?' Osman asked.

'He can, but if you want to make a change to the leadership do it now. This stuff-up is your opportunity to move on him,' Wolff convincingly declared, leaving no doubt it would be a strategically wise move.

'It would be too complex to start thinking about a change of leader,' Lowsonne offered. 'They would have to organise the members to vote for a new leader, and that would take far too long.'

'And if he was to have a heart attack?' queried Wolff, staring at Jameson who returned his gaze, pursing his lips and running a bony talon-like finger across his chin.

'Messenger would get the call, and we don't want him yet. He's far too young and untested,' Jameson finally replied.

'We would want Hughes before Harper. So, it is way too difficult to do it right now, we shall have to stick with Stanley.'

'More's the pity,' Wolff responded. 'It's not impossible for him to win, but I would recommend you have a bit each way by making Gerrard feel a little warmth toward you.'

'He may need money, so he could be willing to listen to us now,' Hancock hopefully offered, conscious his friend hadn't been returning his calls.

'Money is a good motivator. It certainly is for me,' chuckled Jameson, until he wheezed a cough.

'He may need decent media for a change.' Wolff directed his question to Hancock. 'Can you get favourable press going for him?'

'It may have to start with a grovelling apology,' Hancock responded.

'He wants it on page one,' Wolff smiled.

'Best I ring him and calm him down,' Hancock suggested.

'I suspect we should meet with him. I'll get him in to see us tomorrow,' Jameson said, looking to the others to agree. 'Okay Mr Wolff, thank you so much for the work you have done for us so far. You are authorised to mobilise your community organisers to begin work and if you need anything else, call me directly. We appreciate your efforts in working for a better Australia.'

Wolff sat back in his chair and half smiled. 'Well, it's my country. I want the best for it, and I know it's time to get rid of Gerrard.' He then stood, nodded, and left.

As he was stalking through the foyer, the executive assistant interrupted his assessment of the meeting.

'Mr Wolff?'

He stopped and looked at the woman, smirked, a little embarrassed, and slowly sauntered over to the desk. 'My father was called Mr Wolff,' he smiled. 'My father is long dead, so Wolff is just fine.'

'Well, Wolff…' The assistant hesitated for just a moment breathing deeply, her cheeks a little flushed. 'It seems there has been an opening made available in the dating roster you enquired about earlier.'

CHAPTER
9

DAY THIRTEEN – TUESDAY

'Professor, this operation manual they've sent us is brilliant.' Robert Wong was sitting at a chair in the university library working through initial campaign plans, studying very closely the manual that had been delivered from campaign headquarters earlier that day. 'It covers in great detail everything we need to know.'

Jaya chewed the end of her pen as she scanned research papers, head resting on her hand, thick hair trailing to the table. 'Well, that's good. I suspect we will need every bit of help we can get.' She then looked up with a quizzical frown. 'Do you think I need to be across every policy?'

'I suppose you should be across tax rates,' Wong replied. 'From my research of previous campaigns, the standard questions journalists usually to try and catch candidates out on is tax.' Wong looked to see if the professor understood. 'You know – so they can create a political storm against the leader. They apparently call them gotcha moments, but it seems like stupid journalism to me.'

'What else does your research tell you?' Jaya, with a smile of admiration, looked over to her colleague.

'They ask questions like the price of milk, which no-one actually knows, but they expect politicians to have the answer immediately.' He chuckled and referred to his notes. 'They also want you to know some basic policy principles of the party, and I suppose you had better get across the current health initiatives. Plus, given we have a traditional green bloc of voters in the electorate, we'd better get across energy issues and where the party differs from government.'

'Where does it differ from government?'

'We want a secure energy supply, and the government doesn't consider that aspect of sovereign wealth to be important.'

'Why would they think energy security is not important? It's essential,' Jaya said.

'No-one really cares, especially young voters, so the government do and say anything to achieve headlines about climate change,' sighed Wong. 'This is a problem with the academic work we do – it never matches political reality out on the street.'

'Well, if we can get traction, avoiding any scandals along the way, then we'll have achieved an awful lot. I think adding an applied campaign unit to the curriculum would be a great result from all of this energy.'

'What is your primary vote expectation?' asked Wong.

The professor sat back, pulling her hair back and tying it with a scrunchy from her wrist. Jaya frowned and said sternly, 'I would like ten per cent.' Then she smiled broadly. 'That would be my best result, if we beat the Greens on the primary that would be an even better result. Ten per cent would be a great result, I suppose, but, if we do the best we can, then that'll be okay as well.'

'Actually, I must confess, it's a little stress free knowing we're going to lose,' said Wong. 'I couldn't begin to imagine what marginal seat candidates must go through.'

'That may be so, but ensure we document everything and apply the right ethics to our decisions. Otherwise, this whole exercise will be a waste of time and resources,' Jaya said. 'Remember, you've promised me a credible campaign, Robert, without any trouble,' she waggled a finger at him. 'I don't want my academic reputation tarnished in any way.'

'Do you think we should do a campaign plan?'

'Do politicians do plans?' Jaya asked, not knowing the answer. 'They just seem to manage the news cycle – I don't recall seeing any plans in the studies I've taken over the years. I don't think handing out brochures at bus stops and train stations is much of a plan.'

'I suppose we should do one if we want to be serious,' sighed Wong again as he flicked over pages of the manual. 'I was just planning to focus on election day and getting volunteers standing at train stations handing out your brochure.'

'What does the operation manual suggest?'

Flicking back to the contents page, Wong was directed to four chapters dedicated to a thirty-day campaign plan. He quickly scanned the information and turned to the professor with a broad smile. 'According to this manual, you need to be outdoor knocking this afternoon.'

'Do you think that's wise?' Jaya was sceptical, crossing her arms. 'I could lose votes if a golliwog like me turned up on a voter's doorstep.'

'You really have a problem with this colour thing, don't you?' Wong asked casually.

'You try living in Australia as a black person,' sighed Jaya. 'You can see it in their eyes. My colour challenges them. They don't expect to see people like me in the supermarket, let alone on their doorstep.'

'I find Aussies to be colour blind,' Wong countered.

'Don't get me wrong, it's not just Australians, it's a human condition to be sceptical and wary of something different. Every culture discriminates against something they don't like,' Jaya said. 'Look at India. One of the most overt discriminatory cultures in the world, but they don't try to hide it. It is what it is. Australia believes it is liberally pure, when clearly it's not – not purposefully, I might add – when you inhibit free speech then thoughts are covert, but you always see it in their eyes.'

'I'm not sure I agree with your view,' smiled Wong. 'But I will defend your right to say it.'

'Touché,' laughed Jaya. 'Now, what happens if we don't do this door knocking thing?'

'They have a section on non-compliance that clearly states if the non-conformity continues, it could lead to disendorsement, and we wouldn't want that being broadcast on the national news. Being a sacked candidate would definitely tarnish your reputation.' Wong paused and gazed at the professor for a moment. 'I reckon we better get the others in this afternoon and allocate activities.'

'Seems like a plan.'

'Did you expect campaigning to be so complex?'

'Frankly, I didn't know what to expect,' Jaya nodded and winced. 'The whole preselection thing was bizarre. Folks asking me weird questions about the food I ate and what books I read. As if that's important.'

'What did you say? You love a curry and a poppadum.'

'No, stuff that. I told them I prefer a good steak from the barbie with a cold beer.' The colleagues laughed a little too loudly and were shushed by nearby staff.

Wong looked at his professor. 'Do you have any regrets so far?'

'Not at all. This is why I was enthusiastic when you suggested it. Learning about the election process from a candidate's point of view is a great idea. I think there'll be enormous lessons for us. If we can educate future candidates, maybe the entire political process could be better organised.

It's really exciting.' Jaya was shushed again as her voice shrilled louder so she hoarsely whispered. 'Just make sure we document everything. That means recording a personal diary about how you feel, and the many challenges you face, which would make a good case study.'

'Well, my first response to that is that we need much more money than we currently have and way more people,' Wong whispered a reply. 'We probably need a campaign slogan.'

The professor immediately responded with her hands blocking the words in the air. 'Jaya Rukhmani – more than black or white?' They laughed and were shushed again by annoyed staff.

The prestigious habourside mansion, Admiralty House, was resumed by the Gerrard government soon after the shock failure of his republic referendum. Once the Sydney residence of the governor-general, the prime minister decided with the strokes of his scrawled signature that a four-bedroom brick veneer house on the river in Parramatta was more appro-priate for the king's representative – banishing the governor to live twenty-five kilometres from the CBD.

Gerrard refurbished Admiralty House to his own specific tastes, including private suites boasting expansive views of the harbour. He then redeveloped the former prime minister's Kirribilli House residence next door into working offices for staff and other departmental advisers, providing a secluded compound away from the hustle and bustle of Sydney CBD, and an escape from Canberra. Gerrard's wife Margaret rarely travelled to Sydney with him. She found it hard to cope with the traffic and the hot humid weather, preferring instead to stay at Yarralumla.

Gerrard's electorate for the last thirty-two years had been the inner-city suburbs and CBD in Melbourne. He rarely visited his loyal staff at his electoral office in Fitzroy, and only did so when he was required in Victoria. He had not lived in the city for over twenty years, and no longer owned real estate there either.

Meredith Bruce, Government Education Minister and Manager of Government Business in the House of Representatives, arrived at the prearranged time for her meeting with the prime minister. She managed herself through security to the foyer of Kirribilli House, looking forward to working with Gerrard to review campaign strategy. Miles Fisher welcomed her downstairs in the foyer.

'Miles, how are you? Is the boss ready to see me?'

'He is over at the residence, minister. He asked me to direct you there.'

Expecting to have met Gerrard in his office, Bruce suddenly dreaded the directions. She lingered for a moment, hoping any delay would encourage the prime minister to come looking for her. 'Good work in overcoming the shameful media yesterday.'

'It's easy when it's fake news. So disappointing to have it happen, but increasingly common in politics these days.'

Fisher began to move away.

'I have to admit the trend is toward this type of rubbish reporting,' continued Bruce, keen to stall. 'The media have to do better than that.'

'We tracked the delivery of the forgery to Brisbane. It was a Mr Paul Keating who sent it,' Fisher snorted and held his nose, prompting Bruce to join the laugh. 'There was no CCTV of the transaction unfortunately.'

'Why would someone use that name?'

'It's delicious, isn't it,' smiled Fisher. 'The greatest treasurer in our history. Someone's idea of a joke, I suppose. A good one though, we all had a laugh.'

'Given he was eventually dumped by the punters, I reckon the forgery came from the other side.'

'You think someone from the opposition set up Stanley?' Fisher was surprised by her suggestion.

'The poor dear, I feel sorry for him,' mused Bruce, then looking about asked. 'Is he planning on coming back here soon?'

'No, the boss has another meeting in an hour, so you had better get a move along.' Fisher walked her to the door leading to the path to Admiralty House.

'Thanks,' Bruce said, without much excitement.

The walk through the garden showcased the harbour and the white sail traffic bobbing about, fighting with the ferries for passage on the water. As Bruce strolled slowly, taking in the vista, she wondered if there would be a chance for another woman to reside at the house, scoffing cynically at the thought it could be her, although she did wonder.

She recognised the females in her party were not as highly regarded as the media pretended, and she knew her ambition for higher office would need to be carefully managed. Her recent assignations in Canberra with the prime minster unsettled her a little, but she liked the idea that she was now favoured by him, which helped with any occasional regrets she may have about her behaviour. 'Whatever it takes' was the clichéd advice from her mentor – she just privately wished it was not as often as the prime minister was increasingly demanding.

The housekeeper directed her to the pool deck, advising the prime minister was enjoying the sun after this flight from Melbourne. She walked the sandstone paving until she came across Gerrard in a private alcove surrounded by lush greenery. He was laying on a lounge enjoying the sun, a mirrored sheet beneath his chin. He heard Bruce approach and looked up, shielding his eyes, and folding away his reflector.

'Ah, Meredith. Thank you for coming over. Please, take a lounge and get a little sun on those gorgeous legs,' Gerrard pointed to the next lounge. Still close enough to talk comfortably, she preferred a chair in the shade away from the prime minister.

'Andrew, I would have preferred to see you at the office. This is a little inappropriate. Is Mrs Gerrard about?'

'She's in Paris for the duration and wants me to have a continental tan when I join her for Christmas, so out here will have to do,' Gerrard paused, and then leered. 'You're uncomfortable with a near-naked man. I thought we overcame this silly shyness in Canberra?'

Bruce sighed, 'If we are to remain "friends", Prime Minister,' she used her fingers to emphasise the quotation. 'Then we cannot be seen in these types of settings.'

'Fair enough,' Gerrard curtly responded, sitting up. Adjusting his skimpy red swim trunks, he said, 'Always remember who pays your bills, Meredith.'

'Prime Minister, I will never underestimate your influence on my career, and I will continue to be grateful when time and circumstance permits,' she smiled coquettishly to relieve the sudden tension between them.

Gerrard smirked and leered at Bruce, 'Okay, we can discuss these issues when we are in Canberra again, but I'm sure a sleepover at Admiralty House would help your career no end.'

'Prime Minister, can we get to business, please. I feel a little uncomfortable.'

'What's the current status of the campaign?' Gerrard felt a little chided and pulled a towel over, readjusted himself and left a hand for the moment under the towel.

'Yesterday's forgery scandal has been the best thing to happen for us, quite frankly.' Bruce referred to papers from her satchel. 'You have increased your preferred prime minister rating by ten points and it's now better than the last election. The two-party preferred is now at a level where we are likely to win by ten seats, which is a terrific achievement given the circumstances.'

'Why would you have expected anything less?' Gerrard scratched his head and stretched, reaching for the sun before resting his hands behind his head. 'Stanley is useless, and I would think he has been set up by someone. I wager it was Harper – it's what I'd have done if someone had shafted me.'

Bruce continued to scan her notes. 'We have candidates out campaigning and we are placing extra resources into the marginal seats.' She flicked over a page and continued. 'The debate is yet to be confirmed, but we are insisting on the last Thursday as we normally do. It's almost a tradition now.'

'I don't want to do more than one, so resist the media's demand for more. Get the ministers out if we have to. Debates will just give Stanley a leadership platform he doesn't deserve,' counselled Gerrard. 'Why should we gift him an increased profile? They're just for television ratings anyway and have no relevance for the punters. I don't know why we still bother with them.'

'I'll advise the opposition.' Bruce took a note. 'Do you want to announce any policies before the end of the campaign?'

'Not particularly,' sighed Gerrard. 'We wouldn't even be having this election if it weren't for that stuff-up in parliament. How did you miss it?'

'I was taking instructions from you at the time if you remember.' Bruce was keen to move on. 'Are you planning on spending any time in your electorate?'

'Nope. I don't particularly want to travel out of Sydney, why should I?'

Bruce smiled. 'Oh, to have your confidence in the good people of Melbourne.'

'Are they running a candidate this year? They haven't bothered for the last two elections.'

'I'm advised they have a university professor running against you, a female in her forties.'

'Really?' Gerrard sneered slightly. 'What does she look like, any good?'

'What do you mean by *any good*?' sighed Bruce.

'Is she a looker?' Gerrard asked. 'That would make a difference to my vote. Mind you, not much, but it would help.'

'Since when has looks got to do with politics?'

Gerrard raised his sunglasses to look at her and smugly smiled. 'Oh, you are so naïve, Meredith. Looks have everything to do with successful political careers. That is why you are doing so very well,' said Gerrard, seemingly oblivious to what he was saying. 'You don't think you're a minister because you're smart, do you?'

'I thought it might have something to do with it.'

'I choose my ministers by faction first, locality of their seat second, then looks.' Gerrard beamed. 'Look at Angie Gasper. She comes from the Teachers' Union, she's in the centre-right faction, just like you, and unlike you, she is a Doctor of Education. So why isn't she Minister for Education instead of you?'

'Okay, I'll bite. Why isn't she?'

'Television appeal,' smiled Gerrard. 'She has it all over you with experience, policy grunt and just about all political capabilities, but she would frighten people if she ever got on the frontbench.'

'You're kidding me,' said Bruce, mouth agape. 'I can't believe you just said that. Is that how you make decisions on political careers?'

'It's called political patronage and it's the way I do things,' Gerrard responded. 'You either comply with the system or there is no career for you. You complied with my request, and your career is laid out for you. Gasper, on the other hand, has little chance of becoming a minister because of her frumpy looks, so sadly, we're missing out and wasting her talents – but that's politics.'

'That's bullshit, actually.'

'Well, when you are leader, change it. Until then, enjoy the spoils my leadership provides for you.' Gerrard said, reaching over for a glass of water. 'Now, what else have you got for me?'

Peter Stanley was at his desk resting his head in his hands when Anita Devlin knocked gently on the office door. Stanley looked up, grimly smiled, and waved her in to sit at the desk.

'Mr Stanley, sorry to disturb you. They said it would be okay—' Anita began tentatively pointing over her shoulder. 'I just wanted to get a few details from you to add to a feature article I'm writing on the campaign.'

'Not sure I would be much good with this,' sighed Stanley. 'Perhaps Chris Hughes would be a better choice to talk to about the campaign – he's coordinating the leadership strategy.'

'I've already spoken to Mr Hughes,' smiled Anita. 'I wanted to speak to you, actually.'

'I sometimes wonder if I'm suited to politics.' Stanley noticed Anita taking notes and quickly added. 'All of this is off the record unless you ask me to place something I say on the record.'

Anita understood and nodded her head. 'Where do you think the forgery came from?'

'I wouldn't put it past Gerrard to have set me up,' sniffed Stanley. 'The police have advised it originated in Queensland, which means Gerrard probably didn't do it.'

'Could it have come from your side?'

Stanley gawked at Anita, thought about the proposition and finally said, 'Probably not. I mean who would do that?'

'Someone who wanted to hurt you and the campaign.'

'So not one of ours then?' Stanley leaned back into his chair, slowly rocking it, he rested his face on his hand, his elbow on the arm of the chair.

'Who stands to gain most from it?' Anita asked, having guessed the answer, and hoping Stanley would think it through.

'The government, so maybe it was them. Bastards.'

'How will this affect your campaign?'

'Jack says it will put us back a few days,' said Stanley, the other hand now clawing roughly through his hair. 'He says the local campaigns won't be affected.'

'The Hyphen says that?' Anita tried her luck.

'Yes, he has the campaigns working their programs and we begin active community engagement from the weekend.'

'He must be a busy man.' Anita reeled out more baited line, hoping for a bite. 'What, with all his international projects and the like?'

'We're lucky to have him, quite frankly.'

'So, who's paying for him?'

Stanley stopped and gazed at the journalist. 'You're being a little tricky today, aren't you, Anita?'

'Just doing my job,' she smiled. 'How do you think the campaign is going? Do you think you'll win?'

'Let's see, I crack an innocent joke with so called friends that ends up on the front page. I make a public statement calling for the resignation of the prime minister about a letter that is a forgery. We have very little money in the campaign account and the polls are heading south. Jack has suggested we don't do any debates, he doesn't want me out in public anymore, which I tend to agree with.' Stanley was not smiling. 'How do you think we are travelling? We might have a chance, but we are coming from a long way behind.'

'Where do you reckon Gerrard gets his money?'

'The corporates love him,' Stanley sighed. 'He hasn't

delivered for them for years and he has policy that stifles investment, but they still love him.'

'You didn't tell me specifically,' asked Anita. 'Do you think you can win?'

'If the community campaign goes to plan and I don't stuff up anymore, then yes, we can win it.' Stanley laughed then heavily sighed.

After thirty minutes of chatting, Anita finally said cheerio to Stanley and pondered the information she had noted as she left the building. Who did have the most to gain from a Stanley election loss? The obvious culprit was Gerrard, but the political answer could lie within his own party. She considered the connection James Harper may have had with the forgery – how did he have a copy? When she found a quiet space, she called her boss to discuss her theories, seeking an experienced alternate perspective.

'Cleave, I think James Harper was behind the forgery.'

'Big call, how can you say that?'

'I just wonder how he had a copy before the media conference,' Anita said. 'Who had more to gain from the forgery?'

'Gerrard has benefited most as the polls now place him in an easy winning position. They are talking a ten-seat margin.'

'Yeah, but if Gerrard wins, then what?'

'They have a change of leader,' Cleaver responded.

'Who are the likely candidates?' Anita asked. 'Hughes is the obvious choice.'

'Would they go back to Harper? Not sure they would.'

'But they could if they lost the election.'

'You have a nose for dark conspiracy stuff, don't you?'

Anita laughed, 'Do you want me to put something together? I also have their campaign operative confirmed by Stanley, so we can move on the article Hancock is stalling.'

'I can only ask.'

'Why would he hold it up, anyway?' asked Anita.

'Put something together on the Harper thing, and maybe we can roll it into your previous story and get a feature from it.'

'I actually feel sorry for Stanley,' sighed Anita. 'He's a good and generous man and doesn't deserve to be treated like this.'

Cleaver snorted. 'He's a freakin' politician, Anita.' Cleaver chuckled. 'Never trust them, and never feel anything toward them. They go into this political business focused only on themselves and their own egos. They really don't care about the country, just their own legacy. So, no, don't feel anything for the miserable bastards.'

When Anita finally ended the call, she thought about Bart and wondered if what Cleaver had said of politicians was true of him.

CHAPTER
10

DAY FIFTEEN – THURSDAY

'I'm not so sure we're doing the right thing backing Stanley,' Adam Lowry the retail entrepreneur offered to the meeting when chair Kerry Jameson opened it up for discussion. 'The campaign just doesn't seem to be getting any traction in the polls.'

'He's goddamn useless, that's why, and I'm not sure the country needs a moron like him as prime minister,' barked cattle baron Jim Buckley. 'He offers nothing in policy, and he needs an urgent charisma bypass. We've backed a loser, trust me.'

'So, rather than grumble,' challenged Sally Verhoeven, an IT wunderkind, 'What are we going to do about it? I'm sick of wasting time covering the same old ground just talking. Let's do something.'

The twenty-five-year-old's reputation for ignoring stodgy protocols was obvious as she quickly got to the point. Her attitude to business was much the same. With a reputation for disrupting normal business methods, she had grown her brand very quickly. She delivered new and challenging software applications, sending the entire market scrambling for reinvention.

'Sally may be right,' wheezed Jameson, taking a quick dose of Ventolin from his always near inhaler. 'The question I want answered this morning is this: do we stay with Stanley or go back to Gerrard?'

These were no shady commercial operators sitting around the board table trying to squeeze a fast buck from every crevice of corporate deceit, they were the business community's elite, private owners of successful family companies. They were members of an exclusive coterie based on their total tax paid, the stability of their companies, and their plans to expand. It was in their best interests to want what was best for their country and they unapologetically also wanted what was best for them, their employees, and other stakeholders. Their individual wealth placed them among the wealthiest in Australia, and some even entered the stellar heights of global rich lists.

'We've invested too much into Stanley's campaign to jump ship now,' offered Felicity Osman.

'Why can't we swing a leg over the saddle and have a foot in each stirrup?' demanded Buckley.

'Our projects need a prime minister, but he ain't gonna approve them,' sighed Allan Connell, the mining magnate. 'Are you sure we can't get Stanley sacked?'

'And replace him with who?' snapped Buckley a little too loudly, silencing the discussion.

The group looked about their colleagues searching for a response.

'We could go back to Harper. He'll do what we ask him to do, always has,' Osman said.

'It's way too late for any of that; they would need to have a party vote,' said Jameson softly, dismissing the idea.

'What happens if he literally falls under a bus?' Connell taunted. 'We get Messenger for the campaign, and they vote a new leader after the election,' Jameson responded. 'Then they would probably go back to Harper.'

'He's not likely to fall under a bus, this is crap,' interrupted Verhoeven, keen to get into her busy day.

'What would happen if he was pushed?' queried Lowry, and the room fell silent.

No-one dared say anything and they sat quietly avoiding eye contact waiting for a braver colleague to respond.

'Maybe we should invite Gerrard back to meet with us?' suggested Verhoeven. 'He may be more conciliatory and open for a deal.'

'It would be a foolish move – we would appear desperate.

He would stick it to us big time,' Connell said, shaking his head. 'You heard him last time, threatening us.'

'Yet, if he wins, then what?' Osman asked.

'We could be in a worse position,' suggested Lowry, twisting his face at the thought.

'Then it makes perfect sense to open up communication with him,' Verhoeven looked to Jameson, eyes agog, nodding encouragement. 'A bit of a shit sandwich now might mean less crap we have to take when we go cap in hand after the election.'

Jameson didn't respond.

'I vote we at least give him a call,' asserted Buckley. 'What's there to lose by speaking with him?'

'Agreed,' said Connell.

Jameson gazed around the room seeking responses and head nods prevailed, so he picked up the handpiece on the black telephone in front of him and punched a number. 'Tanya, could you please connect me with Prime Minister Gerrard.'

The business associates remained silent as they waited for the connection.

Wanting to change the subject as they waited, Hancock said, 'One of my journos thinks Harper was responsible for the forgery. She's written a column on it.'

'Are you going to publish it?' Osman asked.

'No, of course not,' snorted Hancock. 'We support Stanley, and an article like this would cloud the campaign with leadership speculation.'

'Who wrote the piece?' asked Jameson.

'Anita Devlin. She also did an investigative feature during the recent kerfuffle in parliament suggesting Gerrard was about to rip off the government for personal gain.'

'You're shitting me,' Buckley spat. 'What was that all about?'

'She thinks he had a deal with the president of Indonesia to have the funding for detention centres pushed through without parliamentary scrutiny.'

'That guy is the biggest con artist going around, he has his fingers in every pie,' said Connell. 'He took cash from me for a new mine license approval just the other month. Screwed me big time.'

'Are you going to print it?' Verhoeven asked.

'We had it scheduled but the governor-general sacked Gerrard, stuffing the entire deal,' responded Hancock. 'So, we put it in the wait-and-see file to use after the election if we need it.'

'Can we use it now?' asked Lowry.

'Well, we could, if we think it might help the campaign,' said Hancock. 'She also wrote a piece on Wolff.'

'Say what?' asked a stunned Osman. Others around the table looked surprised. 'Who is this woman?'

'She's had Wolff's role confirmed by the opposition as a campaign operative, but she is yet to identify who he really is. It's okay, he's operating under an assumed name to slow any investigation to his association with other campaigns. She's begun to research who may be paying him.'

'You've done what?' hissed Jameson, turning to him ready to strike like a snake.

'I've done nothing,' Hancock shifted in his seat. 'A journalist is doing her job, but I won't be printing any story she may write about him.'

'Wolff must be protected at all cost,' Jameson said, seeking to ensure agreement. 'It will be on your head if he is exposed. We have too many connections internationally to lose him as a loyal servant.'

'I'll do my best,' insisted Hancock. 'But I can assure you, I approve everything she does so nothing will get passed to print without my approval.'

'You're into us for too much money to just do your best, Anthony,' sneered Jameson. 'You'll not allow her to learn anything more about Wolff.'

'Can we use Wolff to nullify Gerrard?' asked Verhoeven.

Jameson swiveled his chair to look at her. 'He can do whatever we want him to do.'

'Can he push someone under a bus?' joked Buckley.

'He does whatever he is told to do,' assured Jameson in a chilling whisper.

The telephone buzzed, and Jameson prodded the speaker button. 'Prime Minister, how wonderful to speak to you again. I see you are doing very well in the campaign ...'

'What the fuck do you want, old man?'

·   ·   ·

Two hours later, the nominated delegation of four waited in the foyer of Kirribilli House for the prime minister, already thirty minutes past the agreed meeting time. Jameson, Buckley, Verhoeven and Hancock had been escorted to a room with no chairs and the group was growing impatient as they waited or paced the room. Verhoeven had slunk to the floor in a corner and was working her smartphone. Jameson was struggling to maintain his balance, leaning heavily on his walking stick with Buckley moving in to support him, allowing a weakened hand to rest on his shoulder.

The door suddenly whished open and a polite staffer escorted the delegation through to a formal meeting room where Meredith Bruce greeted them.

'Please sit down,' smiled Bruce. 'Sorry to keep you waiting, the prime minister has been required to attend to some minor affairs of state.'

'Is he still able to make any decisions while in caretaker mode during the election campaign?' asked Hancock, pulling a chair out and steadying it for Jameson. 'I would have thought there was little he could be doing prior to an election.'

Before Bruce could answer, Gerrard swept into the room in a gym suit zipped open to his lower chest, hair wet and white gym towel wrapped around his neck. 'Sorry to keep you, I had a few things I needed to attend to.'

'All okay now?' a compliant, smiling Jameson asked.

'Swimmingly,' Gerrard joked. Jameson sneered, grasping why the prime minister's hair was wet. 'How can I help you?'

'Prime Minister, we would like to apologise for the manner in which our last meeting transpired. It seems we were not able to convince you of our hope for you to retain office. We also failed to reinforce our commitment to your government,' Buckley nervously said, staccato like. 'We've come here today to discuss your campaign to determine if we can help you with anything you may need.'

'Oh, that's very nice of you, Jim,' smiled Gerrard, leering at Verhoeven. 'Who are you, gorgeous? Have we met?'

'I'm with them,' responded Verhoeven, thumbing to her colleagues.

Gerrard smirked at the rebuff. 'Meredith, can you please give us the latest? You all know Meredith, of course?' The others concurred.

Bruce opened her leather folder and flicked over a few papers and settled on a data sheet. 'The current status of the campaign is this. The government is likely to be returned with a fifteen-seat majority – our best result for the last three elections.'

'Really, that many? How wonderful,' grinned Gerrard. 'Now, what is it that you think I need. You were saying?'

'We want to support your campaign,' said Verhoeven.

'Who are you, again?' Gerrard persisted.

'Sally is the founder of World Communications and has significant locations throughout Europe and the United States,' Hancock offered.

'How nice,' mocked Gerrard. 'So, tell me, Sally, are you able to communicate with Hancock Media and get them to cease publishing rubbish about my government and begin to expose Peter Stanley for the cheap political fraud and forger of letters he truly is? Are you able to do that, sweetheart?' Gerrard smiled at her. She took his gaze and stared back. 'Are you able to use your no-doubt worldly communication skills to get this current stupid media strategy corrected so that you can begin to support my campaign?' Gerrard beamed a cheesy smile at Verhoeven, making her a little uncomfortable.

'Andrew, this is not really necessary,' said Jameson.

'Prime Minister to you. Thank you, Kerry,' barked Gerrard without moving his gaze from Verhoeven. 'Well, Sally? Can you provide any support? Or are you here just to tempt me?'

Verhoeven flushed and looked away. Saying nothing, she avoided the prime minister's smarmy glare, a little shaken he could be so openly provocative.

'Prime Minister, as you know, we have been writing pro-opposition pieces,' stumbled a contrite Hancock. 'This is what we do, we have to report.'

'Not sure I was talking to you, Tony.' Gerrard tossed a withering look toward Hancock.

'Prime Minister, please be reasonable and accept our mea culpa,' Jameson said softly, offering his hands up in a surrender.

'Sorry?' Gerrard bombastically looked at Bruce. 'You're sorry?' Gerrard mocked Jameson. 'You want to kiss and make up do you, Kerry? You want to kiss my arse and you think that giving me whatever I want will return our cozy relationship back to normal, is that it?'

'We're wasting our time listening to this crap,' said Buckley, making a move to get up. Verhoeven was quickly to her feet.

'No, you're not wasting your time, cowboy,' sneered Gerrard. 'I'm wasting mine.'

The remaining delegation struggled to get up and Gerrard beat them to the door. 'When you come and see me after the election, bring your cheque books, because if you ever expect to laud it over my government again it will cost you big time.'

Gerrard swung the door open. 'You backed the wrong horse this time, Kerry, you doddery old fool. You'll need a hefty payout on the result to get a place in the next race. And you, little girl,' he pointed at Verhoeven. 'Wear something shorter next time. Now get the fuck out.'

As they left, he slammed the door.

'Wow, Andrew, that was hot.'

Gerrard turned to Bruce and slowly pulled the towel from about his neck. 'So, do I lock the door and cool you down, or is this not an appropriate time or place?'

Bruce smiled approval and shifted backwards onto the edge of the table as the prime minister snibbed the door and advanced toward her.

CHAPTER
11

DAY SIXTEEN – FRIDAY

Hancock media retained an editorial office in all capital cities and major regional centres throughout Australia, usually in the prime real estate commercial district. Journalists assigned to a city desk were usually found among piles of papers, files and hordes of newspapers cluttering desks and work nooks. Post-it note reminders were strewn about the edges of computer screens, bins overflowed with empty coffee cups, and the odd half-empty bottle of vodka or whiskey was stashed in the corner.

For travelling journalists, they were assigned hot desks, usually a small workstation with computer cabling for the laptop but no fixed network telephone. Anita normally avoided the facilities, preferring a cafe or an outside cosy table to work far away from nosey colleagues with their constant social interruptions and inane conversations about family and children.

Sydney was turning on a typically humid November day, and although Anita normally fought the need to work inside, she surrendered to the increasing muggy heat and retired to the relief of air-conditioning. Her choice of cargo pants and sneakers would have her melting quickly in the morning humidity.

She had been on the phone to Cleaver in Canberra questioning why her recent columns were not being published. They had disappeared into an abyss of editorial delay after being sent to the owner for his approval, receiving zero response. She was getting no quality feedback from anyone, speculating that Hancock's editorial direction to pump Stanley's tyres remained the newspaper's strategy.

Exasperated, she said, 'Just let me know what's going on.'

'Hancock hasn't given me any direction on these articles.' Cleaver worked to placate her. 'I've had them legalled and they look okay with minor edits, so we're ready to go.'

'Does Hancock want me to continue to investigate Sinclair-Browne or not?' asked Anita, annoyed by the continued avoidance of a direct response from her editor. 'I've tracked a similar campaign operative to a Queensland election a few years back, when there was an unexpected result. Apparently, a Simon O'Brien was the leading campaign operative then, but I've been given a description that seems like our man. No photos though.'

Cleaver gasped a strong draw from his cigarette. Holding his breath he asked, 'How did you manage that?'

'You know those things are bad for you, don't you?'

'So, they say.' The editor blew out the smoke, sounding as if he was blowing a balloon. 'Where did you get it?'

'I have my sources and I tap into them whenever I want this type of information.'

'You're doing a great job with Stanley.'

Cleaver blew out again so heavily into the phone that Anita felt as if she could smell it.

'No, I'm not, so stop mocking me,' sighed Anita, exasperated by the regular patronising of men with power. 'I'm just sick of this constant delay when I know there is a story to be had.'

'Anita, look. There are times when we go hard and times we need to back off,' said Cleaver. 'This is one of those times. Just step back a little on the style and tone of what you're writing.'

'I can't stand dishonesty, you know that,' Anita moaned. 'It's what drove me to the corruption story on Gerrard in the first place. I still think we should have published that story. It's the same now. I can feel it, Cleave, there's something going on and I think Harper is behind it.'

'What does your boyfriend say?'

'For heaven's sake, how many times do I have to tell you, he's not my friggin' boyfriend,' barked Anita. She hesitated to calm herself and took a long draught of water from her bottle. 'Anyway, he knows nothing, and even if he did, he wouldn't tell me.'

'Who's paying this Hyphen chap?'

'I'm yet to find out. I've sourced it to a printing company out west of Sydney, but I'm yet to see any connection with its proprietors and politics.'

'Do they have investors?' asked Cleaver. 'Maybe there is a connection there?'

'I've looked at the government company registry. On the surface it offers nothing,' Anita responded. 'It does list a Michael Buckley as a director, but he's not listed on their website.'

'Buckley?' Cleaver was surprised. 'Nothing to do with the Buckley family?'

'Who are they, some eastern suburb socialites?'

'Quite the opposite,' scoffed Cleaver. 'The Buckley family own the Northern Territory and most of far-north Queensland. I'm surprised you don't know them.'

'Country business is not my business.'

'They run cattle and have the major share in live beef exports into Asia. They also have international assets. South America, I think.'

'So why would they invest in a small printing plant in western Sydney?'

'I don't know, but you could find out, couldn't you?' Cleaver chided.

'I suppose so, but why bother if the boss is too damn lazy to read my stuff?'

'Anita, if you want a move to television, I suggest you put more effort in. And can you have a look at the Gerrard campaign?'

'Why don't I check out his local campaign. I hear the candidate is doing some interesting things on the ground?'

'Like what?' Cleaver seemed distracted and Anita felt it.

'They're working on a documentary. I thought I'd write a column on it.'

'Yeah, sounds good. I have to go, see you.' The phone went dead.

'And so ends another unfulfilled discussion with my editor,' Anita said to no-one, tossing her phone on to her workbench.

'Sounds like you need a drink.' The voice of Bernie Brereton drifted over the grey partitioning. 'Shall we go out for one?'

'Bernie, it's eleven o'clock. A little bit early, wouldn't you say?'

A head appeared above her, full of grey hair and twinkling blue eyes, although a little bloodshot. 'It's never too early, and besides, it's after midday in Auckland.'

'I could go for a coffee, does that suit you?'

'I'll have a wine and you can have a coffee, let's go.' Anita caught up with her scruffy colleague at the lift foyer. 'Do you ever wear anything else other than those bloody sneakers?'

'They're comfortable, and I can't stand wearing high heels, not to work at least.'

'Good job then. Too many girls think it's looks that get them ahead in this business.'

'I've never met any girls who think that,' smiled Anita. 'Mind you, I don't get to meet too many girls in this organisation.'

'Good thing too.'

'Bit of a misogynist, are you?'

Brereton raised an eyebrow and shook his head, punching the ground floor button and dragging a cigarette from a crumpled pack he pulled from his mustard linen jacket. As soon as they were outside, he lit up, sucking it deep into his lungs and stirring a significant coughing fit. 'I've got a cold,' he gasped, as he saw Anita's look of reproach. 'True.'

Anita ignored him and walked on. 'Let's go to the quay and sit by the water,' Anita suggested. 'It's a bit hot here.'

'A bit far to walk for a drink, don't you think?'

'Come on, it's only a block. The fresh air will do you good.'

Brereton started spluttering again with a wet cough. 'That's what I'm worried about.'

The colleagues eventually settled into a shady outside table by the Museum of Contemporary Art, Brereton insisting on the smoking section. With views directly to the Opera House and the towering bridge to the left, the sun could turn the harbour into a delight for the weariest, most cynical journalist. The coffee and glass of red arrived quickly, and they pondered what to say after their convivial small talk dried up. Brereton lit another cigarette, saving his lighter by using the end of the butt.

'I was a little surprised you didn't know the name Buckley,'

Brereton said, clearing his throat before sipping on his wine to taste its quality. 'They not only own most of the export cattle business in Australia, but the old man also has holdings in Argentina, Canada and Texas. Not only that, but he also has significant abattoir holdings throughout Asia and recently announced plans to move into Europe.'

'As I said to Cleaver, I'm no country business queen,' Anita sipped her coffee. 'I specialise in politics and policy.'

'Well, again, that surprises me you don't know the name.' Brereton took a large mouthful of wine, swished it, and swallowed, seemingly enjoying the immediate effect, before taking another large gulp almost draining the glass. 'Buckley's been active in politics for years and commands a lot of clout in Canberra.'

'Ultimately the minister makes the decisions, driven by the department. This Buckley chap would just be another voice among all the other lobbyists.'

'You're kidding me?' mocked Brereton. 'I thought you were the gun investigative political journalist?'

Anita was a little taken aback. 'What are you saying?'

'What I'm saying is this.' Another long hard suck on the cigarette almost saw the end of it. 'The government might think they manage policy, and they probably do on social services and community care programs such as education and health, but it's the big dollars that control the economy, not the politicians.'

'Are you saying the Buckley family runs Australia?' Anita scoffed. 'I find that hard to believe.'

'I didn't say old man Buckley runs the country, but he belongs to an exclusive group that does.'

'How come I don't know about it?' Anita asked. 'Come to think of it, how do you know about it?'

'I've come across them a few times, but I've been warned off,' Brereton said, draining his glass and calling the waiter for another. 'Bring two please.'

'I said I didn't want one, thanks Bernie.'

'It's not for you, love.'

Anita looked at her colleague and considered his comments. 'What do you mean you've been warned off?'

'When you play with the big boys and they want to manage you, then best you do what they ask.'

Brereton pulled another cigarette from his packet and lit it, coughing again when he drew it deep into his lungs.

Anita scoffed, 'Rubbish, you're a killer dog when it comes to getting a story. I wouldn't have thought you would be frightened of anything.'

'At my age, the only thing that scares me is not having a job.'

'What are you saying? Has Hancock threatened you? Over what? Why would he do that?'

'Let's see. Why would Tony Hancock, and before him his father, want to stop me from exposing his business cabal?'

'Rubbish. That wouldn't be right.'

'Ask yourself this. How come I've never got off the news desk?'

'Because you're lazy and a drunk,' Anita grimaced at her unkind retort.

Brereton ignored the verbal slap. 'Maybe so, but I was like you once,' he gulped another mouthful of wine. 'I was eager and keen to get ahead, just like you. I discovered a story about old man Jameson, to do with a gambling deal he was trying to execute in Macau. Apparently, he wanted to build a major casino complex with a significant residential and office tower. He was implicated in manipulating the approval process with certain government officials − apparently money was being left in hotel rooms for certain guests of his casino when they transited in Hong Kong. When I tried to get the yarn published, the whole tower came crumbling down on me.'

'What happened?'

'I was sent to Vietnam as Hancock's correspondent. Not for the normal two years − I spent ten in the lousy, stinking place. Cost me my family and I discovered things an addictive personality should never discover. No wonder I have a relationship with alcohol.'

'Why didn't you leave?'

'Hancock's old man threatened me. He told me in no uncertain terms that if I left the company or spoke to anyone about the Macau deal, I would never work again.' Brereton gazed out into the water. 'I tried to leave, but no-one would touch me. I even went overseas to try and get work, but it seems there are these same pathetic exclusive networks everywhere. The Australian group is related to other fucking business groups around the world all doing favours for each other.

So, if I wanted to write, I was their man forever. Downgraded to obituaries and shipping news. That's why I'm lazy and a drunk.'

'Rubbish!' Anita didn't know whether to believe him or not.

'You're idealistic, I get that. You want everyone to do the right thing, I get that. But you need to look a little deeper into the political system than you're currently doing to find out how it really operates.' Brereton sucked more smoke into his lungs and spluttered it out. 'You did a good job on Gerrard, and what did you find? Corruption and fraud. It'll never get published; I can guarantee you that. Just remember, there are folks who can hurt you. Be careful.'

'Hurt me, how?'

'You're looking at how.' Brereton opened up his arms and bowed. 'Why do you think Hancock has sat on your stories?'

'I don't know.'

'The cabal, my dear, the fucking cabal.'

'Why?'

'My guess is that you're probably close to something they're managing, and they don't want you to expose them.

'Who's in it, this cabal?'

'It changes. I reckon there are about ten, maybe twelve. Not sure who, but I reckon Hancock would be in it. Buckley and Jameson for sure. Those three are definitely in the group. It's like a secret society. They believe they're doing good for the country but ultimately, they're only ever looking out for themselves.

'They have some weird name that I can't recall, but the Merchants sounds familiar, or maybe I'm confusing it with something else. They seem to be up themselves a bit and over-state their influence. I mean, why wouldn't you be arrogant if you thought you ran the country. Check the files, and you'll always see those three together with the prime minister at major business events.'

'This is rubbish. The politicians run the country, not some flakey business group.'

'Don't kid yourself, love. They manipulate campaigns and when they do, they get their priorities attended to.'

'Rubbish. What examples have you got?'

'Years back, in Queensland when the entire country was against a new coal mine, what happened?' Anita shook her head. She hadn't heard of it. 'Let me tell you. Even though the media, the local first nation tribe, environmentalists, celebrities and even the king expressed a view to stop the development, what do you think happened? Gerrard approved it. His mate Allan Connell got the approval to develop the mine and he made a fortune from it. He's another one, I'd wager.' Brereton drained his second glass and took up the third. 'Mind you, it's been an economic bonanza for Queensland and created thousands of jobs. Who would have thought?'

Anita crossed her arms and looked at Brereton a little cynically. 'But there are always the same people hanging around with the prime minister and other ministers at events and fundraisers.'

'Not with the clout over the government these people have.' Brereton gulped down his third glass and stood, a little shaky. 'Don't take my word for it, do the research. But remember what I told you, be careful.'

Brereton carefully sauntered over to the checkout register, paid for the wine and coffee, and began to slowly walk back to the office. Anita watched him go and felt a little sad for him. Was this just another one of his legendary colourful stories, or was there some truth to it? It seemed fanciful that a cabal of businesspeople could influence policy, and have legislation created and enacted to their advantage without anyone knowing about them.

The Manly ferry steamed into the Circular Quay terminal, secured itself and disembarked its passengers as Anita watched, reflecting on the election campaign. She worked through the snippets of information she was collecting. Why was Hancock holding back her columns? She tapped and swiped her way through her phone contacts and called Messenger.

'I'm coming down to Melbourne tomorrow,' she said after their friendly pleasantries. 'Can we have dinner? I'd like to see you.'

'Of course, we can have dinner, so long as we don't talk politics. I've literally had enough of it.'

Anita changed her tone to business. 'Barton, I need to ask you a question about government, do you mind?'

'Fire away.'

'This may seem really silly, but does the government actually rule?' It did sound silly, and she flushed anxiously, hoping he wouldn't think her stupid.

'Of course, they do, who else rules us?' Barton seemed a little surprised by the question.

'What influence do lobbyists and special interest groups have?'

'We listen to them, we have to – we don't know everything,' said Barton. 'Although, Gerrard thinks he does.'

'So, when a group comes to see you and they suggest that you do something for them otherwise they'll withdraw their investment from the market, what is the usual response?'

'We listen, we test their statements, and we make a decision. Lobbyists play an important role in securing government funding or protecting the interests of their clients, but they never direct the government, or the opposition for that matter.'

'So how do you determine what to do as a government?' Anita felt embarrassed by her question. 'I hate to ask, but I've never thought about the process before.'

'We have reviews, we have inquiries, and we seek feedback from the electorate and other interested parties. We consider the information and generally, we respond with funding or enacting legislation. When we see a problem, we more often than not genuinely need to intervene.'

'So, if lobbyists are organised, they can influence government legislation?'

'Well, when you put it like that, then yes,' said Barton. 'Why the interest?'

'Have you heard of a group calling themselves the Merchants?'

'No, nothing like that, although retailers have various groups. There are formalised groups, such as peak bodies that represent their industry. They put a lot of pressure on us to respond to issues affecting the market. The car industry for years took government funding handouts to stay in Australia, but ultimately we couldn't afford them anymore.'

'Is that fair?'

'How do you mean?'

'Well, it seems those with the most money and the loudest voices get listened to by the government,' said Anita. 'Wouldn't that put limitations into the political system and allow corruption to potentially raise its ugly head.'

'That's why there's an anti-corruption watchdog.'

'That never gets the head of the serpent though, does it?'

'They've had some big scalps.'

'But no-one of any consequence. Like Kerry Jameson, for instance.'

'Jameson pays his taxes and has never had any allegations made against him, so I'm not sure what you mean,' queried Barton.

'That's the point,' insisted Anita. 'He's powerful and always seems to get what he wants. How does he do that?'

'He maintains friends, I suppose.'

'So, if you or I, or some Joe Public, wants to right a wrong, we would find it difficult, but if you have money and powerful friends then it's okay.'

'That's rather cynical, don't you think?' asked Barton.

'Maybe, but I'm learning more and more each day about politics and the subterranean world of power. Although you'd reckon I'd know this by now.'

'Well, let's talk more over dinner tomorrow.'

After saying goodbye, Anita left the cafe to stroll back to the office, past the ferry terminal toward George Street. As she turned the corner, opposite the Four Seasons Hotel, she saw Tony Hancock walking in the forecourt. She called to him and waved but doubting he would hear her above the traffic noise, she telephoned him. As she waited for the connection, she saw Hancock stop and look behind him to see a man in black with a shaven head quickly walk up to him and shake hands. Hancock looked at his phone, held up a hand to the man to wait and answered.

'Hi Anita, what can I do for you?' Hancock said. 'I'm out of the office so you need to be quick.'

Anita stepped into a nearby cafe opposite keeping her eyes on the men. 'I just wanted to know if there has been any movement on the Stanley campaign operative story.'

'I'm still considering it. I have a meeting with Stanley this afternoon so I can chat to him about it then. I'll keep an eye out for anyone suspicious. Do you know what he looks like?'

'He's shortish, wears black and is totally bald.' Anita described the man standing in front of him.

'Okay, I'll get back to you after my meeting if I learn anything. Bye for now.'

Hancock rang off, returning his phone into his jacket and resuming his attention to the man in black.

Anita watched the men in an animated discussion from behind the cafe window. It seemed from the exaggerated hand and arm movements that Hancock was getting a strong lecture. The man in black pointed a finger then pressed it firmly into Hancock's chest, ending the conversation and quickly stalking off, leaving Hancock to watch him go. The man trotted through the traffic across George Street, running straight toward the cafe where she stood concealed by the door. Anita panicked and quickly sat down, stumbling over a chair with a crash. Expecting the man to come in, she looked away from the door. Had he seen her? After anxiously waiting until she thought she could wait no longer, she stood to survey the scene. He was nowhere to be seen.

Maybe Brereton was right, maybe she needed to be a little more careful.

CHAPTER
12

DAY SEVENTEEN – SATURDAY

The rickety corrugated iron door crashed behind Anita. She had cautiously stepped through the opening and into the warehouse in a west Melbourne street full of derelict, abandoned factories. Looking for Jaya Rukhmani for their prearranged meeting, she thought she may have the wrong address so checked her smartphone to confirm she was in the right place.

The warehouse was dark with little light coming from the sparse, grimy windows high above. The concrete floor looked as if nothing had been on it for years other than dust, dirt, and scattered rubbish. As she walked further into the depth of darkness, somewhere high above her birds fluttered and a small feather drifted to the floor.

'Hello?' shouted Anita. There was no response, although a faint scurrying sound from a dark corner startled her a little.

'Hi.'

Anita yelped, and quickly turned toward the voice coming from a metal balcony high above the entrance. A young man was looking down with a beaming smile.

'Are you the journalist?'

'Yes, Anita Devlin. Hi.'

'Come on up, the stairs are over there,' said the man, pointing to steep metal stairs running up along a brick wall. 'We were expecting you a little later. Jaya and Robert have gone for coffee.'

'I can come back,' said Anita, looking up to the man.

'No, they won't be long. Please, come up.'

Anita walked to the stairs and clomped up, her sneakers on the metal steps giving out an echo. When she got to the top, the young man introduced himself.

'Hi, I'm Steve Calwell. I suppose you could call me the election day coordinator for the professor's campaign.'

'Hi Steve, pleased to meet you,' puffed Anita, the unexpected effort had her breathing hard. 'That's a nice workout.'

'We figure it will keep us fit. How do you like the place?'

Anita scanned the floor below and then looked through the glass into a large single office. 'Well, you certainly have enough room.'

'We thought we only needed an office, so we were going to work from Rob's spare bedroom, but the campaign manual recommended we would need space for the election day material. Given the list of gear we must accumulate we thought we would hunt around for a warehouse. We got this beauty for a month for almost nothing.'

'It looks great. Are you going to put signs up out front?'

'Hadn't thought of that, maybe we should,' Calwell said. 'There are a lot of things we haven't considered. We naïvely thought we could easily run an election campaign, but it seems democracy takes a little more effort than we thought.'

'Who would have thought?' laughed Anita, as she followed Calwell into the cluttered office. 'You look busy.'

'Yes, we're trying to match the data we've been given with the mailing program so we can get the data and community groups linked. Power isn't connected so we're running off our batteries. It only becomes a problem at night. We thought we might get a couple of gas lanterns if we need to work through.'

'So, this computer program, who wrote it?' Anita asked.

'It was given to us by campaign headquarters a few days ago. They sent us a community organiser the other day, who is out and about talking to community groups right now, basically getting us organised.'

'So, everything is done for you?'

'Yeah, how sweet is that? We just fill in the blanks. The only task we have to do is mobilise people and attract money,' said Calwell, moving papers for Anita to sit. 'We've started online recruitment for campaign workers, which is going gangbusters. The professor's alumni of former students seem keen to help, and money is slowly coming in from a crowd-funding site.'

'Sounds impressive.'

'It's easy, so far. We're concentrating on election day and making sure we get that right because the manual says fifteen per cent of voters make up their minds at the polling booth.'

'I find that hard to believe.'

'Yeah, me too. But unless we do what headquarters say, they could cut us off,' Calwell sat opposite. 'Apparently, Jaya signed a statement agreeing to follow the manual otherwise she could be sacked.'

'The electoral commission closed nominations last week and declares them, I think, next Wednesday, so it would be too late to sack anyone if they didn't comply,' Anita explained. 'Once you're declared, that's it. You'll be on the ballot paper as the endorsed candidate no matter what happens.'

'The professor is of the view we should do everything we can to validate the material. She hopes to use it for a documentary and the material she is developing for her academic course.'

'Good plan.' Anita looked around at the chaos and noted maps on various pinboards marked with coloured pins and shaded in various colours. 'When's the professor due back?'

'Any time,' said Calwell, who abruptly jumped up hearing a noise from below and stepped out on to the balcony. 'In fact, here they are now.'

Anita waited, listening to the excited voices and echoing

steps on the stairs. Professor Jaya Rukhmani hurriedly swept into the room, commanding the mood. 'Hi Anita, sorry to have kept you waiting,' Jaya graciously extended her hand and smiled. 'We didn't know if you wanted a coffee, so we bought one for you. Do you take sugar?'

'If you have any, Professor, I take one.'

'Ah, you see how smart my campaign manager is, he buys lattes with one and two sugars in them to cover all bases.' Jaya took a cup from one of the two cardboard trays Wong was carrying.

'What would you have done if I wanted three?' quizzed Anita.

'No-one takes three sugars in coffee, way too sweet,' Wong chuckled, placing the coffees down and extending his hand. 'Hi Miss Devlin, I'm Robert Wong, the professor's campaign manager.'

'Drill sergeant, more like it,' smiled Jaya. 'He has me working way too hard, especially since we have no realistic prospect of winning. But we're giving it our best shot, aren't we, Robert?'

Anita sipped her coffee as the others settled in around her. Calwell stepped off to a desk at the far end of the long office to work on a project with two takeaway coffee cups. 'Hey, nice coffee,' she called.

'It's Melbourne, what do you expect?' smiled Wong.

Jaya caught her eye. 'So, you want to do a story on me?'

'Yes, I thought we could do a profile piece for tomorrow. You have an interesting story.'

'Well, I'm not so sure I'm that interesting, but the reason we are doing this election campaign is,' Jaya said.

'Before we get started,' interrupted Wong. 'Would you mind if we record the interview for our podcast?'

'Not at all, we can do some cutaways as well, which you can edit later if you like.' Anita responded.

'That'd be great.'

'Thank you so much for agreeing to do that,' Jaya leaned across and tapped a thankyou on Anita's knee. 'We are learning every day and we are recording most of it, so we don't forget.'

'Good plan,' smiled Anita, bemused by the mixture of enthusiasm and chaos within the office. The difference between the pragmatic strategy at campaign headquarters and how that planning was reflected in the field provided an interesting contrast. 'I was just having a chat to Steve about your campaigning requirements. Are you obliged to meet campaign standards, and what happens if you don't?'

'We haven't met the campaign strategist, what's his name, Robert?' Jaya looked to Wong who was setting up a camera. 'It's a hyphenated name.'

'Jack Sinclair-Browne.' He responded as he continued his set-up.

Jaya clicked her fingers. 'That's him. He told us in no uncertain terms we must meet standards set out in the campaign manual, so we are.'

'Apparently, he's had all local campaigns subscribe to his program, which we find incredibly interesting,' offered Wong.

'I mean, how can all campaigns be the same? Some are in the city, others in rural regions. There are marginal campaigns and safe seats. And others, like us, have no chance in winning.'

'So why do it?' asked Anita, pulling a notepad and pen from her bag at her feet.

'We're doing it so we can add material to an applied campaigning unit I will design and then teach. We are using the campaign as a case study,' responded Jaya. 'I just didn't realise how complex it would be.'

'But you teach politics,' Anita queried, taking a sip of coffee.

'Theory and policy, but we don't touch hard-core campaigning. The coalface campaigning a politician subjects themselves to get elected is unbelievable,' Jaya responded. 'I'm sure none of us at uni actually know what real politics is about.'

'Numbers, I suspect,' said Anita. 'Who has them and who wants them.'

'So, you reckon it's just about arithmetic?' asked Wong as he placed a camera on a tripod. 'Whoever has the numbers wins.'

'That's it,' said Anita as the corner of her mouth lifted.

'That is no way to run a modern parliament,' sighed Jaya. 'I mean, of course votes count. But if it was just about numbers then they could be manipulated to support any just cause,' Jaya said. 'Though history tells us that not all causes are just.'

'I reckon politicians work too hard,' suggested Wong. 'At least some of them do – if this campaign is any indication of what needs to be done to renew their contract every five years with the community.'

'The question then becomes, how do they pay for it, and who's paying their bills?' Jaya said. 'When they need money and people to win, surely it becomes easy to corrupt them.'

'There is no evidence of that in Australia,' Anita said.

'Really?' Jaya was genuinely surprised. 'Let me remind you of Brian Burke and Alan Bond. The State Bank fiasco in Victoria, the debacle in South Australia and Premier Barry O'Farrell's demise in New South Wales. Eddie Obeid's influence, and the chap who ripped off a hundred thousand from claiming false allowances in Victoria, wasn't he the speaker?'

'What do those cases have to say about politics?' Anita asked.

'Sadly, political corruption exists. We just have to look harder to find it – and call it out rather than covering it up and protecting the party brand.'

'We're all set to go,' interrupted Wong.

Anita reflected on the professor's comments. She thought about her unpublished story on Gerrard's attempt at manipulating the parliament by doing the deal with Indonesia. Perhaps Jaya could be right. Maybe corruption does exist, and we just don't investigate to find it or eradicate it.

'Rolling.'

Anita switched on her recorder and asked, 'Professor Rukhmani, I wonder if we can start by sharing with me a little about your background. When did you immigrate to Australia?'

'I'm not sure I'd call it migration.'

'What would you call it?' queried Anita, a little confused.

'My parents sold me off to be married to an Indian family from Melbourne who paid them a considerable amount of rupees,' sighed Jaya. 'I was twelve at the time.'

'Sorry, what?' Anita was even more confused. 'You were a child bride and sold to your husband?'

'Yes,' sniffed Jaya, waving her hand dismissively. 'My culture encourages it, and my parents were given a significant reward for their sacrifice. My husband's family was very pleased to have such a young bride.'

'How old was your husband?'

'Thirty-three. He was an architect in Melbourne and couldn't find a wife here, so his family organised it. He visited India to marry me and then brought me to Melbourne on a family reunion visa. The first time I met him was at the wedding.'

'You're kidding me?'

'No, this is very true and still happens, even now.'

Anita began scribbling shorthand notes. 'So, you landed in Australia as a married girl. Could you speak English?'

'No, only Hindi.'

'Which school did you go to?'

'Anita,' Jaya scoffed. 'I never went to school,' she laughed. 'Within a month of my marriage I was pregnant and gave birth to a beautiful boy, Gurudo. Now a handsome, strapping thirty-year-old man with two children of his own.'

'How many other children do you have?'

'Gurudo is my only precious child. Once I'd given birth to a son I was excluded from my husband's family. I became their bonded housekeeper until I was eighteen, and then told to move out. They haven't done much for me, in fact, I haven't seen them for years.'

'Seriously?' Anita was astounded, shaking her head while quickly scribbling notes in her pad. 'How is it that you are now a university professor if you were not able to go to school?'

'I worked two, sometimes three, jobs until I was around twenty- two. I then sat an adult assessment test for university under the government's new citizens scheme and voila,' Jaya clapped quickly. 'I haven't left.' She beamed a broad smile.

'That must have been difficult being a single mother, working and studying?'

'I only saw my son once or twice a year when he was growing up. Once he left his father's house, we've been able to get to know each other again.'

Anita vigorously scratched the back of her head with her pen, trying to understand what happened to her. 'How did you learn English? You speak it so well.'

'Thank you, you're so nice,' Jaya crossed her legs and cupped a knee with her clasped fingers as she leaned back. 'A lot of television, I can tell you. I really enjoyed Play School; it helped a lot.'

'This is unbelievable; how did you survive when you were moved out?'

'I worked and the government helped. Migrant services were very supportive. The best thing I did was work and mix with other people.'

'Have you been back to India?'

'No,' Jaya snapped, then self-consciously looked at the camera as if caught in a secret, before adding. 'I haven't seen my parents or any family since my wedding. In fact, I don't want to, quite frankly.'

'This is really sad, I didn't know,' Anita hesitated. 'I feel terrible, this must have been awful for you.'

'Oh, don't be like that, it wasn't that bad,' reassured Jaya, smiling. She gently touched Anita's hand. 'Sure, looking from your perspective it's awful, but that is from your place of privilege. If I didn't have the opportunity to come to Australia, I would not be living the remarkable life I now am. I wouldn't be campaigning against a prime minister. I would not have my academic books read. I would probably be breaking rocks for a living in some lost village alongside my mother.'

'But your story is dreadful.'

'To you, maybe it is,' Jaya said. 'To me, it has been bountiful. I have a son, grandchildren, and I live in a safe place. If I had stayed in India, my life would have been completely different.'

'Have you suffered discrimination?'

'Have I been called a wog or a black bastard? Of course, I have,' Jaya dismissed the query. 'And in Australia, the words used are the same as they are in India. There, people threw stones and big rocks at me, they would beat me ... in Australia they throw words, not rocks.'

'Still as painful?'

'Of course, they are, but they are only words of ignorance. One must forgive the ignorant and help them to learn.'

'I find your attitude utterly remarkable,' smiled Anita, shaking her head.

'You do because you're pale skinned, living a life of privilege, with free health and education. It's not remarkable to me, it's my life.'

'I don't know what to say,' Anita was perplexed and quickly brushed an unexpected tear from her cheek.

'Then say nothing and move to the next question. Perhaps ask me about the campaign.'

'One last question before moving on,' Anita smiled. 'How important is culture within a political system and how does political culture relate to the community?'

'This is an important question because the entire economic system was developed on the patriarchy. I blame the French,' Jaya smiled at her clichéd joke. 'They were the first I think to separate women from men in the workplace, observing women were a distraction. Can you believe it – women a distraction, who would have thought?' Jaya laughed at the irony.

'Men developed the systems of power and trade. They planned for the participation of only men and built institutions and their rules around the culture of men.' Jaya moved into familiar territory. 'Over the last century we see greater female participation, but the principles of patriarchy remain when it comes to culture.'

'How so?' Anita scribbled notes.

'Not many brown faces or Asian names in the federal parliament. Not many in boardrooms or even universities for that matter. We seem to exclude certain cultures to our great disadvantage. If Australia is to truly engage with our region, we should have greater representation from the Asian diaspora. Diversity is not just about gender as my sisters would have us believe. It's about all things, including culture, age and access.'

'Interesting.' Anita chewed on the end of her pen as she considered the professor's comments. 'It's refreshing to hear a politician talk like that.'

'It's a shame I won't be elected because it could be an opening for others to follow. That is why we're doing the documentary.'

Anita couldn't help but feel a buzz of admiration toward the professor. She continued to question the professor about her campaign; how the development of the documentary was progressing; and if there had been troubles campaigning. She scratched lines around key words like ethics, equity, and political power as she asked questions of Jaya until Wong called for a final question.

'Okay, last question,' smiled Anita. 'If you were prime minister for the day, what would you do?'

Jaya didn't answer immediately, she leaned back in her

chair, eyes closed, working her way through a response. She then dropped her head and connected eyes with Anita in a searing look. 'I would toughen the immigration laws to exclude those who cannot contribute to Australia. It seems to me that for too long we accept people who contribute nothing. They don't bother to learn the language and often disrespect our laws. We should ask them to do more if they want to stay. If I can do it, why can't they?'

Anita wasn't expecting her answer. 'But this is contrary to what you said earlier about gaining from other cultures.'

'We can, absolutely, but not if we constantly live in a community focused on the lowest common denominator. We have selection processes for almost everything in Australia, but not our social welfare programs. So, let's go to the source and select better people to come settle here. Sure, we have a role in resettling refugees and those who need us, I'm all for that, but our immigration program should stop bringing in the deadbeats.'

Anita didn't respond, shocked at what she had just heard, challenging her own thoughts about the issue. Perhaps she never thought about it as it didn't impact her, and she rarely spoke with that segment of the community – she just never thought about it and preferred that Australia was a home for anyone who wanted to come. This was an interesting perspective from someone who had lived in the system.

'That last answer is totally off the record,' Wong jumped in and sternly said.

CHAPTER
13

DAY SEVENTEEN – LATE SATURDAY

As Melbourne woke from its cold winter slumber with the two-week Spring Racing Carnival, Anita mused almost daily how she could relocate to this handsome European style city. As the days progressed during the campaign, Anita enjoyed wandering the city's laneways, past cafes and restaurants, savouring coffees while observing rushed city folk and sauntering tourists.

The prospect of having a stable relationship with the handsome Barton Messenger was often on her mind, and she thought about how she felt whenever they were together. Maybe she enjoyed his company a little more than she would care to admit, especially to him.

She couldn't explain it, but he had her dropping her guard a little too much. They had shared a clumsy, drunken embrace at the parliamentary mid-winter ball while waiting for a taxi. She didn't like to admit to herself she may have been the initiator and didn't want the dashing shadow minister to think of her as anything other than a competent and respected journalist.

Yet, since that time, he had persisted in breaking down her professional resistance. It meant a lot for her to provide him comfort at his most vulnerable point after his party killed off James Harper's leadership just a few short weeks ago, when he had been unexpectedly elected deputy to Peter Stanley in the alternate government. He was comfortable and agreeable, but she remained anxious about stepping into a relationship with him, and harboured reservations about getting involved with a politician.

They met for a quiet cocktail before dinner at the River-land Bar beneath Federation Square. It was across the bridge from her Melbourne office, and she simmered with anticipation for most of the afternoon, distracted from her work after her interview with Rukhmani.

Barton leaned forward, quietly confiding, 'You know what it is? I just worked it out,' Barton smiled. 'You're hesitant about us getting involved because I'm deputy leader and a heartbeat away from being leader.' His cheesy smile broadened further. 'I could be prime minister one day, and that scares you a little.'

'What worries me?' Anita coyly asked, leaning into the table on her crossed forearms.

'You, dating the future prime minister,' declared Barton. 'I mean, if I was not a politician, would you date me?'

'Hmm,' smiled Anita, lowering her head before chewing on her cocktail straw. 'Maybe.'

'You see!' acclaimed Barton proudly, slapping his fingertips across the edge of the table. 'If we had met prior to me being a politician, this impasse we now have before us would not be an issue.'

Anita looked away, seeking comfort by snuggling her chin into her shoulder, noticing a rowing eight stroking gracefully along the river. 'It must be beautiful to be out on the river exercising every day.'

'You would have known me, as me, and not as a politician,' Barton persisted, ignoring her attempt to distract him.

'Barton, I would never have dated you before you were a politician. I hate lawyers.'

'Ah.' He was a little crushed. 'So, you prefer dating a politician?'

Anita peered over her glass as she held it to her lips. 'Are we dating?'

'I would have thought we might be given the current position of our chairs, your knee against mine, the fabulous twilight sky and the sound of romantic music playing quietly in the background.'

She pricked up her ears to pay attention to the music, smiled and then said, 'You think the Rolling Stones are romantic?'

Barton sat back and gazed at her. She shifted in her chair, smiled a little self-consciously, and then drained her glass.

'I can't get no … satisfaction,' Barton followed the lyrics along with Mick Jagger. 'No, no, no.' He grinned at her, resisting a smile, and held out his hand, 'Shall we go have dinner?'

'Sure,' laughed Anita as she stood collecting her satchel bag and following Barton toward the bluestone stairs to Swanston Street.

Antony Lorenzino's Bulgarelli restaurant, opposite Victoria's grand Parliament House, was a refreshing ten-minute walk from the river. Antony came rushing forward to warmly welcome his guests as they stepped through the wood and glass door.

'Mr Messenger, so very good to see you again, and who is this lovely lady you have brought to see me?' Antony was being the gracious host.

'This is Anita Devlin, she's from Canberra.'

'Ah, so beautiful.' Antony clicked his heels and bowed. 'If I'm not mistaken, you are the leading political commentator for the Hancock Media Group, am I right?' He took her hand and placed a charming light kiss on her knuckles.

'I'm not sure I'm their leading commentator,' Anita said, nodding her head with a smirk that belied she was impressed by his gracious generosity.

'Not yet,' Antony reassuringly patted her hand. 'Come, I have the best table for you this evening, Mr Messenger.' Antony led them back to the window alcove so they could look out on to Spring Street. 'All good retailers have their very best products on display in their shopfront, and as you are a very good-looking couple, no doubt you will attract more customers for me this evening.'

'Thank you, Antony. This is a first for me,' grinned Barton and winked at Antony.

'Mr Messenger, if you brought a beautiful woman like Ms Devlin to my restaurant, you would always be getting the best seat in the house. Unfortunately, you only ever bring ghastly politicians, so I do not want to scare people away.' Antony fussed over seating Anita, drawing the serviette from the table, and draping it over her lap. 'Now madam, a drink? Allow me to get you a glass of our finest champagne. And for you, Mr Messenger, I have your usual waiting.'

Antony stepped away and Anita cupped her face in her hand, moving closer to Barton. She smiled, and he leaned over. Kissing her on the cheek, she gave a small sigh before saying, 'You are quite the political hotshot, aren't you? And he has you wrapped around his little finger with his European chivalry.'

'It's close to the parliament and the Federal Parliamentary Offices are just down the street a little, so I come here a bit. But you're the first lady I have brought to dinner, and he seems impressed.'

'Sure, Bart,' scoffed Anita. 'As if you haven't brought a girlfriend here.'

'Anita?' Barton sat back a little offended. 'I can absolutely assure you; I've never brought a female date here.'

'A *female* date?' chided Anita. 'What aren't you telling me?'

'I mean girlfriend,' said Barton, a little embarrassed, he looked out into the street.

Antony arrived with drinks, and they clinked glasses. 'I had an interesting meeting with Professor Rukhmani today, what an interesting woman she is,' Anita said as she leaned closer.

'Oh yes, what did she have to say?'

'Plenty. I was utterly surprised by her background, such an impressive story. She also has a few weird ideas on immigration.'

'Let me guess,' Barton took a sip from his glass. 'Like keeping the peasants out?'

'Exactly!' Anita exclaimed. 'I must say, I was a little surprised,' she said taking another sip of champagne then rubbing the tip of her nose. 'She would create a media storm if I printed what she said. I'm not sure we're ready for an immigrant criticising immigrants. There seems something decidedly odd about it.'

'She's probably right in a lot of ways,' said Barton. 'Our whole immigration model is very dated and needs reframing.'

Anita slunk back into her chair mouth agape. 'I don't believe you just said that.'

'What?' mocked Barton. 'I can't have a view on immigration?'

'No, of course you can,' apologised Anita as she straightened up.

'I mean, I can't believe you think we have a problem with who we bring in.'

'Some aren't going to adapt to our culture, our laws and the way our society operates, consequently they really are unsuitable as immigrants.'

'So where do they go?'

'If they're in trouble or danger and safety is a concern, then of course they come here or another UN signatory country,' Barton responded cautiously. 'If they are economic refugees, that is another matter, and we should shut the door. It's better for them to stay in a community they know rather than come to a country where they will not be able to participate.'

Not saying anything, Anita just grimaced at Barton.

'What's wrong, did I say something inappropriate?' he asked.

'No, I'm just thinking through the issue. Maybe I'm missing something. I must be if a professor of politics at a prestigious university and a federal politician, the alternate deputy prime minister no less, share the same view on immigration, which is totally different to my own thinking.'

'Anita don't get me wrong. I care about the plight of folks, but I also retain a responsibility to the nation. This means making tough policy decisions on provocative issues like immigration when they could in fact be contrary to the way I think.'

'That's interesting,' mused Anita, a little sarcastically, her head resting in her hand. 'I know politics is all about the art of compromise, but how can a politician make a decision on policy that goes against their personal values?'

'It's never about me,' Barton said glumly. 'It's about what is best for Australia.'

'So, you'll make a decision that you don't believe in?'

'It's not as simple as that, but yes, if I need to compromise my beliefs for the betterment of the country, then I will.'

Anita took a drink then said, 'Crumbs, I'd be a hopeless politician.'

'It's not as if it's every decision,' justified Barton. 'It just means that sometimes, particularly on social issues, we have to be flexible in our own beliefs.'

'Conviction politician without any convictions?' Anita cynically asked.

'Let me give you an example.'

'I hope this is good,' smiled Anita, attempting to relax Barton.

'I hate war and all its symbolism. I hate it. I've had family affected by it, maimed by it, even killed by it. I would speak against it and seek peace at every opportunity,' Barton slowly, persuasively, punctured his words. 'But I would support increasing our defence force, and if my country was at threat, I would have no hesitation in defending it.'

'Crumbs, I must be going around in some sort of ignorant haze,' chortled Anita, trying to lighten the discussion. 'I've never considered the pressure our politicians must be under when it comes to making decisions. No wonder they age so quickly.'

'Do I support euthanasia? No, I don't.' Barton's voice trembled slightly. 'Would I have requested assisted death for my mother to ease her pain, contrary to my beliefs? Yes, I did.'

Anita looked at Barton and watched as he struggled to regain his composure. She slid her hand across the table and squeezed his. He gripped it hard in response. He was a man with commendable beliefs that attracted him to the parliament, and yet he seemed so very conflicted, and right now, exposed. Anita pondered if the rough and tumble of politics was truly a vocation for such a sensitive man and stroked the back of his hand with her thumb.

After a few moments, allowing the charged lingering emotion to subside, Anita softly said, 'So, I was wondering—' Barton looked up. 'I was wondering how the election campaign is going and what the current polling is suggesting?'

Barton laughed at her attempt to lighten the mood, quickly dabbing his eyes with his napkin, and smiling at her. 'If I told you, I would have to kill you.'

'Ah, but I thought you were against domestic violence?' Anita suggested coyly.

'Domestic? What are you suggesting?' Barton smirked and dabbed his eyes again. 'Let us achieve couple status first before we talk anything domestic.'

'How long will that take?'

Barton's eyes widened, and he openly bit his tongue within a broad smile. 'Well, Miss Devlin, you're being quite forward at the moment and you're terrifying me a little. I'm not sure how to take you.'

'Oh Barton, you kill me,' laughed Anita. 'Come on, let's eat and get out of here.'

As if on cue, Antony appeared and served a bountiful antipasto plate. After checking their preference for wine, he suggested a chef specialty of crackled pork ribs for main course. He bowed and withdrew, leaving them to eat and enjoy traditional Tuscan pickled foods, dips, olives, and prosciutto-wrapped asparagus.

Having slowly worked their way through their sumptuous meal, a bottle of red from the Mornington Peninsula, and shared laughs following audacious declarations, the couple settled into a final coffee and chocolate.

'So how is the campaign actually going?' Anita asked again.

'Not well, we're slipping in the polls, and I suspect there is no way back.'

'How do you feel about that?'

'Disappointed, of course. This is our best chance in years to win government, and I fear if Gerrard wins the election, it may be years before we get another opportunity,' said Barton pessimistically. 'Which means, if that happens, I may give it away and go do something else.'

Anita was surprised. 'Seriously? You would give it up?'

'If I want a life, to have a family and do the things others do, then yes, I would give it up.'

'But you can make a difference.'

'Maybe I can do more to get things done outside of the parliament,' Barton said. 'I mean, perhaps I can influence policy and legislation more if I wasn't a politician.'

'Like Jameson?'

'I reflected on what you were asking yesterday, so I did a little research.' Barton smiled and tapped his nose with a finger as Anita stopped enjoying her chocolate for the moment. 'I've never really thought about it, but there have been all sorts of groups throughout history who have influenced laws and demanded change.'

'What sort of groups?'

'Unions are the most obvious. Churches have a significant influence as well, so do many industry groups. But there are so many now it's hard to know who represents who. In newer democracies like us – and the United States, for that matter – there is less emphasis on established culture and more focus on community groups that impact society. This may indicate we're not subjected to cultural and class influences, ignoring tradition and the practices of—'

'Barton?' interrupted Anita.

'Yes?' Barton stopped talking and looked about expecting a surprise.

'Get to your point will you, you're mansplaining.'

'Oh sorry…'

Anita smiled. 'So cute.'

'What I was saying was, even during the development of Federation, there were special interest groups developing the hegemony, protecting their interests.'

'Do you think they still exist, like the unions?'

'Industry groups? Yes, they do exist.'

'Who is the most influential?' Anita asked. 'Groups or individuals? Where would I go to get this sort of research?'

'Ask the Parliamentary Library, they should be able to help.'

'That's a great idea, I'll check it out,' said Anita sitting back. 'So, listen, how is your campaign operative going, this Sinclair-Browne chap?'

Barton shifted in his seat. 'How do you know about him?'

'I'm an investigative journalist, it's what I do.'

'He's very well organised and has most electorate campaigns running around frenziedly following his plans,' Messenger sucked his teeth slightly. 'But the good news is he's getting results – although not in the polls at the moment.'

'There is only one poll that counts,' laughed Anita. 'So, is he worth the money?'

'We're not paying him; a printing company is. It's a win for us no matter what happens. Hopefully he gets us across the line. Totally off the record, of course.'

'Of course,' Anita stretched and held Barton's hand. 'Off the record, why don't we go?'

CHAPTER

14

DAY EIGHTEEN – SUNDAY

The warmth on her face disturbed Anita, waking her. Rolling back into the crisp sheets away from the sun streaming across the bed, she looked up to see if Bart was still sleeping or working his phone. He was neither, so she leaned on an elbow and looked about the room. 'Bart? Are you here?'

There was no answer, and she flopped back into the pillows disappointed. Turning her head to where she had last seen him, she saw a slip of paper on the bedside table and leaned over to snatch it.

Good morning, gorgeous. Anita smiled and rolled over to the edge of the bed to read the note. *I have two church services to get to this morning. Sorry, didn't want to wake you. I'll be back for a lazy late lunch if you're available, I have the afternoon off. Call me. B*

Anita fondly placed the note back on the bedside table and walked to the windows to see what the day was offering. She pulled the remainder of the curtains back and looked out on to the western suburbs of Melbourne, following the coastline she found Williamstown, where no doubt Barton was singing the praises of the Lord. She smirked at the thought then checked out the city far below. Not much traffic on a Sunday morning and the late spring November sun was filtering through the tall buildings casting appealing light on the street cafes and their late breakfast guests.

She took a step back from the window and looked about the room for the morning papers. Seeing none, she went to the door and carefully opened it, peering outside to see if they were delivered. The three Sunday editions would be challenging to pick up without opening the door fully, their multiple magazines and lifestyle supplements adding to the awkwardness, but she decided to risk it.

She tossed the papers on the bed, fired up her computer, grabbed a juice from the fridge and settled in for the remainder of the morning. She quickly flicked through the Hancock newspaper and was pleased her piece on Professor Rukhmani had been given a prominent page so close to the front. A breakout box quoted Prime Minister Gerrard welcoming the challenge of the first opposition candidate in many years. The accompanying photograph of Gerrard was recent, and she recognised it as Admiralty House with the Opera House in the background.

Anita wondered if Gerrard ever bothered coming back to Melbourne, speculating if he even had an address in his electorate. She quickly logged in to the Hancock server and tapped her password to expose meticulous files on her every thought, report, and facts about the politicians she dealt with.

She entered Gerrard's file and clicked on pecuniary interests, bringing up the most recent report. Anita confirmed what she had assumed. Gerrard had no property registered. How does a politician represent a Melbourne electorate and have no property in that city? She pulled her notebook and pen from her leather bag on the floor, taking a note for a future column: why doesn't the prime minister live in his electorate; does he even visit the place?

She then flicked through the competition's Sunday editions trying to get a flavour for what their editors' thought were important election campaign issues. Health, education, and immigration seemed to be the constant themes and one respected columnist had gone early, calling a Gerrard government win. 'Brave decision,' muttered Anita as she tossed the supplements and magazines to the floor, pulling her computer back onto her lap.

She remembered Bart's advice and after another log-in process, clicked into the Parliamentary Library and began searching various articles concerning business policy. Anita wanted to research any patterns from various government policy announcements. She recalled her university studies high-lighted the 1980s as a period of radical change to the economy and searched documents from this era. She found details of an economic summit in 1983 and a tax summit in 1985.

She even found the origins of the Australian Business Council, which was founded in 1983 at the urging of the then prime minister. What struck her as interesting was the invitees to the economic summit included various business groups, respected business executives and unions. From this summit it was agreed that a prices and incomes accord between the government and unions would give economic and investment certainty for business – an idea initially floated by the Mercantile group.

Anita then searched for listings of the Mercantile group within the library's resources and was astounded to find more than five hundred entries identified. Though there were many listings from formal parliamentary inquiries, the apparently covert organisation seemed to shun the media.

The very first reference to the group was during the Henry Parkes' self-government campaigns during the 1850s, when the issue of the transportation of convicts to the New South Wales colony and universal suffrage was a provocative issue for the fast-growing British colony. The Mercantiles supported a move toward self-government to reduce taxes being paid back to England and demanded citizens should have the right to self-determination including the democratic right to vote.

Decades later, they fought the federal government's

protectionist policies and considered instituting a basic wage for workers an economic disaster. This led their chairman, an armaments manufacturer William Thackeray, to write:

I do not agree with the concept of this basic wage. In my view, it is each man according to his ability and capacity, not every man the same. God did not make men equal – we should not make laws as though He did, or to pay people according to their needs instead of according to their services they bring—

They lost the argument, but it did not stop them from submitting a declaration against the concept in every arbitrated wage case until the prices and incomes accord.

The most recent entry for the group was their objection to the amendments of the Native Title Act that transformed the entire compensation program for Indigenous peoples. The Mercantiles argued miners should cease negotiating individual agreements and enjoy unfettered rights to mine.

In return for these rights, they recommended all Australian ratable land be taxed with an Indigenous reparation levy allocated to the United Indigenous Congress, which would allow Indigenous peoples greater economic self-determination and distribution of funds. It was a stroke of policy genius to shift the responsibility of funding Indigenous services from the farmers and miners to every Australian property owner. Indigenous groups supported the successful parliamentary passage of the policy, allowing greater funds to flow to the first nations.

Anita researched for the next few hours, taking plenty of notes, learning more about the shadowy business group until the echoing shriek of her phone recharging in the bathroom startled her. She dashed to answer, pushing her computer aside, slipping on the strewn papers on the floor and scrambling to answer before it was sent to message bank. The screen displayed a smiling Barton, and she was happy to speak with him. 'Have you found Jesus yet?'

'Just finished with the happy clappers. They were really charged today.'

'Are we catching up?' Anita asked looking at herself in the mirror and fidgeting with her hair.

'Sure, let me shower and change at home and I'll come in, what do you want to do?'

'I don't mind, so long as we get out of here. I've been researching all morning and I'm feeling a little soggy.'

'What have you been working on?'

'Have you ever heard of the Mercantile Group?'

'Sure. My mother's father was once a member.'

'That would be your grandfather, darling,' Anita laughed.

'I suppose technically he is. He divorced my grandmother when mum was three and Gran quickly remarried. Mum considered her stepfather to be her dad and had little to do with her actual father.'

'So how do you know him?'

'He contacted me when mum died, and we catch up every now and then. He lives in the mountains. Say, here's a thought—' Barton paused for a moment. 'I've been meaning to get up there to see him, do you want to drive up this afternoon? It's a beautiful day and we can take the roof off. It would be nice to catch up with him before Christmas. You can ask him about your research.'

'I'd only do that if you want to, I don't want to intrude. I don't need to talk to him, and anyway, I'd rather spend time with you.'

'I'm not sure I'll see him before Christmas and no doubt he'll want to give me a few views about the campaign. He usually has an opinion on most things and would probably like to meet you. It'll be a pleasant drive. I'll give him a call. I'll pick you up in about an hour. Let's have afternoon tea with the old bloke and we can have an early dinner afterwards. Have you eaten?'

'No, I'm fine,' Anita said softly. 'Call me as you approach, I'll meet you in the concourse.'

Two hours later, Barton's blue Mercedes sports car crunched the pebbles as they approached Arthur Hamilton's rambling home. As the couple climbed the wide sandstone steps to the house, Hamilton shuffled to the edge of the broad wooden veranda to meet them, leaning heavily on a brass-handled wooden cane.

'I saw you coming up the road, my timing is impeccable as always.'

'Arthur, this is Anita. She's down from Canberra for a few days,' said Barton, hugging Hamilton.

'Miss Devlin, I follow your columns assiduously. I must say you're a little bit of a troublemaker,' chuckled Hamilton, as he held out his hand in welcome.

'From what Barton has said about you on the way up,' she said good naturedly. 'I suspect you're the troublemaker here!'

'Only believe half of what a politician says to you, and then question that half,' laughed Hamilton. 'Please join me and help yourself to some nibbles, you must be hungry.'

They settled into the heavily cushioned cane lounges, pouring tea, and enjoying a quartered sandwich and slice of cake. Chat included the weather, aged care, immigration, and taxes, with Arthur providing valid arguments as to why all of Barton's party's policies were wrong for the country.

'How do you think we are doing in the campaign?' Barton tried switching away from the policy earbashing he was getting.

'I think you'll lose,' said Hamilton, as he settled further back into his large wicker chair, propped comfortably by large colourful cushions.

'That's a little provocative. We're working hard to get our message out,' said Barton, slightly regretting talking politics in front of Anita.

'From what I can see, Gerrard is working harder than you lot. Stanley is unknown and a total loser with the way he is campaigning. Coming from Western Australia, what would you expect? No-one really knows what the heck they do over there. I've only been there a few times myself, could never see the point really.'

'You have a lovely place here, Mr Hamilton,' said Anita, catching on to Barton's discomfort.

'Yes, I bought the bush block almost fifty years ago and

established the gardens. The house has been added on to over the years, it truly is the grand mansion I envisioned when I first purchased the land. But it's too big for me now. Can you see my road where it meets the highway at the bottom of the mountain, over there to the left? It always gives me a good view when folks are coming up. I saw you two coming, so I got this spread out for you. My carer arranged it for me earlier. She did a great job, didn't she?'

'Let me pour another for you, how do you have it?' Anita asked.

'Thank you so much, milk with one,' Hamilton said smiling at her then glancing at Barton. 'You've got yourself six numbers and the supplementary there, Bart.'

'Yes, I'm very lucky,' laughed Barton. 'I suspect she is trying to impress you though, softening you up a little – she has questions.'

'Oh, has she?' Hamilton cheekily said. 'What about?'

'The Mercantile group,' Barton responded.

'The Mercs?' laughed Hamilton. 'We called ourselves that silly name and some of us even drove a Mercedes Benz. Young and stupid we were.'

'You were a member of the Mercantiles?'

'Yes, for around twenty years, maybe thirty,' Hamilton said. 'I forget these days. I was invited in and then years later they kicked me out.'

'Why did you get kicked out?' asked Barton, surprised by the admission.

'My tax receipts fell below their acceptable benchmarks

for membership, so I was politely asked to leave.'

'Did your tax receipts ever go back up?' Barton asked, a little puzzled.

'Yes, but once you're rejected from the Mercs, you never get a second chance.'

'How many were in the group?' Anita asked, stirring the tea for Hamilton before passing it over to him.

'Twelve, only ever twelve,' said Hamilton, nibbling at a slice of fruit cake. 'Sometimes they're active and highly influential on government policy and at other times they're unobtrusive. When I was with the group, they were quiet on government policy but still actively supporting various politicians. Their idea is to identify a potential minister and connect with them early in their career so when they are promoted, the Mercs have an easier route of influence.'

'How come they haven't come to see me?'

'Maybe they don't see you as influential,' Hamilton tenderly smiled. 'Although, I would have thought you could expect to hear from them very soon given your recent promotion to deputy leader. We would get government ministers in and have a chat about issues important to us, but we never exceeded our welcome. That all changed when Gerrard became prime minister, but I was long gone by then.

'How did you get invited to join?' Anita asked.

'Well, as I said, it had to do with tax receipts. They wanted the collective of the Mercantiles to be paying around twenty-five per cent of government revenue, which you could imagine is a huge contribution from such a small group.'

'Tax on profit?' asked Barton, surprised.

'No, it was total tax, which also included employee taxes and other levies such as sales tax – and now the GST – we were required to pay or collect,' replied Hamilton. 'We had influence because we were the twelve highest tax-paying private family companies. Politicians tend to listen to folks with a cheque book.'

'And did you influence any policy?' asked Anita.

'Oh yes, we achieved great things for this country. Mind you, we wouldn't have done it unless it favoured us – why else would you want to influence government policy?'

'How long has this group been operating?' asked a perplexed Barton, slightly shaking his head.

'Not sure, I think around mid-eighteen hundred,' said Hamilton. 'Its membership doesn't change much, and you're only invited in if there is a vacancy. I came in with Kerry Jameson, although technically he wasn't invited, he was just replacing his father. He must have been around twenty-five then.'

'What industry were you in?'

'Recycling and paper. They try to have one representative from each industry sector, but as I said, it depended on how much tax you paid.'

'So why did you get kicked out?' asked Anita.

'The market collapsed, and we needed to retool. Our revenues were hit hard, and expenses went through the roof. After three years of poor returns, they let me go.'

Anita stretched for the last curried-egg sandwich. 'Do you think they still have an impact on policy?'

'They run the joint.'

Barton snorted, cynically. 'They don't run the country.'

'I keep telling you to open your eyes and see what's around you,' Hamilton said, giving a half smile. 'Most folks think the government runs the place, but that's not my experience. Most of the innovative things they do can be linked to the Mercs, especially economic and trade policy.'

'That's rubbish,' Barton rejected the claim, crossing his legs and arms.

'Trade policy?' Anita was surprised.

'Oh yes, the group is affiliated in other countries, and they have a strong interest internationally. For instance, you don't think Trump's idea to erect a wall with Mexico was his idea, do you?'

Barton asked. 'Why would the Mercantiles want a wall?'

'It's not the wall, it was the symbolism.'

'What do you mean?' asked Anita. 'I thought it was to control their southern border.'

'The Mercs want a better deal for all private companies, not just theirs,' Hamilton sipped his freshly poured tea. 'What they got with Trump was a presidential focus on the American economy for the first time in decades, probably since Reagan, actually. They needed him to win but giving a tax cut to the wealthy wasn't going to get him the support of the working class. So, Trump starts talking about immigration and suddenly mentions a wall – changes the entire election campaign. The rest is history.'

'His policies killed foreign investment over the years,' Barton replied. 'So, they lose. They were lucky to get rid of him when they did.'

'How have the Mercantiles faired?' chuckled Hamilton. 'Not only the affiliate in the States, which I think is called the Union, but also their members here?'

'Well, if I knew who they were, I could tell you,' Anita said.

'Let me tell you this. Most of the Australian members have assets here, but all of them trade with foreign countries,' claimed Hamilton. 'It's in their interests to have governments working for them favorably in other countries.'

'So, they influence elections?' asked Anita, somewhat bewildered by what she was hearing.

'I thought you were smart?' smiled Hamilton. 'Of course, they do. Not only here, but internationally. They are into everything, let me assure you.'

'So, you think they're influencing this election?' asked Anita, captivated by the disclosures.

'Of course, they are. Ask yourself this – which party will give them what they want? Gerrard has in the past, but I'd wager they're shifting to Barton's mob because Gerrard has got too arrogant and probably tells them to get fucked. Excuse me.' Hamilton brought his hand to his mouth, then glanced at Barton. 'Take it from me, Bart, they're already running your campaign.'

'Yeah, but according to you we're losing, so they can't be too much of an influence.'

'Do you know the name, Sinclair-Brown?' Anita asked as Barton shifted slightly in his chair.

'No, I don't. Why?'

'He is a new campaign operative for the opposition, using techniques Harding used in a recent election in the US,' Anita responded.

'Well, if that's the case, then by all accounts he needs to work a lot harder in this campaign,' laughed Hamilton. 'Who's funding him?'

'We don't know,' said Anita.

'A printing company from western Sydney,' offered Barton.

'A company no doubt owned by a Merc,' smiled Hamilton. 'Check it out, I'm sure you'll find a link to either Jameson, Buckley or Connell.'

Anita wished she had brought her notebook to scribble notes and worked over the information silently as Barton and Hamilton talked further about the campaign. Her suspicions about the loose pieces of information had come together: Sinclair-Brown was probably a Mercantile operative.

'Can I ask just one last question?' Anita had waited for a break in the conversation.

'Just one?' joked Hamilton. 'No, ask as many as you want.'

'Is Tony Hancock a member of the Mercantiles?'

Hamilton guffawed, 'Is the Pope a catholic?' He coughed from his laughter. 'Well, let me qualify that. His grandfather was the chairman when I first came in, then his son was invited when the old man died. I assume since he is now dead Tony would have taken over, but don't quote me. In fact, if you don't mind, never quote me. I haven't got many years left and I don't want to threaten whatever time I have.'

'What do you mean?' asked a perplexed Barton.

'They have been known to take the law into their own hands in the past, if you know what I mean.' Hamilton softly said, tapping the end of his nose with a finger.

The mood dampened abruptly as the three looked at each other wondering how to respond. Nothing needed to be said, but Anita doubted the businessmen were as vindictive as Hamilton was suggesting. Surely, they wouldn't influence their power position by initiating violent political outcomes, not in Australia. She was confused with the news about Hancock yet seeing him with the Hyphen now made sense – and could explain why her columns weren't being published.

When she returned to her hotel, Anita tapped all the information she could remember from the conversation with Hamilton into her files. Barton was just as confused and insisted he didn't know them as a collective but guessed he must have listened to them as individual business owners and they may have been to various fundraising events.

Anita accepted she had more research to do on the Mercantiles. If she could link Sinclair-Brown to the group, it could feasibly uncover another political exposé and lead to a possible journalist award – not that she considered awards important. She smiled at the thought. Of course, she did.

CHAPTER
15

DAY NINETEEN – MONDAY

Meredith Bruce, the elegant government Education Minister and – if things went to plan after the election – the next deputy prime minister, slowly stalked the foyer waiting to meet with Kerry Jameson. She hadn't made an appointment and hoped an audience would be granted spontaneously, although it had been a while since the receptionist had left her. She ignored the Whiteley again as she circled the room.

'Minister, Mr Jameson will see you now.' The tall woman had returned and was holding the door for her to enter. Bruce walked through to be greeted by Jameson, standing shakily by a leather lounge setting.

'Meredith, what a surprise. So nice to see you again.'

Jameson ushered her to a lounge chair. She sank into the soft leather while he struggled to sit in a rigid wooden chair opposite. 'I didn't think I would see you again after last week's meeting with your boss. How can I help you?'

'Mr Jameson, I have a proposition for you.'

Jameson didn't answer, instead considering her for some time. Bruce shifted in her chair as if she might have said something wrong. 'I'm intrigued,' he smiled thinly. 'I'm always interested in political propositions. Please, go ahead.'

'I want you to get the outcome you want, as we discussed last week,' said Bruce, looking straight into his eyes. 'And in return, I want you to give me what I want.'

'Still intrigued, what is it you think I want?'

'You want influence, and you want a responsive government,' Bruce replied. 'You also want to get a number of your projects up, and you're concerned the prime minister will not support you.'

'Go on.' Jameson relaxed back into his chair, crossing his legs, his lean arms draped along the wooden chair arms, his hands drooped at the wrist, one bouncing his cane.

'I can give you both.'

'How would you manage to do that young lady when Gerrard has already clearly indicated he does not share our views?'

'We win government.' Bruce smiled as if about to tell a secret. 'There are two possible options – one is that Gerrard is no longer prime minister.'

Jameson didn't respond immediately, tapping the silver

knob handle of his cane against his chair as he looked at Bruce. 'This is an interesting idea, but your party colleagues will endorse him as prime minister after the election, will they not?'

'They can't elect him leader if he is no longer a member of parliament.' Bruce was almost smug with her reply, crossing her legs and relaxing a little.

Jameson slowly got up and hobbled as if in pain to the window. He looked out onto the city as Bruce waited patiently for his response. 'So how does this very unlikely plan get me what I want?' he finally said, eyes fixed firmly out of the window.

'That's the second option, and it doesn't need the first option to succeed. With your influence, I stand as deputy leader. I win the ballot and you get your confidante back into the leadership group.'

'This sounds very enticing Meredith, but it is only the dream of a political lightweight,' Jameson turned to look at Bruce. 'You offer me nothing I don't already have. You have no influence, you have no political aggression, and in the past, you just say and do what you're told. You talk a big game, but you are not in the big league.'

Bruce was slightly unsettled by the analysis. 'That's a little unfair, I've achieved a lot since coming into the ministry.'

'No, you haven't. There are others more qualified than you. You are only there because you're a favourite of the prime minister, a pet if you like. Let's not overstate your worth.'

Taken aback by Jameson's comments, Bruce retorted. 'That's a little sexist, don't you think?'

'I think not, we know all about you.'

Bruce was unsettled and pulled herself forward in the chair. 'Why do you think we are having a general election right now?'

'The parliament was prorogued, something to do with the speaker not allowing questions. The prime minister didn't act fast enough to stop the clerk from shutting the parliament down.'

'Why was that do you think?'

'Gerrard was full of himself as usual and missed what was going on.'

'I'm the manager of government business, you'd think I should have known what the clerk was doing.' Bruce gazed at Jameson, who felt a little uncomfortable and pushed off the windowsill.

'And did you?'

'Yes.'

'You knew the parliament would be sent to an election?' Jameson resisted the idea, thinking it couldn't be that simple. 'So why didn't you stop it or inform Gerrard?'

'It's in my best interests to have an election right now.'

'Interesting.' Jameson turned and shuffled back to his chair. 'So, you consider your ambitions will be enhanced by an election?'

'We win and then all positions in the government are up for negotiation. But if Gerrard is elected as prime minister, then it's the same misogynistic rubbish it has been for years. More importantly, your grip on government influence is lessened even further.'

'You knowingly sent the government to a general election? I find that hard to believe.'

'Let's just say I facilitated it.' Bruce waited for a response but received none other than a withering stare from the old man. 'So, you see, perhaps the opinion you have of me is a little skewed by the veneer of my long legs and pretty frock.'

Jameson gently rubbed the silver knob of his cane against his cheek. 'Gerrard has let you down, hasn't he?' he eventually said. 'After fucking you senseless for a few months, and you getting nothing from him, you've decided he's not going to satisfy your ambitions and give you what you want so now you seek your retribution, is that it?'

'This has nothing to do with Gerrard's alleged relationship with me.'

'Bullshit lady!' barked Jameson provoking a cough. He then took a few moments to calm his breathing and softly added. 'If we are to be friends, Meredith, you must always speak the truth.'

Bruce flicked her eyes about and considered a response. 'Okay, if we are to be open and honest − we may have had a relationship, but that is now over. Yes, he may have promised me a promotion and now he says nothing about my future,' Bruce seethed through gritted teeth. 'I can't trust the bastard and it seems neither can you − so let's get rid of him. We're a good government, so let's win the election and get rid of him at the same time.'

'How would we do that?'

'Defeat him in his seat,' Bruce said. 'We politicians must win a seat to retain our position in the parliament, after all. If Gerrard loses, you have nothing more to worry about.'

'He has a large majority in his electorate. This is a silly idea. I would have expected better from you.'

'He has won elections in the past because no-one of consequence stands against him. Curiously though, the informal vote is around twenty per cent, almost three times as much as any other seat.'

Jameson narrowed his eyes. 'What does that tell you?'

'People would rather vote for an empty chair than vote for Gerrard.'

The old man smiled at Bruce's analogy. 'So, you think he can be beaten in Melbourne?'

'If there is a credible independent candidate against him, then yes. I think we can mount a good campaign and he can lose. If the independent can get second on the primaries and Gerrard's vote is taken to preferences, then he most certainly could lose.'

'I like your optimism, Meredith.' Jameson smiled. 'So how can you help me?'

'With Gerrard out of the way, I stand for deputy leader and be your eyes and ears in government,' Bruce responded. 'You must recognise if Stanley gets elected it'll be bad for the economy. We would be at another election sooner rather than later.'

'It may be time to give the opposition an opportunity,' Jameson suggested.

'You have to admit, it's only time for Stanley's mob if the prospect of Gerrard as prime minister is real.' Bruce pulled herself further forward in her chair. 'I need your help to get rid of him and I know you have the resources to make it happen.'

'I'm not sure I know what you're talking about.'

'You know and I know the influence you wield. If you make it happen, the country will be a better place, you must know that.'

'It's an idea worthy of further consideration, I grant you that, but I'm unsure if I can do anything. Let me think about it and I'll call you in a few days.'

'Mr Jameson, I can promise you this—' Bruce stood, making ready to go. 'I will do whatever it takes to ensure Gerrard is not elected.'

Jameson paused for a moment, looking up at Bruce who stood before him. 'Anything?'

Bruce looked directly into his eyes. 'Anything.'

'Goodbye Meredith, thank you for coming to see me.' Jameson held out his hand. 'I shall consider your proposition and be in touch.'

'Thank you, I look forward to hearing from you,' Bruce said, softly shaking his hand before leaving the room, confident the meeting influenced her leadership ambitions.

· · ·

After Bruce left the room, Jameson waited for a few moments before speaking. 'What do you think?'

An amplified voice answered. 'I think she's genuine and not a Gerrard stooge. I think her idea has some interesting merit and might be worth considering. I'll crunch some numbers this morning. I also think she is a little young to be deputy prime minister.'

'How old should a deputy be?' queried Jameson.

'She's early forties, that is too young.' Wolff's reply came from a speaker in the ceiling. 'She'll be useful in the future, but I suspect she'll need to operate to our timetable rather than her ambitious goal.'

'According to the polls, they'll win,' declared Jameson. 'We may need to groom her if they do.'

'They won't win; the campaign is back on track. Polls have improved significantly because Stanley is not in the public eye as much as he was a week ago.'

'Can you investigate the nominations for Melbourne and determine if we can alter the result? It would be difficult to oust him, but it's a truly wicked idea.' Jameson smiled, reflecting on the prospect.

'Anything is possible. We have done it in the past, but we may be running out of time,' Wolff responded.

'Let's do whatever we can to get rid of that bastard,' Jameson scornfully whispered.

'You're the boss. I'll be in touch.'

'Let me know by tomorrow, nominations are declared Wednesday.'

'Leave it to me. Speak soon, bye,' Wolff said, and then a dial tone echoed through the room.

Jameson sat quietly for a moment, already regretting he would have to stand and creak to his office. Finally, he muttered, 'I'm getting too old for this bullshit.'

Jonathan Wolff ended his call to Jameson and walked from his small office toward the back of campaign headquarters to talk with Harry Lester. 'Henry, do we know the candidates in Melbourne yet?

'Please don't call me Henry,' Lester said, looking up from his research.

'Just a little fun Harry, lighten up, for heaven's sake. This is serious shit we're dealing with. We need a little humour every so often to break the tension.' Wolff smiled as he stood in the doorway of Lester's office, leaning on the metal frame. 'Now, do we know the candidates in Melbourne, do we have one?'

'Yes, we do, she's a university professor and I have a list of the other nominations. The Greens are running a candidate for the first time.' Lester passed him a file.

'Thank you, Harry,' Wolff patronised him. 'I'll get this back to you.'

Wolff walked back to his office, stopping by various busy staff, mostly volunteers, discussing any campaign issues they had, answering questions, providing direction. He was pleased with the energy and although Lester still resented his authority and influence, the campaign was gaining community momentum just as he had anticipated. He squeezed into his desk and flicked through the file looking for a potential winner.

It's time for a change of government, thought Wolff, who agreed with Jameson and remained disappointed in the competence of the leadership group surrounding Stanley. Wolff was annoyed with himself for hesitating when Jameson asked if Stanley was up to being prime minister. He always wanted the best for his country and agreed Gerrard was past his use by date to lead the nation, but he remained unconvinced the alternative prime minister was made of the right stuff.

He grimaced when he flicked to a campaign photo of Jaya Rukhmani. *She has no chance.* He quickly dismissed the Family First Party candidate and didn't think much of the Shooters and Fishers aspirant. The Greens had a likely choice and wondered if he might be able to get the candidate to say and do what he wanted. He doubted it. If this idea of Gerrard losing was to gain momentum, he would have his work cut out for him to convince voters to change their vote. He needed an issue that would polarise the community so they would question if Gerrard had their best interests at heart. He speculated his local community organiser in the seat could make a difference but was dubious the professor could attract enough votes.

Nothing in the file excited him so he swept it up and walked from the office, needing to talk strategy with someone who could make a difference. He stepped out on to Exhibition

Street and made his way to the cafes on Bourke Street so he could have a private conversation. He thumped his file on to the street side table and settled into his favourite seat, admiring the girls walking past in their summer frocks. He called for a peppermint tea and pulled his phone from his jacket, punching in commands to connect his call.

'Hancock? It's Wolff. I need to talk to you about a shift in strategy.'

'I thought we were glued to Stanley?'

'We are, but Jameson wants a little insurance, so we need to discredit Gerrard. What have you got?'

'Why do we need to do that?' Hancock had been feted by the prime minister for twenty years; they were friends. He felt anxious about taking a personal attack position against the godfather to his daughter.

'We need to discredit him somehow. Does he have a shady past with the ladies?' Wolff asked. 'Has he been up to anything irregular?'

'He's had many dalliances, but little evidence. Rumours persist about his promotion and patronage techniques for ministers and appointments, but I don't have any hard evidence to support them.'

'Has he said anything that could be misconstrued or are there any inconsistencies in his speeches?'

'We're talking about the most accomplished politician ever to enter the Federal Parliament. He is the consummate performer and oozes confidence from every pore on his body,' Hancock replied.

'He must have a weakness somewhere. Surely.' Wolff brushed a hand across his bald head.

'His wife is in Europe, which could imply a strained relationship between them?'

'Why is she in Europe?'

Hancock sighed, not wanting to continue to discuss his friend. 'Margaret Gerrard is a Francophile and is reportedly spending Christmas and New Year in Paris. We're yet to confirm if the prime minister will join her. He probably will after the election.'

'What?' Wolff pulled a pen from his jacket and doodled a note in the file. She just up and left him during an election campaign? That's weird.' Wolff watched a young woman walking toward him, the morning light was behind her, and he smiled when she caught him gazing at her silhouette. 'Why would he let her leave? She should be here.'

'She left the day the parliament was prorogued. One of my journalists floated a theory she was going to Europe to open a bank account.'

'Did she go to Switzerland?'

'No, she flew to Milan, just a few hours from Zurich by train. There was talk of her opening an account, but nothing can be confirmed.'

'Interesting,' mused Wolff. 'Why would they do that?'

'My journalist wrote a solid piece on it. She insinuated the prime minister was about to complete a funding deal with the Indonesians that would deliver him a secret commission.'

'He was about to do a deal with the Indonesians, with what?'

'Offshore immigration detention centres. Ten of them, apparently.'

'Is he tough on immigration?' Wolff asked, flicking open his file and pulling out the professor's candidate profile. 'Is he a racist? Does he have an immigration problem?'

'You mean, does he have a Muslim problem?'

'No, I don't. Does he have a thing against blacks and Indians?' Wolff asked, toying with an idea. 'Has he said anything controversial about Indians?'

'He loves them. He loves curry and loves to beat them at cricket. He did the uranium deal with them when no-one else would,' Hancock said. 'But he won't do or say anything about their human rights, especially child marriage laws, which has caused a few problems here in the past.'

'Really?' Wolff looked through Rukhmani's profile sheet. 'If I suggested he might be a racist, would that work?'

'No, he isn't.'

'Okay, if I ran a racist against him, would that drag votes away from him?' Wolff asked.

Hancock didn't answer immediately. 'The seat is full of progressives. He could probably extend his margin, but the demographics are swiftly changing so a candidate against him would need to be a nationalist.'

'Interesting.' Wolff sipped his tea. 'If a populist ran against him, leveraging nationalist policies, could we gain traction against him?' Wolff turned to watch a woman continue her journey over his shoulder.

'The greenies and the hipsters have mostly left his seat. It's been gentrified with new immigrants, mostly from Asia. We could run a campaign focusing on open borders.'

'So why the offshore detention centres?'

'We asked that question of him. He gave us the standard security answers and a willingness to end the people-smuggling trade. The way he sells the perils of people smuggling, there's never a dry eye in the house.'

'Are you prepared to run the story your journalist put up?' Wolff finished his tea and pulled the Shooters party candidate profile from the pile. 'Can we run it next week?'

'It will create a shitstorm if we do and the Mercantiles could be vulnerable.'

'Let me worry about that. Just be ready to run it when I have set the conditions for it. I want it on page one.'

'Shouldn't be a problem.'

'And can you get the journo you have working on Stanley's campaign to shift focus to Gerrard's local campaign? What's her name?'

'Devlin. She did a profile on Stanley's candidate last Sunday. She'd prefer to be in Melbourne anyway.'

'Okay, gotta go. Talk soon.' Wolff prodded the stop button. Company had returned.

CHAPTER
16

DAY TWENTY-ONE – WEDNESDAY

The air-conditioning was cranked to its maximum, working hard to cool the bus travelling south. It was ferrying journalists to an unknown location for the daily campaign policy announcement of the leader of the opposition, Peter Stanley. Every day the media pack assigned to follow Stanley would board a bus. They were told nothing about where they were heading, the policy to be announced or even how long they would be away from the city. The journalists were virtually held captive for the day, allowing the opposition party to be in complete control of what media was reported about them for that day.

The bus refrigeration unit struggled to win the fight against the heat and Anita regretted her decision to wear her cargo pants, but she only had her black sneakers in her travel bag and would have looked foolish in a frock, not that fashion was ever her forte. The bus was full, there were no curtains and the traffic slow. She truly regretted coming as the sun pounded her.

After fifty minutes battling the traffic, the speakers kicked into action with the jolly amplified voice of Sussan Neilson providing a briefing about the event. 'We are visiting a recycling plant today. This company turns plastic milk bottles into contemporary office and garden furniture. We will distribute a briefing sheet as you get off the bus so make sure you have one with the background information you may need.'

Michele Kingsley, a columnist with the Sun shouted from further back. 'What is the policy announcement supposed to be today?'

Neilson replied. 'We shall be making that announcement at a presser once we arrive.'

'Why?' asked Kingsley. Neilson didn't respond, which Anita thought was a perfect metaphor for the opposition's campaign – they just didn't have any answers.

Fifteen minutes later, about two kilometres north of the bayside suburb of Frankston, the bus pulled off the Nepean Highway. They travelled along an unsigned road for ten minutes, eventually turning into an industrial estate, and swung a few bends before parking in a bitumen lot beside a clean and welcoming factory. A welcome party of company staff was out front, and an older man – smiling in his shirtsleeves and a shortened tie that didn't reach over his large belly – tentatively took a few steps forward.

Anita watched as Neilson walked over and shook hands. After a brief discussion the man retreated to his staff, obviously not interested in journalists. Neilson returned to the bus and from the front step, without the microphone, asked the journalists to disembark and venture along the side of the building to the roller door where refreshments were waiting. She then stepped off and worked her phone, probably wondering where the leader might be.

Anita was the last off, shoving her recorder and notebook into her pockets, she left her bag on the bus. As she jumped off, she sidled over to Neilson. 'Do you have the briefing notes?'

'We'll distribute them when the leader gets here.'

'Can you tell me who owns this plant? Is it part of the Hamilton Group?' asked Anita.

'Not sure, but I'll find out for you.' Neilson took a note and Anita joined the others for water and a scone.

'This is massive, look at the size of the place,' said Kingsley as Anita settled in beside her for an idle chat.

'What the heck are we doing wasting our time here?' Anita slurped on her water from the chilled bottle. 'This is an unbelievable waste of time.'

'This is what they do, you know that. Keep us isolated and busy to stop us snooping,' Kingsley said. 'They don't want to alert the rent-a- crowd who monitor our Twitter feeds to avoid any demonstrations.'

'Doing our jobs, you mean?'

'While a good fight makes for good television, they don't want a mob spoiling their announcement.'

'So, no anarchy on the news tonight,' said Anita. 'Just more hard hats and high-vis and Stanley smiling, shaking a fat businessman's hand.'

'Such a cynic, Anita,' chortled Kingsley. 'Given the signs, this will obviously be about the environment babe, and how the opposition will protect us from nasty polluters.'

'So, nothing to do with the twenty-four-hour news cycle and managing the media with the right messages.'

'Of course, it has,' sighed Kingsley. 'Gerrard spoilt it way back with this campaign-management trick.'

'I might get a train back to the city, it would probably be quicker.'

'No money for a cab?' asked Kingsley.

'Even splitting it with you would be way too much for my daily allowance,' smiled Anita. 'But I can't waste time here, once Stanley goes, I'm off.'

'Then let's go together. I'll chat up a staffer for a lift to the station.'

'Mish, you're such a revolutionary.'

'No, but if you're going to break out, you'll need company, girlfriend.'

A rush of camera shutters flickering erupted as Peter Stanley, Barton Messenger, the smiling manager, and an unknown man emerged from the administration block. They walked to a designated spot and cameramen positioned themselves. Journalists held microphones on poles out of shot, other press journalists stood in the created semi-circle.

'Are you ready?' Stanley asked, looking about the group. Messenger stood behind him, the stranger and the manager opposite, but still in shot. 'Okay. We're here in the seat of Dunkley supporting our dedicated candidate, Billy Phillips. I must say it is a wonderful time to be here.' Stanley said turning to acknowledge the other man.

'Billy has insisted the leadership team visit this fine recycling plant to announce our policy on our proposed initiative to drive economic growth into the recycling sector. I'm very pleased to be with Terry Pettersen, the manager of this innovative plant, and recognise him and his hard-working team for the work they do in significantly reducing our carbon footprint. They are recycling the everyday plastics that make our lives easier, but ultimately impact our environment in such a negative way. If not for the Australians working in this plant, and indeed similar plants throughout Australia, our plastic pollution would be much greater.

'It is the innovators, like Progressive Plastics, who make our country great – and a Stanley Government would like to support them to continue their good work. I'm pleased to announce today that within twelve months of the election, the Stanley Government will bring forward to the parliament legislation for mandatory management of plastic waste.

'In other words, we will require all businesses in Australia to send their plastic waste to recyclers. We will also regulate local governments to send residential plastic waste to recycling plants, and we will provide investment opportunities for local governments to establish their own recycling plants. This innovative program will create new job opportunities within all local government regions throughout Australia. A Stanley government will always be focused on jobs, and this is a positive step toward creating new industries.

'We estimate this new initiative will directly provide ten thousand new workers within the recycling industry. We also believe logistic suppliers and associated infrastructure will also increase opportunities for employment. All in all, we estimate an increase of twenty-five thousand new jobs within the first term of a Stanley government from this significant policy initiative.

'Funding grants will vary depending on scale, but we believe this will ensure we get on top of the nation's increasing plastic pollution. We have seen other government programs try to encourage the population to mobilise in this truly beneficial cause, but sadly, it seems many of us continue to believe someone else will take responsibility.

'My government will no longer accept excuses. We will act to provide financial incentive and punitive inducement to get on top of this environmental issue that impacts us all.' Stanley paused for a moment as he looked at his papers and shuffled pages.

'The government invests significant taxpayer funds with the purchase of furniture and other office fixtures. These items are usually made from wood products, adding further to the reduction of our forests. In my view, if there are alternatives we can use, we should.

'Today I announce that in the future, my government will only purchase general furniture items for community building projects throughout Australia that are manufactured from recycled plastics. Our cost estimate is two hundred million dollars a year.

'This figure will be offset by decreasing government capital spending on furniture as we begin to look for cheaper alternatives, such as products from Progressive Plastics who specialise in recycling plastic into modern office furniture.' Stanley turned and pointed to an impressive display of modern furniture. 'As you can see, modern design and modern materials for a modern government.'

Anita took a note of the iteration and smiled as she wrote it – modern government with a mistake-prone, stodgy leader.

'If the community continues to use plastic, like milk containers, then let us redevelop that wasted resource into community use. You will see on your tour of the plant and with the display of quality products Progressive Plastics are already exporting to China and India that this innovative industry will deliver high value to the Australian taxpayer. You will also see there is no good reason these products cannot be used within government.

'Our policy will reduce expenditure and help balance costs of the program. Are there any questions?'

The media pack was not overly enthusiastic with their first question until Michele Kingsley asked, 'Mr Stanley, why have you not issued an apology for your gaff about domestic violence?'

Stanley was not expecting it. 'A private conversation has been taken totally out of context. I will not be commenting any further.'

'What does that say about your party's respect for women?'

'I have nothing further to say.'

'You don't have a comment about women?'

'That is not what I said, you know that is not what I said, and I ask for further questions.'

Another journalist asked. 'Where will the money come from for this initiative?'

'We have fully budgeted this innovative program. Our costings will be released before the election.'

'Will you guarantee no new taxes or levies?'

'There will be no tax increases for this initiative?'

'What about levies?'

'As I said, there will be no new taxes for this initiative.'

'And what about levies?'

'I have already answered your question, another question?'

'There is a report today that a boat has left Indonesia with two hundred asylum seekers on board,' said Kingsley. 'If they arrive in Australian waters, what will be your position on these desperate people seeking our help?'

Stanley swayed slightly from foot to foot. 'I am unaware of those reports and will not be commenting specifically on operational matters.' Stanley said, looking about for another question. After further consideration he added, 'Let me be clear on this issue of asylum, versus immigrant, versus refugee. Our party has well established policies and we have pushed Prime Minister Gerrard to join us, and to his credit, he has. We support offshore detention and processing to stop the scourge of unlawful people smuggling and our humanitarian intake is set much higher than the government's. Our immigration policy is clear: we will bring migrants who want to make Australia an even better place to live. We have no regret or dark hearts when it comes to immigration policy.'

'Mr Stanley?' called Anita. Messenger looked to her and gave a half smile. 'Your campaign seems to have overcome its early strategy and resources weaknesses, is this because the Mercantile Group is now managing your campaign?' Messenger pursed his lips slightly.

'Our campaign is fully funded, fully staffed and is run by our campaign team headed by Harry Lester.'

'Not Jack Sinclair-Browne?'

'Not sure I know that name,' Stanley tried to brush Anita off. 'The campaign is doing its job and we are seeing a lift in the polls. But I must remind all of you, the only poll that counts is election day.'

'You say categorically, the Mercantile Group is not involved in your campaign and campaign operative Sinclair-Browne has little influence?'

Stanley didn't respond immediately, and Messenger passed a severe look back to Anita. 'I can say I'm unaware of the name you mentioned. The Mercantile Group, I have not spoken to for some time, and have had little to do with them over the last ten years. They are a fringe business group, just like any other special interest organisation.' Stanley looked away from Anita and smiled, looking about the other journalists. 'Are there other questions regarding this exciting initiative?'

Another journalist asked a question about the company and Stanley called upon Terry Pettersen to step forward, who then waxed lyrical about the company history and how it had evolved over the last thirty years into a recycling specialist.

'Who owns the company?' Anita wanted to check.

'It's a private family company. They have other interests throughout Australia.'

'The name?' Anita asked. Pettersen hesitated slightly, checking over his shoulder, looking for support from the politicians and getting none. 'It is only for a reference. I mean, I could search the corporate records at the securities commission. I just thought you may like to help, given this exciting initiative,' Anita smiled at Pettersen.

'Top End Pastoralists.'

'Thank you.' Anita took a note, ignoring Barton's glare. She was done and wanted to go, so moved to the back of the pack. She saw Michele laughing along with an employee. 'Do you want to go, or shall I call a cab?'

'Sally here said she could take us to Seaford train station, they run every ten minutes.'

After collecting her bag, the run to the station took five

minutes, and Anita thought it better than completing an excruciating tour of a plastics factory. She was going to take the opportunity to talk to Sally, who drove a hotted-up, early model Ford. Anita lazed in the back seat as Michele excitedly talked about the car.

'When was this event organised, Sally?' Anita asked when Kingsley took a breath.

'Monday. There was so much we had to do to clean up and get things ready.'

'Did anyone come out and inspect the plant?'

'Yeah, a weird dude. Bald head, dressed in black. I remember him because he had a decent scar on his head.' Sally changed down a gear to go around a corner and the engine throttled a throaty growl. 'You don't get scars like that without some sort of trauma.'

'Do you remember his name?'

'Nope.'

'Was it hyphenated?

'Could've been.' Sally gunned the beast, the road with the station another kilometre away. 'I honestly didn't take much notice.'

Within seconds the car came to a throbbing halt outside the station entrance.

'Thanks babe, that was great,' Anita said as Kingsley got out.

'Here's my card.' Kingsley said, closing the door, 'Please call me and we can catch up for a drink or something.'

The journalists watched the car drive off and gave a final wave.

'Man, that was so hot.'

'Such a revolutionary,' smirked Anita as they walked into the station, figured out the ticket machine and strolled onto the platform as a partial express train to the city came whooshing to a halt.

'What's all that garbage you were asking Stanley about?' asked Kingsley as they settled into their seats for the sixty-minute trip. 'Who is this Mercantile Group?'

'Nothing really.'

'Crap, Anita. You never ask a question unless you've got the answer.

Tell me.'

'I can absolutely assure you it was nothing,' Anita said. 'I was more interested in what Sally had to say.'

'Yeah, me too.'

Anita's phone abruptly interrupted them, and she checked the caller ID. 'I had better take this, sorry.' She pushed the receive button. 'Hello grumpy, what's up?'

'Where are you?' Barton asked.

'On a train to the city. I thought I'd leave you to manage the most exciting initiative you have done today.'

'Don't be like that, I thought it went well.'

'Bart, it was terrible.' Anita was surprised by his response. 'Surely there are better things to talk about at the moment than the environment and plastic recycling. It was boring, and you'll be lucky to get more than five seconds on the news tonight. I won't be doing anything on it. Total waste of time for me and that's why I'm on a train.

'Okay, smarty-pants,' Barton said. 'What should we be talking about?'

'Immigration, especially with this potential boat arrival. Gerrard's period in government. Shonky deals with Indonesia, which is the reason for the election. I don't know, something that excites voters.'

'Okay, thanks for that,' Barton said, changing tone. 'Why did you ask Pete about the Mercs?'

'Because I think I'm onto something. And you know me, when I get a sniff of a story, I'm onto it.'

'What? You don't want a change of government?'

'I don't care to be honest with you,' said Anita, quickly adding, 'I care that you win, and you are a minister, but frankly, I have to report the parliament and I don't take sides.'

'Fair enough, I have to go.' The phone went dead, stunning Anita who wondered if it was a reception problem. It rang again immediately.

'Hello? Sorry darling, I didn't mean to say that.'

'Say what?' Tony Hancock asked, further unsettling Anita.

'Oh, sorry Mr Hancock, I thought you were someone else.' Anita pulled a face to Kingsley who fell about the seat behind her in hysterics, stifling a raucous laugh.

'I hear you've been creating a bit of a stink in Frankston. Asking Stanley questions about campaign strategy instead of the environment.'

'News travels fast.' Anita shook her head. 'I must say – don't believe everything you hear.'

'I won't.' Hancock moved to business. 'Anita, I want you to change your focus a little.'

'Oh, yes? From what to what?'

'From the campaign generally to a campaign specifically.'

'In what way?'

'I want you to focus on Gerrard, specifically in his electorate, rather than the bigger national issues. I hear the candidate against him is getting traction.'

'She's interesting. Did you read the profile piece I did on her?' asked Anita, waiting for cues. 'I don't think she'll win, but she is a quality candidate.'

'We've done polling and we think Gerrard is exposed to a potential loss.'

'You're kidding. There's no chance he is going to lose Melbourne.'

'I'm running your piece about the shonky deal he nearly pulled off with the Indonesians,' said Hancock. 'That should set the hares running.'

'Why? Why do we need to set the hares running?' asked Anita. 'Surely we can't influence an election with pure speculation that is no longer relevant. It's a little unethical, don't you think?'

'We want Gerrard to have a strong contest,' responded Hancock.

'Who's we? You mean the media group?' queried Anita. 'I thought you two were mates?'

'Just focus on the local campaign for the next week or so, please.'

'You're the boss,' said Anita, before quickly adding. 'Just a quick one, Mr Hancock. Have you met with Stanley's campaign operative, Sinclair-Browne?'

'No. Why would I do that?'

'Oh, I don't know, maybe to discuss how the media group could help the campaign,' said Anita. 'Never caught up, perhaps in Sydney?'

'No,' Hancock snapped. 'And don't bother asking me again.' The phone went dead.

Anita looked across to Kingsley who was looking out on to the suburbs flashing past. 'Fancy a late lunch with a chardonnay, Mish?'

'You bet, girlfriend.'

CHAPTER
17

DAY TWENTY-TWO – THURSDAY

Only three candidates eventually nominated for the seat of Melbourne, surprising the commentators who were expecting a robust contest. The day before declarations, Wolff visited with the Family First and the Shooters and Fishers candidates. Both candidates displayed little political ambition and Wolff easily persuaded them with inducements to withdraw.

His methods and offerings were contrary to electoral law, but both candidates were clearly advised on their rights if they spoke about the arrangements – they had none. Wolff had a unique set of skills he'd developed over many election campaigns. When he wanted something done, his persuasion skills got him what he wanted. In Melbourne he had the candidates focus on more important things in their lives other than politics, such as protecting their families from the rough and tumble of politics, and he was pleased with the negotiated outcomes.

With the two minor parties out of the running, the voters could now focus on a clear choice for the first time in many elections. There remained a core group of Greens voters keen to save the world with their unrealistic radical ideas that could reach twenty per cent of the primary vote. It was then up to Wolff to achieve a significant share of the remainder to change their vote away from Gerrard, or at least make a commitment to vote in the case of the high informal voters.

His plan was simple enough. Finish second after the primary vote count and have the third candidate's preferences allocated to Rukhmani. But he knew politics wasn't always that straightforward. Finishing second also required Gerrard to fall below fifty per cent in the primary vote so voting preferences could be counted – no point finishing second if Gerrard had an absolute majority greater than fifty per cent.

Getting preferences from the Greens would also be problematic – they never allocated preferences to a conservative party candidate. They often spruik about electoral fairness and supporting a candidate based on merit, yet coincidentally send their preferences away from conservative candidates, no matter their position on environmental or social issues.

Preferences were usually finalised about a week prior to the election so how-to-vote cards could be printed, so there was a window of negotiation opportunity of five days, six maximum, for Wolff to secure a preference deal.

Rukhmani received the coveted top of the election ballot paper position when it was drawn after nominations closed, which meant she could receive a big share of the donkey vote. These were usually residents who didn't care about voting and only did so to avoid a fine. Not caring about who was standing, they usually marked their ballot from the top down in numerical order.

Wolff's strategy to win the seat was also very risky. The Greens remained a strong threat, harbouring an ambition to win the seat. The candidate was an engineering PhD student who specialised in online gaming technology. A graduate of Melbourne University, Wolff liked the synergy between him and the professor. The young man was buoyant when Wolff spoke with him about his political ambitions, and he remained confident about a positive result for the Greens. He was yet to realise their core group of support had moved from the electorate, pushed out by the changing gentrification driven by hard-working new immigrants, weakening the Greens' traditionally strong first-preference vote.

Wolff's plan to achieve votes for Rukhmani was straightforward. Raise her profile and get people to advocate, convincing others to support her. There was a little over two weeks to generate momentum to convince fifty thousand voters to give their first or second preference to her. Not so easy considering she was running against the longest serving, most highly respected prime minister in the nation's history.

She's also in the conservative party, and – black. Walk in the park.

Private polling Wolff had instigated confirmed the national campaign was going well. The plan for community engagement was ticking along with positive outcomes in the majority of campaigns and targeted marginal seats. On the other hand, Stanley was not doing so well in polling. Wolff had been involved in enough campaigns to know when a national leader was beyond help, and when creating as much media attention as possible toward him was needed to steer the focus away from the real election campaign.

Allow the lazy media to give Gerrard a false confidence he was doing well. Allow the commentators to nominate the winner and say the election will be a walkover for Gerrard. Let the pollsters believe their data reflects the electorate – because when it comes to election day, the result will be embarrassing for them. Whenever Wolff was involved, there was always a result the experts didn't predict or understand – there is only ever one poll to be concerned about.

Wolff's election strategy insisted that early in a campaign a public meeting should be organised in every electorate. His idea was for the community organisers to rally public interest for a public meeting where candidates could deliver a speech and then take questions from concerned local community members. Sitting politicians were very experienced at these town hall–type meetings and welcomed the opportunity to compare their experience and profile to those inexperienced candidates.

Conversely, novice candidates were usually shy and overly nervous, often causing a negative perception. It would be a challenge for conservative party candidates pitted against seasoned politicians, but his campaign manual set out in detail how to prepare and who should write the speech.

The Melbourne electorate's debate was scheduled for later in the day. Wolff learned from operatives that Gerrard wouldn't be attending. He also learned Gerrard had not asked any of his senatorial colleagues to represent him. It seemed he was annoyed he was even asked to attend, and therefore no-one should go. He was not leaving Admiralty House for anyone on such a sunny day in Sydney. Good news.

Robert Wong was instructed by Wolff to request the organiser, the local newspaper, to have three chairs on the rostrum just in case a government member showed up. He then urged Robert to prepare and then tape a sign reserving a seat for Gerrard prior to the candidates taking their seats. Wolff also advised he would be sending a prepared speech that he insisted should be read word for word without modification. Although concerned about the tone of the message, Wong acquiesced and assured Wolff that Jaya would deliver the speech as written.

Wolff 's next call was to Hancock. 'Mr Hancock, have you redirected your journalist?'

'Yes. I've also told her we are likely to run the Gerrard piece tomorrow.'

'Very good, but you may want to hold it back until Monday or Tuesday. The shit is going to hit the fan after an event in Melbourne tonight. Tomorrow will be a huge media distraction and we don't want to be diverted from our plan.'

'What's going to happen?'

'Best I do not tell you, otherwise it might lessen the surprise and your editorial tone may not be right. Can you get your girl to get to the public meeting in Melbourne tonight?'

'I'll make sure she's there. Where is it?'

'Too much information for you to know, tell her to get it from the local campaign office.'

Anita was trying to draw together a narrative that could answer her suspicions about the outside influences of the election campaign. She'd worked in the federal parliament for years, never once considering the influence outside power and money could have on politicians and the political process.

Of course, she understood the role of lobbyists and registered organisations working hard to influence and communicate their point of policy view. The many voices were indeed prolific and loud in the media around May when the federal budget was announced. Each group held their own self-interest, but she hadn't considered there may have been a murkier arrangement of covert influence not seen by the public.

Gerrard always resisted the idea of a federal commission against corruption, believing the current strong regulatory system within federal politics was adequate. He often cited as evidence the state governments funding such bodies using their Supreme Court jurisdiction for little need for a federal watchdog, especially when it came to matters of land development. The prime minister argued the senate held significant anti-corruption powers and there was no justification for such a body in the federal system. Yet Anita was beginning to think there may be a case for a federal body, especially with the influence of lobbyists on federal parliamentary decisions.

What better place to set out her research than the prestigious State Library? She was ensconced at one of the eight long timber desks laid out like spokes in a wheel converging to a central information hub. The four-level octagonal atrium sat under an enormous glass dome. Allowing natural lighting, it was the perfect place to reflect and search through old newspapers. Anita always liked to have a direct link to history when delving into a research project. Google was a good resource, but she considered it shouldn't be her only source when seeking creative ideas. She liked the libraries.

Methodical as ever, Anita noted a list of what she knew:

The Mercantiles – since mid 1800s

Membership – highest taxpayers and collectors

Private family-owned companies – no shareholders

Membership by invitation only – changed if tax level reduced

Hancock may be a member – grandfather definitely was

Twelve members?

Likely members Jameson (gambling) Buckley (beef baron) Connell (mining)

Other members? Check property? Finance? Manufacturing? Export?

Influence on government policy

Prominent when negotiating the prices and income accord in 1980s

International affiliates – especially US

Trade benefits from influencing other governments

She then listed what she knew about the campaign and the mysterious man in black.

Campaign operative paid by printing company – Acclaim (Sydney)

Policy launch in pastoral company business – is this Buckley?

Hancock denies knowledge of operative yet confirmed sighting with him

Hancock defers stories critical of Stanley campaign

Assigned to Gerrard's local campaign

The list may have been interesting, but Anita was getting nothing other than a headache from studying it. She searched the Mercantiles on the internet with over sixteen million results but zero relevance within the first ten pages of searching. Arthur Hamilton told her about Hancock's grandfather being the chair, so she began searching Sir Frank's achievements. She typed his name and the prices and income accord into the search engine and five entries linked both.

It seemed Sir Frank Hancock was outspoken, publishing editorials every day that supported greater labour regulation. Anita retained a grasp on this information from previous research, but what she didn't expect to find was a social entry within the Melbourne Herald linking prominent businessmen at a political function in Melbourne to mark the first agreed pay rise under the accord. She clicked on the entry and was advised the page was no longer available, so swiped back to note the details of the event and the date in late September

1983. She then asked an information attendant stationed at the central hub if he could help, and within thirty minutes Anita was flicking through an original newspaper from the 1980s. The paper and print quality almost seemed as if it was printed that morning, let alone decades previously.

The news of the day highlighted Australia winning the America's Cup, a nuclear catastrophe averted, political troubles, unions on strike and the mighty Hawthorn Football Club winning another premiership. What Anita was looking for was in the social pages, which she found after searching thirteen editions without luck. A handsome photo of twelve business executives at a dinner for the then prime minister. It was one of those staged photographs before the advent of the smartphone. There were twelve smiling faces and a look from the prime minister that suggested he was not enjoying himself.

Anita smiled as she looked at the credits. It listed the names of all the smiling faces, including a very young and rather handsome Arthur Hamilton. She blessed the subeditors – their companies were also listed. Anita was grateful for the internet, but it didn't have everything an investigative journalist needed. This was a rare photograph of the Mercantiles.

It was a sound starting point, and she listed into her notes the companies by classification. Mining, banking, telecoms, retail, transport, insurance, energy. Gambling had a dashing Kerry Jameson smiling broadly, media was Hancock's grandfather, then there was health and an airline. Hamilton's gorgeous smile was a standout. All men of variable ages, but mostly pale and stale.

Anita then switched her search to the current top fifty privately owned companies in Australia, making a list with an eye to her membership listing decades earlier to isolate the likely members and their proprietors.

Kerry Jameson – Australian Gaming Operators

John Buckley – Top End Pastoralists

Allan Connell – Fitzroy Prospecting

Tony Hancock – Hancock Media

Then it got a little harder as she worked through the list. It seemed to be more a wish list without structure or logic.

Tasmanian Seafood Group

Newfields Property Group

New Women Clothing

United Health Union Bank

Hyatt Transport

World Communications

Buckminster Building Group

From these listings, Anita was able to confirm John Buckley owned the company where Stanley held his recycling policy announcement, adding another line to her conspiracy list. The link was tenuous, but it was a link to the Mercantiles. Hamilton also suggested Buckley might be one of the group behind the Acclaim Printing Company sponsoring the man in black, Mr Hyphen, so Anita transferred her research to company searches within the government commission responsible for all company registrations.

She typed in Acclaim Printing Company and sure enough, as she expected, the Acclaim was owned by another company. She searched that company, which was owned by two further companies. She then searched those companies, then again, with Anita surprised by the web of structure trying to hide the real owners of the company. Why go to all this trouble for an apparent tax dodge? She didn't understand the motives for doing this complex ownership structure.

By her sixth search a company name kept repeating as part owner of many companies within the web of ownership. Harborne Holdings Limited. Anita delved further into this company and looking through the ownership listed discovered it was part owned by Hancock Media.

She fell back into her chair a little deflated and confused by the entry. She removed her smartphone from her bag on the floor and snapped a screenshot. She felt uneasy and a little compromised by what she found; anxious her findings would confirm what she suspected – Tony Hancock was a Mercantile trying to influence the election.

Tony Hancock not only knew the Hyphen. He was paying him.

'Robbie, I'm a little uncomfortable with this speech. Are you sure they want me to deliver it?' Jaya Rukhmani asked her campaign manager. 'Have you read it?'

'Mr Sinclair-Browne specifically told me you must deliver it word for word. In fact, he insisted on it.'

'Do you think it might be a little provocative?'

'Ours is not to reason why, madam candidate, ours is to do what we are bloody well told. It's in the manual, remember!'

'But this might create a media storm. Are we ready for the backlash that will no doubt come?'

'Head office said they will look after us. Let us do the speech, answer the questions, and get on with it,' sighed a grumpy Wong.

Jaya dropped the speech to her side and looked at her student. 'You sound a little tired. Have you been eating properly?'

'Don't ask me these things, you sound like my mother.' Wong brushed his hand past his ear as if swatting away a fly. 'I thought I'd gotten rid of that tough love years ago.'

Jaya smiled broadly, watching him busily tapping at the computer. 'It's only two weeks to go, can you last?'

'Sixteen days to be precise,' he said harshly. 'Then I'm going on a holiday until the New Year.'

'Can I come?'

'No. I've seen enough of you to last me a very long time.'

Anita arrived at the candidates' debate location, a community hall in the popular Carlton Italian restaurant district, flashing her media accreditation to the security attendant as she entered. She was surprised by the media turnout. There were two television camera crews, various radio correspondents and a few political journalists. Surely, they weren't expecting Gerrard to turn up. She surmised they may have been informed the prime minister could be attending so they took a chance. She was there because she was told to attend by her editor, foregoing a date with Barton in his electorate.

Barton hadn't spoken to her since the Stanley media conference, and when she called to cancel, he left her a little cold. She occasionally questioned if her role as a political journalist would compromise their friendship, just as it may have done yesterday. She was doing her job reporting on the activities of the leadership group and should not be compromised by the thoughts she had for him. She was doing her job, that's all. She felt a pang of regret and a little sorrow toward the way he must feel about her reporting and the implications to his career. She hoped they would work it out.

The hall was the community base for the Italian Club and ageing memorabilia, pennants and national flags were strewn across the walls, reminding local residents of their links to the old country. The standard, uncomfortably hard, stackable blue plastic chairs had been set out in rows with a centre aisle and surprisingly, most seats were already taken. Greens supporters were in a group with their signs declaring dismay with the current government, stating they wanted more done to protect the environment. A significant number of young people in the blue and white colours of the conservatives were scattered throughout the audience. The remaining audience seemed to be older local citizens interested in hearing from their representatives.

Anita made her way to the front where there were always seats available. Robert Wong quickly danced across the stage and placed a sign on the seat closest to the lectern – ABSENT MEMBER. An overt reminder to the audience and a subtle jibe against Gerrard, which would no doubt filter back to Sydney. Anita chuckled at the brazenness, and cynically shook her head at the amateurish attempt to ridicule the prime minister.

Within five minutes of the allocated start time, the two candidates were seated on stage with the appointed master of ceremonies, a local councillor. At the exact time for commencement, she welcomed everyone, outlining the rules for the debate. There would be an opening statement of ten minutes from each candidate, twenty minutes of questions, and then five-minute summaries in reverse order.

A coin toss was made to determine who would speak first – the coin bounced and rolled off the stage, bouncing and spinning further to the great glee of the audience and the frustration of the councillor. A staff member looked at the coin and called heads. Jaya Rukhmani walked confidently to the lectern, cleared her throat, and spoke.

'I came to this country, not as a volunteer, nor as a refugee, but as a child bride of twelve years of age, the wife of a husband some twenty years my senior. The marriage was an arrangement and provided my parents a substantial reward. I have not seen or communicated with my parents since my marriage.

'I was brought to Australia under a family reunion visa

and very soon fell pregnant. I had been in Australia for a little over twelve months when I gave birth to my beautiful boy, who is now a strapping thirty-year-old. I am extremely grateful for his love and the manner in which he lives his life.

'After the birth, I was excommunicated from the family and forced to become their housekeeper; at eighteen I was driven from their home into a life of poverty and desperation. I spoke little English and had no education. I had no money, no job and no prospects.'

It was a proud start and Anita smiled at the confident manner which Jaya introduced herself. This was a woman of substance. She scribbled a note, looked about the room and observed the attentiveness of the audience. They were captivated with her story. She scribbled more notes.

'Now I'm a professor of politics at Melbourne University and thankfully, I occasionally see my son and grandchildren. When I reflect upon those thirty years since coming here, I have achieved many things and continue to contribute to this great country, which is now my home and where my loyalties lie. I love Australia for what it has given me and the opportunities it will provide my family. I love its sense of community and the manner in which we care for each other – this is one of the values I hold dear when I think about my country.

'But, ladies and gentlemen, I must say to you in all honesty, I'm saddened by what I see happening to our country. Specifically, the way our immigration laws are flouted by those who would take advantage of my great country.'

Anita was surprised by the statement and looked to see if

the camera crews were recording. This was only the beginning of the speech and after a strong start it was already becoming politically provocative. One crew was filming and the other rushed to reverse the packing they had begun once knowing Gerrard was not going to attend.

'I see international students enter this country illegally to take advantage of our nation's generous soul. I say illegally because they have no intention of studying their chosen course or degree and lazily turn up to register each semester sitting the required exams to maintain a pass. I have person-ally seen incidences of imposters sitting exams for students and, of course, university professors are acutely aware of the trade in writing academic papers for marking.

'Instead of studying, these fake students are working in this country, sending the money they earn back home to support their families. The working conditions these so-called students suffer under are less than the standards of legitimate workers and because they're here under false pretences, they accept less money, never complaining. But let me tell you, even working in this illicit trade of foreign workers and suffering extreme work conditions, it still allows them to earn more money than they could ever dream of earning back home.

'These students – no, let me call them what they are – these illegals, are using this country to increase their family wealth back home, sadly at the expense of Australia. By any measure, this is a community and government moral scandal for it certainly devalues our tertiary education system and disavows the rights of other students who have missed a university place because of these so-called international students. It must stop.

'Yet, when I read the policies of the major universities in Australia, it is clear their attitude is to accept increasing revenue from the international student market. It seems to me academic standards are slipping and perhaps our universities do not consider if they are acting ethically or not. Unfortunately, it seems it is only about the money for them, which is sad. But what is worse is when I look to government policy for a solution, I see nothing.

'The immigration policy in my country is essentially an open borders policy with little control of the visa program. They care about stopping refugees but pay little attention to the real people smuggling in Australia.

'The visa system, particularly the student visa system, encourages itinerate workers to take Australian jobs. It allows some international students to lower the academic standards of our universities and deny Australians opportunity.

'Our immigration system permits the wretched of the world's economic disasters to claim immigration rights and live a life on the generosity of the Australian taxpayer. They have more money and services provided to them by the government than they can ever earn back home and living here is a safer option. Why wouldn't this country be the honey for the those who think work and effort is so last century.'

A number of positive interjections from the audience

interrupted Jaya's flow and she paused for a moment, calming further comment.

'Australia is tough on so-called boat people who pay top dollar to smugglers to skirt the regulations and process of immigration. These are the people who take advantage of our laws and courts by using litigant lawyers who increase their own wealth, generously funded by the Australian taxpayer. By gaming the system, these people fraudulently seek to position themselves ahead of legitimate immigrants. As a result, we see a developing queue of wasters, leaners, and people who don't care about Australia and its people – rather, they only care about plundering the taxpayer riches it offers.

'Yet, if anyone deigns to speak about these matters in a considered way, we are branded to be racist or phobic in some way. It is not racist to protect our people. It's not racist to help our people. It's not racist to call out wrong government policy, and it is not racist to ensure new immigrants earn the right to live in this great country.'

Scribbling quickly, Anita tried to get the words down. Photographers were now sitting on the floor in front of her snapping the professor, checking ISO and white balances before snapping more from different angles. The Greens candidate stopped looking at his notes and seemed stunned by what he was hearing.

'Australia is duty bound to provide sanctuary, but we are not duty bound to let this sanctuary become a haven for the unscrupulous, the dishonest and the fraudsters.

'Government statistics clearly indicate there is a wave of

migrants we have welcomed for the last twenty years, under the management of Andrew Gerrard, spiralling into a ghetto of welfare recipients taking advantage of the free and easy social security system we have created.

'Why wouldn't you want to come here? Free education, free health, subsidised housing, subsidised utilities, subsidised public transport. We offer funding incentives to have more children so that a family can live comfortably on welfare and have no-one work for generations. We offer free childcare support, aged care support, and support for carers on this merry-go-round of taxpayer subsidy. My country provides too much to these cheats and we place zero requirements for these phony Australians to contribute to our nation.'

Someone interjected, 'Hear, hear.' Anita swung around to see how the audience was reacting. Many seemed captivated by the professor's words as there were plenty of smiles, surprising her. The paradox of a migrant criticising immigration was compelling, and yet Anita wondered if this was the language the community should be listening to.

'I would like to see the government place a cap on international students trashing our universities, demanding academics like me to pass them in their subjects no matter their academic standard. I would like to see a cap on social welfare benefits for new immigrants set at three years – either contribute to Australia or go home.'

One or two audience members clapped enthusiastically.

'I would like to see the reduction of suburban enclaves and criminal ghettos springing up in various suburbs and regions across the country.' Jaya paused for a moment and looked out into the audience. 'Friends, if we are appalled by many of the grand European cities with their noble history being trashed by immigrants from countercultures, then see the early signs of this silent invasion happening right here in Australia. I do not want to fear going into a suburb because I'm female, yet this is how I'm made to feel by these ugly enclaves. I encourage the government to get actively involved in settlement planning and allocate new arrivals to cities and regional towns that are not deluged with the leaners and takers of our society.

'These issues of immigration, segregation and cultural change are not new. They were here thirty years ago when I arrived, and there has been much political debate and community hand-wringing over that entire period since. Yet there is very little change to government policy and action to resolve the many critical issues within the community that face us all.

'I was a victim of racism and ostracised from the Australian community when I first arrived here, but I was able to do something about it and change my world. I did not become a victim. The difference between talk and action is significant, and for me it has been very rewarding. My country supported me, now I give back to my community in many ways.

'While Andrew Gerrard has talked, I have acted.

'I've contributed to this great nation, yet I started with absolutely nothing. No support, no family, and no future.

Friends, if I can help myself, why then cannot others? If new immigrants won't use their God-given skills like I did, why then do I, as an Australian taxpayer, pay their indulgences and put up with their conflicting cultural attitudes?

'Australia should not be a soft target for those who come to take advantage. Yet sadly, this is the position of the government, and it is also the stated policy of the Greens. We must all earn the right to live here. There should be no free rides in the name of human rights and racial discrimination.'

The Green candidate said something to the professor, but Anita could not hear him. His supporters tossed a few interjections disputing her claims, but Jaya ignored them.

'Of course, we must care for those among us who need our support. But all of us must work together to grow this fine country and ensure we are all rewarded for our efforts. It's not just the taxpayers who have that responsibility; it's everyone.

'It ought to be hard to be an Australian citizen – it's tough work and for those wanting to come here, it should be earned. Yet evidence suggests we are a very soft touch when it comes to immigration. Evidence clearly shows we are losing our culture to those who take advantage of our willingness to provide help – evidence confirms we turn the other cheek when the worst of society rages against us by continually demanding more from us. They take our money and soon they will take our culture and then Australia will be left as a failed experiment. England sent us their dregs over two hundred years ago and we built a great nation. We cannot allow the dregs of other nations to drag us down to their lowest common denominator.

'Friends, I weep for my country. Australia has been taken advantage of by those who see us as an easy prey for the charlatans and cheats. As our national anthem says, if we are to provide wealth for toil, then we must stop this sit-down money concept Andrew Gerrard and his government wants to continue. This namby-pamby hand-wringing policy on immigration is supported by the regressive left, who have taken my dream for my country and turned it into a nightmare.

'Ladies and gentlemen, I seek your support as your member of parliament so that I may bring sense to policy and reject this notion of taking before ever giving back to the community.

'American President John F. Kennedy said it well in his inauguration speech long ago. "Ask not what your country can do for you, ask what you can do for your country."'

'I am sad to say we have stopped asking what we can do for our country because these ungrateful leaners have started demanding from us. Unfortunately, political correctness drives us to ignore what is happening because we're too afraid to speak out, too afraid to say no, and too afraid to demand a review of our immigration policy.

'I ask you now, send me to Canberra to be your voice so together we can ask the questions that need truthful answers.

'Thank you.'

The audience immediately exploded as Jaya backed away to her seat. Many in the crowd got out of their chairs clapping, cheering and whistling salutation. A minority sat stony faced, intimidated by the response. Instinctively, Anita knew this was a front-page story and dashed to the back of the room looking for any Rukhmani staff who may have a copy of her speech. 'Provocative, Robert,' she said as he handed her sheets of stapled paper. 'Whose idea was this?'

'All part of the strategy to unseat Gerrard,' smiled Wong.

'My guess is Jaya's speech will move beyond this seat and create a significant national story. Good luck – she will be hung out to dry for it.'

CHAPTER
18

DAY TWENTY-FOUR – SATURDAY

Wolff arrived at campaign headquarters early to read the media editorials about his candidate's speech. The cramped office didn't allow him to kick his feet on the desk, so he sunk back into his chair with a big smile on his face. All the major newspapers were reporting the speech with expert political commentary denouncing the xenophobic tone and the damaging message the obscure candidate had delivered to the government and even her own party.

One editorial implied Jaya Rukhmani was a racist and recommended she should be stripped of her tenure as professor of politics. Apparently, it was an affront to humanity and the ideals of tertiary education to have such an unqualified person talk about the culture of other countries.

While Wolff was pleased with the editorials, he was more interested in what the prime minister had to say. Gerrard was condescending in suggesting the public meeting went ahead without his appearance. Apparently, he could not remember receiving the invitation and would not have hesitated in making time to come and speak if he had received it.

He further asserted the meeting was organised by right-wing groups who want to stain the fabric of Australian culture and had used their puppet to provide a voice for the deplorables within the community. Gerrard also claimed the speech was outrageously racist in tone, delivering racist intent, by a racist.

He also said it was no worse than a fascist totalitarian diatribe with little foundation to support her claims, instead focusing on the most marginalised who were unable to defend themselves. He also suggested Rukhmani was loose with the truth about her background and implied her credentials should be checked.

A perfect result.

Wolff read Anita Devlin's column with interest. She claimed nothing in politics is ever spontaneous, and the speech was delivered with passion and grace with no hint of racism. 'How could it be racist?' she questioned. 'The person delivering it had the authority to speak on these issues due to her own history of discrimination and the manner she was mistreated as a child by her family and her own culture.' Devlin described nefarious activities in politics were always evident at every event and questioned why the community should blame the candidate when it may be the conservatives raising immigration wedging against the government.

'She is too smart this girl,' said Wolff as he flicked to the cartoon to see Rukhmani raging from a pulpit with a stylised Nazi flag draped behind her yelling for equality.

Perfect.

At the prearranged time, Wolff moved to the boardroom for a regular campaign meeting, hoping a decision about the speech could be made without his input. He wanted the party to act decisively without his influence but didn't hold out much hope.

After Stanley called the meeting to order, Harry Lester asked for the results of overnight polling. Andres Jorges reported there had been a significant spike in the primary votes with the over forty-five demographic toward the party, and away from the government. He couldn't say why this was the case but did advise calls were made after all the news programs had reported Rukhmani's speech.

'This is unbelievable,' said Stanley, a quizzical look on his face. 'Voters support us more because we are racist? I'm not sure this is the party I lead.'

'It's not an act of racism to question immigration,' Lester affirmed. 'The party does not have racist policies, never has and we would never ascribe to anything remotely culturally intolerant.'

'Maybe that's our problem,' sighed Messenger, sparking Wolff's immediate attention as he sat quietly in a darkened end of the table in the windowless room. 'We're too soft when we should be making bold statements about culture, immigration and the misuse of social welfare. We're too scared to upset the minorities, so we let it pass, getting smashed in the media because of it.'

'I would have thought that was good politics,' suggested Christopher Hughes on a speakerphone from Sydney. 'Anything to do with immigration scares the electorate.'

'You mean it mobilises the vocal left, who tag every considered comment as racist, stifling debate,' chided Messenger.

'How the heck did our candidate get that speech approved?' barked Stanley.

No-one responded as they glanced at each other.

Eventually Sussan Neilson offered. 'It wasn't – we had no idea she was going to do it. Candidates are strongly advised to say nothing publicly unless pre-approved by the campaign team.'

'Has anyone spoken to her?' asked Hughes. 'What does she have to say for herself?'

'She has gone to ground; no-one can find her. Her campaign staff are not returning calls either,' said Lester. 'This could turn into a significant media crisis for us.'

'Could?' Stanley barked. 'It's the lead in every media outlet and the trolls are killing us on Twitter.'

'We've done nothing, said nothing, and our polling has gone up,' said Messenger. 'Which could suggest she might have laid the golden egg for us.'

'It could fry us,' chuckled Hughes from the machine in the centre of the table. 'Or we could all be poached.'

'Not funny, Chris,' sighed Stanley. 'This is serious. It could change the campaign if we don't respond, we can't just continue to scramble about doing nothing. What do you think, Jack, you're unusually quiet?'

Messenger cringed a little at Stanley's poor choice of words.

'Your campaign was going nowhere until this issue,' Wolff said.

'That's not entirely correct,' ventured Lester. 'Our poll numbers were improving before last night.'

'That's my community strategy gaining traction in the mind of voters, but as a broadcast message on leadership, we're going nowhere.' Wolff tossed Lester a vicious stare, making him feel uncomfortable. 'If we can change the leader, we should. We would have a better chance against Gerrard if we did.'

'Hang on…' Stanley blurted.

'Shut the fuck up, will you, and let me explain—' Wolff snapped as he leaned into the table. Stanley dropped back into his chair, his jaw slack. 'There have been too many stuff-ups from you to give you any credibility in running the country as prime minister. In fact, I wouldn't even vote for you.' Wolff stopped talking. No-one moved or offered a view. Stanley was defeated. 'But you're all we have and surprisingly you might have a chance on an issue that'll give your personal brand traction and get your name recognition up,' Wolff continued. 'Any increased name recognition for the leader will help the local campaigns. My strategy, which you folks resisted, has begun to turn in our favour, according to Andres's polling.'

'What are you suggesting?' stumbled Stanley softly.

'I'm suggesting the electorate is looking for leadership on this issue of immigration. They are so desperate for leadership they will vote for anyone providing it. They want strong borders and have wanted government action for years, but what they get is soft policy and see their culture diminishing. Gerrard will justify his government's policies, so you need to make a strong statement and leverage the issue.'

'We could launch our immigration policy tomorrow,' suggested Stanley.

'What will that do other than give us crap from the media for being opportunists,' said Hughes echoing from the speaker. 'We need to attack Gerrard.'

'Was he not doing something shonky with Indonesia?' Neilson tentatively asked, looking about the table. 'Isn't this the reason we are having the election now?'

'Nothing was ever proved,' replied Messenger. 'It was only a conspiracy driven by some in the media.'

'Does it need to be proven he is corrupt?' queried Wolff. 'Just a sniff of a political fraud would be enough to show Gerrard doesn't truly care about the security of our borders and only thinks about himself – just like any other politician.'

'We can't say anything; the media wouldn't accept us

raising it,' Stanley said. 'After all, it was our candidate who started this bushfire, not us.'

'Maybe we don't have to,' Wolff smirked. 'I hear from a reliable source Hancock Media will be running a piece on Gerrard's alleged Indonesian fraud next week.'

'You're kidding? I'm not sure this is good or bad news,' groaned Stanley as Messenger disengaged from the discussion, pushing back from the table, and slowly rubbing his face.

'This issue of immigration is the hotspot in the electorate, not so much politicians doing fraudulent things,' contributed Jorges. 'I would recommend we ignore Gerrard and run hard on immigration.'

'We can do both,' smirked Wolff.

'How can we do that when our policies are very similar to the government's? What line can we say that is different?'

'We tell the big lie.' Wolff delivered it with so much authority the other's fell silent.

'I don't want to be involved in anything illegal,' offered Julia Laretsky, the women's division president.

'Of course not, Julia, we wouldn't support anything like that,' said Stanley quickly in response. 'It's not illegal to politically exaggerate a statement, which is what I think Jack is referring to – it's a common campaign tactic. Gerrard does it all the time.'

'It might be time to return the favour,' suggested Hughes.

'What do you suggest, Jack?' said Messenger, now engaged again.

'Andres said immigration is the electoral hotspot, so what

big lie could we say about that to get them excited against Gerrard?'

Lester stood and moved to the whiteboard on a stand opposite Wolff at the end of the table, ready to record notes with a marker as the others considered the question. 'Any ideas?'

'What about this – immigration is run by criminal organisations fronted by the immigration agents' network,' suggested Hughes. 'There seems to be a lot of money being made in the market.'

'Not bad,' said Wolff, as Lester wrote the suggestion on the board. 'Could in fact be true.'

'It's not true, is it?' Laretsky queried Messenger, who shrugged.

'Gerrard plans to increase Muslim immigration numbers,' said Stanley.

'An old one, but still a good one in many communities,' laughed Jorges. 'At least that is what my polling indicates.'

'Let's go the opposite way. Gerrard is about to ban immigration from Muslim countries,' said Messenger.

'Or maybe he is going to ban immigration altogether for two years,' Neilson suddenly suggested. 'Or maybe he wants to increase the price of immigration.'

'Would he lower the current price for entry?' asked Laretsky.

'This is good,' said Lester as he noted the ideas. 'Any other thoughts?'

'What really scares Australians?' Wolff asked.

'Foreigners,' said Jorges, creating a spontaneous laugh among the group. He shifted in his seat embarrassed and leaned forward into the table. 'No seriously, it's foreigners. We are all immigrants; the paradox is we hate the fact others get here much easier than we did. They have greater access to welfare than we did, and they speak louder on issues that undermine our democratic culture. Australians hate it. Mix that with their ignorance about Muslims and border security and it is a hotspot for a clear majority within the community no matter their voting preferences, especially in the regions.'

'We aren't racists,' wailed Laretsky.

'Sadly, based on what Andres just advised, we might be,' Stanley said glumly.

'Xenophobia is not racism,' interrupted Wolff.

Stanley scoffed, still smarting at Wolff's previous attack. 'Okay smarty, what is it?'

'It's nationalism – if we use it, and use it well, we can turn that slow upward trend in the polls into a significant win on election day.'

'Yeah, but if we do, what do we truly win. I don't want a polarised

community.'

Wolff shook his head, sneering at Stanley. 'We need to change the hearts of the community to have them vote for you.'

'I'm not sure we should be doing that,' replied Stanley.

'You either want to be prime minister or you don't, Pete,' said Hughes.

'Yes, but will it be tainted, and will I be portrayed as a racist?' asked Stanley.

'Who cares? You'll be prime minister,' Hughes replied.

'That is an excellent point,' said Wolff. 'If we construct the big lie after you have shown strong leadership, you could be sitting in Yarralumla for Christmas.'

'So, everyone,' interrupted Lester, still standing at the whiteboard looking at his list. 'Which of these could be the big lie?'

'We can't mention the Muslims, so cross that off the list.' said Laretsky.

'Why?' asked Messenger as he stared at the board.

'It will create too much hurt and pain in the community,' said Laretsky.

'I agree with Julia,' said Stanley.

'So, we don't mention them,' smiled Wolff. 'And yet we do.'

'How would that work – everyone hangs out to criticise the Muslim community.' Laretsky queried.

'How about this as an idea?' Wolff proposed, and the others looked to him, waiting for a response. He slowly rose and paced to the whiteboard as if figuring out a plan. 'Gerrard has a secret plan with the Indonesian president to declare open borders for free movement of citizens between each country.'

No-one responded immediately, thinking about the idea.

Stanley quickly jumped in. 'Whoa, wait a minute – free

movement between both countries?' Stanley quickly looked for support from his colleagues. 'It would never work.'

'It doesn't have to, it's a lie,' scoffed Hughes. 'I like it.'

'Just listen. We suggest the Gerrard government has secret plans to restructure a free movement pact between Australian and Indonesian citizens based on the successful program we already have with New Zealand,' said Wolff.

'How would we control movement?' Messenger asked.

'We don't – just like the kiwis,' Wolff smiled.

'No-one would ever believe a predominately Muslim country would ever have open borders with us,' suggested Laretsky.

'The region is a haven for various covert groups with spurious links to terrorist organisations,' said Hughes, warming to the idea. 'Talkback radio would go nuts if this was implemented.'

'And that's the point.' Wolff clicked his finger and pointed at the speakerphone.

'Why would anyone believe that preposterous idea?' Stanley asked.

'Because Gerrard was not able to get his money from his deal with the president, so it's payback time,' smiled Wolff. 'It's so outrageous, I'm beginning to like the idea myself.'

Stanley was still not convinced. 'The community would go berserk. Gerrard would deny it, and no-one would believe us.'

Wolff returned to his chair. 'We don't need the whole community to believe us, we just need four per cent.' He leaned back in his chair satisfied and waited for a response.

Stanley looked around the table unsure of what to make of the idea. His colleagues just stared at the whiteboard not wanting to engage. He finally asked, 'So what is this leadership thing I should do to distance myself from this lie?'

'Let's have a decision on this strategy first,' asked Lester as he also resumed his seat. 'Does anyone speak against the idea?' No-one engaged, the staff members averting their gaze. 'It is agreed then. We will dangle this strategy out there in the media no matter the backlash against us?' No-one responded; thus agreement was assumed. 'If this is what you want then I want it clearly minuted that this was a decision of the group because if it goes bad, I'm not wearing the flack.'

Everyone sat silently for a moment as the group processed what they'd just decided.

'What happens if Hancock doesn't print the story?' Messenger asked. 'Do we still go ahead?'

'Yes, I think we do, but I have it on very good authority they will print either Monday or Tuesday,' said Wolff.

'Who will run the campaign? It shouldn't be Peter,' said Hughes. 'It needs to be the deputy,' said Wolff looking at Messenger, getting a shoulder shrug and nod of the head in agreement.

The group paused for a moment and Stanley poured himself a drink of water, revealing a shaking hand.

'So, what's the leadership action Pete will need to be doing?' asked Messenger.

Wolff looked around the table. 'The leader needs to make an unequivocal statement befitting a prime minister and therefore must make an announcement today about the candidate in Melbourne.'

'What do you think I should say?' asked Stanley, taking a large draught of water.

'You sack her.'

'It's way too late for that, nominations have been declared. We can't replace her.' Lester was adamant and quickly began flicking through his papers. 'Even if we sack her, she will still be on the ballot paper – and we won't have anyone.'

'You terminate her as a candidate this morning.'

'It would be a strong response,' agreed Hughes. 'It would shut the media up about us and flick the focus to her.'

'She may not want to continue,' said Messenger. 'This has always been a case study for her, and all of this media attention may create enormous ethical issues for her with the university.'

'And her stupid speech would not have created the same ethical issues?' Laretsky jibed sarcastically.

'If you want to become prime minster, you must sack her this morning,' reaffirmed Wolff. 'This is not a time for hesitation. This is a time for leadership, and you will display it at a press conference within the hour. Sussan and I will provide you speaker's notes. You will emphasise the conservatives are an open and liberal party, and you will not tolerate outspoken ideas that do not embrace our core philosophies of cultural tolerance. Do not mention her by name and do not move into any discussion about her. Short and simple. She is gone.'

CHAPTER
19

DAY TWENTY-FIVE – SUNDAY

The metal stairs yielded to Wolff 's light touch as he quietly climbed to the campaign office of Jaya Rukhmani, his eyes scanning for sudden movement and unexpected threats from the dark warehouse. The campaign team never heard him coming and was surprised to see him pushing open the door. Everyone's attention was immediately drawn to the stranger, but no-one responded to the intimidating man in black as they were unsure what to do.

Wolff disarmed them with a smile, hoping to break the increased anxiety in the room. 'Hi, folks. I'd like to speak to Jaya,' he said, stepping into the office and looking about. Jaya was pulling a poster from the wall and hadn't heard him. 'Would you be Professor Rukhmani?'

'I have no comment to make. I'm no longer running for the election.'

Wolff looked about the others as Jaya continued disassembling the campaign material. 'Yeah, I heard. That's why I came over. Can we talk?'

'Who are you?'

'Hmm, that could be problematic for you,' said Wolff. 'I'm Jack Sinclair-Browne from head office.' Jaya turned and stood gazing at him. Wolff was unsure what to do so smiled broadly. 'Can we talk, please?'

'Get out, you moron,' howled Robert Wong as he quickly walked between them and almost chested Wolff with fists on his hips.

Wolff stepped back a step. 'Ease up, mate, I'm here to talk,' said Wolff, then re-engaged with Jaya. 'I want to explain what happened and talk about strategy.'

'It's over, mate. We've been let go. Disendorsed. Sacked,' Wong barked. 'We're no longer the candidate and it's because of you, you fucking moron.' The others in the room took a few steps toward the confrontation to support him.

Wolff still held Jaya's gaze, then scratched his jaw. 'I just want to talk. I have a proposition for you.'

'I'm not sure I want to hear it,' Jaya responded, dropping a poster to her feet, and taking a step toward Wolff.

'It'll take no more than ten minutes,' Wolff assured her, then waited. 'The only reason I'm here longer is if you ask me to stay. Nice poster, by the way.'

Jaya shook her head in disbelief at the comment. 'My

reputation has been shredded. The university has demanded a review of my tenure. My case study has gone up in flames. I get weird calls from nut jobs and the media has hounded me for days. And you have a proposition for me?'

Wolff held out his hands, spreading his fingers in a gesture of submission. 'Ten minutes.'

Jaya walked toward him and sat on a nearby desk. 'You're on the clock, go.'

Wong stepped back from Wolff and lingered at another desk. The others went back to what they were doing.

'Do you disagree with what I wrote for you?' Wolff got no response. 'Was there anything you said at the community meeting you considered wrong?'

'You're going to have to do better than that.' Jaya sniffed and crossed her arms.

'I wrote that speech because I think I know you.'

'You don't know me,' grunted Jaya. 'Don't for one moment kid yourself that you know anything about me because you don't.'

'I wrote it for you because it was time for someone to say it. To beat Gerrard in this seat, someone has to say it,' said Wolff. 'Gerrard is beatable, maybe not as prime minister, but he is very beatable as the local member. And you are the only person who can achieve that.'

Jaya remained unconvinced, raising an eyebrow. 'Why?'

'Because you raised the big elephant that has been stomping on immigration policy debate for many years, and frankly, you're the only one who is entitled to speak about it.'

Jaya slowly shook her head incredulously. 'You sacrificed me, my project and quite possibly my job so I could start a debate?'

'I haven't sacrificed you,' grinned Wolff. 'I've elected you.'

'You must be mad.' Jaya shook her head, stood, thrust her hands onto her hips and walked the floor a couple of times. 'Surely you know I'm no longer the candidate. Are you for real?'

'All part of my campaign strategy. That's why I wrote the speech, initiated the community meeting, had the media there, and got you sacked from the party.'

Jaya vigorously scratched her head above her ear and with a pained expression asked, 'Please explain?'

'Look, Jaya. May I call you Jaya? Nice name, by the way, what does it mean?'

'Are you completely mad?' Jaya was tempted to call time.

'No. Humour me, what does it mean?'

'Victory.'

'Exactly. That's why you are going to win, Jaya, because your name means victory.'

'Oh look, I've heard enough of this rubbish. Are we done?' Jaya flicked her hand at Wolff and turned away. She took a moment then turned back to face him, quickly averting her eyes from his gaze.

Wolff stood. 'Did the party fully support your candidacy during your preselection?'

'What?' Jaya looked up from the floor, directly at him.

'Did they want you as a candidate and would you have

won preselection if they had a white candidate?' Wolff had her attention. 'No matter if you won this seat or not, do you think the party would have supported you?'

Jaya assessed the questions and thought through a response. 'They weren't overly enthusiastic, let's put it that way.'

'Would you have won the election as a conservative candidate against Gerrard?'

'No.'

'Would you like to win?'

Jaya snorted. 'Sweet dreams, mister, but useless to even think that way now.'

'If I help you with resources, foot soldiers, manage your media and your statements, would you consider continuing to run against Gerrard as an independent.'

Jaya didn't respond immediately, looking toward Robert who returned a doubtful look. 'Why would you want to do that?'

'Three reasons. You're no longer under the weight of the conservatives and the dill they call their leader. You're now free to say and do whatever you want without the restriction of party policy. You're now a very clear independent candidate with a higher profile and name recognition than Stanley in the electorate. Two.' Wolff held up two fingers. 'You are a female on the coveted top of the ballot paper running as an independent against two male candidates who represent the swamp of party politics and political correctness. And three, because I think you can win the seat.'

Jaya didn't respond and looked to the floor, thinking about what she had heard. With her head still bowed she said, 'We don't have any money.'

'If I can get you as much money as you would ever need, would you then consider running as an independent candidate and with some dumb luck become the first woman to be elected in the seat of Melbourne?' Wolff's phone started making a noise. 'That's ten minutes, thanks for listening to me.' He started to walk from the room, leaving Jaya to watch him go. The others glanced at each other, wondering what to do. He was halfway down the metal staircase before Jaya stepped out onto the landing.

'You really think I can win?'

Wolff stopped and looked back up to her. 'I can't guarantee you'll win, no-one can – but I know you are a quality candidate and with the right local campaign you are very capable of winning. At the very least you will take Gerrard to preferences for the first time.'

Jaya didn't respond, and Wolff began to step down the stairs again.

'Well, you had better come back up and have a cup of tea,' Jaya smiled then called over her shoulder. 'Robert, put the kettle on, will you please.'

Over the next three and half hours, Wolff ran through campaign strategy, outlining what was likely to happen during the next two weeks leading to election day. He told them about his plans for the party and how Jaya's campaign could leverage off it with clear messages he assured would resonate throughout the community. He encouraged the team to continue filming their documentary but on the strict proviso he would never be identified or referred to at any time during or after the campaign, no matter the result. Wolff suggested he needed the assurance to not confuse his employers and any media. If his involvement was exposed, it could mean Gerrard wins. It was in everyone's best interests if he remained anonymous.

Wolff emphasised the importance of the team to remain focused on door knocking, street meetings and community group meetings. He wanted Jaya to smile more whenever cameras were around her. He wanted her in summer frocks and away from her dowdy black university garb. 'You have a nice figure, flaunt it.'

Both Jaya and Robert immediately objected to the sexist comment. Wolff calmed them with a smile and conceding hands, explaining it was important to make a statement to women that Jaya was a positive role model for them and their daughters, so using her femininity was legitimate. He also suggested wearing traditional costume to community meetings, especially cultural groups, and meetings with councillors. 'Take plenty of photos and get them on your Facebook page and Instagram.'

Jaya laughed. 'I don't have any saris.'

'Then get some, especially vivid vibrant colours. You'll look terrific in them, and it will be a point of difference to Gerrard,' Wolff smiled. Jaya blushed.

'Are you sure this is the type of behaviour required?' Wong asked. 'It all sounds a little cynical and sexist to me.'

'Mate, listen. I shouldn't have to tell a young dude like you that social media will play a significant role in this local campaign,' Wolff said. 'Bombard the Twittersphere and Instagram with everything and have your university groups begin a retweet campaign. Let's get your message out there. We want Twitter going crazy with the exotic independent candidate from Melbourne. So, we tweet everything and every hour we must have something to say. I'll write them, but you must tweet them. Photos on Instagram linked back to Facebook are in addition to those comments, as are the polit-ical comments you'll be making on Facebook.'

'How much will that increase my profile?'

If you get your local folks to retweet and like the entries, I'll get a few trolls to begin responding, good and bad to your entries, which will promote good and bad discussion. This builds momentum.'

'Do I need to make any policy statements?'

'The only thing for you to focus on is drilling down on what the major parties are announcing, and spin a negative impact for your local voters,' said Wolff. 'Dumb it right down so anyone can understand it. You must remember most folks have not been to university, so get it back to a street language you would have used prior to your doctorate. What did you do your doctorate on by the way?'

'I examined the use of push polling within a local political campaign.'

'Which one?'

'A Costa Rica presidential campaign.'

'Oh, yes? Was it the Jose Vargas campaign?'

'How would you know that campaign, did you read my thesis?'

'I probably wrote it,' Wolff smiled shyly.

'You are an interesting man, Mr Sinclair-Browne,' grinned Jaya, then smiled more demurely as she looked away from the intensity of Wolff's return look and smile. 'Very interesting.'

'Look, folks, I could talk about these things for hours, but I'm starving and have other work to do,' said Wolff as he stood and stretched out any aches. 'You have my number, so stay in touch. If you have any questions, no matter how stupid, call me.'

'Do you fancy a vindaloo?' asked Jaya. 'There's a khaane kee dukaan nearby.'

'A what?'

'An Indian restaurant,' Jaya smiled. 'If you like curry, that is.'

'Sure, let's do it. I would love something hot and spicy tonight.' Wolff smiled at his own joke as he started walking out. 'Coming, Robert?'

Wong looked up at Wolff then passed a quick flick to Jaya, who pursed her lips with a very slight shake of head. 'No, that's very kind of you, but you have given me plenty to do here. I want to get on top of it tonight.'

Wolff smiled at his enthusiasm. 'That's fine, just make sure there is no reference to me anywhere, okay?' He was at the bottom of the stairs before Jaya, and he turned to watch her descend.

Jaya liked being watched as she slowly came down the stairs. 'I'm really pleased you came when you did, Mr Sinclair-Browne,' she said as she slowed, nearing the bottom step, and letting Wolff watch her more closely. 'You made my day.'

Wolff ran his tongue by the corner of his lips.

CHAPTER
20

DAY TWENTY-SIX – MONDAY

Taking in the view from the leafy Commonwealth Reserve in Williamstown across the bay to the tall buildings of the Melbourne CBD, Anita sipped from her water bottle. As the setting sun transposed the greys of the skyline into vivid contrasting colours, she released a sigh. The old warship museum moored at the pier added an unusual dimension to her view, as did the swaying masts from the nearby Royal Yacht Club.

She was waiting for Messenger, who was at a community function at Customs House Hotel, a local beer barn across the road from the park. The bench was hard but comfortable as she tapped her way through a draft critique of the Mercantiles. A story she conceded would probably never be published, she was nevertheless committed to it being written and was already five thousand words in.

The noise from the seaplane about to take off on a scenic tour over Melbourne distracted her, and she watched as it glided out past the moored yachts to clear water. The grunts of nearby players at the tennis courts behind her had her thinking the little village would be an ideal place to live.

Just across the bay from the most livable city in the world, it was still far enough away to provide the laziness of a bayside small town. From the remarkable colonial buildings in the nearby streets to the old anchors and cannons along the foreshore, the village obviously had a rich maritime history. Anita speculated if she would ever have the opportunity to share in it with their local politician. She whimsically sighed again, a little distracted from her work.

Another slurp of water and Anita began watching the late afternoon strollers and the families stretching out on the lush lawn of the park. Wondering if she would ever be up for the enormous challenge, responsibility, and obligation of family life, she shifted in her seat a little uneasily.

Bringing her mind back to her research, Anita focused. *Were there organised business groups in Williamstown when it first established itself as a major port of Melbourne?* she wondered. *Were the Mercantiles active in the region almost two hundred years ago?* She knew the Mercantiles were committed to the economic development of Australia and set out to work with government to get what they wanted, so they probably were interested in the new port.

She thought about how they must have endured many economic challenges over the years, including constant disruption to their markets, claiming government over-regulation and increased interventionist legislation interfered with their operations and, as a consequence, their wealth. They were looking after themselves and working together for a better future, just like any family. She tapped the idea of familial values into her piece.

The question she couldn't quite frame an answer to was the ethics of what they do and why they do it. Was it ethical for the Mercs to influence policy and legislation for their own benefit? No different to other lobbyists, especially unions, she supposed. Unions stopped at nothing to get their way with government on issues they considered important, so why couldn't the Mercs do the same?

The community doesn't complain too much when militant unionists shut down the docks or building sites, so why would it be a problem for business owners to negotiate better market conditions? The unions often used violent demonstrations to get what they wanted, including alleged large payoffs, but it seemed the Mercs used their money more covertly to gain influence. They both worked for outcomes that suited themselves, they just had different styles of negotiation – one group has capital for investment, the other has control of their labour. Both powerful levers in the economy.

Based on recent history, Anita considered whether muscle had more influence in political debate than money; certainly, the public knew more about union disruption. But she also believed monied people with power and access used more sinister means because of their lack of transparency.

Was it a good or a bad thing for the community to have politicians influenced by business owners and their money, especially in the covert manner the Mercantiles go about it? Does the community care about what goes on backstage politically? So long as they don't pay the government too much and governments provide more and more services to the community to ensure they enjoy a settled and safe life, who really cares? Can you have ethics in politics and still get things done? An interesting no-win question. She took a note in her journal to reconsider the question at a later time.

What piqued Anita's interest about the Mercantiles even more was their international connections, like a large interwoven web of networks working for the benefit of each other. No different to international lobby groups and statutory authorities like the International Labour Organisation, just a little more secret in their actions and influence. Why did they see the need to hide the work they did? She tapped further thoughts into her column. *Is international trade influenced by the Mercantiles' international network, and do they influence government elections in sovereign states?* She scribbled another question in her notebook.

Anita looked up from her computer. Catching sight of

Messenger, she watched him walk across the lawn toward her. She smiled fondly with a touch of excitement as she watched his poised swagger and aloofness. He spotted her looking and waved. When he reached her, he bent in and kissed her cheek before sitting.

'How was your meeting?'

'Rowdy,' sighed Messenger. 'There was a lot of chatter about dumping the professor. I was a little shocked, quite frankly, about the comments from people I consider friends and thought I knew.'

'What did they say?'

'Some people think she was right while others argued she didn't have the right to say anything. Red-necks started getting stuck into her because she's black, which totally shocked me. Immigration is a hot topic, more than we realise.' Messenger leaned on his knees and looked out into the bay. 'I must say, I heard things tonight that make me question if I really need friends like that.'

'Well, I guess the community debate's been suppressed for way too long,' said Anita as she closed her computer and put it into her overly large bag. 'What the professor said the other night was spot on. The irony is that an immigrant was actually saying it and then gets sacked for saying it,' she gently rubbed his shoulder. 'What's for dinner?'

'I thought we might go Croatian, there is a fantastic restaurant over there,' Barton flicked a thumb over his shoulder. 'They serve a wicked pork rib you must try.' He then paused for a moment and looked at Anita. 'Tell me about your article on Gerrard.'

'What article about Gerrard?'

'The one you wrote a few weeks back about the detention centre funding in Indonesia that's going to run in your paper, probably tomorrow.'

'That story's dead.'

'Not from what I've heard, it was going to run today, which must mean it's in tomorrow's edition. We've been waiting for it so we can make a strategic announcement.'

'Who told you it was going to run?'

'Sinclair-Browne told us on Saturday,' Barton said slowly, a little unsure how much to say. 'I'm not sure how he knows, perhaps he has a contact.'

'First I've heard of it,' said Anita. 'What do you think of the Hyphen?'

'He seems to know what he's doing. Polls are showing a strong trend toward us.'

'Did he have anything to do with the professor's speech the other day?'

'Don't know. He refutes Jaya's claims about head office,' said Messenger, shifting in his seat and looking about. 'He was the first to call for her dismissal, so I would suspect he had little to do with it.'

'Operatives like him always work to strategy. I wouldn't be surprised if this speech response and the public outcry is deliberate. Maybe it forms part of his election strategy against Gerrard.'

'What? Start a race war on immigration?' Messenger looked back to Anita who provided a querying shrug. 'I don't think so.'

'What's your view?' Anita reached out her hand and he quickly clasped it, running his thumb along her palm. 'Do you think this is a debate the country should have?'

'No, I don't. I feel really uncomfortable about it.'

Anita squeezed his hand. 'The Australian community hasn't had the opportunity for a long time to talk about culture and what we expect from each other.'

'That's a different debate,' Barton said. 'What we now have is an us-versus-them fight and sadly I don't think anyone will feel better for having taken part.'

'Why do you feel so anxious about it? Surely we're mature enough to talk about these things.'

'We are, but in the heated battleground of an election, passions run high and sometimes we say hurtful things we later regret,' Barton looked off into the distance again. 'I could have supported Jaya more than I did, and I question why I didn't. Was she just expedient to the cause, a convenient political kill − or was there something in me that said she was not appropriate for the party?' He dropped his face into his hands and sighed heavily. 'Maybe she's right − she told me I was like any other white man with zero understanding of what people of colour go through.'

'You're being way too harsh on yourself.' Her soothing words helped him, and he looked up at a smiling Anita. 'It's politics at its ugliest − people get hurt.'

'Government is for everyone and out of control immigration debates like this don't help anyone.'

'Yes, but sometimes we need to talk about it.' Anita leaned over and kissed his cheek. 'If you're concerned, why don't you get your team to back off.'

'Too late I'm afraid, we're preparing to drive it hard.'

Anita leaned back and asked, 'Bart, you just said you hate this debate. Why are you pushing it harder?'

Messenger didn't respond immediately, watching a family walk past, then looking off to the distance. 'Politics is about having the power of government to get things done. I suspect if we need to separate the two leaders in the minds of the voters by a toxic issue like this, then so be it.'

'Win at any cost?' Anita was a little surprised by his comment and she felt a twinge within her.

'Yes,' Messenger shifted in his seat. 'I told you the other night at dinner that politics is about compromising your values sometimes. For me, this is an example.'

'I can't believe you just said that.' Anita paused for a moment. 'Do you truly believe you must say and do anything to win government?'

'Yes.'

'This immigration thing is potentially very dangerous,' Anita said sharply. 'If the Hyphen has activated this polarisation in the community that we are seeing by getting the professor to speak, then sacking her – well, that sounds like strategy to me. A very dangerous one.'

'Look, Anita.' Messenger turned and faced her. 'Gerrard has been in power for too long, it's time for a change.' He gripped her hand. 'We're coming from a long way behind in the polls and perhaps we will do and say things that may disappoint many of our followers, perhaps even our family. This is politics. It's the manipulation of perceptions and nothing to do with reality.'

'Why are you telling me this?' Anita unexpectedly felt concerned for Barton. 'What are you going to announce in the next few days?'

'All I can tell you is that we're going hard on Gerrard and his soft stance on immigration, suggesting he has a new policy so voters can make a judgement call on him before they vote.'

'What policy? I've heard nothing.'

'Just because you haven't heard it, doesn't mean it isn't true.'

'Is Gerrard announcing a new policy?'

'We are saying he is about to.'

Anita crossed her arms and gazed at Barton a little frustrated. 'Do I understand you correctly that you are going to allege a new government policy.'

'I've said too much.'

'Are you going to tell a lie?' Anita shook her head. 'I can't believe what you're telling me.'

'It'll be up to the voters to determine.'

'On what?'

'What's fact or fiction.'

Anita was cross with the disclosure, vigorously gnawing her bottom lip as she waited for Barton to look at her. 'You know the Hyphen and Tony Hancock know each other, don't you?'

'I wasn't aware of that, no.'

'Would it worry you that Hancock is actually paying him to coordinate your campaign.'

'I thought a printing company in Sydney was the generous donor?'

'Hancock owns it, or at least one of his many offshoot companies does.' Barton still avoided looking at her. 'Would it surprise you to learn the Mercantiles are working against Gerrard?'

'Well, other than Sinclair-Browne, I don't know what else they're doing for us.'

'I don't think it's Stanley they particularly want as prime minister. I think they just want to get rid of Gerrard.'

'Wouldn't surprise me,' Barton slyly looked at her. 'Everyone in politics is self-interested. Dare I say, even you.'

Anita leaned back in the bench a little perplexed by his comment. 'What makes you think I'm self-interested?'

'If you think Sinclair-Browne is a Mercantile operative paid by Hancock then why haven't you publicly called it out?' Barton had changed his tone. 'If you think there is a conspiracy with Jaya being sacked, why don't you call it out?'

He waited for a response, but Anita looked away.

'You don't because it may cause you to lose your television opportunities, and perhaps if you did call it out, you'd risk losing your job. You would rather write stories making fools of politicians than write the truth,' Barton looked away. 'You're the same as us. You'll do or say anything to get what you want. Just like us.'

'That's totally unfair.' A squealing kid distracted Anita for a moment. 'I don't think that way about you.'

'No? Then why all this fake news.'

'I have a code of ethics I subscribe to—' Anita crossed her legs, turning them away from Barton. 'I just wish your colleagues had a similar code.'

'I don't recall ever reading in your code the need to humiliate politicians. To try and catch us out by using shifty wordplay and creating gotcha moments.'

'You're being ridiculous.'

'I don't remember the media supporting James Harper when he lost his leadership just a few short weeks ago. But I do seem to recall you raising issues with Stanley when you knew he would stumble over them and not know the answer. Is that ethical?'

Anita teared a little, shocked by Barton's aggressive comments. 'What has got you like this?' She bit her lip. 'What's wrong?'

'Nothing,' said Barton, staring out across the bay. After a little while he added, 'I have to do something soon that I think is wrong. It'll cause a political shitstorm.'

'Then don't do it.'

'If we want to win then I have to,' insisted Barton.

Anita looked at him and saw he was struggling with his

thoughts. 'You don't have to do what it is you say you have to – no-one can force you to do anything.'

'Sadly, in politics, yes they can.'

Families were breaking up and heading home, paying little attention to the couple on the park bench sitting like strangers, looking out into the darkening bay with the distant city lighting up.

Anita was suddenly flustered and wiped her eyes. She didn't know what to do. Politics was suddenly becoming too hard for her to mix with her personal life. What started as an innocent conversation was now sliding into an abyss and she didn't like it. She had an ache in her stomach and was anxious about what to do.

'I have strong feelings for you, Anita, and I really want to explore those feelings with you,' Barton said softly. 'Remember that when you are soon faced with having to write about me.'

'When am I going to do that?' Anita quickly wiped a finger across her eye, just above her cheek.

'The day after your Gerrard column appears.' Barton stood and held out his hand. 'Just remember, it's all politics and has nothing to do with us.'

Anita stood and stepped into him, falling against his chest, kissing him like it was her last chance. They hugged hard and then both released clumsily, stepping back a little awkwardly, feeling it may be a while before they felt the same again. They crossed the park hand in hand with the contrasting mixture of grey, blue, yellow, and striking orange in a band across the western sky. 'What did you write about Gerrard, anyway?' asked Barton.

'I provided solid evidence that exposed him ripping over forty million dollars out of the deal with Indonesia for the detention centres.'

'Wow! Gerrard won't be very happy when he reads that.'

CHAPTER
21

DAY TWENTY-EIGHT – WEDNESDAY

The buzz of the media room was disordered as photographers prepared cameras and checked flash units, and television crews scurried about positioning boom microphones and setting lighting, arranging recording gear. Journalists arranged recording devices toward a clear space on the lectern and waited for the deputy opposition leader, Barton Messenger, to make an announcement in response to the incendiary story in the Hancock media of a corrupt prime minister.

The national broadsheet's morning edition published a front-page story accusing Prime Minister Gerrard of an alleged corrupt deal with the Indonesian president, linking government funding for offshore immigration centres with commuting the death sentences of two convicted Australian drug smugglers.

Bylined by Anita Devlin, the article alleged the prime minister was about to skim a secret commission of forty million dollars, but the fraudulent scheme was foiled by the parliament, forcing the prime minister to an election. The article alleged the deal would still be completed if Gerrard were to be returned as prime minister.

Anita hadn't written the published story, but her initial draft and incisive research were used to provide substance to the claims. A photo of the prime minister lounging by his pool with a drink in his hand at his Sydney residence was used under the headline: I WIN, YOU PAY.

She immediately telephoned Tony Hancock to complain about the use of her name for a story she didn't write but was quickly dismissed by the owner. 'It's called editorial license,' said Hancock in response to her complaint.

'My column said nothing about the drug traffickers and my research touched on Gerrard's wife going to Europe with him retiring soon. You never mentioned it. You've just said a deal is done and he needs to win the election to get his money, which is absolutely wrong.'

'Your research implied there was something going on, so that's good enough for me.'

'There's nothing going on and that's the point,' barked Anita before taking a few deep breathes through her nose to calm herself. 'Where did you get that hideous photo of him?'

'He always loves lying by the pool in his skimpy bathers. I

used an old shot of him I had on my phone. Do you like it?'
Hancock laughed. 'I was at a summer barbeque last year. He's
going to hate it.'

'That's the point. He won't hate you, he'll hate me, and
that stuffs up my future access to his government colleagues.'

'I rewrote the story using your material and I thought
giving you credit would probably help your future access.'

'You think this byline will help my access?' snapped Anita,
shaking her head. 'Making these allegations will be a disaster
for my access.'

'Not in our television division.' Hancock was firm and
short, leaving Anita looking at her telephone with incredulity
when he suddenly disconnected.

Gerrard was yet to respond to the allegations, so as
planned by Wolff, Messenger was to add another dimension
to the story with the big lie agreed by the leadership team.
The media assembled for the morning briefing after being
advised the opposition wanted to add to the story with new
allegations.

'Ladies and gentlemen, thank you for coming.' Messenger
took his place at the lectern. 'After today's startling revelation
in the Hancock media, it's important to remember the
coming election is about leadership. Who do Australians trust
to lead them for the next five years? Who do they trust to
provide good government in all its dealings? What ethics and
standards do Australians expect from their political leaders;
and what transparency do they want from their government?'
Messenger paused for emphasis.

'Do they trust a prime minister with unanswered damning allegations hanging over his head as referred to in this morning's press, or do they trust a new era of integrity, honesty and transparency?' He quickly referred to his notes. 'A Stanley government will ensure at all times we are open and honest with the Australian people. We believe in strong relationships with our neighbours based on honesty and mutual obligation to respect each other's customs and culture.

'Indonesia is a strong, long-term friend of Australia and we welcome our free-trade agreements and the cross-border cooperation we share with them. We see our relationship as enduring, and we are very conscious of the ongoing vital need for our governments to work together for the stability of the region. We do not expect to involve ourselves in Indonesian domestic affairs and we do not expect our friends to intrude in ours.'

Cameras clicked rapidly as Messenger moved his pose, looking to various parts of the room. 'Today's allegations against Prime Minister Gerrard are disturbing, and if found to be true, should condemn him from ever standing for public office again. I note the prime minister has failed to respond to the allegations, therefore adding weight to the veracity of the story in the Hancock media. Why hasn't he responded to the allegations – does he have something to hide?'

Messenger looked up from his notes and gazed directly at the television cameras. 'We call upon Mr Gerrard to immediately respond to these serious allegations made against him and explain himself to all Australians by answering the following questions.

'Why did the prime minister, during a period of national mourning, attempt to force the parliament to approve funds for the construction of detention centres contrary to other government announcements? Was there a secret deal concocted by the prime minister with the Indonesian president? What guarantees can the prime minister give to the Australian people that there will be no further dirty deal when parliament resumes? And, under what circumstance is Mrs Gerrard now in Europe instead of Australia supporting the prime minister during this election period? These are the questions the opposition will seek to have answered before election day next week.

'If the Stanley opposition is successful in gaining the Australian people's trust and we are given the privilege of being asked to form government, then we will establish an Auditor General inquiry to investigate this sham deal and determine if there was a secret agreement, reviewing the money trail before we approve further funds to Indonesia. That is our commitment to the Australian people, and we will not let you down.'

Messenger paused, swallowed harshly to clear his throat, and coughed, quickly taking a sip of water from a glass positioned on a shelf within the lectern. 'The lack of transparency by the Gerrard government is not new and we have come to learn over the years that it is standard practice to keep the

Australian people sidelined from major decisions, especially on significant policy.

'I can now disclose more startling evidence of the Gerrard government potentially overstepping its mandate when it comes to securing our borders, again, more specifically, with Indonesia, and we have to ask – why?' Messenger looked about the room and settled his eyes on Anita, but she looked down at her notebook, quickly doodling, anxious about what she was about to hear.

'Sources close to cabinet have recently briefed the opposition about a top-secret policy paper being considered by the government and it has been virtually ticked off for immediate implementation after the election. I have it from very reliable sources close to the government that a re-elected Gerrard Government will immediately begin to negotiate with the Indonesian government a new border and immigration agreement between the two countries. A new policy has been proposed to cabinet that a re-elected Gerrard Government will open the borders for the free movement of citizens between our two countries.'

A sudden noise erupted as journalists and cameramen commented to each other and cameras shutters clicked continuously. Messenger waited for the din to subside before continuing. 'This new open border management agreement, similar to the immigration arrangements we already have with New Zealand, will mean open borders to the largest country in our region and allow their citizens to enter Australia without restriction just as our New Zealand cousins enjoy.

'This proposed Gerrard government initiative will mean the years of tight border controls will be relaxed and allow any person with an Indonesian passport to enter without visa and reside in Australia without restriction. As a consequence, the anticipated surge in residency from citizens of our northern neighbour will see a significant increase in the demands for government services and support.

'We are advised by these very reliable sources close to the government that this secret policy proposed has been prepared and will be legislated within two years of the re-election of a Gerrard government.'

Messenger gnawed his bottom lip and continued reading. 'This proposed government policy is at best a slap in the face to all Australians who have directed their governments for many years to maintain strong borders and stop the scourge of people smugglers taking money from illegal immigrants to get access to Australia.

'The Australian people are strongly opposed to free movement of nationals from other countries to ours without following strict guidelines for residency or citizenship. This proposed new immigration plan continues the arrogance of the Gerrard government toward Australian culture and follows today's allegation of corruption at the highest levels of government.

'We call upon Prime Minister Gerrard to immediately address these serious allegations and either confirm or deny his secret plan for an open border policy with Indonesia and come clean with the Australian people.

'Who do the Australian people trust – a government too friendly with our neighbours to the north, or a Stanley government who will bring honesty, integrity and transparency back into government?

'Thank you very much.' Messenger quickly left the media room as journalists shouted questions.

Anita Devlin sat at the back, arms tightly crossed over her chest, wiping a tear from her cheek with a thumb.

'Boss, you need to respond. We can't have this rubbish out in the electorate for too long.' Miles Fisher was frustrated with Gerrard's lack of response to the increasing news broadcasts announcing a secret government policy to open the borders with Indonesia.

'It's a fucking lie, so why give it air!' Gerrard growled.

'If you don't respond they will keep pushing it until you do.'

'It's Hancock and Jameson who are behind this, I fucking bet you,' said Gerrard. 'Those bastards have done the big lie thing before, about twenty years ago.'

'What was the result?'

'I was elected,' snarled Gerrard. 'And I've been paying for it ever since. They think this will hurt me, but it won't. We're still way ahead in the polls.'

'I'm not sure this issue left without a response will play out well in the electorate,' said Fisher beginning to pace. 'There is already an anti-immigration mood and the candidate in Melbourne has stoked the heart of the racism beast. The Islamophobes will be out next. You urgently need to publicly respond, boss. Or at the very least, issue a media statement.'

'Okay, let's do a release. Let me dictate the wording,' retorted Gerrard angrily. 'Are you ready? And use this word for word – Prove it!'

Wolff was standing in the night shadows across the street from the all-night convenience store. He had taken extra care not to be seen, avoiding CCTV in various properties and traders. He'd walked the final half-kilometre and now he waited. Watching who was coming and going, waiting for the moment when the right people would turn up. He figured the late crowd would be filtering in soon for supplies, but he wanted the right kind of citizens to be in the store when he acted, so he waited.

Earlier he had watched the news broadcasts with their expert editorial commentary regarding Messenger's allegations of open borders with Indonesia. The political commentators had called it for what they believed it to be: a huge lie.

The condemnation in the community was universal and many groups came out to speak on the issue, suggesting Messenger was a fascist causing increased racial tension within the community. Perfect. There were suggestions of xenophobia by the Greens and the Human Rights Commissioner asked for citizens and residents offended by Messenger's highly provocative remarks to contact his office with a formal complaint.

Meredith Bruce defended the government, denying any plans for an open border policy with Indonesia and calling the allegation a lie. She accused Barton Messenger of knowingly and willfully besmirching the government with garbage political allegations causing irreparable damage to international relations and adding fear to many in the community. 'This is a lie and Messenger knows it. I would have thought he was better than this rubbish.'

The Indonesian Ambassador denied any knowledge of the plans, but left the issue open by saying, 'These are things for the Australian government and not for Indonesia to comment on at this time.'

A spokeswoman for a right-wing extremist organisation called for an end to Muslim immigration and Rukhmani's speech highlights were being replayed on various broadcasts. The Australian Broadcasting Commission commentators claimed Messenger was a racist with anger in his heart, not worthy of being in the parliament let alone deputy leader of the opposition and called for his immediate resignation.

The nightly news current affairs programs left an empty chair at the interview desk, accusing Messenger of being too frightened to appear to answer questions. 'We live in a multicultural society where we have accepted diversity for many harmonious years,' opined Barry Meagher, the respected commentator. 'There is no evidence of racial tension in the community and this allegation from Mr Messenger is ill considered and totally without foundation. I would go so far to say it is a deliberate lie.'

A perfect result for Wolff.

The elites were disparaging the allegations as a deliberate lie, but citizens in the suburbs hearing the story second- or third-hand from workmates or at school pickup would not have heard the denial of the story and the lack of evidence to support the Messenger claim. They only heard the message that the borders will soon be open. Wolff coveted a difference to the election narrative so there was a clear choice between the parties. He told Messenger that a lie will be someone's truth and to dismiss the negativity being heaped on him and get back to campaigning. 'You don't have to raise it again, and if folks ask you to recant, then refer them to the prime minister's lack of response.'

A group of laughing young people approached the store, prompting Wolff to prepare for his attack. Wolff assessed the young Asians would be the perfect witnesses. He wanted them on the early morning news broadcasts anxiously talking about the frightening incident and how they were now too scared to walk the streets at night. They would be perfect players in his campaign strategy to win Melbourne by potentially provoking a racist response from the viewing public. The group innocently filed into the store, moving to the various shelves for their late-night food supply.

Wolff picked up the glass bottle at his feet and lit the inflammable cloth wedged into its neck that dangled into the petrol liquid inside. When the cloth was strongly alight and warming the bottle, he stepped from the shadows and hurled it high toward the store. He aimed for it to land on the gas bottles for sale stacked in a metal guarded pallet by the front door. Hoping for chaos if it smashed into the gas storage, he knew the ignition wouldn't be enough to cause an explosion, but the fear of an explosion would make great television.

The bottle bounced off the window and dropped into the display, smashing, and exploding. He watched as the customers began yelling and gesticulating to the cashier while moving deeper into the store away from the door. The cashier ran to the fire with an extinguisher, but it was already out of control, quickly spreading to other products on display out front with flames licking up the wall and into the roof, rendering the fearless cashier's firefighting efforts almost negligible.

Wolff could hear the distant wailing sirens of the first responders and began to move away as spectators assembled to watch. He was very pleased with his first efforts and moved off to extend his strategic urban attacks to his next location, the local mosque. He planned to daub graffiti decrying Islam and then move on to the nearby Catholic church spraying similar messages about Christians, making sure his spelling was questionable. He had already smeared anti-immigration slogans on the cenotaph in nearby botanical gardens and once the Catholics were insulted, he figured his little battle waged against the community was enough for one evening.

When he reached his hotel in Carlton, he called

Rukhmani. 'Jaya, I have written a press release I would like you to post this evening. Do you have a problem with that?'

'What am I calling for this time?'

'You're seeking assurances from all political parties they will refrain from inciting racial violence and come to the negotiation table to resolve the increasing community conflict.'

'What conflict?'

'There have been a number of various incidences of community unrest in your electorate this evening and the news will be carrying it in the morning, so if you get this out now you will be invited to comment.'

'What unrest?'

'Fires and the desecration of churches.'

'My god, anyone hurt?'

'I wouldn't have thought so, but I suspect it will stir up a fight in the community, especially driven by radicals on either side. You need to be seen as the calming influence,' said Wolff. 'Our country and its culture are under attack in your electorate, and you need to lead on this.'

'But I'm an unelected independent candidate.'

'You are also an immigrant, highly articulate, a university professor and you can provide a solution to these troubled times for the voters of Melbourne.'

'What's that?' laughed Jaya.

'Overthrow Gerrard.'

CHAPTER
22

DAY THIRTY – FRIDAY

Vitriol and extremism were the calls coming into talkback radio and being stoked by announcers after two nights of targeted fire-bombs in Gerrard's electorate of Melbourne. The community was angry and wanted action, but the police were finding it hard to find the perpetrators and the politicians were ducking for cover, trying to avoid the media.

The broader Melbourne community was on edge with increasing signs of anxiety and chaos. A sense of fear hung like a storm cloud over the city, persuading citizens to stay close to their homes at night with the streets becoming still as if a curfew had been enacted. Daylight brought people from their homes, but their heightened anxiety was evident in their nervous interaction with each other as they wondered what was going to happen next in their suburb. Discussions about the urban terrorism was dominating the media. Community leaders demanded police protect their citizens and called upon the government to stop talking and act to stop the violence. Gerrard was nowhere to be seen, preferring not to comment on police procedural matters.

Perfect.

This was a campaign playbook Wolff had used before when he needed to focus the electorate on issues that would change their vote. He wanted chaos, but violent demonstrations were not his preferred strategy. He much preferred the media and social media to create a wave of dissent and anger but given his strategy to shift large numbers of votes in Melbourne, he needed a quicker emotional response from voters.

He didn't want to target a specific ethnic group – he wanted to scare them all. He firebombed ethnic businesses after smearing uncivilised racial slogans across their windows calling for a cleansing of the culture. He recruited groups of Sudanese youths to stalk the city during the evening rush hour creating a nuisance with their numbers. He paid them to skylark, enjoy themselves and be loud. They were harmless, but within the community they were to be feared.

Disturbed and increasingly anxious commuters and visitors to the city were extremely worried by the youths' presence, providing excellent footage for the provocative media of scared citizens worried for their safety. The youths didn't engage in any direct conflict and followed Wolff's careful instructions to just provide a menacing presence. In response, other extreme gangs had begun to muscle up their presence in the city streets thinking it may be a good idea to assert their own ethnic identity. The tension between the ethnic groups was palpable with police and church leaders insisting on calm.

Deploring the violation of their city, concerned citizens entered the Twitter debate and gained immediate community traction with #notmycountry. Wolff mobilised his many Twitter trolls to begin a sustained program of hate speech inciting emotional and at times unbalanced responses from various community groups, which threw social media out of control with outrageous claims. Other racist hashtags began to appear, as did #notmyprimeminister #closetheborders and #Jaya4pm.

Perfect.

Wolff strategically mobilised a further twenty covert operatives with the direction to take at least four taxi trips before midday throughout the city. They were to sit in the back seat and fake a telephone call complaining about immigration, saying racially provocative comments against Indians immigrants. 'Talk about curry and cricket and the way our national symbols are changing – blame the immigrants.'

He wanted to organise a public backlash from the tight and supportive, yet frequently anxious, community of Melbourne Indian taxi drivers. During the lunch period, Wolff directed his Twitter and Facebook trolls to initiate messaging news of a public protest by taxi drivers at four o'clock in the city – word spread quickly of the demonstration with drivers and their supporters congregating in the major intersection outside Flinders Street Station, bringing city traffic to a standstill. Gridlock soon took hold of the city and the streets ground to a traffic nightmare.

The demonstration was vocally hostile toward the government with chants including anti-racism cries such as, 'What do we want? A safe city. When do we want it? Now!' Commuters supporting the demand for action to end the violence joined the massive throng and soon they were singing the John Lennon classic song about peace and giving it a chance

Perfect.

The mob was pining for leadership, someone to listen to their needs and speak for them. As instructed by Wolff, Jaya Rukhmani gave it to them.

Robert Wong cleared a way through the throng to the centre of the intersection and set up a stepladder with a platform so Jaya could easily address the crowd and be heard. Wolff provided speaker notes and she took the megaphone offered by Wong before nervously climbing the ladder and standing on its platform.

Wong then raised a hooter above his head and pushed the button that emitted a piercing wail, silencing the crowd, most turned toward the noise to see Jaya high above her audience just like at speaker's corner.

'Fellow Australians,' she started nervously, waiting for the crowd to quieten and listen. With an even louder voice projection she started again. 'My fellow Australians, we have a simple principle in Australia that draws upon the values of modern democracies: freedom, equality, community. We hold these values to be true and we have fought many battles to uphold them. Battles here in this country right throughout our history. Indeed, Australians have also supported other countries against attacks to their democracy.

'We Australians pride ourselves on our culture and we welcome people from all lands to come and work with us to build our wealth so we may provide for all of us – together. We have built a magnificent country and for those who wish to contribute, there are ample rewards.'

The crowd fell completely silent listening to the woman before them. 'My name is Jaya Rukhmani. I came to Australia thirty years ago as an immigrant, just like many of you. I could speak no English and I was bonded under arrangements from India. I was in a position of poverty, but Australia gave me a chance. I worked hard to repay the debt I owed this country for providing me the peace and love of which you speak. I've worked hard.' Jaya paused for a moment for emphasis. 'But many do not. I'm sad to say there are people who take advantage of Australia and its people. They take advantage of all of us.'

'You got that right!' yelled a Sikh taxi driver in a blue turban and the crowd around him cheered agreement.

'There are those in the community who come to this country and take advantage of those who work hard and pay their taxes. There are those who come here to take government money, your money, as if it is their right without any contribution to the community.

'Friends, these are not just random individuals rorting the system. No, this is a culture of entitlement, and you have the privilege of paying.' A sudden vocal agreement ripped through the crowd.

Jaya paused to take a calming breath, looked around behind her, smiled and then continued. 'It's not their fault. It's the government system that is giving our money to them. It is the government system insisting hard workers, like all of us here, must pay. We pay those not willing to work. We pay those in the community demanding more money and demanding greater government services.'

Jaya paused and the crowd cheered its agreement again. She was gaining confidence and slowed her words so they could be clearly heard. She looked behind her and waited for the noise to calm.

'Let us not blame individuals. Nor should we ever blame any race nor ethnic group or religion. The people to blame are the politicians.' Her voice rose and the crowd erupted agreement again. 'Politicians ignore us. The elite tell us what to think – even what to say – suppressing our views. The elite never hear us; they don't want us to tell them the truth. They sit quietly in their glass houses while they open our borders to the takers, the leaners, and the entitlement generation. The elite are not listening, and it needs to stop.'

The mob was now in unison with Jaya's words and again cheered and clapped when she paused.

'We must restore Australia's freedom, equality and community and rid ourselves of the policies that promote a culture of entitlement. We must demand our government listens to the people. A government must provide leadership. A government that does not weaken to the call of the elite. We need a government to take responsibility.

'We, the people, should be participants – not watchers and not the victims we are becoming. We, the people, are the rightful guardians of this great country along with our first nation people. And we, the people, must regain control so we all share equally in its abundance.

'Friends, we need to take control.' Jaya paused and looked out on the expectant faces. 'We don't take control by stalking and demonstrating in the streets. We don't take control by fighting and waging war against each other. We don't take control by burning our businesses. We don't take control by complaining—

'We take control by voting.

'We, the people, can take control of this policy mess the government has given us that is our immigration policy. We can take control of this mess that is the misuse of government funds – our taxes. We can take control of the policies that affect us all—

'We take control by voting for a change of government next week.'

A supportive cheer erupted.

'Over the next week, Prime Minister Gerrard will present his plans for the future. But rather than listen to what he has to say about the future, I ask you to consider his past. What can he do in the next five years that he could not have done in the last twenty? Gerrard will come to you with false promises asking for another five years, but in five years' time he won't be here. Gerrard will have retired long before then and we will be left with nothing. Again.

'Friends, I ask you to maintain the rage you have. Not on the streets of Melbourne but in the ballot box next week. Let's all Make A Difference and use it as an acronym. Let us be MAD about the government; let us be MAD about Prime Minister Gerrard. Let us not be little m mad and disrupt our community, let us be MAD and disrupt government by changing it.

'I stand before you as a candidate at this next election wanting to make a difference. I want to serve the community in Canberra. But I need your help. I need you to take your rage for action off the streets to the ballot box and vote for change.

'It's time for Australia to change government. It's time we, the people, took back control, and it's time for all of us to end the days of privilege and entitlement. Together, we can achieve a future we can all be proud of. Let us change the government and vote.

'I thank you.'

The crowd erupted with applause and cheering. Several

strategically placed Wolff-paid operatives began to chant her first name as she stepped down from the platform.

Perfect.

Wolff smiled as he watched Jaya move through the crowd being stopped, hugged, and touched by appreciative supporters.

Anita looked out upon the cheering crowd with respect, initially convinced the professor would have struggled to be heard, but she delivered a measured yet electric speech, matching the mob's angst and fervor. She had positioned herself on the steps under the famous clocks at the entrance to the iconic metro station with its yellow façade and arched entrance and looked out on to what seemed to be the entire Indian taxi driver community of Melbourne. Ironically, Flinders Street Station was built using 1906 plans originally meant for New Delhi, and Anita thought it appropriate as a location for the Indian community to meet.

After Jaya stepped off the stepladder, Anita followed the professor's progress through the milling enthusiastic crowd, with Wong carrying the folded aluminum steps, leading the way toward Federation Square on the opposite corner. As she watched, she caught a glimpse of a bald man dressed in black waiting by the traffic lights. She had seen him weeks earlier at a Stanley event and recognised him with Hancock. Now he was hugging the professor, kissing her on the cheek and shaking Wong's hand.

'Who is this guy?' she muttered to herself. She pulled out her telephone and called her editor, Peter Cleaver. 'Cleave, I've just listened to a speech at a public demonstration the likes of which astounded me.'

'Who by, Gerrard?'

'No, his opponent, outside Flinders Street Station with around five thousand protestors.'

'Did they give her a fair hearing?'

'Like a pin drop.'

'Really?' asked Cleaver. 'I thought she was Indian?'

'She is, but this was not about immigration, this was about getting rid of Gerrard.'

'Will she?'

'Not in Melbourne, but the crowd responded, and I think it was a great nod for Stanley,' said Anita. 'So, what story do you want me to write? A demonstration story promoting chaos, or a story about leadership and a change of government?'

'If it's going to help Stanley, let's go with leadership.'

'Do you know what else is interesting?' smiled Anita. 'The Hyphen was supporting Rukhmani.'

'Really? What do you make of that?'

'Conspiracy!' laughed Anita.

'You and your damn conspiracies, surely you're done by now?'

'Always good for a front page, Cleave,' joked Anita.

'Get your story in and take care please.'

As Anita pressed the end call button the smartphone rang. She recognised the caller and tossed up whether to answer before doing so. 'I'm not sure I should be speaking to you.'

'Anita, its politics,' Messenger said.

'That's crap. You know it wasn't true and yet you still did it.'

'Anita please, let me explain.'

'No, I don't think so. Just tell me this. Is the Hyphen still on your campaign?'

'Yes, why?'

'Was it his idea for the lie?'

'I can't say.'

'You just did.' Anita pushed the red button and didn't respond when Messenger immediately rang back. Soon after, her phone pinged with a message.

Please call me

She didn't hesitate in deleting it.

Anita looked up to see the man in black cross the intersection toward Saint Paul's Cathedral and saunter along Swanston Street toward the university. With the crowd now dispersing, she made a quick decision to follow him, sticking to the opposite side of the street some twenty metres behind. There were enough people in the busy pedestrian mall to obscure any direct detection of her stalking him and anyway, he didn't turn around, so she felt confident in her strategy of keeping a reasonable distance between them.

The man walked past the entrance to the Metro underground, crossed Collins Street passing the Town Hall before heading right into Little Collins Street. The manoeuvre was problematic for Anita as significantly less pedestrians were going about their business, creating the possibility of detection, so she dropped back to fifty metres.

The man was yet to look over his shoulder and when he turned into Royal Lane, Anita quickly scampered to the corner. Her sneakers luckily allowed her to run unhindered. When she got to the corner, she was panting from the uphill run so took a moment then peered around the edge of the building to watch the man. He was ambling, checking out store windows and looking into cafes.

There were just a couple of pedestrians walking toward her, so she waited until he turned right into Bourke Street and then she quickly dashed to the end of the lane, again creatively peering around the corner, her breathing rapid from the quick run and the increasing excitement from her covert activity. More people on the footpath in Bourke Street encouraged her to re-engage the stalk.

He stopped at the traffic lights on Russell Street, waiting for the green pedestrian light. Anita stopped and looked at the shoe display in a store advertising a summer sale. The stilettos didn't impress her, and she positioned herself so she could observe him from the reflection of the window.

The man stepped off the kerb when the traffic lights

turned green, and Anita made a dash to catch the lights so she could cross before the flashing red. When she reached the other side of the crossing, she was now much closer to her quarry so again looked into a store display for a short time, allowing the man to move further ahead. He then unexpectedly darted to his right, bouncing up stairs at the entrance to Southern Cross Lane heading back toward Little Collins Street, which Anita thought a little odd given he had already been in that street. She quickly caught up by running to the stairs – he was nowhere to be seen.

She hurriedly spun about, scanning the outdoor tables of the cafe full of busy executives discussing business over a coffee. The foyer of the Australia Post head office showed no sign of him. She checked the back-entrance foyer of the state government building. Nothing. She stood looking about her wondering what to do, quickly dismissed entry into the government buildings and checked out the cafe again. Still nothing. She walked slowly then more quickly to the end of the lane but didn't see him. He had disappeared, and she looked about wondering where to go.

Anita then realised the next street to her left was Exhibition. The opposition's campaign headquarters were nearby, almost around the next corner, so she surmised he could be going there. She scuttled up a rise toward Exhibition, wondering why he had taken the deviation unless he stopped for business further back in the lane and she had missed him. She stopped and looked back but could not see the man so went with the idea that he was heading for the campaign headquarters. She dashed toward the corner opposite the party's headquarters at 106 Exhibition.

Distracted by her intent to look across the street to the building entrance to see if the man was about to enter, as she turned the corner, she almost collided into pedestrians scurrying about. She didn't notice the man in black waiting for her who stepped out from an alcove forcefully manhandling her off the street and into a recessed doorway of an abandoned store, thrusting her hard up against a wall. Panting from her run, Anita was now choking for air as the man squeezed his hand firmly around her throat, digging into skin. Pushing her against the wall up on to her toes, forcing her to gasp and look down her nose at him, his eyes squinting with effort as he stared back.

'Why are you following me?' Wolff hoarsely whispered.

Anita struggled to speak. 'Who are you?'

'I'm your worst nightmare, lady, if I ever see you again.'

'Please… you're choking me…' Anita struggled to say as she felt his squeezing fingers dig deeper into her throat. Her hands were gripping his wrist, rapidly trying to lever his fingers away and attempting to kick or knee him but needing to keep balance as he pushed her higher. Her frantic attempts to stop him were fading.

'If I ever see you again, I will do worse than choke you.' Wolff was nose to nose, staring into her eyes. 'Do you understand?' Anita couldn't answer. Wolff squeezed her throat tighter. 'Do you?'

'Yes.' Anita's voice whispered as she gulped and gasped for

breath. Her hands were scratching at the man's fingers trying to relieve pressure, but she could not budge the tight grip. 'Please ... I can't breathe.' It was the last thing she could remember.

What seemed like moments later, Anita was aware of a woman bending over her asking if she was okay. She was lying crumpled among papers and rubbish in the corner of the doorway, her bag still slung on her shoulder. The woman helped her to her feet and asked again if she needed medical aid.

It hurt to speak as Anita struggled to get the hoarse words out. 'I'm okay, thank you.' The woman helped her to a kerb-side iron bench seat, and she was grateful for the assistance. Anita took a bottle of water from her bag, uncapped it, and tentatively sucked in a mouthful, unsure if it would hurt when she swallowed. It did.

'What happened? Were you assaulted?' the woman asked. 'Shall I call an ambulance?'

'No, I'm okay. I must have fainted, but I feel fine now.' Anita wanted to be left alone to collect her thoughts. 'I appreciate your kindness, but I'm okay now, really.'

After staying a few more moments the woman left reassured Anita was recovered. Anita looked around wondering if the man could still see her. Her throat was sore, and she gently rubbed her thumb and finger along her voice box. She took another drink and looked about, still nervous about seeing the man. She never wanted to see him again – ever.

She brushed down her trousers and straightened her

jacket, then took another mouthful of water. It still hurt to swallow; she tried to clear her throat, which also felt uncomfortable as she coughed.

She thought about going across the street into 106 and demanding an answer to her assault claim but thought better of it. What was she to say, a campaign worker tried to kill her? No, she had a story to write about the protest and wanted to link this mercenary thug she assumed accosted her with the Mercantiles. Her revenge would be with her words.

CHAPTER
23

DAY THIRTY-THREE – MONDAY

Forty minutes into the federal police presentation, Prime Minister Gerrard was cranky and increasingly agitated. He was restless and angry, tired of seeing photos enlarged onto the screen of rioting youths, firebombed businesses and what the police were calling anarchy in the streets. He had been invited to return to Melbourne for the presentation and either ignored, or failed to grasp, the enormity of the challenge before local police and wondered why he was wasting his time.

'Why is this a federal issue?' snapped Gerrard when another victim of violence was flashed onto the screen. 'The local police need to restore law and order, not the feds. The local hospitals are a state government responsibility – not the feds.'

'This is turning into an election issue, Prime Minister,' advised Miles Fisher sitting behind him.

Gerrard scoffed. 'No-one else in Australia gives a stuff about Melbourne, trust me.'

The police commissioner was a little uncertain what to say and began speaking before having to clear his throat and start again. 'Prime Minister, there is no relief from the chaos we've had to deal with this last week. Our investigation has determined that it is strategic and well organised and seems to be escalating within your electorate.' The commissioner paused for a moment. 'We need a statement from you.'

'Why would I want to make a statement and take pressure off the state government morons?' sneered Gerrard. 'This is a local law and order issue and has nothing to do with me. Let the state government fix it.'

'You're the local member,' suggested Miles.

'So, what? If they want to wreck their own neighbourhood let them, nothing to do with me,' Gerrard responded sharply. 'It's not my community, I only come here to vote.'

'Sorry Prime Minister, you don't live in the electorate?' asked the perplexed commissioner.

'Just like many fine upstanding politicians who rarely live in their electorates, most preferring to live in up-market suburbs. Some even forget they own investment property in their electorates, although in most cases it wouldn't be much of an investment,' responded Gerrard. 'I live interstate – in a government-owned property.'

'We have to say something, Prime Minister,' encouraged Miles. 'This issue could impact your local vote.'

'You fucking moron, Miles, haven't you learned anything over the years?' Gerrard dismissed his adviser, then added. 'If I speak then it becomes a national event and it gets blown up out of all proportion by the media into a racial debate. As it stands, this is contained to Melbourne and has yet to get the national prominence it would if I were to comment,' justified Gerrard.

'If I speak it will raise the profile to a national debate then it would affect the national vote, and I can't afford that. I secured more than seventy per cent of the primary vote at the last election, this may cost me ten per cent, but no more. I know my people.'

'The ones you never see?' provoked the commissioner.

Gerrard frowned and didn't respond before standing to leave. 'Let me talk to a few people and I'll try and calm things down, but don't expect a public comment.' He walked to the door. 'I'll be back in Sydney this afternoon. Call me if you need me.' Gerrard and his adviser were gone.

'We need you, Prime Minister,' muttered the commissioner to his colleagues.

Gerrard stormed from the building, jumping into the waiting government car with his adviser running to get into the front seat. 'Get me Jameson, will you, Miles.' When the car was on the freeway to the airport, Miles passed back the connected phone call. 'What the fuck do you think you are fucking doing you fucking moron?' barked Gerrard into the phone. 'Call off your fucking dogs otherwise I will make it my goal in life to ensure you never get the things you want from the government or anyone else again.'

'What are you talking about, Andrew?' whispered Jameson, a little anxious about the vitriol of the shouting prime minister.

'Call off your dogs in Melbourne and stop this anarchy you're stirring up, otherwise I will pull your fucking eyes out of your head. You will never know when it is coming, but if you don't do this today, then it will be before fucking Christmas.'

'Andrew, I don't know what you're talking about.'

'Just fucking do it!' shouted Gerrard before throwing the phone back at Miles. He gazed out the window as his driver rushed through traffic.

Anita sat at her computer in a quiet Italian cafe in Lygon Street, staring at the screen. She had a story to write but was missing a piece of the puzzle. Who was the Hyphen? Nothing could be found on social media, not even LinkedIn. She had searched everywhere. She doodled in her notebook and pushed arrows to names and companies. She was missing a link yet didn't know where to look.

She had doodled a dollar sign representing the Mercan-

tiles at the top of the page, with a list of the probable companies associated with them. It was a guess, but she wondered
how close she may be to the total number of members; she
had confirmed at least seven so far.

She rested her fingers at the base of her throat as she
looked at her stick man and the lines squiggled from it
connecting the opposition, Hancock, and the recent addition
of Rukhmani. She wrote the word Hyphen beneath it, with a
question mark. Who was he?

'Did you enjoy that, love?' a waitress began clearing away
her half-eaten food.

'Yes, it was beautiful, thanks,' said Anita, paying little
attention to the waitress.

'Then why didn't ya eat it all?"'

Anita looked up a little surprised. 'I wasn't hungry.'

'Sore throat, have ya?'

Anita gently stroked a finger along her neck, conscious of
the heavy bruising. 'I had a little trouble.'

'Best ya leave him then, love. Men are no good, trust me.'
She began to move away after clearing the table of the dishes.
'They never change.'

Anita watched her go. She mused on her words that
seemed harmless enough but stimulated an imaginative worm
in Anita's mind. Men never change. Maybe this is not the
Hyphen's first campaign, but any search just doesn't bring
him up.

'Wanna 'nother tea love, or would ya like a coffee?' Anita

looked up and smiled, unsure if it was an intrusion or good service. 'Come on, you're workin', it's a tax deduction.'

'Sure, I'll have a cafe latte, thank you,' smiled Anita. *What a strange thing to say to upsell. What's a coffee got to do with tax?*

Anita continued to doodle and linked the Hyphen stick figure to the Acclaim Printing Company with a line back to Hancock and another line to the Mercantiles. Tax? The tax system would absolutely have the Hyphen in it, so Anita pondered how he would be paid. Surely, his expense would be paid by the opposition, and they would treat the money from Acclaim as a donation for tax purposes.

Anita searched Google on her phone looking for the printing company. She sourced the contact number and pushed the connect button.

'Good afternoon, Acclaim Printing Company. How can I help?'

'Accounts payable please.' Anita didn't like assuming someone's identity but needed information. When the clerk answered she said, 'Hi, it's Sussan Neilson from the Conservative Party in Melbourne, I'm trying to invoice money for the sponsorship your company is paying us, and I wonder who I make it out to?'

'What donation are you referring to?'

'Apparently, you are sponsoring a campaign consultant we have working with us, and I want to pay him.'

'I was under the impression we were paying the consultant directly, let me check the ledger.' Anita felt an ethical twinge of guilt wash through her, but she was about to get a connection for the Hyphen, maybe. 'Yes, I have the account up now, Sussan. It seems we have already advanced him three hundred thousand in two payments so far. I'm to expect more expense, apparently.'

'Just to make doubly sure, is the person you are paying a Jack Sinclair-Browne?' Anita grimaced. Did she push too far?

'No, the person we made payment to was Jonathan Wolff. Has he not been consulting to you?'

'Oh Jonathan? Well, that explains it then. Thanks for letting me know. Sorry to trouble you.'

What a fluke, an absolute fluke. Anita couldn't believe her luck and quickly tapped the name into her search engine. To get the actual name of the Hyphen was just the clue she needed to piece the puzzle together. Her enthusiasm was flattened immediately as nothing of interest came up on the first three pages. Over fifty listings in LinkedIn, a character in a book called The Assassin's Creed and entries for renown composer beginning to outnumber any other entry by the time she got to page six.

She searched through the first twenty pages before she found an entry from thirteen years earlier with a reference to a bloodless coup d'état in an obscure Paraguayan province. It seems a man named Wolff was implicated in a successful conspiracy to overthrow the local provincial government. It was reported he was arrested and held for two months before being exonerated by the president of Paraguay.

Anita hastily tapped in detail and searched for further information about the coup. Local farmers had been complaining about climate change laws impacting cattle grazing rights and no matter what they did, the local politicians and police would not act to help reduce the increasing presence of political demonstrators impacting the farmers' livelihood. The farmers had an opportunity to export premium beef good enough for emerging world markets such as China, but the protestors and other eco-warriors had convinced a town mayor and the provincial legislative congress to listen to their concerns about the overuse of land for cattle grazing.

The farmers eventually received increased protection from police when an unexpected change of the provincial government redirected policy to safeguard the farmers' land holdings. Anita zeroed into the province and the industries supporting its population. She found beef production had more than tripled over the last decade since the change of government. Additional processing plants now employed a substantial number of local citizens, significantly reducing unemployment and providing economic growth for the region. Anita searched for a listing of the cattle producers and one of the twenty- two names stood out. Top End Cattle.

'Fuck me.'

'Is that a request or a direction, love?' smiled the waitress as she cleared Anita's cup.

'Sorry? Oh, no, I was talking to myself,' a scattered Anita responded as she quickly collected up her computer, notes and bag.

Wolff was resting in his room, working through his plan for the evening's anarchy. Tasks had been assigned to his groups of disparate youths; keen for money, they were prepared to do anything to earn it. He focused the insurrection within the federal electorate of Melbourne, sheeting home responsibility for the violent troubles on the man everyone was beginning to blame – Andrew Gerrard.

The plan was simple enough, but multifaceted in its delivery. Deliver as much mayhem and street theatre as possible to align any subsequent media outrage and debate with the government's failure on immigration. The ultimate strategy was to get the message out, calling for a temporary pause on all immigration with advocates calling for an immediate review of immigration policy.

His rent-an-urban-warrior concept came from a previously successful campaign in Spain that convinced the government to change policy on migrant workers. The Spanish Mercantiles wanted amendments to temporary visa conditions allowing only skilled migrants into the country. This increased skilled workforce caused competition for jobs within the local workforce, which subsequently pushed wages down. Paradoxically, the change in government economic policy attracted increased investment from international companies entering the market because of cheap labour, allowing greater work opportunities and prosperity for the locals.

His social trolls were highly active in foreshadowing

violence, and the campaign was scaring people. Social media was explosive with comments from people emotionally triggered by the wild commentary and expressing fear for the wellbeing of the community. Twitter messages were targeting the blame on the prime minister by focusing on him living in Sydney and not caring about what was going on in his electorate. Tonight, the plan was to focus on greengrocers and nail bars in the region of Fitzroy.

Other trolls praised Rukhmani for her leadership in bringing the community together and recommended support for her campaign so the electorate could pass a judgement vote on the lack of government action. For those Neanderthals still resisting Twitter rage, Wolff was planning a mail drop overnight at various high foot-traffic areas, pasting walls with posters calling for a change of government at the coming election.

The police struggled to contain the nightly demonstrations and the milling gangs of youths looking for trouble. They never seemed able to identify where violence would be created next; it was as if the gangs knew police strategy and steered clear of their patrols. The police were forced to take an assertive policing strategy, arresting benign innocent protestors who came out onto the streets each night supporting harsher immigration laws or conversely supporting an open borders policy. Either way, the chaos theory was gaining traction.

Wolff recognised the number on his phone when it displayed.

'Wolff?' a familiar voice whispered.

'Hey, boss. How're you doing? Do you like the campaign so far?'

'Let's end it tonight. Keep the media trolls and the local campaign active but stop the violence.'

'Oh, really?' queried Wolff, gently caressing his scar. 'We planned to have a car fire tonight; we got one the other day from the wreckers and were going to blow it up outside the local police station.' Wolff laughed at the thought.

'End it. Now!' barked Jameson.

'Consider it done, Mr Jameson.' The phone went dead. Wolff tossed it on his bed. Looking out the window he surveyed Fitzroy, the battleground for votes – but not tonight.

The front yard didn't look inviting – strewn with large dirty plastic tubs, a rusting bicycle frame, waist-high, out-of-control wild grass looking for a harvester not a mower, and an impressive Harley Davidson in the driveway. Jaya hated door knocking for votes and only persisted because Wolff insisted that she share herself with the community. Everyone who came to the door was very polite, but she never left a front door thinking she had achieved anything, let alone secured a vote. Some residents bluntly responded to her door knocking with a rude 'Go away', but she didn't know if this response was because she was a political candidate or if they didn't like her colour.

She had discussed these rejections with Robert Wong over a quick sandwich and a bottle of water an hour earlier, arguing racism thrived behind most doors of suburban Melbourne. Wong hotly disagreed and said, 'Just because people didn't like you doesn't mean they're racists. Maybe it's your beaming smile they don't like, or your clothes, or your hair, or even your politics.' He argued it was too easy to call out racism if people didn't like what you said. Jaya thought she might add an extra mark to his next assignment for bringing her back to the reality of political discourse.

The textbooks she'd read never covered real-time campaigning where the reality of grassroots politics met the voters; most books were strong on political theory and heavy with reference citations, but very weak with relevance to politics on the street. For instance, experts never explained the anxiety felt by a candidate walking up to a stranger's front door to talk to whoever lurked behind it. Anything could happen, and for Jaya, most things did.

She learned it was better to be cautious when approaching an open front entrance with a wire door the only protection from whatever prowled inside. Savage snarling dogs had killed her enthusiasm over the last few weeks, and she always listened intently for the fearful sound of scampering paws on bare floors.

As always, Jaya placed her sneakered foot at the base of the wire door of the Harley house and gently knocked on the wire doorframe, expecting a pit bull to stir into action. It wasn't a dog that scared her this time but a Siamese cat that flashed down the passageway and leapt straight toward her head. She squealed loudly as she ducked away from the door, fearful of the cat coming through the wire. When she recovered her poise, she straightened to find the cat still pinned to the door, its extended claws stuck through the wire. A massive hairy man came to the door. Filling the entire opening, he politely apologised and pulled the cat from its capture, tossing it back down the hall.

'What can I do for you?' the man asked.

Breathing deeply, Jaya took a few moments to recover before responding. 'Hi, my name is Jaya Rukhmani. I'm standing for the seat of Melbourne at the election next week, and I would like your vote.'

'You know something lady, you're the first politician to ever come knocking on my door,' smiled the man. 'So sure, I'll give you my vote.'

'Can I leave you a brochure?' Jaya said, holding up a card.

'Sure, be happy to read it,' said the man, unsnibbing and then opening the wire door, then taking the card from her. 'What are you going to do for me?'

Jaya didn't know how to respond to the request and suddenly became more nervous, if that was possible, and took a cautious step back. 'What do you mean?' she gulped.

'When you get to Canberra, what are you going to do for me?'

She breathed out heavily, a little relieved, 'I'll be your voice.'

'Do me a favour then.'

'If I can, I will.'

'Tighten up the laws on Indian immigrants. We have too many coming in – and keep the kooks out as well.' The man smiled. 'What did you say your name was?'

'Jaya Rukhmani.'

'Well, Jaya, good luck and just keep those fucking Indians out of the country.'

She stepped back from the door, smiled, and left with a small, thankful wave. As she walked back along the path she almost broke into laughter from relief, not quite believing the reality she had just put herself through with the Harley rider. He wants to stop Indian migration and he was telling an Indian to do it. She wondered what the heck had she gotten herself into with this political nonsense if that biker boy was a typical voter.

Wolff punched the numbers into his phone and waited for a pickup. 'Hi Jaya, I need to talk to you about an event I want you at tonight. There's going to be a public demonstration against racism, and I've got you on the speaker's list.'

'You know I don't like those things; they scare me.'

'It'll be good publicity – Indian girl calls for halt on immigration to stop racism.'

'That sounds bizarre, are you kidding me?'

'No, I'm not. Look, I've written a speech that I'll send to Robert,' said Wolff. 'Just stick to the key messages. Tell them you've spoken with many of the rioters, and you've calmed them down.'

'But I haven't.'

'That doesn't matter – tell them you have and that you've negotiated an agreement to stop the demonstrations.'

'I can't promise that,' snapped Jaya.

'Yeah, you can. Just don't go into any detail.'

'So, you've stopped the riots, is that it?' asked Jaya. 'What did you have to promise?'

'Nothing,' said Wolff. 'They'll listen to you tonight. Tell your story and talk about people ripping off the system through the fraudulent visa application system. You're not suggesting banning it, just deferring it, slowing it down.'

'Will they shout me down?'

'As I said, I've written a good speech and I can promise you they'll be clapping,' assured Wolff. 'I'll have people there to support you. Keep working hard.'

'Cleave, I think I have a good story.' Anita was excited to be pitching it.

'Let's hear it, and it had better be good.'

'You may recall I've been following the campaign guru with the Stanley team. I've been able to dig up more information on the Mercantiles, a business group, which to my reckoning appeared for the first time in politics around two hundred years ago. They're now an exclusive group of twelve private business owners very active in policy and influence with governments all over the place.'

'I thought you said this story was good, sounds a little repetitive to me.'

'Just be patient, okay. I reckon the Mercantiles are running the Stanley campaign driven by an operative known as Jonathan Wolff.'

'Wait up,' queried Cleaver. 'I thought you said this guru had a hyphenated name?'

'He's working under an alias.'

Cleaver blew a small raspberry of disbelief. 'Are you making this up?' His tone suddenly changed. 'I hate it when you do this, Anita.'

'No, I'm not kidding,' snapped Anita, taking a deep breath before continuing. 'Wolff is a hired gun and works on their behalf in the shadows with election campaigns all over the place. I've tracked him to campaigns in South America, the States, the UK and Spain.'

'Is that all?' Cleaver was yet to be excited.

'That's what I've been able to find so far,' said Anita referring to her notes. 'In every campaign, while yet to be confirmed, he has represented special interest groups linked in some nefarious way.'

'What are you saying? All these mysterious campaigns are linked in some way to the same special interest group?'

'Yes.'

'What proof do you have?'

'The Mercantiles are members of various international groups either individually or collectively.'

'This is beginning to sound like one of your conspiracies,' Cleaver sighed. 'What sort of groups?'

'I suppose there are no guarantees with any election, but it seems they've had considerable success in establishing real economic growth for the country or region they get politically involved in, which is bizarre.'

'What are we talking about?'

'Mining, energy, food production, IT, and in Jameson's case, gambling interests.'

'Kerry Jameson?'

'Well, it was his father first and now it's Kerry. Over the last forty years the expansion of his international gaming interests always followed a change of government or community campaign supporting gambling.'

'Really? You have proof of that?'

'It's circumstantial, but compelling, wouldn't you say?' questioned Anita.

'You think this group is involved in this federal election?'

'Most definitely. More than that, they're running everything in the opposition's campaign.'

'How are they running everything?' mocked Cleaver.

'They're running Stanley's campaign, driving policy announcements, and managing his media. That's why you rarely see him out and about now.'

'He's also a goose, which could be a reason.'

Anita ignored the provocation. 'They set up Rukhmani

with a controversial racist speech then sacked her. But here's the curious thing, they are now running her campaign as an independent.' Anita flicked further into her notes. 'Then the opposition announces the big lie about Indonesia, which was the Mercantiles' idea, I'm sure of it. I also reckon they facilitated the immigration anarchy we've seen on the streets in Melbourne. The demonstrating is the work of this chap, Wolff. I'm convinced of it. There's no doubt in my mind they want Gerrard to lose the election, but to ensure he leaves the parliament, they want him to lose his seat as well.'

'What's this about Ruki whatever her name is?'

'They set her up with a speech about immigration, critical of government policy. Stanley had no option and was forced to sack her, but coincidentally, it was after the declaration of the polls, which meant it was too late for them to select another candidate to replace her,' Anita paused for a moment. 'I suspect they thought it would show Stanley as a strong, fearless leader, politically above all the racist accusations flying around. Anyway, they dumped her, but intriguingly, this Wolff chap is now advising her campaign, which has clicked up a notch.'

'Sounds like wild speculation to me.'

'You know what is really remarkable, Cleave? I found out who's paying Wolff.'

'Who? Don't tell me it's one of the group!' Cleaver said mockingly with a laugh.

'Worse than that,' Anita said, pausing before going on. 'It's Hancock.'

'Bullshit,' was the immediate response, then, 'No way that's right.'

'There is a complex web of deceit associated with the ownership of the printing company paying this chap Wolff, but I've discovered the majority owner is Hancock, or at least his media group.' Anita waited for a response. It took some time coming.

Finally, Cleaver said, 'Are you sure about these allegations? Can you confirm with solid evidence?'

'I have evidence and confirmation from the conservatives that Wolff is operating under an alias, that he is paid by a Hancock company, which probably explains why we have gone soft on Stanley. And I'm certain he's leading the management of their strategy.'

'Do you have him linked to Rukhmani?'

'Yes, I have them together at a demonstration in the city and I'm certain the street demonstrations and isolated rioting is instigated by Wolff. It's the same methods he's used in other elections.'

'And you have evidence he is paid directly by a company in our media group?'

'I have that evidence confirmed directly from the company,' Anita referred to her notes. 'They have so far transferred three hundred thousand dollars to him and they're expecting more payments in the next few days.'

'Write everything as you know it to be, put a conspiracy line around the immigration issues. We can tie it to Gerrard's deal with Indonesia. Part two of the story, as you've just explained it, can focus on the campaign operative, linking this chap Wolff to the Mercantile group and other work he's done.'

'I can do that, when do you want it?'

'I can't guarantee we'll run it before the election, but it could make a great two-part feature,' Cleaver advised. 'Oh, and one other thing, leave any reference to Hancock out of it.'

'Cleave, I can't do that.'

'I'm not asking you; I'm telling you.'

'But I can't withhold the truth.'

'That's bullshit, Anita,' Cleaver snapped. 'It's what we do. We run stories that suit us, you know that – and outing Hancock will not suit us.'

'That's not fair, Cleave. Hancock is up to this neck in this and for our own credibility, it needs to be exposed – for my credibility.'

'If you don't do as I suggest, the story will never be published – and you'll never work in the media again, trust me.'

'Wolff? It's Hancock. My journalist is on to you.'

'How close is she?'

'She has you named, knows who's paying you and has you in the Rukhmani campaign.'

'Thanks for letting me know.'

CHAPTER
24

DAY THIRTY-SIX – THURSDAY

O ver the years, opposition leaders have asked for more than one opportunity to debate the economy and policy differences between the parties. Gerrard always refused, but as an alternative, he offered up his ministers to debate their opposition shadows at various venues around the country and never cared if they were televised. Right now, was Gerrard's big, orchestrated moment of the campaign, and in the past, achieved a huge viewing audience just a few days before the election.

'Punters never start paying attention to the election until the last few days so that's when I want to speak to them,' Gerrard often boasted to interested staff.

The National Press Club stage was dressed like a television studio set with subtle lighting and national symbols across the back wall. A centre podium reserved for the adjudicator was flanked by matching lecterns on either side of the stage for the leaders. Gerrard's media adviser always brought a rubber mat for him to stand on. Gerrard said the soft pad helped relieve his ageing legs, but covertly increased his height by three centimetres, ensuring a towering leadership figure compared to his opposition.

The leaders relaxed in separate rooms for final preparation, fidgeting with tie knots and pacing the floor. Gerrard was familiar with the pressure of these events and warmed his voice with vocal exercises given to him years before by his wife, Margaret. Opposition leaders came to the debates ambitious and confident, but always left with greater self-doubt after Gerrard's commanding performance. It was their time to shine, yet more often than not their reputation was trashed by Gerrard's razor wit and thorough understanding of all government policy in every ministerial portfolio.

Peter Stanley nervously flicked his shoulders of unseen fluff. He checked his image in the mirror again, straightening his tie then pacing the floor again.

'Do you have your key economic points to deliver?' Messenger asked him.

Stanley held up his leather binder. 'Yes, I do. Are you sure these are the points I need to be talking about? They seem silly to me.'

'Sinclair-Browne sent them through this morning; they're matched to the overnight polling from the focus group.'

'Where is he?'

'He's in Melbourne finalising election day strategy and later today he'll be video-conferencing all campaign managers, polling day booth captains and community organisers,' Messenger said as they stood facing each other. 'He'll watch it live and text through any suggestions as we move through it. If I need to, I will slip you notes during the breaks so keep an eye out for me.'

'I must say I'm a little nervous,' confessed Stanley. 'I've never been any good against Gerrard in the parliament.'

'Just don't get sucked in by his provocative rhetoric. He'll bait you, so don't respond and always keep on message. Just take a few deep breaths.'

'Do you have any questions for me?'

'What is the price of a litre of milk?'

'Good question, depends on where you buy it. Supermarkets offer a different pricing structure but at the local convenience store it's two dollars.'

'That's a good answer, but if it's asked, I would prefer you say the price first. Like, two dollars but cheaper in the supermarkets. It shows you are strong and unequivocal and have a good understanding of day-to-day costs for working Australians.'

'Okay,' Stanley nodded thinking through the advice, swaying from foot to foot. 'What else should I know?'

'The marginal rates on tax might be a good idea.'

'What are they again?'

'Gerrard changed them five years ago to twenty thousand

before the punters start paying tax at a flat rate of twenty per cent, and fifty thousand for the next level, which bumps it up to thirty per cent. Eighty per cent of taxpayers fall within those two rates. Then at two hundred thousand, the rate is forty-seven per cent.'

'Perhaps I should take a note.'

'Pete, you're about to be elected prime minister. This stuff is basic – you should know it.'

'I do, but not off the top of my head,' said Stanley, writing a prompt in his notes. 'What do we do if we do win?'

'Let's just get past this debate first. We can worry about what we do in government if and when we get there.'

Jameson took the call as he was sitting before a massive television screen waiting for the debate. 'Is Stanley ready?

'As best as he will ever be,' Wolff replied. 'It would take years to get him to Gerrard's level.'

'Will he win?'

'The debate doesn't really matter. It'll be close on election day.'

'National polls don't support your view.'

'My campaign teams say to ignore the national figures as they don't reflect the electorate's sentiment on the ground.'

'So, the national polls are wrong?'

'Let me say this,' Wolff tightened his tone. 'It's too close to call the national result but let me reassure you that Gerrard will not be prime minister.'

Jameson didn't respond and shrugged his shoulders of a sudden chill. This was the time to make the decision he'd hoped he would not have to make, so he carefully considered his response. 'How will you do it?'

'I have my methods. I can absolutely assure you if the prime minister wins government, and wins his seat, he will not be up and about on Sunday to enjoy it. I suspect witnesses will report Gerrard celebrated long into the night − perhaps a little too much − and unfortunately, he will not recover from his overindulgence that led to and perhaps caused a brain aneurysm from a fall. It is arranged for the early hours on Sunday at Admiralty House.'

'No more,' insisted Jameson. 'Your money will be transferred if the result is as we want it.'

'As I said, I can categorically guarantee you Andrew Gerrard will not be prime minister on Sunday, so please do not defer any payments.'

Jameson paused for a moment, the menace in Wolff's tone creating anxiety and making him a feel little uncomfortable.

'Do you want your usual link to the debate?' asked Wolff when no further comment was forthcoming.

'If I need to ask a question, I will call you.'

Wolff ended the call, slipping his phone into his jacket pocket before stepping back into the cafe to finish his lunch. He could do no more on the campaign. Everything was in place and with just one last national briefing to provide his key electorate teams the election day strategy, he just hoped the electorate would respond to his tactics and change their vote – and not compel him to act on his assurance to end Gerrard's term as prime minister.

As he looked out onto the street to nothing in particular, he felt a shroud of tiredness envelop him but shrugged it away. He thought about all the things he'd been required to do in the past, the dangerous things that brought no satisfaction to his life. His influence in covert political campaigns meant he was well rewarded, and his accumulated assets were significant enough for him to call time. This campaign might be the occasion to draw an end to the transient lifestyle.

Conspiracy and intrigue can seem glamorous and addictive when mixed with political power, but there were only a certain amount of dills, flakes, and morons he could deal with. Stanley was probably his greatest challenge and added to the appeal of retirement he was playing with.

He popped open his notebook computer and connected to a news feed to watch the leaders' opening statements as the time for the debate ticked over. He connected his earphones and settled in with a bottle of water to watch the entertainment.

He laughed at the awkwardness of the coin toss to determine who was to speak first. Gerrard called heads and with his usual strong and confident statesman speaking craft, he opened the debate by castigating the opposition for being without policy ideas for the future and no effective policy to drive the country toward continued economic growth. He assertively stated the opposition's incompetence would send the country into a depression, and it would be many years before the country would recover. 'Why take the risk? Who do you trust to continue to deliver jobs and growth?'

When he had his opportunity, Stanley jumped right into his monologue, closely following the directions set out by Wolff. Gerrard stood opposite him, smirking like the kid who had stolen lollies from his best friend. This made him a little anxious about what he was saying. Thinking perhaps he was stepping into the prime minister's established game, he stopped mid-sentence.

'The prime minister asks who you can trust. Well, would you ever trust him again with his open borders policy? A policy that will allow our northern neighbours to have open access to our country. I ask why – why has the prime minister allegedly promised this deal with the Indonesian president? Has it anything to do with the allegations of corruption levelled at the prime minister and the very reason why we are now at an election? The prime minister asks who you can trust – trust no politician who asks that question.'

Gerrard bristled with anger as he waited his turn to respond.

'Ya wanna 'nother cup of tea, love?' She was around thirty, the gold-tipped big hair a little wild, and her tattooed arm intrigued him, as did the too short skirt. 'Go on, you're obviously working, you can claim it as a tax deduction.'

'Yes, please.' Wolff smiled as he watched her leave to fetch his tea.

The first question from the moderator had Gerrard speaking about his achievements as prime minister and the many benefits his leadership had brought to the Australian people, challenging Stanley to explain what leadership roles he may have done.

'Whatcha watchin'?' She placed the peppermint tea before him, with a tea bag still dangling its tab over the side.

Wolff pulled an earphone from his ear before replying, 'The leaders' debate.'

'Boring.' She waltzed off, giving Wolff a chance to watch her again as he replaced the earphone.

Stanley's responses to questions were on message. Wolff smirked when he interjected and nailed a question about the price of milk when Gerrard floundered, looking through his notes.

Perfect.

The phone buzzed and Wolff quickly answered. 'Mr Jameson?'

'Get him to ask a question on fracking.'

After ending the call, Wolff texted:

Ask Gerrard the fracking question.

The moderator waited for Gerrard's response about inner city living to finish before calling Stanley to respond to the same question. He then looked down to read a silent text message on his phone. Stanley finished his answer by promising more money to be spent by his government on public transport infrastructure.

The moderator turned to the prime minister. 'Mr Gerrard, coal seam gas is becoming an important component of our energy mix. Do you support increasing fracking extraction licences?'

'Jameson asks and moments later it's on air. Geez, I'm good,' Wolff muttered to himself.

'My government supports energy security—' Gerrard stumbled a little as he searched his papers for an answer. When he found his note, he continued assertively. 'On-land gas exploration and extraction are part of my government's policy platform that will provide jobs and growth. We support further development and reject the notion it is dangerous to the water supply or impacts farming. Jobs and growth are what my government has always been about, and gas exploration is no different.'

'Mr Stanley?'

'This is typical of the prime minister, no answers on immigration, and no answer for hard-working farmers whose land is at threat by the exploration for coal seam gas. Mr Gerrard would rather have open borders then sell all our resources to overseas interests.'

'That's a lie,' Gerrard barked.

The corners of Stanley's mouth turned up. 'Mr Gerrard is no friend of hard-working Australians who, from the sweat of their brow, have created the wealth of our nation. We must protect their farming interests. He pontificates about local jobs while standing there in his finest Italian handmade suit and talks about selling our resources overseas as if they are his to do with as he pleases before he unconvincingly tries to explain that he is tough on crime when he is about to open our borders.'

Wolff chortled. It was a miracle. Five speaking points reinforced in one answer – there may be hope for Stanley yet.

The debate was nearing the end of its televised time and the moderator brought the leaders to a conclusion, inviting Stanley to provide his closing remarks.

'This afternoon we've heard much about Mr Gerrard's approach to the future, but we know that it's not your future he is worried about – it's his own. Mr Gerrard will jump about and get excited about the things he may have done in the past. But the more the prime minister talks about the past, the more he proclaims his embarrassment about the present, and confirms he has nothing to say about the future.'

Wolff smiled. He loved that line and had used it to great effect with other clients in the past, even in Australia.

'The prime minister is fond of talking about history so let us remind ourselves about some important aspects of recent history for which he is responsible. He speaks of jobs, but we have an unemployment rate of eight per cent – even higher in the under thirty-year-old category. Mr Gerrard has presided over the worst economic downturn we have had in forty years. He has given us the highest current account deficit since the turn of the century, and he wants to initiate an open borders policy with a country with a vastly different culture and religious customs to our own. This man has no love for this country. Remember he has stated in the past that he wishes to relocate to Europe whenever he deigns it time to retire, which at this stage, could be in just a few years.

'He has trashed the institution of parliament and the many rules and protocols we hold dear in our democracy – just look at his disdain and treatment of the governor-general. If it wasn't for the recent courage of parliamentary officers, he would have forced through parliament a money bill that is alleged to provide a secret commission deal with Indonesia, providing him with corrupt and fraudulent funds. An allegation he is yet to deny or even explain to the adequate satisfaction of the parliament, the media, or the people of Australia.

'When this man talks of jobs, he only has one job in mind: his own.

'He has no compassion for those languishing in the mire of unemployment. He doesn't care about mums and dads struggling to put food on the table; he ignores the breakdown of our health system; and has no respect for working families. So, it is incumbent upon the people of Australia to let him know on Saturday in no uncertain terms that they are tired of his arrogance, tired of his disdain for them, and tired of his cheap money offers to keep them happy.

'This Saturday, make your vote count. Send a message to the prime minister and tell him it's time for him to go. Tell him we don't like what he has done to the country. Tell him his style of government is wrong for this nation and tell him to pack his bags and go.' Stanley paused and looked at Gerrard before saying, 'Just go.'

Just as rehearsed.

Stanley then looked back to the camera, as he had been instructed to do for his final comment. 'The decision you make on election day will determine if you reward this man or give your country a chance to grow. My fellow Australians, will you join with me to provide a future for our children? Will you join with me to set ourselves free of the limitations of political correctness and free speech? Will you join with me to provide a new direction of which we can all be proud? Will you join with me to rid ourselves of the culture of the elite? Will you join with me to make Australia great again?'

Wolff smiled as Stanley finished his address, pleased he had so convincingly stuck to script. Although the process had been painstakingly slow, he thought Stanley had nailed it, just as he wanted.

The moderator called upon Gerrard to respond.

'It will take more than a decade of old rhetoric to win the election on Saturday. Old words, from an old script, delivered by an old grey head with no plans for the future. The opposition has been talking about the apparent parlous state of Australia for over ten years, and they have just proven they have nothing further to say for the future.

'It was not by accident that the conservatives passed over this man when they elected James Harper as their leader a few years back. Mr Stanley has been in the parliament for decades yet remains unknown to the Australian people.

During his rather long political career he has had few policy ideas, little understanding of how to grow an economy, and since he started his moribund career – and I have been there every day to witness it – he has done nothing, said nothing, to add his name to the list of builders and dreamers of this great country. He was never considered a future leader, yet by some miracles he is now the accidental leader of the opposition – and still unable to talk about the future.

'He strides into this debate and claims he has the answers, criticising Australia and its achievements over the last two decades. He is wrong – wrong when he claims Australia is in some sort of parlous economic state and wrong when he claims he has the answers.

'This man arrogantly believes he is the only one qualified to speak for families. He says he believes in families, yet he doesn't believe in family support and voted against it when my government increased the base rate ten years ago.

'The opposition talk about policy changes and the urgent needs of the community, but it is very easy to promise something in opposition and then never have to deliver it in government. I have served in opposition, and I have had the privilege of serving in government as prime minister, and I can tell you none of the opposition's grand plans will ever come to fruition in the unlikely event of them being elected on Saturday.

'If Peter Stanley ends up as prime minister, God help us. He is an intellectual nobody. He's our yesterday man. His history in the parliament has been known for its universal lack of policy insight and I can't recall him ever presenting a speech that called for any new initiative. I always regarded him as the resident nutter.'

Gerrard was just warming up to the personality attack he was renowned for in the parliament. 'Where is the thought-out policy position? This man is all tip and no iceberg; he has no ideas, no plans, and no future. Unless he is scripted, he is utterly useless.'

Wolff screwed up his face and begrudgingly nodded agreement with Gerrard but had had enough so snapped closed his computer. Final preparations and directions for the team needed attending to in the campaign head office before his video-conference so he shoved his materials into his knapsack. The waitress gazed at him, then cocked an eyebrow.

He checked his Breitling, glanced around the café, shrugged and followed her to the back rooms.

CHAPTER
25

DAY THIRTY-EIGHT – ELECTION DAY

There were long queues at most marginal seat polling booths prior to them opening, with some booths reporting voters turning up an hour before the 8 am start – a good sign for a strong anti-government vote. It was hot early in most regions along the east coast and a jovial holiday mood flooded over constituents as they waited. Community groups stationed themselves at exit doors with cake stalls and enterprising groups fired up gas barbeques for a sausage sizzle, raising funds for the community.

Wolff remained confident of a positive result, especially in the seat of Melbourne, and had insisted his election-day instructions were meticulously followed. Colourful bunting was installed where instructed to provide final messages to

voters as they strolled up to the booth. Booth workers delivered well-rehearsed lines when offering how-to-vote cards as
voters filed into the school hall to register. Booth captains
distributed drinks to their team and fed hungry volunteers
throughout the day to ensure they remained enthusiastic and
provided an anti-government message. Good-natured banter
from conservative volunteers washed over voters as they were
steered through the throng of helpers trying their best to get
voting cards into hands. There was a sense of excitement
toward the inevitable.

Perfect.

Time zones across the nation made it difficult to manage
election day from a central point, but the conservatives had
never been as organised as they were this election. It had the
precision of a military campaign. Every vote was important,
but in marginal seats they were more important as they could
make a bigger difference to the overall result. Win enough
marginal seats and a party wins government. Elections and
governments are only ever about the numbers and Wolff
ensured his marginal seat booth captains were his very best.

Polling booths closed at six in the evening and on the east
coast, television broadcasts commenced at seven after normal
news commitments. The only broadcaster worthy of watching
was the Hancock Channel 5 because of their access to candidates and the quality of its panel of political experts. Anita set
herself up in her hotel room in Melbourne to watch the
broadcast, taking notes about results in various electorates for
the several stories she'd file during the evening. She was keen

to stay in touch with politicians, especially marginal seat members, and was on a telephone rotation to all the key political players. Everyone except Barton Messenger, who she hadn't spoken to for the past week, peeved as she was by the big lie.

Anita remained conflicted with the stories she had been writing about the Mercantiles. Exposing the group might limit her opportunities for promotion to the Hancock television network. None of her submitted opinion pieces on the Mercantiles had been published anyway, disappointing her greatly. She had a suspicion Tony Hancock was blocking them from publication. If Hancock was quashing them, perhaps she was compromising her ethics and values by continuing to work for him, no matter the promotion opportunities before her. She was a little perplexed by what to do and wondered if her integrity was being compromised.

Maybe she could convince her editor to publish some of the less provocative stories after the election when a clear result was known. If Gerrard was elected, they could be used as attack pieces toward the opposition to ameliorate the relationship with Hancock. The media coverage of the prime minister must have driven a wedge between them, so perhaps she could recast them as pro-government. Maybe she should just take Cleaver's advice and minimise all references to Hancock – but if she did, what was the point of running the stories?

Hancock's connection to the Mercantiles bothered her. She fretted over whether to keep writing the stories about them. She was convinced the shadowy group needed exposing as a covert lobby group influencing government policy – she thought democracy and government should not be left in the hands of a few to manipulate their interests ahead of the community. Perhaps she was naïve to think so, but she believed they should be exposed as a danger to the Australian democracy.

The election coverage commenced with Cassandra Rogers, a senior journalist and longtime political commentator mediating the panel. She opened by announcing that the count was underway at the national tally centre and early results were indicating that the Gerrard government would be returned, although it was too close to call at this stage of the evening. She then introduced the panel.

'Meredith Bruce is the Minister for Education and Manager of Government Business in the Gerrard government. We also welcome Barton Messenger, the Deputy Opposition Leader. Also joining us is respected political commentator with the Hancock Network, Maurie Weideman. Another government minister to join us is Western Australian Senator Dean Smythe, the Minister for Social Security. Last, but certainly not least, James Harper joins us, who up until a few weeks ago was the leader of the opposition. A week's a long time in politics, James?'

'You could say that, Cassandra. I'm happy to be here again,' Harper responded.

'I welcome you all. So, to get a clear picture of the current trend, can I ask: what are your early predictions of the result, Maurie?'

Weideman was an untidy overly large man although a highly respected pundit by the political community for his incisive analysis. 'It seems the very early trends on the east coast are to the government. They need to hold their current seats and they will probably increase their margin if they win their targeted seats in Queensland. The opposition needs to win at least six seats to win a majority, but they will need to win more than that to put a clear stamp on the parliament as a new government.'

'So, unless the opposition claim eight to ten seats it will be considered a loss?' queried Rogers.

'Yes, I think so,' said Weideman.

'That's a ridiculous assessment,' interrupted Harper. 'And can I just say this is a normal start to these events. Maurie just can't help himself when it comes to espousing his affection for the prime minister. He has a history of exclusives leaked from Gerrard so no doubt these types of statements are payback for the prime minister. Let's be very clear, the government must increase its margin. Anything less will mean the people have rejected the prime minister's strategy for the future and provide no mandate.'

'Actually, it does matter how many seats you win, Cass,' interrupted a smiling Bruce. 'Politics is all about the numbers and if you have more numbers than your opponents, you win government and have a mandate.'

'Barton Messenger, what is your view?' asked Cassandra.

'I'm expecting the result to be very close. I will go so far as to say we may not even have a result tonight. Our exit polling is indicating that there may be a one- or two-seat margin for any party and that means it is too close to call,' Barton spoke with authenticity and Anita admired his confidence, perhaps chipping away at her soured view of him. He could after all be deputy prime minister in a few hours and his ethical blemish with the big immigration lie during the campaign would be quickly forgotten. Why couldn't she let it go? 'It's far too early to say.'

'Senator Smythe?'

'I agree with Barton, we are jumping at shadows at this early stage of the count, but I think the battleground will be the marginal seats in Queensland and Western Australia, and the polls don't close on the west coast for another two hours.'

Anita agreed so ordered room service and began writing paragraphs of opinion in preparation for various stories to be added to her wrap-up editorial column she had been asked by Cleaver to write.

As Jaya entered the function room the crowd erupted into spontaneous cheering and clapping. Her workers and supporters were crammed into an overly large function room and her progress to the microphone to speak was slow – they wanted to congratulate, touch her, and speak with her.

A large screen on the wall behind the lectern was broadcasting scenes from the national tally room. Individual results were scrolling through, but the news for those hoping for a change of government was not good – the opposition was not winning enough seats from the government, and it seemed the government would be returned.

Jaya's supporters didn't really care who won the election. They were there to recognise the work she had done to change the narrative and tone of the immigration debate that threatened the community, but the celebratory atmosphere in the room only increased her anxiety.

When she eventually stepped up on to the small stage at the front, another round of cheering erupted. With her name raucously chanted, she self-consciously waved to her friends. When Jaya finally stood at the microphone, the room hushed, and she began.

'Friends, this campaign first started as a university project for my students studying politics at Melbourne University.' A small cheer erupted from her students in the corner by the bar and Jaya waved to them. 'We wanted to research real-world campaign experiences, so we decided to stand against the prime minister of Australia – and what an experience that was.

'We naïvely thought we could produce a documentary about our campaign experiences and from our research and experiences, write and design an applied political campaign unit we would teach to assist students and others seeking a career in politics. Little did we know what would happen during the campaign and the results of our efforts – it has been a wild, fabulous ride.

'It's too early to provide you an outcome, but I can announce this—' Jaya paused for a moment with a broad and excited grin. 'For the first time since Andrew Gerrard has held the seat of Melbourne, the voting to determine the local member has been required to go to preferences and will eventually be decided by the second votes of those who voted for the Greens.'

A cheer erupted, louder than before, prompting Jaya to raise her hands outstretched to calm and quieten the crowd. 'During the campaign, we have seen significant disruption in the community, a lot of hate spoken – too much, really. There has been a lot of violence threatened and metered out by strangers who have trashed our community, and yet, we as a community have voted for change.

'A change from the politics of the old, a change to the politics of the new. I stand before you as a proud Australian citizen, a woman – a proud black woman – who wants to fight for her country and end this racial divide within the community. It's okay to talk about the things we must change in our country, especially immigration policy without being labelled a racist, and for the sake of our country we must.'

Another cheer erupted and Jaya smiled broadly, looking about the room and waving to more friends she spotted. 'Our scrutineers are currently wading through the votes, but I can tell you – on advice from my loyal colleague Robert Wong, who has done such a fabulous job – that there are just a few votes in it.'

The crowd erupted and Jaya had to speak loudly over the din. 'So tonight, my friends, the government may be returned, but we may also have a new prime minister.'

'Miles,' barked Gerrard from the lounge at his Sydney residence. 'Do you have any results from Western Australia yet, for fuck's sake?'

Fisher ignored him. He was working his phone getting results directly from the scrutineers in the key marginal seats.

After a few moments, Gerrard – now more interested in the television broadcast as the panel began talking about Western Australia – held up his glass. 'Is there any more champagne?'

'I have good news and bad news for you,' said Fisher, now standing beside the lounge. 'We've lost Petrie, Leichhardt, Blair and Rankin.'

'The speaker lost her seat?'

'Yes, but we have picked up Morton and Griffith.'

'Western Australia?'

'Still early, but we are behind in Cowan and strong in Stirling. Victoria is okay and remains neutral, so is Tasmania. We have a few close ones in New South Wales.'

'What's your best estimate?'

'You have a three-seat majority.'

'Champagne,' cheered Gerrard. 'You fucking beauty! Another victory to me.'

Fisher anxiously studied his figures. 'Prime Minister, the bad news is a little more worrying.'

'What is it lad, come on, speak up.'

'Your seat has gone to preferences.'

'Maurie, it's just gone ten o'clock. Can you please give us a current state of the election?' Cassandra Rogers asked. The panel seemed preoccupied with their smartphones, trying to receive accurate up-to- date information from local electorate operatives.

Weideman stood before a screen with a scrolling result of key seats slowly rotating. 'Cassandra, this election is the closest result we've had for many years. To win government, a clear majority needs to be attained of seventy-eight seats, which allows a one-seat working majority in the one hundred and fifty-five seat parliament,' explained Weideman.

'After my analysis of preference voting trends from the past two elections, I would like to go early and predict the Gerrard government will win the election with a five-seat majority. The final numbers in my estimate will be, eighty for the government, with seventy-five for the Stanley opposition.'

'So, the Gerrard government wins government again. Your reaction, Meredith Bruce?'

'If Maurie's sources are correct about results in the key seats, and I must say they usually are, then this is a great victory for the government and justifies the policy program of jobs and growth we want to continue to implement.

'It also means this election has been a complete waste of taxpayers' money. The parliament had no reason to prorogue in the first place and the presiding officers should not have acted to force the government to an election,' Bruce said, then smiled and looked to Messenger. 'The government has a solid history of achievement and the program we took to the election means we will have five more years of growth with good parliamentary stability. We will have time to transition the leadership before the next election.'

'Whoa,' interrupted Messenger. 'Are you saying we will have a new prime minister during this next term of government?'

'What I'm saying is that Prime Minister Gerrard has clearly and publicly indicated that this may be his last term and he will consider retiring before the next election. I would support his view.'

Anita couldn't believe what she just heard and began to furiously take notes for another column. *Meredith Bruce declaring Gerrard gone in a few years.*

'Will you be a candidate for leadership?' asked Messenger. Anita smiled at the incisive question, quietly thanking him.

'If my colleagues would like to have a competent woman lead them, I would proudly put forward my ministerial credentials and parliamentary experience as being suitable for the job,' said Bruce. 'We haven't had the privilege of having a woman as leader for either party for a significant period, yet women hold fifty-one-per cent of the national vote. I think it might be time to bring the government into the modern world, don't you? Or do you still prefer your male privilege?'

Messenger bristled at the comment. 'I actually find that remark offensive, Meredith, and I ask you for an apology.'

'Toughen up, snowflake,' smiled Bruce as she turned to Rogers cold-shouldering Messenger's request. She then returned to look at Messenger as she remembered to say something with a curled lip of disdain. 'Your sensitivities did not extend to the offensive lies you declared about the so-called open borders policy. You knew it to be a lie and you, and your colleagues have been pushing it hard for the last week of the campaign. We have had anarchy in the streets of Melbourne because of your lies. Where were your sensitivities to businesses being ruined?'

'Can I just interrupt for a moment by saying we have had a couple of results confirmed in Western Australia,' inter-jected Weideman. 'Cowan has been retained by the govern-ment and Stirling has been won by the government, which is a great result and was not expected as the sitting member has been a credible advocate for her local community. So, this could possibly mean a two-seat swing to my calculations and the government's majority could be even greater than five.

'Wolff, what the hell happened in WA?'

'It's way too early to know anything. Calm down.' Wolff

had been taking ranting calls from Jameson since nine o'clock; this one was no different. 'My people tell me it will be close but there will definitely be a change of government. Just be patient.'

'You promised me Gerrard would not be prime minister.'

'As I said,' Wolff lowered his tone. 'If the results don't go the way I expect, then I will deal with him before the morning. I have a plane on standby.'

Cassandra Rogers looked down the barrel of the camera when the coverage returned from a commercial break. 'If you are joining us for the first time, I can report the national election results remain too close to call, although experts are predicting a government re-election. To get a clearer picture in those seats still to be declared, what can you tell us, Maurie?'

'Well, it seems my prediction an hour earlier of an easy victory by the Gerrard government may have been slightly premature. The results now seem much closer than predicted and could come down to just one seat. Scrutineers in the seat of Griffith, as you know a former prime minister's seat, indicates a late surge in preferences from an outer suburban district and it's now being predicted as a likely retain for the opposition.

'But what is even more baffling, we have been told the seat of Melbourne, the prime minister's own seat, has surprisingly gone to preferences. This is the first time the prime minister has not had an absolute majority since he first won the seat. This result is highly unusual, but I'm still predicting he'll win his seat. The prime minister has secured just under forty-five per cent of the primary vote and that should see him win on preferences, but I'm advised the preference trend is going away from the government.'

'What does that mean?' Cassandra asked.

'It could mean if it continues to favour the independent, no matter the national result, we could have a new prime minister. We just don't know from which party just yet.'

Rogers raised an eyebrow, smiled, and turned to Bruce. 'Would you put your hand up, Meredith Bruce?'

'I would seek advice from my colleagues, but this is way too early to predict. I have heard from our scrutineers, and I remain confident the prime minister will be returned.' Bruce was troubled, quickly jumping on to her phone to seek clarification of the current position.

'I think he's gone,' said Messenger. 'There is a strong independent candidate in Melbourne—'

'Who you sacked,' interrupted Smythe.

'—who we disendorsed over comments she made contrary to our policy. She ran a strong campaign and if she wins, she'll be a very good member for the local community.'

'She's a racist,' snapped Smythe.

'She is an Indian immigrant with an African heritage – how can she be racist?'

'She said students were ripping off the country. Her

comments focused on Indian students,' added Smythe. 'She implied new immigrants from the sub-continent were ripping off government programs and by making these untrue allegations, tarnishes an entire race of people; therefore, she's a racist.'

'Can you actually hear yourself?' Messenger shook his head. 'Jaya Rukhmani is a university professor and said students signing up for her classes were not attending. How does that make her racist?' asked Messenger. 'This is typical of any social debate within Australia, those with a different view are shouted down with this ridiculous political correctness using terms such as racist.'

'What is your view, James Harper?' Cassandra wanted to move the discussion on.

'I think Australians will have a new prime minister in the morning, either Peter Stanley or an empty chair from the current government.'

Midnight came and went. The electoral commission announced they would stop counting at one, advising a clearer result may be determined by then. Anita chose to ring Robert Wong for an update of the count in Melbourne, but when he connected, she had trouble hearing him from the noise in the background. 'Tell me again, I couldn't hear you. What was the result?'

'Rukhmani fifty-one per cent two-party preferred. She did it. The professor won!'

Wolff struck a lonely figure as he walked from his hotel in Collins Street looking for a late-night cafe. He knew Pellegrini's in Bourke Street would still be open and there was always the casino, but his preference was for pasta, and he didn't want to push and shove among drunks on Southbank. Grossi's was closed but a few diners could be seen in a celebratory mood as he passed the dining room. Before he entered the cafe, he took a call from Jameson. 'What did I tell you? I said we would win.'

'That move to cut off Gerrard was brilliant, but I preferred Stanley as prime minister. Now, at this stage at least, we don't have anyone.'

'You can still get him, but you also told me that under no circumstances did you want Gerrard as prime minister. I delivered you what you wanted, yet again,' said a chuffed Wolff chuckling silently, walking to the kerb, and looking out on the traffic moving slowly past. 'What deal you do now with the new prime minister is entirely up to you, but I would encourage you not to support Bruce to stand. She's not ready and could be problematic for you.'

'We will have to think about it. This is not what I wanted.'

'You said you didn't want Gerrard as prime minister.'

'Yes, but I also wanted a clear result, not this rubbish we are likely to have now. A hung parliament is not what I asked for.'

Wolff sharply turned and focused on the discussion, changing the tone. 'I delivered what I promised so I expect my money will be transferred overnight.'

'I will wait until I see who forms government.'

'That is not our agreement, and you know I'm a stickler for doing what is promised.'

'You promised a change of government.'

'No, Mr Jameson, I promised a change of prime minister.'

'We will wait.'

'Mr Jameson, I'm sorry to have to tell you this, but as you know I have certain capabilities that you have used to your benefit over the years.'

'And you have been adequately rewarded.'

'I also have other attributes that can be used effectively to get what I want, as you well know. So, if I say I want my money transferred tonight, that means do not delay. Otherwise, sir, I can absolutely assure you I will be on the first flight in the morning, and I will meet with you face to face. I promise you; it will not be a pleasant breakfast.'

'I only want to know who wins before I pay.'

'That is not my problem. I got the result you wanted and now unless I have my money, you will not benefit from my win.' Wolff tightened his lips and lowered his voice, adding a shroud of dark menace. 'Are we clear?'

Jameson didn't respond and Wolff checked his phone to see if he was still connected.

'Are we fucking clear, old man?' Wolff yelled into the phone.

'I will transfer it within five minutes.'

Wolff quickly relaxed and said gently, 'Thank you, Mr Jameson. It's a pleasure doing business with you.'

Tony Hancock took the call at his desk as he was setting out the front-page layout, unsure whether to claim a Stanley victory or a huge election stuff-up. 'Hello, it's Tony.'

'It's Jameson. We have ended our arrangement with Wolff. I have transferred the contract amount and the agreed bonus to him. Get the invoices out to the others.'

'I'm onto it, anything else?'

'Run the Wolff piece your girl wrote.'

'Are you sure? Gerrard is gone, why would we want to upset the apple cart? We have what we want, why expose him now?'

'Run it.' Jameson snapped as he finished the call.

Hancock dropped the phone onto his desk and pondered what to do. He looked out into the design room and saw editor Peter Cleaver in an animated discussion with his sub-editors. 'Hey, Pete?' yelled Hancock. Cleaver stopped his discussion and slowly walked to Hancock. 'Run the Stanley campaign operative story in the next edition as a feature linking it to the win, and let's go with a Stanley victory headline.'

CHAPTER
26

SUNDAY

Admiralty House, the Sydney residence of the prime minister, seemed unresponsive as Miles Fisher approached the front portico keen to talk to his boss about what to do. The government didn't win, nor did it lose; it was a tie. An independent had won the deciding seat and would hold the balance of power to determine who would form government. There was no-one about the grounds other than formidable security by the front gate and his heavy knocking on the front door brought no response.

Fisher walked through the rose garden to the small administration block where he met Gerrard's housekeeper who directed him to the pool where he would find the prime minister. He quickly skipped along the cobbled footpath, past the freshly trimmed hedgerow to the pool where he found Gerrard sprawled asleep on a lounge, a bottle of brandy lying beside him. He coughed as he approached, disturbing the prime minister.

Gerrard looked up and shielded his eyes from the sun. 'What the fuck do you want?'

'Prime Minister, I need you to get changed and ready for a media conference in ninety minutes. You have to make a statement about the election.'

'I don't have to do a damn thing.'

'The media are waiting. They want to know what you're going to do.'

'Miles, my sweet little darling, I'm not going to do a damn thing,' said Gerrard as he picked up the bottle, uncorked it with his teeth and took a generous swig. 'Not my government anymore.'

'You are the prime minister, and the nation needs to hear from you.'

'They should've thought of that before casting their fucking vote,' snarled Gerrard. 'I'm not their prime minister anymore.'

'We need to negotiate a resolution as to who will form government.'

'Don't care, so piss off, will you.'

'Prime Minister, this is a very serious predicament, and you need to pull yourself together,' pleaded Fisher. 'The country has no leader, and it needs to hear from you.'

'I've been prime minister for almost two fucking decades.

I've done all I could to make them proud, and this is what they do to me. I will not be saying anything to anyone as I'm no longer their leader and I'm no longer a member of the fucking commonwealth parliament,' sighed Gerrard. 'The ungrateful fucking morons.'

'Prime Minster, please. I implore you – we need you to say something.'

'Let me say two words that will allow you to clearly understand my position. Fuck off!' barked Gerrard.

'It's Peter Stanley,' said Robert Wong, passing the phone to Jaya.

'Hello Mr Stanley, how can I help?'

'Congratulations on a great victory, Jaya, your win in Melbourne created history.'

'It was a good result, wasn't it? I have many people to thank.'

'Jaya, you worked really hard. We are very proud of you.'

'Proud of me?' queried Jaya. 'That's funny. You weren't so proud of me a few weeks back when you sacked me.'

'Jaya, you have to understand, the party could not sanction the things you were saying,' a contrite Stanley explained.

'Your people gave me the original speech and asked me to deliver it word for word, which I did, and that speech started it all,' said Jaya. 'What do you mean you could not sanction what I said?'

'I'm not sure I know who would have given you the speech,' a confused Stanley responded. 'Are you sure it was from us?'

'Hmm, let me think – your head office email account was used to send it to us. Is that good enough for you?'

'You don't need to be like that, please Jaya, you are a member of the commonwealth parliament now.'

'What's that supposed to mean?'

'There are different standards we have to adhere to.'

'You're kidding me?' snapped Jaya. 'Standards? You people have none!'

'This is all part of the political process; let's not get personal. We all need each other.'

'After you set me up, you publicly treat me like a racist. Now you don't want me to take it personally being called a racist by the party that gladly endorsed, then sacked me. You never called me to talk to me about it. You created a shitstorm for me at my university, threatening my tenure, and now you want me to calm down?' snapped Jaya, thinking about what more to say, then changing her mind before softly adding with a heavy sigh. 'What do you want?'

'I want to talk about forming government. You have the deciding vote.'

Jaya's jaw dropped in disbelief. 'So now you need me? What irony.'

'Gerrard has not made a statement and I need to advise the media if I am able to form government. If you can let me know what you are thinking, I would appreciate it.'

'I'll tell you what I am thinking, Stanley,' growled Jaya. 'Under my current thinking, you will never be prime minister.' Jaya winked at Wong.

'What do you want?'

'Already you are trying to buy me?' responded Jaya sarcastically. 'What type of person do you take me for? Do you think you can buy my vote? I'm not like the rest of you − thank God.'

'Amen to that,' Stanley immediately said, then slowly added. 'I'm sorry if I disrespected you, but the country needs leadership right now and you are the king maker.'

'Well, rather than you trying to convince me, I think I'm more than capable to make a decision and that's what I will do later today after the electoral commission finalises the vote. I will call a media conference and announce who I will be supporting once I discuss my options with my advisers.'

'There is nothing you need?'

'There is plenty I need, but you won't be giving it to me.'

'Will you let me know your decision before your media conference?'

'No, why the hell should I?' snapped Jaya. 'Goodbye, Mr Stanley, look for my answer in the media.' She ended the call and tossed the phone on some papers on her desk.

'You go, girl!' smiled an admiring Wong, his feet resting among a stack of papers on the desk.

Jaya smirked at her campaign manager, wearily shaking her head. 'Well, you got me into this mess Robert, no-one expected us to win,' said Jaya as she gazed at Wong. 'I'm now a federal member of parliament with the balance of power. What do you suggest I do?'

'I suppose the first thing we should do is find out what we can do,' said Wong. 'I mean, what does the balance of power even mean?'

'It means the government needs my vote to get legislation passed. I have to decide who is going to be government. Do we stay with Gerrard's mob and their experience, or do we give it to the inexperienced Stanley who sacked us?'

'Who do you trust more than anyone, who could give you the advice you need to make a decision?'

'I have no-one, that's my trouble,' sighed Jaya. 'Perhaps a parliamentary officer, the governor, I met her once. Politicians are a little too biased and our campaign guru is nowhere to be seen. So, who? It seems like it's just you and me.'

'Who are you favouring?'

'Stanley is utterly hopeless, so if it were a choice between him and Gerrard, it would be a no-brainer, Gerrard would be my choice. But now he's gone, I have no idea who will lead in his place. So, both parties are at the same level.'

'Who will give you the policy outcomes you want?'

'But you see, Robert, this is the trouble with the dilemma I'm faced with,' said Jaya as she sat forward, resting her forearms on her knees, and wringing her hands together. 'If I were to favour one party over the other because of what they offered me, I would be a political fraud. I'd just be one of them and I promised I would be different. I would rather judge them on their legislative agenda and let my promised private member's bill on the immigration matters be judged on its merits.'

'If you are not going to ask for anything in return for your support that means you are probably the only independent who is truly independent, ever.'

'I suspect it will be a tremendous burden.'

'And dreadfully taxing on you, your career and your friends. I'd hate to be you.'

'Yeah,' smiled Jaya as she looked up at her student. 'I've been meaning to ask – do you want to join me?'

The Hancock Media Melbourne offices were located in the office towers by the casino on Southbank. It now made perfect sense to Anita given the covert business links she discovered between Hancock and Jameson. She had arrived at the office early in the afternoon to try and get an opinion piece completed for the next day's morning edition and work the phone to confirm which party would form the next government.

Speculation had not allayed since the tied result was confirmed by the electoral commission early in the afternoon, and the independent Jaya Rukhmani was yet to announce which party she would support in government. A press release announced a four o'clock media conference to announce who she would be supporting.

Gerrard was refusing to appear before the media, and she

couldn't blame him. After a long political career with almost twenty years as prime minister, it must be shattering for his ego to have lost government and his own seat in the process, she mused.

She was taken completely by surprise to have her feature article about the Stanley campaign operative printed. She was yet to learn from her editor why the change of heart about her column and considered many options as to why. It was a blistering exposé of Sinclair-Browne, suggesting a new trend in political campaigning being taken out of the hands of politicians and transferred to furtive public opinion manipulators. She wasn't happy with the positioning of the column away from the reporting of the election result, but she was pleased it exposed the tactics of the Stanley campaign.

The covert manipulation of the political system she had discovered needed spotlighting, she felt, and she hoped it would provide salient lessons for the community to be more aware of the dark art of political campaigning. The use of specialised campaign groups was not a new strategy – social media campaigns had been successfully organised and operated by so-called independent community groups and lobbyists in the past, but this was the first time an operative strategically managed an entire campaign for a political party.

Anita was now convinced the people had little say in government policy. Their vote was important in deciding who would ultimately govern, but governments seemed to be increasingly manipulated to obtain an outcome for whatever special interest group had the greatest voice and impact in the campaign. The unions, the business groups, environmental groups, and even regional organisations forced their way on to the political stage to influence government policy and funding decisions.

She assumed her story would have ramifications during the examination of the election result and hoped questions would be raised on seeking assurances of greater transparency during future election campaigns, as well as restricting spurious community groups that claimed to be independent from acting as front groups for other political organisations.

Politics in its purest form excited her, but she was saddened by what she had discovered during the campaign. The vengeance of Harper, the manipulation of Jaya, and Barton's big lie were blatant examples of covert politics manipulating public opinion – and added to her disappointment. What caused her more angst than her loss of respect for the political process was the blatant cover up and editorial control of her boss toward her opinion columns. She even wondered if the story on the campaign operative was just another manipulation by Hancock to achieve a political outcome.

'Cleave, what line do you want me to take in this editorial?' Anita had called her editor seeking support. 'Who do you think will form government?'

'I have no idea, sweetheart, and to be frank, I really don't care.'

'Can you tell me why my opinion piece on the campaign

operative with the Stanley campaign got a run today – why didn't you tell me?'

'It was a late decision; I pulled a story and needed a filler and thought it was a good discussion piece.' Cleaver avoided letting her know the true reason.

'Will the others get a run?'

'Not sure they will; the boss doesn't support them.'

'What am I doing here, Cleave? What's the point?'

'Anita, it's been a torrid few weeks in politics for everyone. You have been doing a fantastic job and I'm very proud of the work you have done for me. I wouldn't be making any snap decisions about the future.'

'Will I be promoted to television?'

'I don't know.'

'I've done everything I was asked to do and then some,' moaned Anita.

'I agree, but I can't tell you anything – I just don't know.'

'Why am I suddenly out in the cold?'

'Hancock makes the decisions, you know that.'

Anita screwed her face, frustrated with the response from her boss. 'It's to do with the Mercantiles, isn't it? I'm too close to exposing them,' snapped Anita, thrusting her hand through her hair. 'Hancock should have nothing to fear. Surely, he is smart enough to know if he helps my career, I have a conflict of interest and wouldn't do anything to hurt him.'

'I don't know,' Cleaver softly said. 'Listen, just get the editorial done and then take the rest of the week off.'

'Who do I declare the winner?'

'Call it a draw and recap on the best and worst of the campaign. That should be enough until we actually know.'

'I'll fly home to Canberra tomorrow and come see you.'

'Don't stress, it'll all be okay.'

'Yeah, then why do I feel like it won't be?'

'Anita, listen. You're making this bigger than it really is. You've done a great job and so what if we don't use all your stuff. We haven't in the past, you know that. There's no point in getting yourself tied in knots about this.'

She slumped her head into her hands. 'I guess you're right, Cleave. We got some good stuff out there and I'm pleased the way it went.'

'Write the column and get it to me as soon as you can.'

'Thanks, Cleave. See you.'

She dropped her phone to the desk, slumped back into her chair and looked to the ceiling. She was anxious and felt a dull ache within her. She began to question her future and felt a need to get away from the Hancock media.

Brereton's advice unexpectedly filtered back to her; she didn't want to be Hancock's captive. Maybe she needed to get away from the media totally, or go overseas, or start a new career. Policy always interested her, as would working for a minister. Most of them could do with improved media advice.

Sitting up, Anita chuckled as she considered the thought of working for Peter Stanley. Nothing she could ever do would improve his status, yet here he is, perhaps just a media conference away from being announced prime minister.

She opened her computer and went to a new document,

typed a suggested headline, and then looked at the blank screen for the next thirty minutes thinking about what to say. Fingers hovered above her keyboard waiting for journalistic inspiration and then fell away, frustrated at the lack of enthusiasm.

Anita's timer disturbed her, reminding her the four o'clock media conference was about to start so she moved to a room with a television to watch the anointing of the new government. She was impressed with Jaya's manner and noted her increased confidence as she waited for the media to finally settle down before she began. Jaya was dressed in a traditional sari, which Anita assumed was a deliberate statement about her history. She liked the symbolism – a confident woman about to announce a new government.

'Good evening, and thank you for coming,' Jaya began reading her speech. 'Australia has voted for a government yet the result of who will lead that government for the next five years has yet to be decided.

'I am a political novice of little consequence, some fifteen hours after being announced as the new member for Melbourne. I have been given the task of determining who should lead us for the next five years and under what circumstances that decision will be made – no easy task for someone so junior.'

She paused for a moment and then looked at the television cameras before her. 'I would like to take this opportunity to thank the previous member for Melbourne, Andrew Gerrard, for his long service to the local community. I can assure him his hard work will not be forgotten by the people of Melbourne and I will ensure his legacy is remembered.'

Anita thought it odd she would only refer to Gerrard as the local member and not prime minister. Perhaps she truly was focused on her electorate and not concerned with the disquiet of the nation seeking a result.

'Democracy is not perfect. It's hard work, but as a community we must stand for what is right and vote for the people who we trust and can best represent us. I have been elected to represent the people of Melbourne and I promise them I will work hard on their behalf and represent their views to the national parliament. I will raise their issues and I will fight as best I can to ensure they reach their ambitions for a community that cares and shares for each other.

'To be elected a member of parliament is a great privilege and it is an honour for me to be able to be the first Indian migrant to be elected to the Australian parliament. I take this honour very seriously and will ensure my decisions in the parliament will benefit the people of my electorate.

'But—' Jaya suddenly stopped talking, stepped back from the lectern and then forward again to fidget with her papers. 'I am placed in an invidious position where I alone have to decide who should form government. This is entirely unfair for any member of parliament, especially a novice like me. Clearly this decision and task should not be mine alone for I have little experience as a parliamentarian to draw upon to make such a momentous decision.

'Yet such is the democratic process I now have to make that decision.

'I give fair warning that I will only support the government on supply bills. This does not mean expenditure bills – only supply – and I will also support them on matters of confidence. For all other legislation, I will consider my electorate first and my country second. If it is good for my constituents, then I will consider it will be good for all Australians. But if my electorate rails against any government decision, policy, or legislation, I can assure you, I will not be supporting it.

'I have made this decision about who to support in government after speaking with Meredith Bruce from the government and Peter Stanley, the leader of the opposition. Both advocated a compelling case and I'm respectful of their arguments. Both offered me an open list of requests to be satisfied by them should either of them form government.'

Jaya paused for a moment as she looked directly into the cameras. 'I rejected both offers.' Anita was confused; surely a politician in this position can and should ask and get whatever she wanted.

'I rejected the offers principally because power should not be bargained. Power should be won through the quality of the argument, not the largesse of the treasure chest of government. I also thought that if I could be bought by an incoming government then I would only ever be negotiating price the next time there was an important decision or policy negotiation.

'So, I have rejected all offers and therefore I will not be placing a price on my vote. Rather, I will be evaluating the quality of the policy and legislation and voting accordingly.

'I listened very carefully to the government, and I'm convinced they have the policies and experience to run the country.'

The decision didn't surprise Anita; she was expecting it and stood from her chair, prepared to return to her desk to write the story. The Mercantiles had rid themselves of Gerrard now, but they maintain their government links – a win-win for them. What a surprise.

'The government clearly has many polices that benefit many Australians. They also have policies, which in my view, they should have taken greater care with such as protecting our borders. I point to their immigration laws as an example of their policy failure in meeting community expectations. Having sound policies and experience should not guarantee the government benches.'

Anita suddenly stopped and paid more attention.

'I want to see change in so many policy areas. I want improved immigration laws, increased tertiary education funding, and I want a real effort in primary health care. I want the community to benefit from government not just the special interest groups and those wishing to take advantage of the Australian community.

'These are the issues my constituents told me during my campaign, and they have sent me to Canberra to provide those outcomes on their behalf. These are my priority issues and I have decided to support the party I think is best placed to provide these improvements and outcomes.'

Anita walked back to the television. Hands on hips, she waited for the announcement.

'I therefore consider a Stanley government will deliver the needs of my constituents. For this reason, I will support Peter Stanley as the next prime minister. I call upon him to visit the governor-general and ask her permission to form government with a letter from me providing him with the numbers to do so.'

Anita placed her hand over her mouth as her eyes transfixed on a smiling Jaya. She could hear a distant shout and heard a few telephones begin to ring. The media group at the press conference erupted with questions, but Jaya waved them away. Protected by Robert Wong, she moved from the room.

A stunning political performance, Anita considered it strong and forceful leadership, which was rare and sadly needed in the parliament. The strong message she got from this very raw political novice was not to compromise your values but to remain true to your beliefs. A timely reminder for her too.

Just a few short weeks ago she was happily investigating the machinations of parliament, trying to understand the reasons and motivation for specific legislation. She had found wrong deeds being perpetrated by politicians and discovered systemic failures when the politics of good policy were trashed, and dutifully reported on them. Her own happiness included a blossoming romance, and she was looking forward to the future.

Now, just a few weeks later, she felt she had lost everything. Her whole world had been turned upside down and she had witnessed some horrible politics, exposing ugly people. An empty dread slowly enveloped her.

When she returned to her desk, Anita tried to begin a column but couldn't frame the words. She deleted one attempt after the other as she tried to find the right narrative, struggling to identify anything the conservatives had said during the campaign that would be worthy of a new direction for the nation.

The election campaign had been vacuous. Swamped by the immigration debate, the violence and racism of the street demonstrations had exposed an ugly underbelly projecting racial tension and conflict. She didn't know what to write and was too saddened by it all.

Forty-five minutes before her deadline, she had only cobbled together five hundred of the three thousand words she needed. She felt overcome with exhaustion from the effort of writing about something she didn't totally respect anymore. She had been exposed to the dark side of politics – the one not many knew or even cared about – and she didn't know how to respond.

Should she cynically accept it like Brereton had done and lose her identity doing what she is told to do? Or should she continue to fight the darkness by trying to shine a light on the nefarious activities of the political system?

Her phone buzzed and when she saw caller ID, anxiety hit her hard. She questioned if she should answer it. Finally, she pushed the accept tab. 'Congratulations, you must be very pleased with yourself.'

'Actually, I don't know what to think. It's been a whirlwind for a couple of hours.' Messenger was clearly anxious. 'How are you?'

'Oh, I'm fine. I'm struggling to put a story together about the new government, but I'm fine.'

'I've missed you.' Anita didn't respond. Finally, Messenger asked, 'Are we okay?'

'I'm not sure,' Anita quickly whispered, touching her eyebrow.

'What have I done; can you tell me?'

Anita thought about her response, and she struggled to find an answer. 'Bart, I'm just a little bruised by the whole campaign. It's not what I expected.'

'It's politics.'

'No, it's not.' Anita countered. 'This drive for power, dumping on everything that gets in the way to achieve it – it's ugly.'

'It's what we have to do to get the votes. As I said, it's only politics.'

'You think the public wants the ugliness?'

'They don't know what goes on. They vote for the team they think will benefit them the most. As I said before, it's all about self-interest.'

'So, the people get ignored.'

'Politics is never about the people. It's about those few who live in marginal seats and what they think. We talk to them and hopefully they vote for us.'

'So, the big lie you claimed was just a message for a few people in some marginal electorates. You don't care about the damage you've done to the country.'

'There was no damage to the country,' insisted Messenger. 'There has been a change of government, and sure there will be challenges over the next five years, but we are up for the challenge.'

'You take no responsibility for the damage in Melbourne?'

'We put a view out there, and whether it was right or not, it was up to Gerrard to deny it and he never did,' protested Messenger, then he paused. 'Hey, let's not get into this now. How about we have dinner tonight?'

Anita thought about the offer, smiled, and said, 'I don't think so, Bart.'

'Are you okay?' asked Messenger, a little surprised. 'What's up?'

'You know something?' Anita replied. 'You are part of the political pack, and I was always wary about getting involved with you – but we did, and I was really happy for a while. But then you went and spoiled it by spinning this incredible lie, which you knew to be wrong, but you still did it. Now I actually regret ever being involved with you.'

'Anita please, can't we talk about this?'

'No. Goodbye, Bart.' Anita ended the call. Dropping her phone, it clattered onto her keyboard. She began to weep.

The phone buzzed again, stopped, and then buzzed again. Her tears flowed a little longer.

When she had emptied her sadness, Anita sat back in her chair, looked at her screen and deleted the work she had struggled to write. She then opened a new email, addressing it to the editor of the *Political News*, the independent web-based political service specialising in government reporting that promoted increased transparency within the political process.

She attached all the files she had written during the election campaign; the ones Hancock did not want published and all her notes. She wrote a quick memo outlining the stories, pointing out the connections between Hancock and the Mercantiles. She pointed to the international connections and directed them to her research. She also outlined the manipulation of the campaign strategy to get Gerrard terminated from his seat of Melbourne. It was a grand conspiracy and Anita was convinced it should be exposed – it just wasn't going to be her.

Her finger hovered over the send button.

If she pushed the button, her media career was over; Hancock would see to that. Her opportunities within politics would no longer exist. She would be tainted and no-one in government or the parliament would want her. She understood the ethics she had fought so hard to uphold when she worked in the parliament would be trashed and there was no place for her – if she pushed the button.

The political caravan moves on very quickly. Whoever is popular one day can be quickly thrown aside the next by a comment, an out-of-place suggestion, or an election. The public does not suffer fools and there is nothing more foolish than a politician trying to regain relevance.

Cynicism is a skill that helps insiders in the dance of politics. Combine cynicism and a thick skin to deflect the constant barrage of negativity and it is little wonder too few choose to join the caravan. Anita pondered if her ethical reputation would help her, or not. Perhaps she needed to accept being cast adrift from the moving monolith of federal politics. If she were to remain, she would need to be an outsider. There was nothing left for her in the media and she no doubt would be treated as a pariah by politicians.

Perhaps Jaya would give her a job; two outsiders working together for the betterment of parliamentary standards and principles. It was an interesting thought. Jaya might need help finding her way around the protocols and expectations of the parliament. There was no doubt she would be bombarded with demands by a variety of lobbyists and special interest groups seeking legislative support. She would also have enormous challenges within her electorate who had had an absent member for over two decades. Perhaps there was opportunity for her after all. She decided to make the call to the new member tomorrow.

She pressed send.

Anita watched the screen pass her email through the system and took a heavy breath before slowly freeing herself of the anxiety she had collected. Strangely, she felt an immediate relief and quickly collected her things to leave the building. She needed fresh air and time to think about the future – and close the door to her past. A walk to her hotel would be the perfect remedy to the malaise that had shrouded her for most of the afternoon.

The Melbourne twilight was in its last stages and the balmy evening had drawn plenty of people out to celebrate the Christmas season of joy and goodwill. Such a paradox to the previous day's change of government. Political careers were ending and some, like Bart's, were just beginning.

Life just goes on – no-one cares about a change of government and the likely transformation of a safe and settled national political environment to one of intense scrutiny and possible chaos as the new government settles in. Maybe her worries about the Mercantiles were exaggerated; maybe her priorities and the angst she felt about the political system were not shared by others.

Rather than cross the river and walk past Flinders Street Station, Anita decided to take a little longer and stroll along the river, past the rowing sheds toward the sports precinct before crossing the river at Swan Street. She would then head back to the city along the river and eventually to her hotel in Collins Street. Joggers and cyclists were active along the path and families who had come for an evening barbeque were packing up and preparing to go home.

The evening air and the distance from politics was clearing her head. As she watched the local families, she thought about what the future might bring her. By the time she reached the Swan Street Bridge she was feeling a little better. She stopped halfway across the bridge and looked back toward the city, the dark towers silhouetted against the orange, grey and blue twilight sky. A more positive future seemed to be beckoning her and she felt good to be ridding herself of the shrouding blanket of the past.

As she crossed the river, she had no regrets about ending her media career. Anita smiled as she admired the reflections of the city in the water, wondering at the little things in life, complete in the moment. Perhaps this great city of Melbourne was indeed a city she could get used to.

Stepping down on to the gravel path leading back to the city, she became even more certain about her future. She would call Jaya, and yes, she would call Barton when she returned to the hotel, perhaps there was still time for dinner. She watched as couples walked by, arm in arm, an older couple holding hands. She smiled at the thought of them.

As the last of the sun flickered through the tree canopy, she started to look forward to dinner with Barton. Her increasing joy washed over her face, brightening it in a smile not seen for weeks during the campaign. The gravel crunched under her feet as she quickened her step even further; she wanted to get to the hotel, freshen up and make the call.

Suddenly, a bald man dressed in black appeared some twenty metres ahead, blocking her path. It was only a shadowed outline, but her renewed enthusiasm fell from her. She slowed as she recognised him, a sudden urge to run rushed through her. Panic gripped her. Her breathing halted and she almost slipped on the gravel.

She looked about for others to help, but the path was momentarily quiet. A woman across the river squealed as she was chased by a male friend. Her hand slowly moved to her bag thinking about her phone and where it was amongst the clutter. Her eyes flicked about, wondering what to do, what to say – what did he want?

Her breath quickened and she became rigid, her hands wiped her palms against her trousers. She tightened her shoulders and gripped her bag, greedily gulping in air to calm her, watching, like a startled animal, as the man came before her, a look of nothing on his face – no emotion, just a certain resolve in his eyes.

'I warned you.' The voice was pitched low and menacing.

'Let me pass, I have nothing for you.'

'I said, no more.'

She began to weakly respond with a shake of her head, her throat suddenly dry as she tried to say something.

The punch to her throat was sharp and swift. No-one watching the lonely couple on the path would have seen it. Anita wasn't expecting it. There was little pain, but suddenly she couldn't breathe. Although she dropped her jaw to try and gain air, nothing was flowing into her lungs. Her eyes wide in shock, she collapsed.

The man caught her as she fell to the path and carried her to a tree. Sitting her up carefully against it, he arranged her as if she was enjoying the sunset. As the life drained from her, he walked away.

No-one noticed.

DID YOU ENJOY THE READ?

Authors thrive and rely on the opinion of readers, and I wonder if you could help?

I would be extremely grateful if you let other readers know what you thought of *Duplicity* by considering leaving an honest review on Amazon or Goodreads or posting a review on your social media including the tag, @852press.

If you would like to communicate with me then please do.

I always respond to emails and enjoy chatting about future projects and seeking opinion about some of the issues raised with my writing.

If you would like to be added to my Advanced Readers list, then please let me know.

readers@richardevans-author.com

Best wishes
Richard Evans

DOOMED

THE THIRD EPISODE OF THE DEMOCRACY TRILOGY.

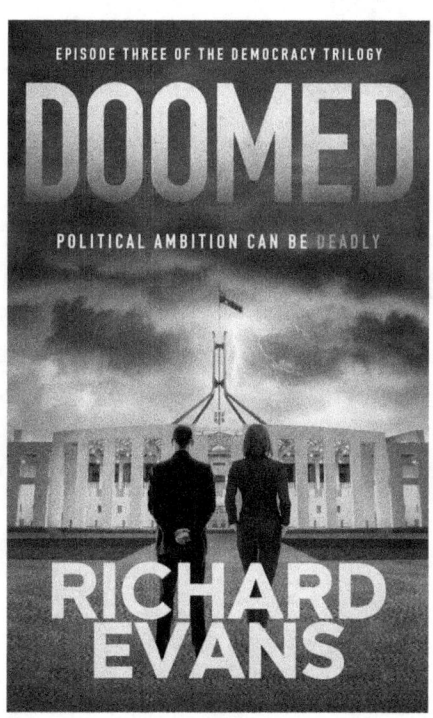

CHAPTER

1

W ords didn't flow intuitively for her; they never have done. She struggled for most of her career to get them out, but always finished her assigned stories on time. The dread of approaching deadlines often helped, as did the prospect of failing her colleagues. Couple this sense of dread with the anxiety of it being found out she wasn't as good as many thought, and stress grew. Perhaps the hype of being the celebrated political journalist at Hancock Media overstated her reputation and talent. She often wondered about that. Did she have the talent? Or did male patronage advance her career?

During lonesome nights, Cassandra Rogers often pondered whether she had sacrificed too much. Her husband gave her up when story deadlines became too much, so he left, taking the children. He gave her the option: the family or the job. It was the wrong time for him to ask because she chose an exclusive interview with the King. She assumed she could charm her way back. She never did. Her teenage children seldom see her now.

She calculated the sacrifice and tears would pay off once promoted to a long-promised national current affairs hosting role. But right now, her dreamy gaze out of her office window interrupted her writing. She was following the billowing sails out on Sydney Harbour, the stiff breeze challenging the yachts proving too fascinating.

'Not much inspiration out there, I reckon.'

Cass didn't respond. She just glanced over her shoulder, then said, 'Get stuffed, Charlie.'

He laughed. 'You can't say that anymore.'

'Say what?' She swung her seat to face him.

'You can't be using harassing language anymore,' he mocked her. 'Your mob changed that years ago.'

'My mob?'

'The sisters doin' it for themselves were always going to overreach and spoil it for everyone.'

'Not a fan of equality, Charlie? Happy with your privileged patriarchy, are you?'

'You see… we just can't talk anymore without being accused of micro aggressions and slagging off each other.'

Cass sniffed. 'Respect is a virtue we all could learn.'

'Respect means nothing amongst this hustle and bustle. You, more than anyone know that. We all want the front page or the lead story on the news.'

'Hustle and bustle?' Her lips turned into a mocking smile. 'Have you done a creative writing course like everyone else?'

His eyes glazed over, then he sighed. 'You know what I mean. Ambitious people eat each other in the newsroom. They aren't majestic lions. More your snarling hyenas.'

'You blokes have had it too good for too long.'

Charlie scoffed. 'And that there, ladies and gentlemen, is the damn problem. Tagging everyone as a predator. This anti-male thing will wear thin, and the backlash will be dramatic.'

'Rubbish; it's been going on for way too long.' Cass crossed her arms over her chest. 'We never called out the sleazy morons amongst us.'

'Yeah, maybe,' said Charlie, his head nodding over and over. 'But the line has moved to the extremes. Everyone seems on edge these days, not knowing what to say anymore.'

'Rubbish.'

'You reckon it's okay to use abusive language?'

'Oh Charlie, it's not about language, it's about power and its misuse.'

'Yeah right, so why is there an increasing culture of fear in workplaces?' He moved away. 'Let me prophecise for one moment; I reckon workplaces will become separated again as they were hundreds of years ago.'

Cass stood, moving towards him. 'Hey, are you going to editorial?'

'I have nothing to say; I've got nothing. My dry run is making me nervous.'

'Don't worry, you'll get a lead soon enough. You always

do.' Cass checked over the cubicle screen to see if others were about, then in a hushed tone asked, 'Do you know why Hancock is coming?'

'Nah.'

'You think he's announcing a certain government appointment?' Cass winked. 'You know what I mean?'

'Harper would never do it. Why would he?'

'Foreign Affairs wants a celebrity in Los Angeles. I suspect Hancock will give them what they want.'

'Those type of consul appointments go to former politicians.'

Cass moved closer. 'I'm looking for a trail.'

'What?' Charlie shook his head. 'Are you mad?' He moved closer. 'Could be a poor career move.'

'Career is going nowhere at the moment.'

'Do a job on Hancock and it'll be over.'

Cass tapped her nose. 'Let's call it karma.'

Charlie moved off. 'I call it madness.'

Cass watched her scruffy colleague wander off before swivelling and returning to her desk, pushing against the chair, and stretching her back. Her camo pants and black t-shirt fitted snuggly as she stretched, touched the toes of her red Dr Martens, and forced her head into her knees before reaching high for the ceiling, then shaking off the movement. She resumed her seat, ignoring the harbour to finish her story for the evening news.

Words now flowed, and thirty minutes later she emailed the editor her revelation of the government's rejection of the

United Nations Climate Council demand for greater action in reducing greenhouse gas emissions in Australia.

She quoted Prime Minister Stanley: *Place your enthusiasm towards India and China before coming to the easily bullied fruit like Australia.* She had no wish to frame Stanley as a moron, but mixing metaphors was dangerous when going on the record.

With a few moments to spare before leaving for the editorial meeting, she mulled over her chat with Charlie. They had fumbled a romance years ago and remained close, sharing struggles with her marriage and his addiction to drugs. The point he made about her career was a little too close to the bone. He knew about her brief liaison almost seventeen years ago with the proprietor, Tony Hancock. She never regretted the relationship and never confessed her enthusiastic participation. But now she remained annoyed by the memory, conceding she might have leveraged her career from the dalliance.

He transferred her to the New York office but became mortified when her engineering fiancé dropped everything to move with her. His lasciviousness for his protégé then dropped off. He redirected his leering gaze to junior staff. Although his energy for office romance shifted to others, he did not put an end to directing and boosting her career.

Now she was Hancock Media's political editor for television and the national newspaper, delivering exclusives, uncovering government scandal, and exposing unwelcome publicity to any wayward politician. As soon as Cassandra Rogers strolled into a government media briefing, ministers fretted about what she might know and how she came to know it.

Notwithstanding her fierce reputation for exposing a political story, she sometimes wondered if her acclaimed position stemmed from patronage or talent. Discovering exclusives was no simple task.

She found what she thought was absolute truth was a shade of truth when a story published proved to be wrong. An impeccable source once told her politics was more about perceptions than reality, and the real dark art of government was to manipulate those perceptions, often leaving truth behind. She could either play the game and bear its scars or she could go write restaurant reviews.

She did what they asked of her, working hard, doing whatever it took to get the story. Cass considered herself a serious journalist, the flirtatious fluff of her youth now long gone. She didn't want to be a celebrity; she wanted respect.

Now the pinnacle of her career, to host the national current affairs show, was within reach. She waited for the nod from Hancock, but the sleepless nights and family regrets didn't make the wait any easier.

A little after four, senior Hancock Media editorial staff assembled in the plush board room, its floor-to-ceiling expansive windows providing a stunning outlook over the towering iconic bridge and the opera house. Whilst Cass enjoyed her own outlook over the harbour five levels down, this view was impressive.

The dishevelled fashion of the assembled editors was typical of the industry, with the solitary necktie worn by an administration manager. The few women who sat around the table were there on merit and wouldn't allow distracting boorish repartee to interfere with their day, let alone their lives. Cass was never comfortable with the shallowness of her male colleagues, detesting their loathsome observations and sarcasm. She sometimes speculated on whether the childish nature ever matured; if this small cabal of colleagues was an example of what women endured in the broader workplace, then there was much work to be done.

She glanced across the table and smiled at Helen Rasminski, raising an eyebrow when loud laughter broke out from the group of blokey colleagues at the other end of the long-polished jarrah table.

Rasminski shook her head, sighing, smirked then asked, 'What's this about, do you know?'

'Not a clue, but it's weird we're all here.'

'Hancock is about to sack us, cut our pay, or maybe announce a new initiative.'

'He's late, as usual,' Cass said, checking the wall clock.

'How's the kids?'

Cass squirmed, shifting in her chair, not wanting to lie. 'They're beaut; I hope to see them next school holidays.'

'Must be hard for you.'

'It's not so bad. I talk to them most days on Zoom.'

'I couldn't do it.'

'Well, I wouldn't be here if I didn't want to be.'

Rasminski smiled, wincing and nodding, then turned away.

The door crashed open, silencing the room, allowing the energy of the charismatic Tony Hancock to sweep in. Editors resumed their seats. He took his place at the head of the table, newspaper staff on one side, television on the other. The most senior closest, with the most junior banished to the opposite end. Cass sat five places down on Hancock's left, facing the enormous windows. He opened his leather folder and lifted several sheets of paper, bouncing them on the table before neatening his stack.

'Gentlemen, thanks for coming up.' Hancock recognised Cass, correcting himself. 'Sorry ladies, thanks as well.'

Cass dismissed it but wondered whether it had been a deliberate slight.

'I've called you here this afternoon because I have a special announcement.' Various colleagues glanced around. 'Yesterday, after thirty-five years, Peter Nicholls paid me a visit and requested he retire.' Hancock chuckled. 'After all this time, an icon of Australian television, greater than Kennedy or Willesee, has requested, and in fact begged, he go enjoy his garden.'

Cass dropped her head, gazing into her interlocked hands, anxious about making eye contact with any colleagues.

'He has agreed to six months' notice, believing I would need all that time to recruit a replacement. He wished us well and hoped our ratings recover.'

A few of the group chuckled.

Hancock waited a few moments, then said, 'We are now in an awkward position of deciding if we have the talent in our newsrooms, or do we go outside, perhaps worldwide, searching for a replacement?'

Anxiety coursing through Cass troubled her breathing as she battled to control her chest, pumping from heavy, rapid breaths. This was it. This was the show she wanted and promised over a decade ago. She sacrificed her marriage and family, but the grand old fart didn't retire when expected, hanging around for another ten miserable years. She peeped at Hancock to read his face and perhaps gain a nod. *Would he now deliver what he guaranteed all those years ago? Had her sacrifice been worth it?*

'We may not take the six months to appoint a new host, but we shall ensure that whoever we select will reflect our values and connect with our audience.' Hancock scanned the room, ignoring Cass. 'Plus, we expect the new host to broaden audience reach and increase revenue. It's our flagship program and we'll ensure we talk to all stakeholders, including you folks.'

Nothing. Cass could read nothing from him, and he didn't cast an eye towards her.

'Questions?'

There was no response. Just a collegiate acceptance of the announcement.

'I'll come see you all, and if you have any recommendations, then I would be happy to receive them. In the meantime, keep doing what you're doing,' Hancock slapped his folder shut, then blurted a little too brashly, 'I'm loving it.'

The grumpy old blokes stood and left with no fuss, while the younger editors had a little chitter-chatter with Hancock on their way out. Cass lingered to share a moment with her boss.

'Cassie, what can I do for you?' Hancock asked. He rocked back in his chair, tapping a pen on his folder.

Cass smiled, stood, and ventured towards him, leaning her weight against the table. 'You recall what you promised?'

'When?'

'You promised me that show.'

Hancock shook his head as if not remembering any conversation.

'You said when Nicholls pulls the pin, you would appoint me to the role.'

'As I just said, Cassie, we will consider all possibles and probables.'

'You said I would be the next host.'

'Not that I recall.'

Cass straightened, glaring at him. 'You promised me.'

Hancock waited a moment, studying her, then said, 'Cassie, we said a lot of things, and we made promises back then. I took you at your word and you changed it by getting married.' He returned her stare.

'You used this job offer to get me into your bed.'

'That's not how I remember it.'

'You bastard,' Cass said, tightening her lips.

'Cassie, I will appoint the position on merit.' Hancock swivelled in his chair, crossing his legs. 'You know it's only ever about merit here.'

'On that basis, announce me as the new host.'

Hancock raised a finger, shaking it. 'Not necessarily.'

Cass shook her head, screwing her face. 'Not happy with my work?'

'Standards have slipped.'

She stepped back, staggered by the comment, gazing out the window to compose herself. 'My standards have slipped?'

'What happened to the skirts?'

She snapped back, facing Hancock. 'Beg your pardon?'

Hancock waved a submissive hand. 'Look, we will treat you just like other candidates, but I can't promise you anything.'

'Will you treat me fairly?'

'Of course. There will be a selection panel appointed.'

Cass stared at him for a moment, her arms crossed. 'What do I have to do to make certain you appoint me?'

Hancock studied her, thinking for a moment. A reflective thin grin crossed his face as he sat forward, then said, 'Just get me political exclusives. You have lost your touch.'

She fisted her hips and stared down at him. 'You want nothing else from me?'

'Noooohoohoohoo,' he said as he smirked and shook his head, crossing his arms tight across his chest. 'Do your job and then we can talk about this gig. You're an important asset to us. You could do the job, but we need to consider the market and what they want.'

'Just make sure it's done under code.'

'Of course, it will be, Cassie. What do you take me for?'

'I know who and what you are, Tony. I just want to make sure I'm not competing with any other... what did you once call me... a distraction?'

'Cassie, it's only ever about merit.'

CHAPTER
2

This was the best time of the day. Dawning light revealing the rolling hills once rich in pasture. The morning mist clinging to the land before being burnt off by the sun yet to rise. The air still, with only a few early riser birds beginning their morning song. No matter the culture, no matter the spiritual connection with the land, it was always at its finest during predawn light before reality squashed the humility of this shared moment with nature.

Tucker Farm had been the benchmark in agribusiness in the region for almost one hundred years. The family didn't waste time meeting standards for beef and wool production; they set higher measures, and their reputation opened doors for them.

Politicians listened. Banks queued to lend money. The industry revered them, bestowing a leadership status the family never sought. Throughout their history, the Tuckers just wanted a secure, sustainable future. They worked the land to produce that prosperity.

Brian Tucker's father was the first to set up a carbon neutralising agenda in cattle country, increasing vegetation and tree management on the vast farm and counterbalancing the farm's carbon footprint with better farming practices. The industry now taught Tucker's methane gas methods in several agribusiness university courses, attracting international interest. Tucker Farm also developed water management practices, bringing a significant change to the biodiversity along the waterways and around the dams dotted over the vast property.

But that was then; now a five-year drought was shredding the once prosperous farm model apart.

Tucker stepped off the expansive homestead veranda and down the stone steps his grandfather quarried, strolling down the slope towards his cattle pens. Ever-alert kelpies trotted in behind his saunter, eager for a little action to start their day. They responded to his calls when needed, a pedigree-line bred for work, no different from their owners.

The forty-two-thousand-hectare farm survived extended periods of drought, but the meticulous historical records showed this one was the most drastic, even harsher than the twelve-year millennium. Tucker managed the property for drought early, sensing a severe rolling weather event when winter rains didn't overflow his twenty-two dams five years earlier. Over time, he reduced his cattle herd to five hundred head and sold off sixty percent of his flock. His pastures were too sparse for grazing, forcing him to ship in feed every two weeks for the last thirteen months at a whopping cost of eighty-six thousand dollars a month.

Tucker's liquidity was falling, pushing him to sell parcels of prized grazing land six months earlier. His financiers were supporting him, along with other farmers in the district, but a recent audit of his accounts showed he would need to reduce his herd and flock even further if he was to see out the drought. Reducing his total cattle live weight kilos meant a significant financial burden, as recovery to a productive herd would be very costly.

Rumours spread throughout the region that Tucker might have to sell everything.

The metal gate chilled him as he laid his crossed arms along the top. To save costs, he had deferred farm maintenance, resulting in the powder-coated metal now showing signs of ageing, flaking rust. He cocked his boot up onto the second rung, gazing out into the paddock where his award-winning bulls mingled. They settled by the stand of Lombardy poplars he planted twenty years ago, some hundred metres away.

'Come on!' he bellowed, waiting for a reaction. Nothing. This time louder and deeper, 'Come on!'

First one bull responded by looking towards him, reluctant to move. Another now moved, and by the time the third call came, they were ambling towards Tucker.

Once a hefty eight hundred and fifty kilos, the bulls still

appeared strong but were closer to six hundred. They moseyed across the paddock, reaching the gate, and waiting a respectful and safe distance, checking the circling dogs and the farmer. Tucker checked his seven prized bulls, looking for any decrease in condition or evidence of salmonellosis diarrhoea. He also studied their eyes, checking for fly infestation and unusual colouring.

Tucker thumbed his hat to the back of his head as he studied his award-winning, money- making machines, speculating when they would be ready for breeding again. He used artificial insemination for his top breeders. His production ratios improved when he kept them apart from the heifers and inseminated at the ripe time. The breeding conversion rate was a significant line of revenue for his farm. With the bulls not producing for the last ten months, it was affecting his income.

'Take 'em back, Blue.'

The older kelpie responded by squeezing under the gate and yapping at the attentive bulls, which pricked their ears and stepped back before turning and trotting to the stand of trees. Blue and his two companions followed, keeping them in order.

Tucker gave a sharp, shrill whistle, scuttling the dogs back to him. He turned away from the gate, tramping to his sheds, jumping into his Mercedes one-tonne pickup. They always left a key in the ignition, and he kicked it into action as his dogs scrambled into the rear tray. Anyone observing the utility could not be sure of the true colour, as the dirt from years of washing neglect caked the duco, making it an unrecognisable red and brown mess.

He gunned the ute uphill towards the dusty dirt road, heading for the sealed bitumen twenty minutes south at Barellan. Once on the bitumen, he mused whether he had time for a hearty breakfast at the Commercial Hotel before tackling the ninety-minute drive to Wagga Wagga. He slowed as he hit the town limits, gliding past the big fourteen-metre tennis racquet statue in honour of Evonne Goolagong, the world champion local tennis player, and then parking outside the pub. He petted his dogs before taking a drinking bucket to the tiny park opposite to fill it with water.

As he placed the bucket in the tray, he snapped a curt instruction to behave, then wandered into the dining room, ordering six sausages with his eggs and hash browns, eating only three and bringing a treat for each of his dogs. It was practically eight o'clock when he hit the road for Wagga.

The Rural Bank had managed the Tucker Farm finances for almost thirty years and promised the family it would never refuse a request when they took the tough decision to shift their accounts. Kevin Tucker wanted a clean break from the big four banks, believing the smaller rural specialists would look after them, and they did. The bank understood the seasonality of farming with the highs and lows of yield and agribusiness demands. It knew the need for fluidity of cash flow. The manager was also aware of the worry and stress of investing capital in farm redevelopment and machinery.

First, Kevin and now Brian valued the bank's understanding of the specifics of cattle and wool production, with its many seasonal variables, and together they forged a solid, rewarding partnership. This partnership helped the Tuckers grow and reject generous offers from large pastoralist companies buying up farms to merge balance sheets of investor companies. The Tuckers were farmers, not business folk. They stuck to what they understood best: cattle and sheep.

Tucker's appointment was for ten o'clock, and he trooped into the Wagga office with fifteen minutes to spare, having had instilled into his life the cliché that if you are five minutes early, you're already five minutes late. Staff directed him to an anteroom, and at a little after ten a woman he hadn't met asked him to join her in her office.

'Where's Jake?'

'Jake?' The woman gestured him to sit as she looped to the other side of the desk. 'Jake retired four weeks ago. They appointed me relief manager and I'm waiting for the announcement of his replacement.'

'He managed our accounts and understood what we could do.'

'What is it you want to do, Mr Tucker?'

Tucker pushed his thumb into the brim of his hat, teasing it back on his head. 'Well, I want rain.'

The woman studied him.

'I'm certain you do; we all do. It would make my job easier, that's for sure.'

Tucker didn't respond straight away, which was his way.

'What's your name?'

'Papadopoulos. Sophie Papadopoulos. I'm managing your account now,' she said, erect in her chair.

Tucker lay back in his seat and crossed his leg, resting his scuffed right boot on his left knee. He removed his hat, draping it on his boot toe. 'What do you know about Tucker Farm?' he asked, unsure why they invited him to Wagga.

'Thanks for coming in. I wanted to meet you,' she said with a broad smile. 'It's rare to meet members of a dynasty.'

Tucker eyed her, waiting.

'Mr Tucker, I can see you are a little nervous. Would you like a drink?'

'I'm not nervous.' Tucker cleared his throat, shifting in his chair, then said, 'Yeah, a tea would be good.'

She picked up the telephone handpiece and pushed a button, making the order.

'Mr Tucker, I have asked you to visit this morning to discuss your intentions and how the bank fits into those plans.'

'Fits into what plans?'

'Your plans.'

'I don't have any plans until rain comes.'

Papadopoulos studied her client, her lips pouting. After a moment, she asked, 'What happens if it doesn't?'

Tucker grimaced.

'If it doesn't rain, Mr Tucker, what are your plans?'

Tucker twirled his hat around his boot, preferring to look at it rather than the bank manager.

'If it doesn't rain soon, Mr Tucker, what do you think we should do with the overdraft we are carrying?'

Tucker glimpsed up. 'Do what you always do.'

'And what's that, Mr Tucker?'

'Add it to our mortgage; we're good for it.'

Papadopoulos waited as a staffer placed a tray of tea on her desk. A cup then poured and passed to Tucker, who took a sip, then another, before placing the cup and saucer on the desk.

'Your mortgage extensions are at capacity.'

'Do whatever you have to do. It'll rain soon.'

'We would like relief on the overdraft and a reduction in the overall debt.'

'What does that mean?'

'We'll keep providing for your family, but the monthly feed cost will need reducing.'

Tucker took in a deep gasp. 'You concede my liquidity is stuffed, don't you?'

'I'm aware.'

'Then why would you ask me to do that?'

'Because my boss in Sydney wants to feel comfortable about the arrangements. A contribution from you may be a shrewd move.'

'Why should he worry? I don't know him.'

'He has bank interests that must be maintained.' She took a sip of tea.

Tucker dropped his head back further, peering down his nose at the manager.

'This drought is placing a lot of pressure on the bank,' she continued. 'Not just you, but most of our rural clients.'

'You are a rural bank and that's expected.'

'Not by our shareholders.'

'I don't understand. What have they got to do with the drought?'

'They lend you the money.'

'You lend me the money.'

'It's shareholder capital we are lending. We are seeing a reduction in our share price, and they aren't thrilled.'

'Everything will be fine when it rains.'

'And if it doesn't?'

'It will. It always does.' Tucker placed his hat back on and shifted from his chair. 'Is that it?'

'No, Mr Tucker, that's not it; please have a seat.'

She opened a leather compendium, tugging a dot-pointed list from her papers and offering it out for him to accept.

'This is a rough estimate of your assets. The second column is a list of your financial obligations to the bank.'

Tucker whistled through his teeth as he studied the list, thumbing his chin.

'We need a reduction in our exposure, and we think you can either sell more property or livestock. The choice is yours.'

Tucker glimpsed up over the paper, frowning at the bank manager.

'You want me to sell?'

'Not everything, just enough to clear a little of the backlog.'

'Are you foreclosing me?'

Papadopoulos smiled. 'No, of course not. We just prefer to reduce our exposure.'

'Your exposure will reduce when it rains.'

'When do you think that might be?'

Tucker screwed the paper into a tight ball without releasing his glare. He lobbed it over to the desk, bouncing it into her lap.

'My family has worked the land for almost a century. Now you want to rip it from us?'

'We don't require your farm, Mr Tucker, we just need our money.'

'You'll get your friggin' money when it rains.'

He stood, towering above her.

'We may need to get it back before then; that's what I'm trying to explain.'

'There's been no problem in the past,' Tucker said.

'The past is the past; a new era exists in banking, which means a different way of doing business.'

'Is that right?' asked Tucker, placing his hands on his hips. 'Well, perhaps I'll take our business someplace else.'

'Yes, please go elsewhere; that would be helpful, but I'm not sure your account risk will be attractive to other banks.'

'You can't treat us like this.'

'You're too geared and we've supported you for too long.'

'Jake would never do this.'

'Could explain his unexpected retirement, don't you think?' Papadopoulos stood, gesturing her hand to the door.

'We want our money and we're happy to discuss better terms with you, but we need to reduce the debt.'

Tucker didn't respond.

'Mr Tucker, please consider what I say. You have two months to decide and make arrangements.'

'Eight weeks? You want your money in eight weeks?'

'It's time to respond or move on to a new venture.'

'You bastard,' Tucker said, frowning.

'Yeah, well…' Papadopoulos said, then sighed. 'If you didn't overcapitalise your herd, you wouldn't be in this position.'

'You gave me the money.'

'Now we want it back.'

CHAPTER
3

'Okay, the next item on the agenda is the drought. Who's leading the discussion?'

'That would be me, Prime Minister,' Barton Messenger said, closing and pushing away the health brief, then opening the next item file from the pile beside him. 'I've consulted extensively and then briefed Jack on this.' Messenger glanced across to the agriculture minister, receiving slight nods encouraging him to continue. 'As the government, there is not much we can do. The affected regions are sourcing stock feed, and whilst the national herd has reduced, it hasn't impacted trade. A relief fund has been established, and the nation seems to be kicking in support, as they often do.'

'The money never gets to the folks who need it,' Wilson Campbell, the regional development minister, interjected.

Messenger glanced over to him and smiled. 'You're right.

I recommend we tighten regulations concerning donations and distribution.'

The prime minister frowned. 'You're not suggesting legislation? We are the party of less government, not more.'

The windowless cabinet room was silent, many of the twenty-three ministers studying Messenger to view his response. There had been unusual tension between the two since the meeting began, with Prime Minister Peter Stanley taking every opportunity to keep his ambitious treasurer in line.

Messenger first glanced at his notes, then frowned at the prime minister. 'No, I'm not suggesting legislation,' he breathed, filling his chest. 'We don't need to over-regulate a severe drought, but we need to act and control the narrative.' He scanned the table, then focused back on Stanley. 'The banks are circling. If one of them gets nervous and moves to foreclose on their loan ledger, then others will come in for the kill. Our farmers will be done over, and communities destroyed.'

'That's an overstatement, wouldn't you say?' the prime minister asked, tossing down his pen and shifting in his chair; he pushed back, crossed his legs, and checked about his ministers for support.

Messenger arched a brow, glancing at his papers, contemplating what he just heard and why Stanley was burning him.

'Prime Minister if I may?' The former leader and foreign minister, James Harper, intervened. 'It seems Bart has the politics right. It frightens folks out on the farms. I suspect city electorates are nervous their country cousins are struggling. Unless we get national leadership on this, it will run out of control in the media.'

'I agree with Jim, Prime Minister,' Christopher Hughes said. 'The media noise will switch to climate change soon. Then the banks. Then it'll move to food security, then water, and then we'll be discussing compensation to the states for desalination plants. If we don't get rain soon, it may shoot our trade balance of payments. This is an enormous political challenge, which may impact the next election.'

'Yeah, and if we lose those regional seats, it stuffs the government, which means the other mob will be back.' Campbell never held back his views. 'Who's to say Gerrard won't stand again and come back as prime minister?'

'He's had enough,' Harper said. 'He lost his seat; he won't be back.'

'He did you over, though, didn't he?' Campbell provoked the former leader.

Harper cleared his throat and shook his head before eyeing Campbell. 'No, you and your mates around this table did that.'

The room fell silent; ministers seemed embarrassed by the claim.

Hughes released a harsh harrumph. 'Look, those things are years ago; no need to go over them now.' He cast a glance towards Harper opposite, smiling.

'We can't afford to lose one seat, otherwise we're back in

opposition.' The prime minister joined the discussion. 'What do we do to control the narrative?'

Messenger waited for a response from a colleague. They offered none. He gripped the arms of his leather chair, lifting himself straight, leaning his forearms onto the jarrah table. 'I think we should have a parliamentary inquiry.'

'What's that going to do?' the prime minister asked.

'I'm surprised you asked.' Messenger cocked his head and Stanley squirmed a little. 'It's second to a Royal Commission, more flexible, allowing quick recommendations.'

Messenger's ministerial colleagues said nothing, waiting to hear more.

'We ask stakeholders to provide submissions and call for the major players to present formal evidence. We get stuck into the banks by backgrounding the media. The inquiry then recommends what we want.'

'That'll be too bloody obvious,' Campbell said. 'We need the other side to help us, and they'll never do it.'

Messenger nodded. 'You're right, Wilson, as always. We need the right recommendations, so we need the opposition's support, but we can't make it obvious.'

'That's what I just said.' Campbell tossed up his hands, falling back into his chair.

'I recommend we appoint the independent member for Melbourne to chair the inquiry.'

'Rubbish. That'll never work,' Jack Stevenson, the agriculture minister, interjected.

'Why is that?' Messenger asked, leaning back, rocking his chair backward and forth.

'Oh, let me think… she's a woman.' Stevenson started numbering off his fingers. 'She lives in the city. She's a humanities professor, she hates us, and she's an immigrant from India.'

'And she's black.' Campbell chimed in, causing several colleagues to wince.

Messenger ignored him.

'Look, I know it's difficult for some of you to come to terms with, but that independent member holds the balance of power that delivers us government. She could switch her vote to the opposition, and we would be stuffed,' Messenger paused for a moment, 'so why not give her a parliamentary title and extra salary with a promotion? She has the academic research rigour to get the evidence we need. She does not have a conflict of interest, and she can open doors others can't. Plus, she can give us the narrative we need, getting us off the front page.'

'Interesting.' Hughes nodded, warming to the idea.

Harper responded, 'You think she has the credibility to be the voice we need?'

'I can assure you, she does. Have you not seen her in the chamber?'

'Any bias amongst all that, Bart?' Stanley teased.

Messenger flicked a quick glance his way. 'She was my politics professor.'

'Nothing else?'

'What are you suggesting?'

'Oh, you know, this place is gossip central.'

Messenger bowed his head then looked across the table. 'Other than helping her with electorate matters, there is nothing untoward between us.'

'When do you think we could get started on this?' Harper shifted the direction of the conversation.

Messenger, still distracted by the prime minister's jibe, turned towards Harper, who was sitting next to Stanley.

'Today, or it would be best to make the announcement tomorrow, setting out the terms of reference.'

Stanley considered Messenger, then asked, 'Okay, does anyone else have a view? If not, who agrees we commence a parliamentary inquiry?'

All hands raised with various levels of enthusiasm.

'Done. What's next?' The prime minister referred to his agenda.

Harper cleared his throat with a cough and opened his presentation folder.

'Prime Minister, I am seeking approval to name the new consulate in Los Angeles. We are seeking to install a person who can open doors for us within the digital communication space. Although the office is based in LA, the appointee will work in San Francisco, focusing on Silicon Valley. This is a two-year sunset appointment and I table my recommendation.'

Ministers flicked through papers to briefing notes, scanning the material.

'Why do we need to specialise and why for two years?' Stanley asked.

'APEC appointed the government to set up a digital broadcasting network for the south-east Asian region. We want to move otherwise our licence will be revoked and turned over to the Chinese. We have eighteen months to source network codes, infrastructure, and security protocols. This is an enormous project needing us to move fast if we are to have access to adequate bandwidths and cloud capacity.'

'What the hell did you just say?' Campbell asked.

Messenger chuckled. Harper smiled at the comment. Stanley waited for an answer.

Harper glimpsed at his notes, then said, 'Unless we secure the right partnerships, we lose management of the network. This means we will not influence content as much as we would want.'

Messenger added, 'This is an important project for us within the region. It will allow us to work with our trading partners, closing the door even further on Europe and the US.'

'Why would we want to do that?' Stanley asked.

'India and China are moving on various economic matters, and we need to leverage broadcasting to protect ourselves against their expansion programs,' Harper said.

'So, is this a security issue? I don't understand,' Campbell asked.

'It is a trade issue. Managing the network will open negotiating doors during trading dialogues; but for us, it remains a high security issue.'

'Who have you recommended for the role?' Stanley asked.

Harper drew a deep breath; conscious colleagues might greet his news with contempt. 'I want to send Tony Hancock.'

The prime minister flopped back into the chair, shaking his head, and blowing out a sigh. Others grumbled to a nearby colleague. Only Hughes seemed to support the idea.

'That's a joke, surely?' Stanley said.

'No, I'm serious.'

'Just because he owns most of the media in the country doesn't mean we should hand him Asia. Anyway, what does he know about digital networks?'

'The very fact he is a media mogul will open doors.'

'He knows all the nerds, does he?' Stanley asked, sniggering.

'Very rich nerds, Prime Minister.' Messenger joined in.

Stanley shook his head again and glanced around at his colleagues. 'Does anyone have a view of this?'

Campbell sat forward. 'Well, with Hancock working for us for two years, it might just help at the next election. He won't be able to influence editorials with his cold-hearted black hand.'

Harper rejected the notion. 'It's not always about politics, Wilson; this is an excellent decision. It's short term and performance based, so he will need to get his skates on.'

'Have you spoken to him about it?' Hughes asked.

'Yes, of course,' Harper nodded.

Hughes cocked his head, nodding, leaning back into his chair.

'Can we defer it? I want to think about it,' Stanley asked.

'We need a decision today, Prime Minister.' Messenger sat forward. 'We have appropriated expenditure and settled on accommodation in San Francisco.'

'You what?' Stanley leaned into the table. 'Money approved before coming to cabinet?'

'We have been waiting on your decision for a few weeks now, Prime Minister,' Harper said. 'You asked us to come to this meeting for a final decision.'

'We need a decision, Prime Minister,' Hughes said.

Stanley shut down, folding his arms across his chest, bowing his head.

After a long pause it was too much for Campbell and he exploded, 'Oh for fuck's sake, Peter, make a damn decision, will you, and let's move on.'

Stanley glanced up at Harper. 'What do you wish to do?'

'I want to appoint Hancock.'

'So be it. Let the cabinet minutes record the recommendation and decision.'

Hughes glanced across the table to Harper, arching an eyebrow and blowing out frustration. Other ministers shared the anxiety in various ways, some whispering sarcastic words to one another.

'What's next?' Stanley moved to the next agenda item.

Hughes straightened, sitting taller, flicking open his brief on the application from the Timor-Leste government to allow citizens to work on offshore rigs in the Timor Sea; a complex, contentious issue, which extended to mining sovereignty rights in the rich gas and oil field.

Ginni Stavloukas, the mining minister, was first to speak.

'Prime Minister, I wonder why Christopher has carriage of this brief rather than my department?'

'You've got your hands full with the coal industry. I wanted Chris to manage this as an industrial relations issue.'

Not impressed with the response, Stavloukas continued, 'The unions are giving me hell at the moment. I don't see your man getting involved in that.'

'Got a thing against men, have ya Gin?' Campbell said, prompting a discourteous stare that shut him up, cutting off his smirk.

'Why aren't you consistent with this policy?' Stavloukas asked.

'I thought I was.' Stanley glanced at Hughes for support, who shrugged. 'Chris is across the brief from his time as industry shadow minister, and I hoped I would save you time.'

'Why?'

'Where are you leading with this, Ginni?' Messenger asked.

'Where am I leading with this? What type of question is that?'

'I just meant; do we need to talk about this now?'

'Yes, we need to talk about this now.' Stavloukas raised her voice. 'Allowing international workers onto our rigs will change the dynamic of the mining industry's labour force. It's not just an industrial relations issue, because it sure as hell affects the entire mining industry.'

Stanley wriggled in his seat as he leaned forward to see Stavloukas at the end of the table, tucked away on his side. 'I just wanted to make it easier for you and lighten your load.'

'Why? Because I'm a woman?' The words hung across the table.

Several colleagues fidgeted, shaking heads.

'You think a woman needs to lighten her load? Is that what you think, Prime Minister? You think a man can lighten a woman's load?'

Messenger gasped, then furiously breathed out.

'You can't make that assertion from what he just said.' Harper came to Stanley's defence.

'You're a man. What do you know about discrimination?'

'Settle down, Ginni; this is not a gender thing.' Stevenson joined the discussion.

'What, you think having someone else do your job, a man, is not a gender thing?'

Stanley dropped his head to his hand, trawling his fingers through his hair. 'What do you want me to do?'

'Start communicating with your ministers for a start. You make these captain calls without talking to the relevant minister too damn often.'

Hughes intervened. 'Look, Ginni. I apologise for agreeing to prepare the brief. I'm happy to pass it back should you think it sensible.'

'I appreciate that offer, Christopher, and will accept it.'

'No, hang on,' Stanley said. 'This is my cabinet and I'll distribute work in the manner I see fit.'

'I have just taken back responsibility for the negotiations over international workers working on our rigs, if that is okay with you?' Stavloukas said with snapping tone.

Hughes looked across at her and smiled. 'I'll get my people to talk to your people. Would you prefer me to finish the brief or would you like to do it?'

Stanley began dissenting, but Stavloukas talked over him.

'You do it.'

Hughes waited for concurrence from the prime minister, glancing back to Stanley, who sat with his mouth agape, nodded, then with a flick of his hand waved Hughes on.

'On the assumption the mining minister will agree, the government recommends an extension to the 457 visas to allow workers from Timor-Leste to be employed on the rigs in the Timor Sea. Australian work conditions will apply, but with a significant difference,' he said.

'Instead of Australian award rates, they'll be offered three times the national wage rate of Timor. This will do two things. One is to step up the production capacity on the rigs and allow an increase in the workforce. The other is to give wealth to workers who will commute from their country and not be connected to Australia.'

'How does this help Australia?' Campbell asked.

Harper sat forward to respond. 'It allows the government to have bargaining leverage when negotiating the maritime borders. In short, my advisers think there will be no appeal from Timor concerning the borders if we allow their workers to man the rigs.'

'Seems a fair thing to do.' Stevenson nodded.

Stavloukas interjected. 'What do you guess will happen when the Indians open the coal mine in the Galilee Basin? They'll prefer to bring their workers in if you do this for Timor.'

'Not sure we should open any new coal mines,' Stanley said. 'At least not until we're re-elected.'

The comment stunned Hughes. 'You want to ban coal mining?'

'The Greens are giving us hell. The UN is insisting we comply. And there is a constant stream of abuse hitting our backbench. We have to do something.'

'That's crap!' Campbell said, slapping the table.

'Ease up, Wilson,' Harper counselled. 'Peter is not suggesting that.'

Harper glanced at Stanley for confirmation, but the prime minister just shrugged, flushing a pained look across his face.

'The union will go ballistic if you even suggest closing any mine,' Stavloukas said.

'India would want compensation from us,' said the finance minister, Helen Cavanaugh.

'The Climate Science Board briefed government the other day, suggesting we act and cease all coal mining,' Maurice Roussett, the environment minister said.

'You can't do this; the Indians will be on the warpath,' said Harper, unaware of his faux pas.

'We are not going to ban mining, are we?' Hughes asked the prime minister.

'It's on the table,' Stanley said.

'Not at this table, I can assure you,' Hughes said, prompting nods from colleagues.

'It's a consideration,' the prime minister said.

'Not if we have to pay liability,' Messenger said. Cavanaugh nodded.

The meeting descended into a vitriolic discussion about the rigour of climate change modelling and the dangerous nature of withholding natural resources from the world. One minister, pointing to history, even suggested a country like China would just come and get it if Australia denied them coal. They ignored the agenda. Further discussion halted when one of the prime minister's staff entered, whispering a reminder of a scheduled briefing. The cabinet then broke when the prime minister scurried away.

As Messenger left the room, leaving Harper and Hughes to caucus views about the meeting, he said, 'This government is going nowhere fast with the current leadership structure. Beware the Ides of March, my friends.'

The two ministers watched him go.

'He's right, you know,' Hughes said.

'A little too ambitious, don't you think?'

'Yes, he is, but his analysis is valid. We may need to ditch Pete.'

CHAPTER

4

The treasurer concluded his answer to the opposition's question on tax rates, prompting the prime minister to replace him at the despatch box.

'Madam Speaker, after another mighty display of unity and competence, I ask that further questions be placed on the notice paper.'

His announcement triggered the House of Representatives to go about its business. The speaker called for presentation of documents, causing the government leader of the House, Christopher Hughes, to move to the despatch box and table documents, including departmental reports, then moved a motion to accept the material.

Ministers sauntered out of the chamber as government members moved off to their offices or to gossip over a coffee at Aussie's Cafe. Opposition members waited for their leader

Meredith Bruce to be called by the speaker to lead the Matter of Public Importance motion, criticising the government's mismanagement of refugee offshore detention centres.

'The question is: that the motion moved by the manager of government business be agreed to; all those of that opinion say aye, the contrary no.'

There was no response from those remaining in the chamber.

'I think the ayes have it,' the speaker said.

Hughes watched the prime minister scurry from the chamber, arms full of files, not wanting to engage in the next debate, and glanced across to James Harper, who was taking his position at the Table of the House and waiting for Bruce.

'I've been thinking about the Ides of March.'

Harper swivelled in his chair, leaning forward to reduce the chance of a curious colleague overhearing.

'What have you come up with?'

The speaker stood, stopping any conversation.

'I have received a letter from the leader of the opposition proposing that a definite Matter of Public Importance be submitted to the House for discussion, namely: the refusal of the government to honour its election promise to stop the people smuggling boats. I call upon those members who approve of the proposed discussion to rise in their places.'

'Hear, hear!' bellowed the opposition backbench as they stood to support their leader.

'I call the leader of the opposition.'

'Maybe we should talk after this,' said Harper, as Bruce stepped to her despatch box.

'Okay, I'll see you at Aussie's for a coffee in half an hour.' Hughes stood and smiled at Bruce as he sauntered out of the chamber.

'Thank you, Madam Speaker, and you will note that those opposite have deserted the government benches for this Matter of Public Importance with even the minister for industrial relations skulking from the chamber too embarrassed to face the truth.'

Hughes turned at the heavy brass and glass door and bowed to the speaker, as was the custom, mouthing a kiss to Bruce.

Harper settled into his seat to listen to Bruce's fifteen minutes; she decried the government's efforts to improve conditions on Ambon following the construction of a detention centre that did not meet Australian standards. She focused on the terrible plight of families with young children and quoted a report from Médecins Sans Frontières suggesting that the mental health of children was at risk. Harper scribbled a few relevant points as Bruce delivered an emotional plea for the government to get active in saving the children. He would have to choose his words thoughtfully in response.

'Finally, Madam Speaker, I ask the minister. What will you do today to save the children? If we have a death, then you will have blood on your hands.'

'Hear, hear.'

'I call the minister for foreign affairs.'

As Harper prepared himself at the despatch box, the chamber emptied, leaving a low-ranking shadow minister at the Table. He thought it ironic that Bruce would plead with the government and yet not stop to hear its response.

'Madam Speaker, passions run high in this place whenever we talk about the desperate lives of refugees caught up in the vile web of deceit and destruction that is the people smuggling trade. But I notice that the opposition leader is no longer in the chamber, having delivered her passionate speech. No doubt she is excitedly talking to the media as I give the government's response to her questions.'

Harper delivered a well-worn response covering the essential government talking points, ensuring those rare folks who might listen to the parliament that the Stanley government was on track with building the second detention centre.

'The Indonesian government has reassured us they will bring all construction to Australian standards.'

Twenty minutes later Harper was sitting with a latte outside Aussie's Café, gossip central of the parliament and the place to see and be seen by those playing the political game. He waited in line for his coffee, then secured an isolated table by the windows, waiting for his colleague. The wooden floors echoed with the shoe heels of rushing advisers always short of time.

Once settled, Harper cast an eye over the huddled suits at nearby tables to find any potential eavesdroppers. He noted a few backbenchers from both parties in discussion with journalists, and others talking policy with various lobbyists, as they often did outside the indoor café. He checked out the window, wondering who was sitting in the sun-bathed courtyard.

He first came to Canberra as policy adviser to a member of parliament, progressing his ambitious career using his boss's numbers against him, challenging his preselection, and securing the safe seat for himself. He had learnt the lesson well over his twenty years' service: never allow staff to manage branch preselection delegates.

He leaned back in his small wooden chair, checked his watch, crossed his legs, and brushed particles of lint from his knee. The television behind him tuned into the chamber, but the volume turned down, and he couldn't quite hear his colleague ripping into the opposition.

A dawdling Hughes acknowledged Harper with a wave, joining the queue for coffee and soon settling in with his colleague.

'Sorry to have kept you; I got held up by Stavloukas.'

'What did the Greek God want?'

'She's a bully, to be honest.'

Harper guffawed. 'That's a joke, surely?'

Hughes beamed. 'She just won't let this Timor thing go.'

'She's under pressure and reckons shifting the goal posts will focus on you rather than stay on her.'

'She's stuffed this whole mining policy.' Hughes sipped his cappuccino, checking over his shoulder for anyone listening. 'I wish Pete would shift her out of the portfolio.'

'You're asking for a miracle. Peter can never make a decision,' Harper said, peering over his glass as he sipped his coffee.

'I think we made a mistake electing him.'

'Ya think?' Harper was still smarting over the way they had ripped the leadership from him before the last election.

Hughes shifted in his seat, peeking over his shoulder again, then leaned forward. 'Look, I acknowledge we may have made a mistake getting rid of you, but we had no choice. You took a leadership vote when you shouldn't have, and we left Peter with the prize,' he paused for a moment, 'but it doesn't mean we can't ever change our mind.' He sat back.

Harper didn't respond. He checked about him to see who was close. 'Are you suggesting what I think you're suggesting?'

'I don't know, but we need to do something. We're getting murdered by Bruce.'

Harper leaned his elbows on the table, steepling his hands, rasping them together as he thought about his colleague's comment. 'You think she'll win?'

'Looks, legs and language,' said Hughes, causing Harper to chuckle. 'She's all-over social media, and the magazines love her. Her idea of changing the tenor of the parliament was brilliant. And we fell for it; at least, Pete did. We have nothing we can do to hurt her. Did you see that outfit she was wearing on the weekend? The media ran stories for days.'

'Politics is not about who looks good.'

'You are kidding me, Jim?' Hughes shook his head. 'It's about perceptions. Bruce is manipulating those perceptions very well. Just look at her polls. How many cover stories can she do? Geezus Christ, she's in the same league as Meghan.'

Harper arched a brow, nodding; he squeezed out his bottom lip, and he pulled at it.

'We need a circuit breaker to change the narrative. That either means policy, or the prime minister has to go,' Hughes said.

Harper smiled. 'You have a way with words, Chris.'

'Look, Jim,' Hughes sat forward, closer to Harper, 'we have a glamour as our competitor, and we have Peter Frumpton as our leader. He ain't showing me the way.'

Harper didn't respond to the joke.

'And frankly, my guitar is gently weeping.'

Harper scoffed and smiled. 'Nice one.'

'No, seriously Jim, we need to do something otherwise we lose the election.'

'He won us government for the first time in almost twenty years. We can't dump a first term prime minister.'

'A drover's dog would have beaten Gerrard,' Hughes said.

'Fact is, we didn't beat him. If he'd won his seat, he'd still be in government.'

'That's the point.' Hughes thrust a finger at him. 'Stanley should have done better.'

He dropped his head into a hand as he studied Harper. After a few moments he said, 'You would have smashed him.'

'Yeah well, shoulda, coulda, woulda.'

'All I'm saying is that it might be time to think about a

strategy for the next election. In the two years we have left, perhaps recast ourselves and focus on policy.'

'Ease up; here comes Rogers.'

The politicians sat back as a beaming Cassandra Rogers sidled up to the table.

'How's it going, boys? Who are you talking about?'

'Hi Cass, what's happening with you?' Hughes smiled. 'Want a seat?'

'Nah, wouldn't be seen dead sitting with a minister in this cesspit of political intrigue,' Cass said as she looked down at them. 'No, I just noticed you were way too serious, which must mean you are about to bone someone.'

'Not really,' Harper said, gazing up at her. 'We're just talking about the next election.'

'You'll be back in opposition so don't worry too much.'

Harper bristled as Hughes lightened the mood. 'You off to military camp or something?'

'Why? You don't think I'm dressed appropriately?' Cass stepped back, looking down at her trousers.

'Well, you're off to camp or you've jumped to the other side,' Hughes said.

'I might as well; not much talent left on this side of the fence.'

'You're yet to have dinner with me,' Hughes said with a boyish grin.

'You're way too old for me, Hughesie. You'd be asleep before the first over.'

'I was a bit of a demon opening bowler once.'

'Yeah, but you're all spin now,' Cass grinned.

'What's happening, Cass?' Harper asked, breaking the banter.

'You tell me. I hear comrade Tony is up for a gig.'

Harper bounced a forefinger off his nose. 'That's news to me.'

'Yeah, I bet. Just fill me in when you decide. That is, if you ever get to make a decision.'

'Fill me in. Yeah, I can do that,' Hughes said.

'You can't say things like that anymore, Chris, you know that.' Cass frowned at him. 'Well, you should know that.'

'Cass, you're old school. So am I.'

'Mate, one day they'll come and get you if you don't modernise yourself. Then your career is dead; trust me.'

Hughes wanted to argue, but a hand resting on his arm from Harper silenced him.

'I could make an announcement soon, so I'll have one of the team call you,' Harper said.

Now uncomfortable with Hughes, Cass stepped away from the table. 'That'll be great. You guys behave now.'

'Sure will,' Hughes said, as she walked away.

'Why do you have to be so provocative?' Harper asked.

'I've fancied her for a long time.'

'You think smart comments like that work for you?'

'Yes.'

Harper raised his eyebrows, wondering if his colleague was serious. He shook his head and smiled. 'You are a dinosaur.'

Hughes watched Cass as she scooted off through the tables and into the corridor leading to the senate side of the building. She was heading off to the press gallery housed on the second floor.

'Yeah, maybe, but she does it for me.'

'Does what?' Harper asked, breaking Hughes' obsessive stare.

'What do you think Messenger is up to?'

'Finish your coffee and let's go ask him,' Harper smiled.

READER REWARD

As the author of this work, I offer you, the reader, the opportunity to redeem a cash award for introducing this work to any literary agent, publisher or producer that offers an acceptable contract Richard Evans for this work. The reward offered is 10% of any initial book advance or option contract for film up to a maximum of AUD $10,000.

Why am I offering a cash reward to readers?

- **Odds:** 98%+ of all works published today initially found their way to a publisher by introduction as opposed to arriving via "the slush pile" so the odds are better doing it this way.
- **Volume:** Writing is an inherently solitary endeavour and as an author I struggle (off the page) to network, mingle, and promote my own work. Offering readers, a reward to do it not only augments my inability but also multiplies the effort as each volume in the hands of reader starts diverse chains of discussion and introduction, one of which will lead to success.
- **Collaboration:** Reading is unique among all entertainment vehicles in that it requires effort from the reader: the author and reader collaborate to tell the story. Hearing what readers enjoy is exciting to any author and the collaboration of this reward program offers the reader a chance to help jump start the career of an author he/she

enjoys. Besides, publishers are much more interested in readers' likes vs. authors' offerings.

Suggestions:

Via this reward, our mutual goal is to introduce this work to literary and publishing professionals or producers. Many are likely familiar with the term *"six degrees of separation,"* the theory that anyone on the planet can be connected to any other person on the planet through a chain of acquaintances that has no more than five intermediaries. This is what I aim to accomplish here with your help.

- Think about who you know in publishing (literary agents, editors, readers, executives, etc.) and pass this volume on to them*.
- Think about who you know and who they might know in publishing.
- Think about who you know that reads and would enjoy this book.

Send any leads, or opportunities, or introductions via the email link below.

rewards@richardevans-author.com

Thank you in advance for your help.

ACKNOWLEDGMENTS

Writing is such a challenging craft and requires resilience, leaving your ego at the door and having a willingness to listen to criticism, then acting on the advice of others who want to help. This project brought together a team of very willing supporters.

Anne and Michael Keaney never lost their passion for my writing and provided valued wisdom during early stages of the writing process. Patty Kavadias always looked forward to reading my first drafts and giving solid feedback and the occasional coffee. Phil Barresi and his fabulous wife Cate were always ready with advice and humour, and my brother Peter enjoyed the unique genre of the book. All these folks provided valuable feedback and support during the process, and I also acknowledge Greg Pelgrave's thoughtful feedback.

The second edition has been enthusiastically developed by 852 Press who enjoy helping Australians tell their story.

Writers Victoria provided a valuable service of manuscript assessment and I encourage any writer serious about getting their story out into the market to first use a similar service. It will help you – trust me.

Thanks to my colleagues at Yarraville writers' group for their patience and enthusiasm displayed toward their own writing. It's an absolute pleasure to learn from you all. For anyone who wants to write, I encourage you to join your local writing group. You may be surprised by what you learn.

Thanks also to the friendly Williamstown locals who give me so much pleasure, who bought my first book, some even reading it! I appreciate the positivity you provide, and I especially want to acknowledge Paul Tyrrell and his wife Denise for their support, spreading the word about the first episode of the Democracy trilogy, Deceit.

I would also like to thank the many readers and fans of the first episode that have contacted me with their positive feedback, and I hope this next installment answers your questions.

Thanks also to my extended family, especially the matriarchs Margaret Ann and Lynne – I appreciate you all for your support. Finally, I thank Julia, and my children Anthony, Kaitlyn, and Taylor for providing my life with so much wonder.

As a political insider, Richard Evans served as a federal member of parliament for Cowan in Western Australia during the turbulent 1990s. He now specialises in writing political thrillers, writing about the exotic characters in the mysterious world of the Australian Parliament. He lives in the coastal village of Airlie Beach, the gateway to the Whitsunday islands, with a view from his writing desk overlooking the Coral Sea.

For more information about his other books,
or to contact Richard please visit:

www.richardevans-author.com

Visit Instagram for updates on
Plots, Publishing, Politics and Personal news.

instagram.com/richardevans_author

Episode two of the Democracy Trilogy

The Mercantiles, a long-established, clandestine group of high-taxpaying business owners have grown frustrated by Prime Minister Andrew Gerrard's failure to meet promises, and decide the nation needs a change of government at the upcoming election. They call upon experienced and ruthless political operative Jonathan Wolff to organise their election campaign and defeat the prime minister.

Realising he cannot win the election his way, Wolff initiates an explosive campaign designed to remove the prime minister by defeating him in his own electorate using an independent candidate.

Investigative journalist Anita Devlin is appointed by her editor to promote the Stanley campaign as the publishing owner, unknown to her, is a member of the Mercantiles. She discovers the nefarious Wolff strategically working the campaign, and endeavours to expose his influence and manipulation.

For more information and purchasing options visit
852 Press.com.au

Episode three of the Democracy Trilogy

Three years after a change of government, the nation is facing huge social, policy, and environmental-related disasters yet the Australian government seems paralyzed on how to proceed. Two senior ministers resolve that a change of prime minister is essential for Australia's future and begin to lay the foundations for his dismissal.

Meanwhile, the parliament is held in a balance of power by the independent, Jaya Rukhmani, who can decide at any time if government legislation will be approved. Upon hearing the news that former prime minister Andrew Gerrard wishes to re-enter parliament, Jaya turns to Barton Messenger as an ally.

Doomed takes us behind the scenes of a parliament unaware of how ambition and political manipulation affect the everyday Australian. When the environment and economy are brought into the mix, which will be the one to flourish, and which one is doomed?

For more information and purchasing options visit
852 Press.com.au

FIRST NATIONS HAVE NEVER CEDED SOVEREIGNTY...

FORGOTTEN PEOPLE

...IS CULTURE WORTHY OF REVOLUTION?

RICHARD EVANS

She wants her culture and country back. Independence was never ceded, and she will do whatever it takes to get it back, including the ultimate sacrifice. When government peace talks stop, revolution begins.

Revolutionary leader, Nellie Millergoorra, campaigns for an aboriginal homeland to preserve indigenous culture by advocating the prohibition of mining in Arnhem Land using a United Nations declaration to convince a disrespectful government to sign a treaty. Nellie will do whatever it takes to finally gain independence and end government regulation over her people.

When there is no agreement, she recruits mercenary special forces to inflame community chaos establishing an explosive aboriginal revolutionary movement.

In a surprising confrontation with a reluctant prime minister, who is threatened with an ultimatum he can't ignore, Millergoorra negotiates a treaty whilst facing her own battle for survival.

Forgotten People is gripping political thriller featuring surprising plot twists, compelling characters, and a kick-arse female heroine.

For more information and purchasing options visit
852 Press.com.au

He's the nation's chief law maker. His daughter is fighting for her life in intensive care, a victim of a terrible crime. Will he ignore the prime minister's demands and his own laws to save her? Or will politics and the Catholic Church prevent him from doing his job?

Treasurer, Parker Osborne, initiates a covert plan, in partnership with Vatican emissary, Cardinal Rosseau, to guarantee proposed euthanasia legislation is destined for failure in the national parliament triggering a leadership challenge.

In a surprising development, the prime minister makes a decision which changes everything.

The Kill Bill is a gripping political thriller featuring emotional and surprising plot twists, convincing characters, and exposes the black-art of politics that will have you questioning the ethics of assisted dying. If you like fast-paced, page-turning thrillers that draw you into the story then Richard Evans' fourth book will not disappoint you.

Buy The Kill Bill today and learn how the black arts of politics really works.

For more information and purchasing options visit
852 Press.com.au

She changes her name but not her attitude.

A streetwise opportunist escapes despair and abuse in the big city by seeking opportunities in the mallee. She changes her name but not her attitude when she discovers wealth and privilege ripe for the taking from the influential Dowerin family of the mallee.

Rose Dowerin replaces her husband as the local federal politician. The subsequent trappings of influence and power as a minister in the federal government suit her ambitions. It's a privileged life, a life very different from the abusive streets of Melbourne from where she escaped and the dry dusty heat of the mallee.

Under threat Rose falls back into her malevolent ways to overcome the forces against her until an unexpected family twist changes everything.

THE MALLEE is an action-packed thriller with a strong female lead featuring emotional and surprising plot twists, convincing characters, and exposes the dark-arts of politics that will have you questioning the system.

If you like fast-paced, page-turning thrillers that draw you into the story then Richard Evans' seventh book will not disappoint you.

For more information and purchasing options visit
852 Press.com.au

They were in the wrong place at the wrong time and will regret it forever. Nothing can change what happened, but only the lawyer can provide justice for them both. Will Anna Booth do it or will it be out of her hands?

A teenager is looking for a good time and meets a young woman who has no interest in him or his friends. Their worlds collide again when walking home. His mistake was not helping her.

After a police investigation exposing his friends, Billy Brown faces his day in court. He knows he is innocent and has little fear of the justice system. But the justice system wants a guilty accused and Billy is their patsy.

Three trials and a media storm later, his lawyer Anna Booth fights for justice for her client and the victim.

Buy *OUT OF MY HANDS* today and bring to light the reality of the American justice system and its faults.
Trigger warning: *Out of my Hands* is a gritty crime thriller and reader 18+ recommended.

For more information and purchasing options visit
852 Press.com.au

**One day to figure it out
Even less time to save his life**

Ryan Kennedy had it all - the perfect family, a successful career, and a life that others envied. But something was missing, and Ryan was determined to find it, even if it meant giving up everything he had built.

In the cutthroat world of politics, the daily pressure to make decisions and face the consequences takes its toll on even the strongest individuals. Ryan never wanted this life of stress and anxiety, but he found himself drawn in, becoming rich and famous in the process.

But as his secret worlds collide, exposing him as the shallow man he hates, Ryan is forced to confront his crisis head-on and make a decision that will shape his future.

Selfish Ambition is the story of one man's journey to find his true identity and live life on his own terms. In the world of politics, a single day can feel like a lifetime.

**For more information and purchasing options visit
852 Press.com.au**

852

PRESS

ABOUT THE PUBLISHER

We are an independent publisher, helping Australians tell their story.

We are keen to share our experiences and processes with Australian writers so they can self-publish their own works. We will be launching a range of resources, services, and events for those with a story to tell.

Visit our website for more information.

www.852Press.com.au